This is a work of fiction. The events and characters described herein are imaginary and are not intended to refer to specific places or living persons. The opinions expressed in this manuscript are solely the opinions of the author in addition, do not represent the opinions or thoughts of the Publisher. The author has represented and warranted full ownership and/or legal right to publish all the materials in this book.

Revenge Cometh Forth

All Rights Reserved

v2.0

Edited by Betty Powell, Linda S. Carr and Jeff L. Carr

Cover Art designed by Eric A. Carr

PUBLISHER'S NOTE

Harrison House Publishing

www.theharrisonhousepublishing.com

info@theharrisonhousepublising.com

Paperback ISBN: 978-0-9855043-7-3

Library of Congress Control Number: 2014947572

Harrison House Publishing and the "HH" logo are trademarks belonging to Harrison House Publishing.

PRINTED IN THE UNITED STATES OF AMERICA

FORWARD

When you read through the story you may find several places where the laws of the land do not jive with what is being said. When I look at other stories, be it in movie, a book or television, I have found that some authors will use "Poetic License" to change things to fit their plot. If you watch the movie, "Liar, Liar," there is a glaring discrepancy where the law does not fit the outcome of the court case. If the proper legal decision were used in the movie it would ruin the plot (plus it might give a lot of minors an idea of how to try to get away with something). In "Star Trek" and "Quantum Leap" they constantly misused the laws of physics. A Certain US Senator said that he was being fired upon by the Khmer Rouge, while he was in Viet-Nam, even though that political group did not appear on any political scene until after the USA was out of Viet-Nam. If other authors of fiction and science fiction can use it - so can I. If a United States Senator can get up and be some kind of historical revisionist then who are you or anyone else to say that I cannot. If you try to say that I cannot improvise, revise or use poetic license, then all I have for you is a very loud, sloppy raspberry.

REVENGE
Cometh FORTH

BY

DARA J. CARR

REVENGE
Cometh FORTH

BY
DARA J. CARR

Harrison House Publishing

San Antonio, Texas

ACKNOWLEDGEMENT

A great deal of thanks to my close friend Sarah and my two nieces Autumn and Amber for their encouragement and support in writing this book.

REVENGE COMETH FORTH

1

The librarian was making the rounds, letting everyone know that it was getting close to the 10 pm, closing time. Christine looked up from the encyclopedia she was reading and thought, 'I've got all the info I need from this one, so this is as good a time as any to go.' She put her history textbook into her backpack, and stretched. She figured her father might be a little upset about how much time she was spending at the library, but he was the one who was always bugging her about her grades, so what the heck.

She left the library and headed back to the house by way of the mall parking lot. It was a late January evening, however in south Texas it was one of those winter nights where the temperature was still in the mid 60's. Walking home was not unusual at this time and she chose the most direct route home - straight across the mall parking lot. She had gone through there hundreds of times without any problems and she did not suspect anything could possibly go wrong.

She never saw who it was, she just heard a few quick thuds of approaching footsteps and then a sharp pain in her shoulder as she was shoved down. She struggled back up to her knee, and then another sharp pain in her shoulder again…

She woke up with a start in total confusion. She was in a somewhat dark hospital room. There was a patch over her left eye, along with some wrappings around her arms. She inventoried the feelings around her entire body, and felt several painful areas on her back and legs, not to mention a very sore spot on her right shoulder.

There were several wires, or something, attached to her body. All of the leads went from her into a machine that was making all kinds of beeping noises. There was a large tube that had been shoved down her throat that made talking impossible. There were some other tubes that were between her legs and she did not want to think of what they were there for.

A young pudgy woman came into the room, turned on a light and started checking all the leads and beeping machines. Christine tried to reach up and touch her to get her attention, however she was too weak to move her arm very much at all. The woman noticed the movement and looked down into the uncovered right eye. "You're awake!" she said in a surprised manner. The woman hurried to the door and said; "Room 16c is awake."

A moment later an older woman with a stethoscope around her neck came in and started to examine Christine. "Welcome back," she said with a smile. "I'm Doctor Price, and I've been taking care of you for the last six days." She sighed and said: "Now honey, I guess we'll be able to find out what your side of the story is."

The pudgy woman came back, "I called the police. They said they will be here shortly to get your statement."

A few moments later Christine's mother came running in looking rather haggard from an obvious lack of sleep, with fresh tear streaks going down her face. All she could do was sob and hold Christine's hand against her face.

While waiting for the police to arrive, Dr. Price began pulling the tubes out of Christine's mouth and from between her legs. The pudgy one, who introduced herself as Tina, helped Christine out of the bed and got her walking around to get her somewhat flaccid muscles working again. Then she was taken to another hospital room, where there seemed to be fewer beeping machines.

When the police arrived she was informed that she had been beaten, raped and left for dead in a wooded area next to the mall parking lot. Someone had found her the next morning, while mowing the grass, reported the finding and she had been comatose for six days. She was informed that she had been completely cleaned out, so there was no possibility of a pregnancy from the rape.

Her parents had been taking turns keeping vigil over her while she was out and they both showed wear from that tribulation. Now that she seemed to be as mentally sound as one could be after a rape, as well as physically healing, her father could not afford to lose any more time from work. Her mother was able to get some badly needed rest, and Christine was left with just Tina to keep her company.

After two days and some of the bandages coming off, Christine was able to go home, where she found her teacher had dropped off some school work to be done in order to catch up with the rest of the class...as if a 12 year old could just laugh off a sexual assault and a brutal beating and get back to a normal life at the snap of a finger.

Three weeks of home studies went by and she thought she was going to lose her mind. Her teacher came by on Tuesdays and Thursdays, checked the previous assignments, and gave her more to do. She was at home. She felt that she did not have to do any of these assignments, however her father was adamant about her grades. She was not going to get lazy now.

2

Her father ordered pizza that evening. Her mother was a little tired after her activities that day, and was glad to have someone else do the cooking. After eating the pizza Christine felt very tired, went to her room and just fell on the bed.

She woke up…maybe. When she had gone to bed everything seemed normal. Now she might be awake and everything was a blur. Sounds were distorted. It all seemed surrealistic. A huge strange orange object was dancing around in front of her. Strange colored strobe lights were all around her. Two people that she could not focus on grabbed hold of her arms, picked her up and carried her somewhere. She was laid on what seemed to be a bed, and it started moving. This moving bed went into a brightly lit box of some kind and she heard a strange wailing sound as well as more movement. Once the movement stopped, she was taken out of the box, into some kind of tunnel with all kinds of blurry people who were chattering incoherently as they milled around her.

She woke up in a hospital room, again. There was Tina, again. But, this time there was a Doctor named Sizemore examining her…and her left wrist was handcuffed to the rail of the bed. This time there were no bandages. This time no one was nice to her. This time no parents worried about her.

The police informed her that she had been found outside of her parents' house on the front lawn wearing nothing but a see-through negligee. The house had been set on fire and her parents had died in the fire. They were accusing her of starting the fire.

When she was brought into the hospital this time, a blood test had been done immediately, and they found a mixture of barbiturates in her system.

This time, like the last time, she could tell them nothing. Last time she had been knocked unconscious by an unknown attacker. This time she had been doped up, and the police would not believe her when she said that she had not taken any drugs of her own free will.

She was informed of her rights. An attorney was assigned to her case, a man named Thomas Reese, who did not seem to believe her any more than the police did.

She was taken into Juvenile Court where a man read off some meaningless docket number, and then read from a sheet: "Lee, Christine, minor, age 12, two counts of murder in the second degree, one count of arson, and one count of illegal use of a controlled substance."

The Judge looked at her and said: "How do you plead?"

She stared in shock at what she was hearing. She looked at Reese and said "I didn't do anything. I wouldn't hurt my parents. I don't know what happened."

The Judge snapped impatiently: "Your choices are either guilty or not guilty. I don't know doesn't work."

"Not guilty," she cried.

Reese looked down and sighed.

"Bail recommendations?" asked the Judge.

The district attorney said: "She has absolutely no known living relatives anywhere, she has no means of support, nowhere to live and she is a 12 year old minor. I recommend she be held in the juvenile facility without bail."

"No objections, your honor," said Reese.

"Very well. The defendant is to be held without bail until trial." The Judge banged his gavel. "Next case."

She was hauled away to the "facility" where they issued her eight bright yellow shirts and pants that were all about 4 sizes too large. She was told that the yellow outfits were a signal to everyone there that she was more or less a visitor and not a permanent resident. They had to provide her with underwear and footwear as well because everything she had owned had been turned to ashes in the fire. All she had was herself with no clear memory of what happened that night.

The first night was a very depressing one. She was new here and did not know anyone. She did not know who to go to for comfort or advice. She had always had her parents for that…and now they were gone. She spent her first night crying into her pillow in the fetal position.

When her lawyer finally showed up to talk over the trial, he had nothing for her but more gloom. Since she could not give him anything that he could look for as exculpatory evidence. He did not ask any specific questions, he just wanted her to give any information she could remember. She had no memory of how the drugs got in her system, no memory of how the fire started, no explanation as to why there had been gasoline on the bottoms of her feet, and no memory of ever owning the sheer flesh colored negligee that she was wearing when they found her. She had no explanation for anything that had occurred on the evening of Tuesday, March 1, 1983.

On Wednesday, April 13, 1983, she was brought up before the Judge with the only thing that her lawyer said she could say: "No contest."

She was sentenced to spend the rest of her "minor" years in a state juvenile facility. On September 12, 1988, her 18th birthday, the state would then determine further…"considerations."

Back to the juvenile facility…for the rest of her childhood.

3

The "juvenile facility" was a monument to "Political Correctness." It was neither a prison nor reform school. It was a state home/school for minors. She was not an inmate; she was a student. They did not have cells; they were bedrooms (with nothing more than a bed, a desk, a chest of drawers, and two shelves on the wall, a sink, and a toilet). They did not have solitary confinement; it was an individual meditation room. There were no guards; they were custodians and counselors. The warden was, of course, the principal. If you were just a "visitor", (otherwise known as a ward of the state) you wore yellow. Long term "students" got orange outfits. If you were on suicide watch, you wore red. If you were a trustee, or *student supervisor*, you wore blue. Habitual trouble makers, or those needing an attitude adjustment, wore khaki. Pink was reserved for the ones who were pregnant. All of the socks and underwear were white. The footwear was nothing more than slippers.

When she had been brought to the facility before - as a visitor - she had not been indoctrinated. Now that she was a "student" she was to receive the full instructions on the institution and the rules that she had to follow. She was given a booklet that contained all kinds of rules. Break the rules and you get demerits. If you get a certain number of demerits you had different punishments (or different amounts of time in meditation). She read page after page about spitting on the sidewalk, or spitting on or in a building and spitting in the grass or bushes. She wondered if there was a demerit if she spit in the sink while brushing her teeth.

Her first night as a visitor had been bad. Now she was really feeling despondent. Now she was a convicted felon. She had no one she could turn to as a friend and she had no relatives to visit her. She was totally alone.

She had been in this "home" since the fire in early March, after a short stay in the hospital, and had been given a class schedule. Since going to class was the only way to kill the boredom, attendance was usually 100%.

The other part was counseling. When she had first arrived, there had only been indoctrination in the school. Now that she had two murder raps, arson and drug use on her record, she had to go to "seminars" on these subjects in order to help her solve her issues. None of the counselors believed her either.

"You cannot expect to get over your issues until you at least admit you have a drug problem that caused all this. If you did not take the drug, how did it get into your system, and why did you burn down your home with your parents inside?" The counselors were constantly hitting her with this. She had no answers for them, because she could remember nothing that happened that night.

After classes, counseling sessions and dinner, each student was sent to their room for private meditation and study. Since there was nothing else to do she studied her schoolbooks and did her homework. Her Grade Point Average was going way up. She always wondered how that would improve her situation any, but being stuck here - she had nothing else to do.

Everything was pretty routine...until early May. The morning wake-up bell rang. She laid in bed feeling more tired now than last night. She got a strange feeling in her stomach. She bolted out of bed dragging the blanket with her, stumbled and crawled to the toilet and threw up. She knelt there waiting for another heave that never came about.

She stood up, went to the sink and washed her mouth out. At first she smiled as she thought that she might be able to get out of the morning calisthenics due to illness. She looked around the room scheming, wondering what she would tell the school nurse.

Then she noticed the unopened box of tampons on the shelf, and it hit her like a sledgehammer. She had not used a single one since her arrival here in March. She remembered from the sex education class that sometimes a girl might miss a period due to stress. 'Probably from the rape,' she thought. There should have been another period starting March 29, but she could not remember that one happening either. Looking at her small calendar, the next one should have been April 26...nothing. The next one was not supposed to be until May 24 and today was only May 11.

Each corridor in the *school*, had 24 rooms, and a *student supervisor*. The *supervisor* for Christine's corridor, a tall lean and vicious Hispanic girl named Blanca Cruz, was coming down the hall hollering at everyone: "Get your lazy carcasses out of bed, get dressed for exercises."

Christine darted to the toilet, stripped her panties down, sat down, urinated and stretched as if she had *just* gotten out of bed.

Blanca pounded on the door and looked through the small window. A loud click sounded as the door was unlocked, Blanca walked in, looked at the blanket on the floor, cocked her head to one side and said: "What! Are you sleeping on the floor now, you little slob? You always seem to have the messiest room." She shook her head. "How can someone as small as you, always be the biggest problem?"

Christine just shook her head. She finished her business on the toilet, pulled up her panties, and started to make the bed in silence. She did not want to give Blanca any chance at a zinger, because Blanca always had a knack for turning what you say against you, and beating you to death with it...not today.

After Blanca left, Christine tried to think if there was any way she could not be pregnant. She had missed several periods, her bra did seem a little tight, and her breasts were rather sensitive.

What could she say to the counselors? What would they say to her for not bringing the subject up sooner?

She decided to wait until May 24. Maybe - just maybe she would have a period and the whole thing would just be a bad experience because of the stress of the rape, the court appearances and being in this school...maybe.

Every day was the same routine: Get up, throw up, put up with Blanca and check the calendar for May 24.

Then, May 24 was here. Same routine and nothing else. She checked her calendar again - maybe on June 21 there would be a different result. Maybe.

Get up, throw up, put up with Blanca and check the calendar for June 21. She would also check her body profile in the mirror. She started noticing a little bit of a paunch on her lower abdomen.

Maybe she was just getting a little fat from not properly doing all of the exercises each morning. Maybe.

June 21 came and went without a sign of a period. Next stop on the big wait was July 19...and she still had not figured out a way to tell anybody.

At the beginning of July, she stopped having morning sickness. She discretely checked a medical encyclopedia in the library and found out, not solving her situation whatsoever, that morning sickness did not normally last the entire pregnancy. 'Great,' she thought. No help at all.

The counseling sessions were not helping her misery any at all. They were trying to make her admit that she had set the fire that killed her parents, but she was adamant that she could not remember anything that happened that night. She figured out that all the blur and surrealistic activity that went on around her that night was a drug fog, but there was no memory of splashing gasoline around (or even where the gasoline came from) or setting a fire. She also, still had no idea where any drugs had come from, or how they got in her system.

July 19 finally came. No period. She did however notice the paunch in her stomach was getting larger. She tried sucking in her stomach, but it did not help. Just let the baggy clothing cover it, walk and sit slouched over and hope for the better on August 16.

She did not have to wait for August 16, or even August. July 28: A normal Thursday...at first. Get up, put up with Blanca, go out for morning exercise, do morning exercises, take a shower, get dressed, go to breakfast…go to counseling.

Ah yes - counseling. Counseling with Dr. Bruce McFarlin. He was a tall lean man with no sense of humor and a permanent scowl on a face that was under a shock of unruly flaxen hair. He was the main pain in the neck that kept hounding her about what had happened on March 1st, 1983. He kept trying to make her admit that she *had* voluntarily taken some drug, that she *had* splashed gasoline all over the house, and that she *had* then set the fire that caused the death of her parents.

Most of the other students in this group session had admitted to their crimes. Christine figured that they had been brainwashed or hypnotized or finally gave in because they were exhausted from the constant badgering. She refused to admit any guilt, because she truly could not remember anything that happened that night. It did not matter how much he harassed her about that night, she refused to change her story.

As usual she sat in the chair hugging her knees up against her chin and, in total defiance, would not look at Dr. McFarlin. It was, however, getting more difficult to keep her knees under her chin in a comfortable manner. Every now and then she had to move her legs a little so she could breathe. She hoped that the doctor would not think of it as anything other than nervous fidgeting…wrong!

About twenty minutes before they usually ended the session for lunch, Dr. McFarlin stood up and stated in his high husky voice: "Everyone, except Ms. Lee, is excused for lunch."

She flushed as everyone stared at her. They all slowly got up and walked away

"Have you got something to say, Ms. Lee?" he said flatly.

"I'm not going to change what I said. I don't remember what happened that night and I have no idea where the drugs came from." She stated it with as little emotion as she could muster.

"I was not talking about your very well practiced lie, Ms. Lee, I was talking about what appears to be something else."

She looked up totally confused and just gave him a dumb, "Huh?"

He adjusted his glasses. His scowl seemed to appear angrier than before. "Stand up!" He practically shouted it at her.

She let go of her legs and let them drop to the floor. She slowly stood up slouching.

"Stand up, *straight!*" he growled.

She flushed again. She sighed, bit her lower lip and slowly straightened up. She saw his eyes staring at her stomach.

He raised his eyebrows: "Have we been overeating a little?"

"No," she said meekly.

He actually got the scowl off of his face as he leaned forward a little and said: "Are we…pregnant?"

She opened her eyes wide, put a cheerful smile on her face. "We? You said we? Are you pregnant? You don't look pregnant to me…" She stopped and bit her lip again. She grimaced and looked around the room for some place to just…hide.

The look on his face told her that he was not amused at all. "Well?" He barked impatiently.

She closed her eyes and sighed. "Maybe," she said dejectedly. "I'm not really sure."

She was now in the nurse's office, lying on an exam bed, in just her underwear. An attendant was checking her blood pressure, while the nurse was moving a stethoscope to different places on her stomach.

'Busted,' she thought!

A "custodian" had been sent to the medical office to keep an eye on Christine. The guard was a tall heavy set black woman who stood there with her arms folded and showed no emotion. The big woman just kept moving her gaze between Christine's eyes and stomach.

The nurse took the stethoscope out of her ears, cocked her head, smiled and said: "Have you got something to tell us, Sugar?"

Christine breathed a deep sigh. She just laid there flat on the bed staring at the ceiling. "Last January, I was raped. When I woke up in the hospital, they said that they had cleaned me out and there was no chance of pregnancy. For the last couple of months, I was hoping, every time I missed my period, that it was just stress." She sighed again and closed her eyes. She tried to stifle it but could not help whimpering. "I guess maybe I was wrong."

"Well, THEY made a mistake and so did YOU. THEY obviously did NOT clean you out and YOU should have said something a few months ago, even if it might have been a false alarm," said the nurse.

The attendant walked up and dropped a set of "pinkies" on Christine's chest. "This is the smallest set we have. Nobody was expecting someone as small as you to get knocked up. Put it on, you're going to town."

Christine sat up shocked: "Town! Why!"

"I am not a doctor." said the nurse. "You did not let us know you might be pregnant and, as a result, there might be some problems. You need to be seen by an obstetrician."

She put on the pink clothing. The attendant was right - it was too big for her. The cuffs and sleeves had to be rolled up several inches and the shoulders of the suit were hanging almost down to her elbows.

The custodian finally spoke up: "I have to take her into town. What are you saying, you can't do the abortion here?"

Christine nearly panicked. She backed up against the wall to keep from falling down (as well as a better defensive position). "What abortion? What are you talking about? I don't want any abortion!"

The nurse gave the custodian an exasperated look. With a strained smile on her face she turned to Christine and said: "You'll thank us later for this. You won't have to be thinking about where any child is, for the rest of your life, and at this point it won't affect your figure."

Christine screamed with tears in her eyes, "I am NOT having any abortion!"

The nurse started to get irritated. "You are a ward of the

state. You are a minor and therefore do NOT have a say in this. The state has the power to order the abortion. The other girls here, that are pregnant, have parents that have decided for them, to give birth and adopt or whatever. I repeat: YOU do NOT have a choice here."

The custodian called for help. Moments later two male custodians came in with shackles and a strait jacket. Her fighting was all in vain. At 5 feet tall and less than 100 pounds, Christine was no match for three large adults. In no time at all they had her in the strait jacket and had cuffs on her ankles. She laid on the floor sobbing pitifully, while they all stood back to catch their collective breaths.

One man grabbed her legs while the other got her around her waist. They carried her out to a waiting van. Two more female custodians were waiting by the open sliding door. One of them, with red hair and a ponytail, came and looked at Christine with a smile, "You're not going to give us any more trouble, are you?" She shook her head when she saw nothing but an angry glare. "Yes, you are planning on giving us a LOT of fun." She looked at the two men: "Hook her up and strap her down!"

They placed her in the middle of a bench seat, in the van, and hooked the ankle shackles into a ring on the floor. Then they placed belts over both shoulders giving her virtually no room to move at all. She just sat there with her head hung down, sobbing, and begging them to leave her alone.

One of the custodians was saying something but Christine just did not care.

"Hey! I'm talking to you!" shouted a blonde custodian. "You are only making this tough for yourself. We are ready for trouble and we can handle a lot more than you can dish out. You're building up a lot of demerits with this fiasco. So stop the nonsense - NOW!"

She could not think of why and could not put it into words, but there was no reason to abort a baby that had not done anything wrong and had not even had the chance to draw breath one outside the womb. Her parents were gone, as were her grandparents. There were no aunts, uncles or cousins, so when this baby was born she would be the only living relative it had. Everybody else has someone they could call kin, why not me? Christine had never felt so alone in her life.

One custodian was on either side of her in the van. Two custodians sat in the bench seat behind her. Now, the long drive to town where her baby was to be destroyed without her even knowing anything about it...not without a fight. She decided to rest as much as possible for the fight at the hospital.

When they arrived at the hospital, the custodians sitting with her did not move. The driver got out and slid the big side door open. Two men were pushing a gurney in the direction of the van.

Before Christine could even think of how to fight them off, the custodians had her restraints in the van off, she was being strapped down to the gurney and being rolled into the hospital. All she could do was scream at them.

When they got her inside, one of the custodians grabbed her head and held it firmly, while another put a mask over her nose and mouth. A hissing sound and strange smell and she got very groggy very quickly. Things started to blur and then nothing.

4

She awakened with a headache. She was shackled to a bed. She could see through the window that the last rays of the sun were disappearing over the horizon. It had been around noon when she was brought in and she started crying, knowing that the worst had happened.

A thin woman with brown and gray hair walked in slowly while reading through a medical chart. She stopped and was about to say something when Christine's stomach made a rather loud gurgling sound. The doctor looked at the custodian then back at Christine: "When did you last have something to eat?"

"Who cares?" Christine sobbed. "You killed my baby."

"Nobody killed anything," said the woman. "All we've done is draw some blood, check your vitals and examine you. Now, when was the last time you had something to eat?"

"She had breakfast, this morning." said the custodian. "Nothing since."

The doctor shook her head, turned and went back to the door: "Bring some food in here for this poor girl, now!"

There was an unintelligible response from the hallway.

"Of course, she's hungry," the doctor snapped. "She's pregnant. Now get her some food or let her gnaw on your arm."

"What are you waiting for? You want me awake when you

cut my baby out or some other nasty thing like that?"

The doctor shook her head. "No, I'm not doing anything. I am a doctor, NOT some back-alley abortionist. If you go to an abortionist, they just start the vacuum and don't worry about the consequences. I, on the other hand, am a doctor who checks the patient completely before I start any procedure...and I obey the law."

Christine stared at her, confused but hopeful.

"Look, sweetie, the abortionists at those 'hatchet shops' have sent too many hemorrhaging messes to me. I've only been able to save two out of about twenty of them. If your caretakers had taken you to a hatchet shop, first, then heaven only knows what could've happened to you."

The custodian spoke up: "If she's that bad off, how can you let a dangerous pregnancy continue?"

"It is only a dangerous pregnancy because of her age and if she does not start putting on some weight," the doctor turned an angry glare at Christine, "...and TAKING BETTER CARE OF HERSELF."

"Wait a minute, we brought her in here specifically for an abortion - nothing else," said the custodian impatiently. "Are you telling me that there is something medical standing in the way of that simple procedure?"

The doctor looked down her nose at the custodian. "I am not going to confuse you with a lot of big words that *you* probably can't understand. I'll make it as simple as I possibly can. I heard her screaming when she was brought in. She does NOT want an abortion. When a woman - or girl - does not want an abortion and you force one on her, the results of that could be devastating to her mental well-being. There is also the fact that she is far into the second trimester. If you read some of the laws that are around here, you will find that an abortion cannot be done AFTER the 24th week. According to this paperwork, the only time that she had sex was the rape that occurred on January 27th of this year. That, now puts her in her 26th week at the very least. I cannot do it legally or ethically."

An attendant walked in with a full food tray. She looked at how Christine was shackled to the bed. "Am I going to have to feed her?"

"Hold on!" snapped the custodian. "This child is a ward of the state and the state had decided that her pregnancy is to be terminated. She does not have the right to say otherwise."

The doctor rolled her eyes and huffed. "Ah yes, the wonderful, always handy-dandy, double standards. If a minor is pregnant and wants an abortion without parental permission, she is allowed to do so in many states. Here is one that wants to continue the pregnancy without permission and you say no! A minor is allowed to stop it without parental consent, but NOT continue without parental consent. DUMB!"

The custodian started to say something, but was cut off with an angry glare.

"As I said: The *patient* has NOT consented to an abortion - at the top of her lungs - and she is beyond the 24th week. This pregnancy is going full term!"

The attendant placed the tray on the cart. "Am I going to

have to feed her or is she going to be untied?"

The custodian let out several grunts, trying to think of what to say. She glared at Christine: "Are you going to behave, now that you got your wish?"

"I'll be good," said Christine meekly.

As soon as all of the shackles had been removed, Christine tried to get off the bed. The custodian grabbed her: "Where do you think you're going?"

"I gotta pee!"

The custodian's shoulders slumped and she waved her hand toward the bathroom.

Christine scrambled to the bathroom and closed the door. While she relieved herself, she rocked back and forth on the toilet while silently giggling. She had finally won a battle against the bureaucracy. "My baby is okay," she thought. "Okay, diet and proper exercise, okay, and my baby will be okay. I may never see my baby again, but that's okay. This baby didn't do anything wrong, so why should it die? I never killed nobody and I'm not going to start with MY baby."

She finished her business, washed her hands, went back to the bed and attacked the food.

The custodian growled and scratched her forehead. "Is there any other news for me to take back to the people at the school?"

"Actually, yes," said the doctor flatly. "She's carrying triplets."

Christine stopped chewing and stared at the doctor, slack

jawed. A large chunk of potato fell out of her mouth and she sat there drooling. The doctor walked over to her, picked up a napkin, wiped her face, placed her hand under Christine's chin and closed her mouth. "You don't want to waste any of that food - you ARE eating for…four. Now, chew thoroughly before you swallow, Sweetie."

The Doctor added, "I haven't figured an exact due date. It should be either late October or early November, however, multiples are usually premature, so once October comes, you need to keep a close watch on her and she'll probably have Cesarean Section."

The guard grunted, shook her head and glared at Christine. "As soon as you are finished eating, put your pinkies back on, girl. We're going to have some interesting conversations when we get back to the school."

5

Christine was moved to the section with all the other "PG's." Life was a little easier in this corridor. The *student supervisor* was also pregnant and did not bully the other students like Blanca had. The exercises that they did here were far less strenuous and they were allowed to eat more - a *lot* more.

Even though this corridor, like the others, had 24 rooms, there were only 11 PG's in the whole school, so it was also a little quieter in this hall.

The main difference in the rooms of this corridor, was an emergency call button. It was a button on the end of a long coiled cord hanging from the ceiling that could stretch to anywhere in the room. If a girl went into labor or was having some problem - hit it. If you hit the button and there was no emergency - well, you did not want to even think of doing that.

Another difference here was that the beds here were more like hospital beds. They could be cranked up for necessary positioning and they were on wheels for convenience.

The *student supervisor* was a black girl named Clarise. The only other black girl, Shalia, seemed to be second in command. There were six Hispanics, one Korean and one white girl other than Christine. The Hispanics had their clique and rarely spoke English. The Korean was angry at the entire world and so she ignored everybody.

The only friend that Christine had was the other white girl Rebecca Gibbs - and Rebecca was a mute. Christine passed away most of her free time learning how to do sign language from Rebecca. Since Rebecca did not have anyone she could communicate with, without a pad and pencil, she was more than ready to teach Christine all she knew.

Other things that Christine found out about this corridor was that she was the youngest and the first due to deliver. Christine was 12, a girl named Angelina Segura was 14, and everybody else was either 15 or 16. The doctor had said that the triplets could come in October, but hopefully not until early November. No one else was due until December.

The only thing that did not seem to change was that pain in the neck - Dr. McFarlin. He still did everything he could to make Christine confess to things that she could not remember. He kept on calling it either lies or convenient amnesia. She refused to budge and so did he.

September 12, 1983. Christine celebrated her thirteenth birthday in jail, 6 ½ months pregnant and little hope for the future.

October arrived. Christine had put on considerable weight and was ready to get these wriggling monsters out of her at any price. They seemed to sleep and move in shifts and all took turns punching and kicking her bladder as well as other internal parts. She suffered all through October and no sign of contractions - false or otherwise.

The doctor that came to the school on a weekly basis, told her that if she had not delivered by November 11th, they would probably do a C-section. They told her that this was the safest way with multiples, because of the danger of an umbilical cord getting wrapped around the neck of one or more of the children. She looked at her calendar with almost a sense of relief. 'Whatever,' she thought. 'Just do it so I can walk without waddling, get rid of this permanent backache and don't have to pee 40 times per hour.'

6

She slowly waddled into her room from the shower. As she dried her hair, she was thinking of how it was only two more days before the relief of the C-section…then her water broke. At first she just stared in horror at the mess on the floor. Then she realized that she was not going to have to wait until the 11th - it was happening now. What to do - oh yes, hit the emergency button. She reached for the cord just as a contraction hit her. She slipped in the mess and went down hard on her hip. While waiting for the pain in her hip to subside, she repeatedly pressed the button. Nothing seemed to be happening. She looked at the cord - lying on the floor. She looked up at the gaping hole in the ceiling. She had somehow managed to rip the cord right out of the ceiling. That was not supposed to happen - but it did. Now what?

She tried to move closer to the door, but just slipped in the muck on the floor. She heard someone walking down the hall and screamed for help. Rebecca came to the door and saw the mess. She came in and started reaching for the emergency cord and then saw the hole in the ceiling where the cord was supposed to be, then looked down at Christine rather confused.

"Right," said Christine sarcastically. "It ain't supposed to break but it did."

Rebecca looked around, not sure what to do.

"Why don't you go to your room and hit your button?"

Rebecca signed that it might get her in trouble, because she was not in labor.

"I AM!" Christine was losing patience. "If you hit a button and it IS an emergency, I don't think they'll hold it against you because it's my emergency not yours. Now go hit it and get me some help!"

Rebecca looked afraid, but sighed and left the room. She came back moments later. She looked around again, went to the bed and got the pillow, went to Christine and put it under her head. Christine signed a "thank you" to Rebecca.

A few moments later they heard several people running into the corridor. They all ran past Christine's door. Rebecca went to the door and started frantically clapping her hands. Then she beckoned with her left hand and pointed into Christine's room with her right. The team came into the room and as if on cue, they all stared stupidly at the hole in the ceiling.

"Yes, it broke," screamed Christine. "Would you mind giving me some help now?"

One of the custodians moved a little too hastily. She slipped in the "puddle" and hit the floor, almost landing on Christine.

"Stop!" The nurse shouted. "Before we have mass casualties, slow down and get organized." She started pointing: "You and you, move the bed away from the…uh, mess. You, carefully pull the patient out of the mess." She looked at the one on the floor. "Since you've already taken a bath in that muck, move out of the mess slowly, then take off your shoes, so you don't track that stuff everywhere, and then go get the mop and bucket."

Everybody did as they were told and then Christine was helped up onto the bed.

"Why are you naked?" asked the nurse, as she covered Christine with a blanket.

"I just came in, from taking a shower, when my water broke."

"How long were you on the floor?"

"Maybe ten minutes."

"Any contractions?"

"Two, maybe three."

"Maybe? That doesn't help."

They rolled her bed out of the room as the "dirty" one arrived with the mop and steaming bucket.

"Has anyone called an ambulance?" asked the nurse.

Everybody shook their heads.

The nurse rolled her eyes and headed out of the corridor. She came back a while later and asked if there were any more contractions. One of the custodians said, "Yes, and they are…"

At that moment, Christine had another horribly painful contraction.

"All right, get her to my office. We'll wait there for the ambulance."

As they were wheeling her out of the corridor, she was wracked with another stab of mass pain.

While waiting in the nurse's office, there were several more contractions. One attendant would stare at her watch, and another would annotate times on a pad. They had chased Rebecca away, so all Christine could do was lay there feeling miserable. None of them would talk to her - just each other.

After what seemed hours, she heard someone say that the ambulance was here. Three men came into the Nurses office with a gurney. One was a gray-haired Hispanic who walked up to Christine and smiled. "Don't worry, my dear, we're here to give you all the help you need. I am Doctor Mendoza, and I have done this many times."

"What?" said Christine sarcastically, "...give birth?"

Mendoza gave her a friendly smile as he put on rubber gloves, "C-section. I was informed that you are carrying triplets, you are only 13 and you are rather small, so instead of sending the usual emergency technician, I came along. I have been practicing OB-Gynecology for twenty-two years. I think that I can handle just about any situation that may occur." He gave Christine a friendly smile.

Christine looked away and scoffed, not feeling very relieved at all.

Mendoza lifted the blanket, and gasped. "Has anybody been checking her?" He shouted angrily.

"For what?" said the Nurse?

Mendoza pointed between Christine's legs.

The nurse looked shocked: "Is that a baby's head?"

Mendoza looked back in mock awe: "Good guess! Okay, people: Birth has already started, we're going to have to do this the old fashioned way."

The room became a flurry of activity as Mendoza was giving quick orders to people who all jumped to do everything he told them to do. Christine was quickly 'rearranged' on the bed, while several other people put on rubber gloves and masks, grabbed equipment, brought in other equipment, and all of them staring at her crotch.

One of the men climbed behind her and started pushing on her shoulders, while another pushed on her stomach. She felt a huge relief of pain, and Dr. Mendoza called out: "Finally!" He looked up at the clock, "9:13 AM, the first one is here."

After a few moments of activity, one of the attendants went rushing out of the room carrying a crying baby wrapped in a blue towel. Christine could not see any arm, leg or head…just blue.

"Okay, people," said Mendoza. "We don't have any time to waste. We have to get her and the child in the ambulance and…" He stopped talking and looked down at her crotch again. "Hold on! The second one is already trying to push its' way out. We can't go anywhere yet."

Push! Relax. Push! Relax. Again that relief as the baby came completely out. "9:17 AM, and the second one is here."

Again a few moments of activity, one of the attendants went rushing out of the room carrying a crying baby wrapped in a green towel. Again, Christine could not see any arm, leg or head…just green.

One of the attendants looked at Mendoza expectantly. "Can

we move her now?"

Mendoza shook his head. "Nope. The third one's impatient as well."

Push! Relax. Push! Relax. Again that relief as the baby came completely out. "9:24 AM, and the third one is here."

Again a few moments of activity, one of the attendants went rushing out of the room carrying a crying baby wrapped in a red towel. Still, Christine could not see any arm, leg or head…just red.

While they gave her the final examination, she sobbed pitifully asking "What are they; boys or girls? How are they doing? Can I touch them? Can I just see them?"

All of her pleas were completely ignored, as they rushed her out for transport to the hospital.

Sometime during the ambulance ride, she passed out. When she awoke, it was evening and she was in an, all too familiar, hospital room. Everyone that came in the room, checked one of the bags or machines that she was hooked up to. They said nothing. If any of them looked at her, they gave her a glance that appeared to accuse her of something. She began feeling like a leper.

7

The doctors informed Christine that there had been a few problems and that they needed to keep her under close observation for a while. They never told her what the problem was.

After four days in the hospital, in walked Dr. McFarlin, with that usual look of disgust on his face. "Are you capable of telling the truth about ANYTHING?"

She looked at him totally confused, "What now?"

"You KNOW, what I am talking about."

She screamed, "No, I don't! I haven't understood any of your garbage, since I first saw your ugly face."

He shook his head. "Those babies are premature. IF you had conceived in January from that rape, then they would have been full term. According to the EXPERTS, those babies are, at least a full month, premature. Conception took place, in MARCH. Where were you in March? Oh yes, you were already in attendance at the school in March. You had sex with someone in the school and THAT is when you became pregnant. Either a custodian or another schoolmate, I want to know. NOW, who were you fooling around with?"

She just stared in bewilderment.

"When are you going to get it through your head that I am here to help you? I AM your friend. But, the only way that I can help you, is if you start telling the truth. As long as you keep telling me a pack of lies then neither I nor anyone else can help you on any road to recovery." He leaned towards her and said quietly, "Now, who is the father?"

"I don't know," she said helplessly.

"Are you saying that you had several lovers at the school?"

"Can I see my babies?"

"Those children are no longer your concern. They will never be your concern. You will never see them. NOW, who is the father?"

"If I will never see my babies, then who cares who the father is? If you're so convinced that someone at the school knocked me up, why don't you start asking everyone at the school who has that capability?" She looked up at him smugly. "That is everyone except you. I don't know what you are, but you're incapable of getting a HUMAN BEING pregnant. First of all, you would have to be human."

He took in a breath and let it out slowly. "Who is the father?"

She ignored him and looked out the window.

He took hold of her chin and jerked her face back to his. "Who is the father?"

"I DON'T KNOW." she screamed as loud as she could.

A woman came in looking rather upset, "What is going on? We don't need any of that shouting here."

"Then get him out of here." Christine growled.

McFarlin was about to say something, but the woman held

up a finger with a stern look on her face. "If you are what is upsetting her, then I need you out of here now. Her screaming is upsetting all the other patients on this floor and I cannot allow that. I don't know what you do at that prison, and I don't care - you are what is antagonizing her right now, and in her condition, I must stop the problem. YOU are the problem! Now GO!"

McFarlin cleared his throat. He looked at Christine, then the woman. "Madam, I am a doctor..."

"So am I. You want to play a pecking order game? This is my turf. If we were at the prison, it would be yours. Here, I am the top dog, between you and me." She gave him an evil glare and spoke softly. "Now...go."

He shook his head as he slowly walked out of the room.

"Okay, Sweetie, he's gone. Are you going to calm down now?"

Christine sat defiantly with her arms folded. "If you want me to stay quiet, keep that thing out of here."

"Fair enough." The doctor went to the door and looked back with a leering smile: "I don't like him either."

She sat there contemplating what Dr. McFarlin had said. Impossible! The only time that there had been any copulation was the rape. She had been knocked out by her assailant and had absolutely no recollection of it at all. If she had done something with somebody else - surely she would have remembered...something. She sat there contemplating the situation for quite a while and was never able to reach any conclusion about how this could have occurred.

She squeezed her nipples slightly. A small amount of milk came out. She licked the milk off her fingers. At least someone had tasted some of her milk. Even if it were only she. Her babies would never taste it. She would never be able to hold and cuddle them or wipe their tears away. She would never be able to see them again, for the rest of her life. She rolled over and buried her face in the pillow sobbing.

8

After only two weeks of 'goofing off' as a patient in the hospital, she was back at the school. What few possessions she had left had been moved back to her original room.

She did have the luxury of being medically excused from morning exercises for a few more weeks or until cleared by a doctor. She thought how wonderful it would be to tell Blanca where to get off at. She was in bed early waiting for lights out. Usually Blanca would call it just before shutting them off. No warning came this night. The lights went off on time with no verbal warning. Christine shrugged, maybe she is hoarse. Whatever. I'll find out in the morning.

When morning arrived, there was a rude awakening. The lights came on and she heard someone bellowing. Not Blanca. Where's Blanca? Maybe she got busted and lost her supervisor status. It happens. So who is this new loudmouth?

Christine was out of bed heading for the toilet, when "SHE" walked in. All Christine could do was stare. This new student supervisor was well over 6' tall, was wearing XXXL Blues, and she was putting a stress test on all of the seams from top to bottom. She had dirty blonde hair that was tied back tight in a pigtail (appropriate). Her fat face had an equal number of freckles and zits. Her big ham hands were somewhat tanned up to the wrist. Her arms were pasty white, showing that most of the time she was usually wearing long sleeved shirts. Her piercing blue eyes might have been considered pretty…by her mother. To Christine, those eyes just looked evil.

The giant lumbered closer. "I've heared about you. I ain't like Blanca. I don't put up with nuthin' in my corridor. My name is Big Sugar. Some of the staff here may tell you my name is somethin' else, but if you call me anything other than Big Sugar or Boss - I will sit on your scrawny butt until you stop squirmin'. They say that you got two murders on your rap sheet and you don't admit to them. Well, I have four murders on mine and I DID 'em! So, don't give me any problems. Now do your stuff, get dressed and get out to the exercise pad."

Christine swallowed hard. She tried to speak but couldn't. She cleared her throat: "I have a medical…uh…I don't have to exercise…" She wanted to say other things, but the look on Big Sugar's face made her stop.

"I knows bout yer excuse. I still says that you got to be on the pad. I can't make you exercise, but at least I knows where you at." Her eyes narrowed. "Any problem with that…runt?"

"No." Christine swallowed hard.

With an evil grin Big Sugar said: "Good." She started lumbering out. She stopped and turned back. "Just in case you're wonderin' what happened to that Blanca - she had some student in her hall that got knocked up and she didn't tell nobody. That got her fired. I don't plan on nobody getting me fired." She then left. She was so large that she had to turn sideways to get out the door.

Christine sat down on the toilet and let her breath out nervously. She started urinating and then realized that she had yet not pulled her panties down. She growled at herself in frustration.

She pulled the panties off, finished her business and went to the sink to rinse out her soiled underwear. After she wrung out the panties and dropped them in the laundry bag, she got dressed and started toward the exercise pad.

Three female custodians met her at the main door of the corridor. Two of them grabbed hold of her arms, and started hauling her off - somewhere. The third followed close behind, just in case the student tried to do something stupid. Since she had no idea where they were going, or why, and they were too strong for her to resist, she just went along for the ride – wondering in confusion what she was going to be blamed with now.

They hauled her into a corridor she had never been in before. This one had no doors. The rooms looked the same as far as furnishing. Everything else looked the same except for a pile of folded clothing on the chest of drawers - RED clothing.

"This is your new room for a while," said one of the custodians. "Get out of the orange duds, and put on the reds, now!"

"Why?" She shouted, "I'm not crazy! I don't need that stuff!"

WRONG ANSWER! Her arms were twisted painfully behind her back. One of the custodians unbuttoned her shirt and pulled it off as they let go of her arms. Then she was thrown on the bed, and her pants were rather rudely pulled off. She pulled herself up in the bed, just in time to get a red set thrown right in her face.

"No more guff - put those on," said one of the custodians.

Christine threw them as hard as she could to the farthest corner of the room. She then stood up on the bed in the corner as far as she could get from the custodians. She was fighting hard to control her breathing and not cry.

One of the custodians crossed her arms and just stood there. The other two custodians left the room without a word.

Then, in walked Dr. McFarlin.

She went limp and sank to her knees on the bed, crouched down and put her hands over her head. "What do you want, NOW? Why can't you just leave me alone?"

"We told you to get an abortion." He had an air of condescension. "You didn't listen. You had to have things your way. Now, as a result, we have to put you on suicide watch. You will never see your children for the rest of your life and girls your age, very often, get suicidal because of that type of situation."

"Go away."

"I'm not going anywhere. I am going to help you through this. That is why I am here."

"Go away."

"Whether you like it or not, I am here to help you." He tried a more tender tone, "I can help you, but you have to help me help you as well."

She pushed herself up to a sitting position and hugged her knees in the corner as far away from him as she could get. She refused to look at him.

"I am going to help you, no matter what."

"You couldn't help me wipe my butt." She turned her face

into the corner.

He came closer trying to sound softer. "I know you're hurting. I can help ease the pain." He sat down on the bed.

She looked at him angrily. "What? Do you want to have sex now?"

He was taken aback and could only come up with a startled: "Huh?"

She stared at him angrily. "Do you want to have sex with me?"

"No!"

"Then get off the bed!"

He put his hand to his forehead and sighed. "This has nothing to do with sex."

"Then get off the bed!"

"All I want to do is communicate with you."

"Then get off the bed! My daddy told me that the only time a man sits on a bed with a woman, he wants sex. Now, do you want sex?"

"No!"

"Then get off the bed!"

The custodian snorted a few times trying to stifle a laugh. McFarlin glared at her as he stood up. The glare only made it harder for her to stop laughing. She turned and left the room, with McFarlin staring a hole in her back.

"You will be on suicide watch until I decide that you are not a threat to yourself, or anyone else."

Christine started giggling. McFarlin was taken aback and stared at her curiously trying to figure out what she was laughing at.

"I just figured it out." She glared at him grinning. "You're mad. You are mad at me because I won a battle. You wanted those babies dead! They are *alive* and it's sticking in your craw. You can't stand the fact that you lost a battle to me."

"I really don't care one way or another whether those boys are…"

"Boys!" she shouted! "All three? Boys? I have three baby boys out there somewhere…alive!" She now had a huge grin on her face and her eyes were dancing.

He stood there with his eyes, teeth and fists clenched. He spun around and left the room mumbling incoherently.

The custodian returned with the smile and giggles gone. She picked up the clothing that Christine had thrown, walked slowly to the bed and tossed them to Christine. "Put them on. Now! If you don't - I will get some help and put them on you."

Christine folded her arms, and smiled. "No!"

Wrong answer - again! Since she was no longer pregnant, they did not have to be gentle with her. During the arduous task of dressing her, she felt (and heard) a painful pop in her left shoulder. Now she was in the Nurses office - in agony - dressed in red - getting her left arm in a sling.

Here in the "Red Zone," you have no privacy. There were no

doors that you could hide behind or shut anyone out. There was no student supervisor, just custodians. The ratio was one to one. She had a constant companion watching everything she did. Eating a meal, taking a shower, using the toilet and the whole time she was sleeping, she was under observation. The only time the parasite companions were not there was during the sessions with McFarlin.

She finally had some ammunition to use against him. The babies were alive. She now knew they were boys and would rub it in every chance she got. "I wonder how Gabriel, Alexander and Jeremiah are doing right now." She would always say it with a state of superiority.

"Hmm...an arch angel, a conqueror and a prophet. Interesting choices of names. Why did you pick those three names and categories?"

She stared at him confused. "A what, a what and a what?"

"The names: Gabriel is a biblical arch angel, Alexander the Great was a conqueror and Jeremiah is a biblical prophet. Why those categorical names?"

"Gabriel was my father's name, Alexander and Jeremiah were my two grandfathers. Now, what are *you* talking about?"

He looked through some of the papers in the file he always had with him, got a sour look on his face and changed the subject.

He would stare at her with a dead-pan expression. "You cannot start on any road to recovery until you admit that you have a problem, and admit to what you did."

She would respond with equally flat tone. "You say that I

killed my parents - wrong. You say I burned my parents' house down - wrong. You say that I took a bunch of different drugs voluntarily that night - wrong. You say I had sex with someone in this prison - wrong. You say I am suicidal because I can't see or touch my boys - wrong. You can't help me because you haven't gotten anything right, and I doubt that you ever will…because you don't know what you're talking about."

This went on for almost a month. Dr. McFarlin finally decided that she was not a threat, and she went back to orange attire and the original corridor.

She often wondered, with all the different students coming and going, why did she always seem to end up in the same corridor and the same room?

9

Two days after New Years Day, the Korean girl from the PG corridor moved in. It was the first time that Christine had heard the girl's name - Honey Kim.

Christine went to Honey's room. She remembered how hateful and solitary Honey had been in the PG corridor, so she tried to be careful. "Uh…hi…uh."

Honey looked at her like she was something disgusting. "What do you want, runt?"

Christine wrung her hands a little, "I was wondering if you could tell me what happened to Rebecca."

Honey looked around the room then back at Christine. "Don't see anybody - who's Rebecca?"

"Rebecca was the other white girl in the PG corridor. I haven't seen her in a few weeks and I was wondering what happened to her."

"You mean the mute?"

"Yes, I was…"

"She's dead." Honey said it without any emotion as she started putting a few of her things on the shelves.

Christine had to lean against the wall to keep from falling. "What happened?"

Honey huffed impatiently. "What happened to her is the same thing that happened to you and that Mexican girl. When labor started, you pulled your emergency cord out of the ceiling. So did the Mexican. When the mute pulled her cord, it came out of the ceiling, only she couldn't scream. She died in her room and the baby with her. Now, get out of here and leave me alone?"

Christine fell into the hallway. She got up and staggered back to her room. She was completely drained. She could not even think or cry or mourn. Rebecca was dead and Honey had been so cold about it.

The next day Big Sugar had to pull Christine out of bed and force her to get dressed. She did no exercises on the pad. She ate no breakfast…and of course Dr. McFarlin noticed the despondency and decided it was because of her children. Christine was back in the Red Zone. She spent three months there before getting over Rebecca's death. The whole time McFarlin kept on her about her children, not knowing anything about Rebecca, and Christine refused to talk to him about her deceased friend.

When Christine was finally cleared and moved back to her room, she found that there was a power struggle going on between Honey and Big Sugar. Big Sugar had the size and strength, Honey had martial arts. Three days of hearing the bickering and it finally came to blows…right outside Christine's room. The two antagonists were shouting and cursing at each other, both bellyaching about who was in charge. Big Sugar slapped Honey who returned the slap with a round house kick to the side of her head. Big Sugar staggered backwards into Christine's room followed rapidly by Honey who gave a flying kick to Sugar's face. Sugar retreated to the back wall, and used it to hold herself up. Honey tried a kick to Sugar's leg to pull her down, but Sugar's tonnage was way too much to be pulled down. Honey then delivered a kick to the left knee cap. Sugar went down trying to land on Honey. Honey was too quick and scrambled out of the way. She then came back with a flurry of savage punches and kicks to any part of Big Sugar that was vulnerable.

Meanwhile Christine had climbed on top of her chest of drawers and was trying to melt into the wall.

Three custodians came running into the room armed with nightsticks. Honey was in an adrenaline rage and quickly turned her attack to them. She flattened one of them with a kick to the chest. Christine turned her face to the wall in terror and heard a sickeningly loud crack. Then she heard nothing but panting and Big Sugar moaning.

She looked back. A female custodian was sitting by the door holding her hands to her chest and taking controlled, painful breaths. Two male custodians were standing over Honey, with their nightsticks raised. She was face down on the floor and not moving. Big Sugar was grunting, moaning and rolling around like a beached whale.

One of the men looked at Christine with anger in his eyes. "Get to your room, NOW!"

"This is my room." Her voice shook with terror as she saw the look on his face.

"Then get out in the hallway."

She started climbing down off of the chest. She had not

responded fast enough for him, so he grabbed her around the waist and tossed her out of the room to the other side of the hallway. He pointed at her with an angry look: "Don't move!"

She sat there frozen the whole time the investigation went on.

An ambulance came and took both combatants away, as well as the downed custodian. There were several people in suits and uniforms who came and took pictures in the room. After what seemed a life time, she was able to go back in her room to clean up the mess.

Two days later she was hauled up in front of an investigation team. All five of them sat there expressionless as Christine was brought in.

"We are here to discuss the incident that occurred the other day between Cassiopeia Tinkle and Hu Nee Kim."

Christine stared stupidly. "Who and what?"

"The two girls that were engaged in combat in YOUR room. The Korean girl, Hu Nee Kim, and the student supervisor, Cassiopeia Tinkle. Who else has been involved in a fight in your room?"

Christine started giggling. "Cassiopeia…Tinkle? Her name is Tinkle? No wonder she doesn't want anyone to know her name."

"…And exactly what do you know her name to be? We don't have any aliases listed here."

"You're kidding!" Christine giggled some more.

"We don't have time for joking or beating around the bush! What is her alias?"

She took several deep breaths trying to regain some composure. She cleared her throat. "The only name I heard her say was…Big Sugar." She fought hard to keep a straight face. 'Tinkle' she thought and started laughing uncontrollably.

While she laughed, all five of the investigators annotated the alias. The head of the team leaned forward: "You had better start taking this matter seriously. We want to know what happened."

"One of the guards clobbered Honey with a club."

"Honey? Who is Honey?"

"Honey Kim, the Korean girl."

"Her name is: Hu Nee, not Honey."

"That's the first I ever heard of that. I thought her name was Honey."

All five again made annotations in their paper. "I am not talking about when Hu Nee or Honey was taken down by a CUSTODIAN. I am talking about the fight prior to that. What did you see?"

"Nuthin'. I heard some yelling."

"Two students got into a fight, where both of them were injured. Don't tell me you saw nothing. It happened in your room."

"I didn't see anything. I was dusting the top of my chest of drawers and heard a bunch of yelling. Whatever happened is their problem, NOT MINE! I didn't see anything."

"You were found sitting on the top of the chest. Just what were you dusting it with?"

"My butt! You just get up there sit on it and move around."

"Don't you have any dust rags?"

"No, you use what you got. All I have is these prison rags, so I don't care if they get dirty or not. As soon as I'm finished wearing them that day, they go in the laundry'"

The investigator was getting impatient. "You said you saw Hu Nee get clobbered."

"I thought the mess was over. I looked up and saw her get belted by a guard."

"If you don't start cooperating, we will hold you in contempt."

"Oh…gee." She said with dull sarcasm. "What are you going to do? Make me have another session with that jerk, McFarlin?"

The chief investigator cleared his throat. "Four weeks individual meditation. Maybe that will make you a little more cooperative."

She sat there with the same dull expression, scratching her crotch. "Eek. Uh…I'm scared. Uh…I think."

Four weeks of heaven. Not once did she see or even hear the voice of McFarlin. She started thinking of other ways to get thrown into solitary confinement. Punch a guard, punch another student or even take poke at the main headache - McFarlin.

When she was released from meditation, they found that she was not going to be any more cooperative than before. They knew that there was a code of silence that they could not break, (unless whoever was dumb enough to talk wanted to end up maimed or dead) so they gave up and went with the scientific evidence that they had.

Christine walked into her corridor, and saw Big Sugar limping through the hall doing inspection. She was behind Big Sugar so she quietly walked into her room, not wanting to hear anything from Big Sugar right now. No good. Moments later Big Sugar was limping into the room. "What'd you tell those people on that board?"

"Nuthin'." She tried to stifle a giggle.

"What's so funny?" Sugar looked at Christine suspiciously.

"They told *me* a few things…Miss Cassiopeia Tinkle." This time she could not stop laughing. She turned away from Big Sugar laughing and then she felt a horrible pain on the right side of her head as well as dizziness. She felt herself falling and then nothing.

Christine woke up - flat on her back in the nurse's office. The entire right side of her head hurt. She had trouble focusing on anything. She had trouble opening her right eye. She finally saw the face of the nurse and was able to focus on that. She was having trouble hearing out of her right ear. The nurse was saying something but Christine was not sure what it was. She heard other garbled voices coming from somewhere else in the room. She smelled ammonia and the room stopped spinning - a little.

"Christine, can you hear me?" said the nurse.

Christine tried to respond, but could only mumble.

The nurse turned away from Christine and talked to someone

else in the room: "Where did you find her?"

"I found her in her room on the floor," said Big Sugar. "Looks to me like someone done busted her in the head and then trashed her room. Maybe they was lookin' for somethin'."

The nurse turned back to Christine. "Can you hear me? Can you understand me?"

"I'm awake," said Christine feebly.

"Okay, good. Now, I want you to follow my finger." The nurse started moving her finger around and Christine watched it. "No, Sweetie, I need you to follow my finger with your eyes only. Don't move your head."

Christine watched the moving finger closely but could hardly see anything out of her right eye. The nurse turned back to Big Sugar and Christine sat up. The whole world started spinning again and she blacked out. Again her nostrils were assaulted by the ammonia.

"Don't try to sit up again," said the nurse sternly.

"I won't," said Christine terrified.

The nurse again turned away from Christine. "I think she has a concussion. She needs to be seen by a doctor."

"Okay," said a man. "Do we need to call an ambulance or can we take her ourselves?"

"There's no blood shed, so I think we can go ahead and do the transport. Just don't let her sit up…by herself."

"Okay," said the man. "Go get the van."

"Can I go with her?" asked Big Sugar.

"Why do you need to be with her?" said the man. "You're not her doctor, or even *A* doctor. No, you can't! Now, go back to your assigned corridor."

Big Sugar made several loud protests, but eventually got the message that the Custodians would escort Christine to the hospital.

One of the male custodians picked Christine up and placed her in a wheelchair. She was then rolled out to the waiting van. They were much kinder to her this time. They did not even shackle her or strap her down, other than the seatbelt. The ride was uneventful.

When they arrived at the hospital, she was placed on a gurney and wheeled in. Two women undressed Christine - completely. She could not figure out why she had to be totally naked, until she realized that they were not just looking at her head, they were looking for needle marks - anywhere on her body. She sighed and just let them do their search, without complaining. After completing their search, they put a hospital gown on her, shackled her to the bed and finally someone started examining her head and counting her marbles.

She was taken into a room where she found out that she would be there for at least two days of observation.

At lunch time, they would not let her feed herself. The same thing happened at dinner. Now she started getting a little worried about just how much brain damage she might have.

The next morning, they got her up out of bed and helped her walk around a little. Once she was finally steady on her feet, she went into the bathroom on her own. She tried to close the door, but the ever-present guard would not give her any privacy. She sat down and did her business. When she got up, she went to the sink to wash her hands and for the first time, since the slap, she was able to look in a mirror. The entire right side of her face was one huge "hand-shaped" bruise. It was then that she realized that she had been lambasted with an open hand slap, by Big Sugar.

She was kept in the hospital for three nights. Finally, when she was able to walk without any assistance, she was released. This time, on the way back to the "school," she was shackled.

It was late afternoon, when they left the hospital and they got back just in time for dinner. After eating her dinner, she went back to her room, to find that her room had been trashed and not cleaned up. Since she did not have very many possessions, it did not take long to clean up. She was more despondent than tired, but she still went to bed early.

The next morning, she was yanked out of bed and slammed up against the wall with her feet a full two feet off of the floor. Big Sugar was glaring at her. "What is my name, you little runt?"

Christine was trying desperately not to wet herself. "Big Sugar! Big Sugar is your name."

"What was that again?"

"Big Sugar...Big Sugar." Christine started crying.

"That's right, runt. Don't ever forget it."

Christine was dumped on her bed. She slowly crawled off the bed and went to the toilet. While she was relieving her bladder, Big Sugar looked back in the room and hollered for her to hurry up and get to the exercise pad. Christine fell off the toilet, still spraying. Now she had that mess to clean up as well.

For the next month, she went everywhere staring at the ground. She let her long brown hair cover the right side of her face.

10

In February of 1985, Big Sugar moved out and was sent somewhere else. She had turned 18 and was no longer to be held in a juvenile facility. The following January, Honey Kim turned 18 and was gone as well. As each one left, Christine thought that things might get a little easier. Wrong! Every time some bully left, there always seemed to be an ample supply of other monsters to take their place, and now she had a new master who treated her like a toy.

Monday, September 12, 1988. Happy Birthday Christine. You are now 18 and because of the recommendations of Dr. McFarlin, a few other counselors and her original 'No Contest' plea - Life in an adult facility. They had a hearing on the issue of what was to be done with Ms. Christine Lee.

McFarlin got up on the stand and used terms like: Chronic liar, remorseless, in total denial and - sociopath.

"What about the stuff on minors and your record being cleared?" Christine asked several times but was ignored.

She just stared off into space as they put the manacles on her. When they got ready to move her out, she just went limp on the floor. A guard picked her up and carried her out to a waiting bus. The whole time the bus was headed to her new home, she just stared at the floor. Even if she had been released, where would she go? She had no home, no family, no possessions, no skills and no hope.

When the bus arrived at the prison, she almost had to be carried again. She could hear a lot of hooting and cheering as she and six other new inmates were taken into the "welcoming" facility. They took her juvenile clothing - all of it. Underwear, slippers, pants and shirt. She was issued an entire new wardrobe. After they stamped Christine's new number on all the items, she was told to get dressed. Since no one in this facility had ever worn clothing this small, she received no hand-me-downs like some of the other women. Everything was new and very scratchy.

She was then given a set of bed sheets, told to wrap all of her clothing in the sheet and then paraded through the prison to her cell. She tried to ignore all of the nasty cat-calls that were coming her way from various sources. When they stopped at a cell, the guard said: "This is your new home. Look at the cell number above the door. Look at it and remember it." She was then shoved inside.

An 8' x 6' cell. To the right was upper and lower beds. To the left were five shelves on the wall. A toilet just beyond the shelves on the left, and a sink with a small mirror above it, in the middle of the back wall.

The lower bed was made up and there were toiletries and clothing on some of the shelves. So there was a cellmate and she was already territorially established. Christine did not want to make waves the first day, so she placed her belongings on empty places on the shelves and then tried to figure out how to get up to the top bunk. The only form of ladder was the bars to the cell. She shrugged, threw the sheets up on the bed, and climbed the bars.

While going through the difficulty of making a bed while crawling around on it, she heard a voice that made her blood run cold.

"Well! Christmas done come early this year!"

Christine looked back in horror. There she was - big as life and even uglier than Christine could remember: Big Sugar.

"My little toy is here at this prison and she's my cellmate. Who would've figured that to happen? Number 2370716 just happens to be my favorite little toy."

Christine laid down on her bed and pressed herself against the wall. "Leave me alone. I just got here. Please, leave me alone."

"Oh no! I got some dealings to do and you're going to figure in real good with them." Big Sugar reached up and pulled Christine off the bed. "I got some people that you need to meet - now!"

Big Sugar dragged her all over the prison. She found out where the chow hall was, the infirmary, the gymnasium and certain hot spots where Big Sugar was going to profit from Christine being here. Everywhere they went Big Sugar was talking all kinds of deals where Christine was a part of each deal. For three days she was hauled around being introduced to people whose names she ignored or forgot after 5 minutes.

11

And the years go by.

Wednesday, April 16, 2008. Just another rotten day in the prison. Christine was sitting cross-legged on a bed in the infirmary. She was about to get her last dose of tetracycline today, which meant that she was going to get dumped back out in the prison population later on. She had been in quarantine for two weeks because of a contagious STD. Now she would be going back out to probably catch another STD for the twelfth time since being bought, sold and used as a sex toy. It seemed that catching, and being diagnosed with, VD was well worth the two week vacation from all the sex fiends and other extracurricular activities that her owners came up with.

The doctor did her normal routine of bringing the last dose, and trying to give the patient some advice (that no one in the prison would follow) on how to avoid STDs in the future. "Why are you so obstinate? Why don't you follow any of the advice that I give you? If you don't stop this you could catch something much worse, like genital herpes or AIDS. So far you've been lucky."

Christine rolled her eyes and then stared at the two pills in her hand. "Do I look like I'm big er strong enough to stop anyone from doin' anything they want to do to me?" She looked at the doctor. "Well? Do I?"

"You're a toy, aren't you?"

"Gee, good guess. What give you your first clue?" She

threw the pills in her mouth and swallowed.

The doctor handed her a glass of water. "Don't try being heroic. I know that if you don't wash those things down, they just hang in your chest. We don't really need the bed right now, so I'll give you a few more hours of freedom from the sexual predators out there. You don't have to leave the infirmary now unless you want to."

Christine was taken by surprise at the nice treatment. All she could say was: "Okay…thanks."

As the doctor walked away, Christine laid back in the bed and decided to enjoy four more hours of rest.

The four hours went by way too fast. She pulled off the hospital gown and put on her prison garb. As she headed for the door to leave, she could see Big Sugar waiting outside, talking to another inmate. She looked down at the floor and slowly took the last steps to the door. When she opened the door, Big Sugar turned and smiled. Christine noticed that Big Sugar had two teeth missing and she had a swollen lip and a fresh bruise on her cheek.

Big Sugar saw the look on Christine's face. "Don't worry about my teeth. You got two weeks of work to make up for."

"Aw, come on! I just got cured. Can't you let me stay clean for a few days?"

"Time is money! Let's go!" Big Sugar grabbed Christine's hand and started pulling her along, giving instructions on who she had to pleasure and how. Christine just let her mind go blank in order to not hear the vulgar details. She was not hearing anything that she had not heard 10,000 times before.

1 2

She woke up the next morning, sore and stiff - and as usual, not in her own bed. Rarely did she wake up in her assigned cell or bunk. Someone abusing her in her own bed at night had a tendency to disturb Big Sugar's "beauty sleep." Christine could not think of anyone who needed more beauty sleep than Big Sugar – preferably about twenty years of hibernation.

Christine got up, put her clothing on, and wandered into the chow hall for breakfast. After some clotted oatmeal, she went back to her cell, to clean herself up as much as possible and change clothes. After stripping and a little cleaning at the tiny sink in the cell, she climbed up to her bunk for some rest. She was too tired to bother putting any of her clothing on to lay down.

No sooner had her head hit the pillow, she heard Big Sugar come into the cell. "Where you been, you little loafer? Come on! They's work to do." Big Sugar grabbed Christine and pulled her off the bunk and dropped her on the lower bunk. Christine got a pair of pants and a shirt thrown in her face. "Put that on, now! Hurry up!" Christine reached for some underwear and got her hand slapped. "You ain't gonna need that, now hurry up!" She looked up and snarled at Big Sugar.

She slipped the pants and shirt on and was getting ready to button the shirt when Big Sugar grabbed her hand and pulled her out of the cell with the shirt flying open. "Will you let me button up and get my slippers?"

"You know you don't need that, we're late."

She tried to button up with one hand. It proved to be impossible while being dragged along. She finally gave up and just held the shirt closed.

The sight of Christine being dragged somewhere by Big Sugar was a very familiar sight to virtually everyone in the prison and hardly got a second glance from anyone.

When they went through the door into the laundry room, Christine grimaced because she knew where they were going: *The Back Room.* A small room behind the laundry where someone had put in a large bed. All kinds of kinky and perverted things with strange visitors happened in there. They arrived at the door and Big Sugar pulled Christine's shirt off, then yanked her pants down and with no hesitation shoved her through the door. She took one quick look around the room to see who was there. She sighed, walked to the mattress, flopped down on it and closed her mind to the smell and what was about to happen.

Sometime later, the door burst open. Big Sugar came in with anger on her face. She looked around at the customers and said: "I'm sorry, but I got to interrupt. Some fancy-schmancy lawyer type just showed up and is lookin' fer her. I know we had an agreement, but this guy is gettin' mad and our whole shootin' match could be messed up if we don't let him talk to her. She'll just have to make it up to you later."

She dragged Christine from the bed and out of the room, and into a makeshift shower stall that everybody called *the pit.* Christine was trying to rub some feeling back into her legs while Big Sugar grabbed the fire hose. "Stand up so I can wash you off."

"I can't feel my legs. Just give me a few..." She was cut off by a blast of water from the fire hose that slammed and pinned her to the back wall.

"We gotta get all that sweaty smell off of you before you see this guy. Speakin' of which who is he? When didja contact him? What's goin' on with you talkin' to a lawyer?" Christine could do nothing but sputter and cough from all the water that had been blasted up her nose and in her mouth.

"Talk to me! I wanna know what's goin' on!"

"I don't know. I ain't contacted nobody. I wouldn't know who or how or why to contact no lawyer. When would I have a chance to contact anybody?"

"You was goofin' off in that infirmary for two weeks - don't tell me you didn't have time."

"Okay, then why? Why would I need to talk to some lawyer? You think that I'm gonna sue you?"

"You best not be joshin' with me. If he's coming on to you for something, you best not be interested."

"He's probably some bleedin' heart ACLU liberal, whats tryin' to make some name for hisself. Just think - if I get out of here, where am I goin' to go? What do I got out there? A home? A family? A job? I'd be spending the next ten years in a halfway house learnin' how to be a minimum wage waitress. Whoop-de-doo! What a life? Then what do I do?"

"All I know is that you had best not cross me." A strange look crossed her face. "Why you peeing on yourself?"

"What?" Christine looked down. "I'm numb from the waist down! I can't feel nuthin'. I didn't know I was…" She got another blast of water from the hose. She sat there sputtering and coughing again while she tried to rub some feeling back into her legs.

Big Sugar started rubbing Christine with a towel. "Where did you get that thing," cried Christine, "it's wetter'n I am."

"Huh?" Big Sugar looked back at the opposite wall. "It musta got hit with backwash." She grabbed Christine and dragged her out of *the pit*, back to where her clothes had been left. "Put 'em on and let's go."

"I'm still soakin' wet."

"We'll go back to the cell and get you somethin' dry there. Now hurry!"

Christine got the pants pulled up and the shirt on and again before she could button up, Big Sugar was dragging her away. Again she had to take the whole trip holding her shirt closed.

When they got back to the cell, again, Big Sugar pulled out a towel and started drying Christine off. "Will you cut that out?! You're scrapin' my skin off and pullin' hair out."

"Well, hurry up!"

Christine started brushing the bottoms of her feet off.

"What are you doin'? Get dried and dressed!"

"You dragged me out of there wet and barefoot. I got dirt all over my feet. I don't like the idea of puttin' my dirty feet through clean panties because I might get dirt in the panties and when I pull them up - not comfortable."

Big Sugar picked Christine up and dunked her feet into the toilet.

"What are you doin'?"

"I'm tryin' to get your feet cleaned so you can hurry up."

"Will you please let me do it? I can do it faster without your help."

Big Sugar dumped her on the bed. She stripped her shirt and pants off and hastily dried herself. As she grabbed some underwear, Big Sugar started straightening Christine's hair.

"What are you doin'? You're pullin' my hair out!"

"Well you ain't movin' fast enough."

Christine pulled away and backed off from Big Sugar. "Look! I can get this done a lot faster if you just lemme be."

"You ain't doin' it fast enough."

"Just go wait outside of the cell…go, go, GO!"

Big Sugar grunted and walked out of the cell.

Christine picked up the underwear, and put it on while she glared at Big Sugar. After putting on the pants, shirt and slippers, she tried to brush some of the messy tangles out of her hair.

Big Sugar came in the cell grabbed, the brush away, threw it down and started dragging Christine. "Come on. You can pretty yourself up later for someone more important." Away they went in the usual way with Christine being dragged by her owner.

When they arrived at the visitation center, Big Sugar pushed

Christine in ahead of her. "Sir, I found her fer yuh."

The guard looked at her rather strangely. "You look like a drowned rat. Where have you been?"

"Sir, I was in that there laundry room. It's kinda hot in there." She shrugged her shoulders and gave the guard a weak smile.

"Yeah. Well that lawyer has been getting awful impatient." The guard looked off to his left. "Prisoner 2370716, Lee. That lawyer in room 4."

Another guard walked up to Christine with manacles. She looked at the chains and shook her head. "Ma-am, what's that fer? I'm goin' to see a lawyer in here."

"SOP," said the guard. "No prisoner is allowed to see anyone without the chains."

She stood there shaking her head while being trussed up with the belly band and chains, wondering to herself just who was the nut-case that made up these ridiculous rules. After being secured, she was led to the room.

13

As Christine entered the room, a building, disguised as the largest human being she had ever seen in her life stood up and smiled. He had very short brown hair, big brown eyes, a boyish face and muscles on top of muscles. He held out a massive hand: "Hello, my name is David Murdoch. I am your legal representative now."

"Hullo, my name's Christine Lee, my hands is cuffed at my side, so I can't shake yer hand and I ain't interested in no legal repersentation." She looked at the guard. "Can I go back to my cell, now?"

"I have a court order here. No, you cannot go until we have had a little chat. Now, have a seat." He handed some papers to the guard.

She frowned as she read what was on it. She looked up at the big man confused. "Is this for real?"

"Absolutely. Will you please make the preparations?"

"Someone else will do that. I have to stay here." She took Christine to a chair by the table. "Sit!" She then went to a phone, picked it up and waited a few moments. "I need Supervisor Berg down here. You're not going to believe this."

Murdoch looked at the shackles on Christine. "Would you please take the cuffs of her hands? I may need her signature on some documents and it will be a little awkward the way she is now."

The guard unlocked Christine's left hand and then locked it in a cuff attached to the table. She then released the right hand. "That's as far as it goes."

"Could we have a little privacy now? You know - attorney-client stuff."

"The supervisor will be here shortly to take care of this. I will be right outside watching."

Christine sat there the whole time itching with curiosity as to what was on that piece of paper and why it was getting the attention of a supervisor.

Murdoch looked at the cuff on her left wrist. "Is all that really necessary?"

"SOP! Here, we have to keep an eye on our charge no matter what. If you are worried about privileged information - I don't read lips." The guard walked out and closed the door. She turned and stared back through the window at Christine.

"As I said; I am your new lawyer. Your old one - Mr. Thomas Reese - is in trouble. One of his great flaws was that he never took any case seriously and for that he may be disbarred."

"So what! What I care about his problems?"

"Because you are going to get a new trial."

"A new trial. After 25 years. Who cares? What are you gonna to find anyway? I still don't know what happened that night. It's still a complete blurred mystery to me."

"If Mr. Reese had looked at some of the crime scene photographs, he might have been able to do something, then. Those photographs and the four boxes of evidence help fill in some blanks. I need you to fill in some of the other blanks."

Christine growled in frustration. "I don't know what happened that night. How many ways and how many times do I have to say it afore someone finally believes me?"

"This is NOT about that night. This is about you, your mother and your father. Any little detail you can tell me about your family history may be crucial to your defense."

"Defend me…for or from WHAT? Even if you do get me out of here, what am I gonna do and where am I gonna go? I got nothing out there. I've been inside since I was 12 years old, and I don't know nuthin' else."

He looked confused for a moment. "Are you telling me that you have no idea what is in those boxes?"

She looked off to the side and sighed. "I didn't even know that there was any boxes. The only thing that I know of that survived the fire is me and some negligee that I'd never seen afore in my life."

"Did you ever see your mother wearing it?"

"Did yer mother ever wear a see-through in front uh you?"

He was obviously surprised with her question. He gave her a strange look, then cleared his throat. "Did you ever see it in the laundry basket?"

She clenched both fists, closed her eyes and talked very slowly through clenched teeth: "I never seed that thing before in my life." She opened her eyes: "And I ain't seed it since."

He looked thoughtful for a moment. "I notice that you have

been offered a chance at parole twice, but turned it down. Why?"

"I'm a lifer. I got no skills other than somethin' that would put me back in here. Who would trust me with any kind of decent job? Where would I go? What would I do? There's nuthin' out there for me. I'd have to spend the rest of my life with a baby-sittin' parole officer lookin' over my shoulder. I'm better off here where I know what the score is."

"I see that you gave birth, while in juvenile detention. Aren't you the least interested in the location of…?"

"Don't you even bring that up again!" She screamed at him. She had grabbed the edge of the table and would have pushed it into him if it had not been bolted to the floor. As a result all she could do was sit there doing a white-knuckle clutch on the edge of the table.

Upon seeing her lose her temper, the guard was in the room immediately.

David gave the guard a condescending look. "What are you doing? Did I ask you to interrupt anything?"

"I saw her…"

"Do you think that this little woman is going to overwhelm me? I am 6 foot 7 inches tall, I weigh 345 pounds, I was a lineman in college football as well as a member of the wrestling team and I still workout regularly. I don't think that she could possibly outmuscle me, especially since she's shackled to the table."

The guard opened her mouth to say something.

"GO! You don't need to come back in here unless you see that she has me pinned to the floor in a choke hold."

At that moment, the supervisor showed up. The guard backed out while closing the door and keeping a close watch on Christine. She showed the document to the supervisor who started reading.

David turned back to Christine. "Well, I have brought it up. I brought it up on purpose. I need to know what happened the day you gave birth as well as what you saw and did."

She looked down fighting hard to keep from crying. She bit her lip as a tear rolled down her cheek. She took long slow breaths to hide any sniffling. "That mornin', I took a shower. When I got back to my room, my water broke. For the rest of the day I's pretty much helpless."

While she was talking he had been doing some quick writing on a legal pad. He stopped writing, and looked at her. "Were you unconscious for the rest of the day?"

"No."

He looked at her more intensely. "…and?"

"I was lyin' on a bed waiting for the amblance. When it finally showed up, there was a head stickin' out, twixt my legs. I had to go through the whole thing, right there."

He stopped writing and looked up. "Keep going."

She leaned back in her chair. She looked up at the ceiling and sighed. "Why? Do you want ALL of the gory details?"

"You would probably be amazed at what can happen. Some of the most incredible defenses and prosecutions have been brought to the final solution, because of seemingly insignificant details. Yes,

I want to know anything you remember."

She stared at him, angrily, trying to read anything in his eyes. She could see nothing helpful. She gave up and started her story: "As I said, the first one was already comin'. The doctor got me repositioned on the bed and then the baby was out. There was a sheet covering what was goin' on, so I didn't even get a glimpse of the baby." Her voice cracked, her eyes watered and she started sniffling again. "9:13 am, he said. The first one was born. They cut the cord. He started cryin'. They wrapped him in a blue towel and run him out the room without lettin' me see any part of him." She put her hand over her mouth to try to maintain any control of her emotions. It didn't work. Several wracking sobs later, she took a deep breath and stared off to the side.

"Go on," he said softly.

She sat up straight and wiped her eyes. "When my second son came out, the doctor announced it was 9:17am. They did their do and this time the nurse ran out with a cryin' green bundle. Then my third baby boy - 9:24am. Then out with a cryin' red bundle." She sat motionless for a while. "I didn't even get to see the afterbirths."

"How did you know they were all boys?"

She started giggling, then smiled triumphantly. "I accidentally tricked Doctor Dumbbell into that'n." She closed her eyes and laughed a little harder. "Oh, did that get him. I don't remember ever seein' him that far off his nut. One of the few times, I got the better part of the argument on that skunk."

"Doctor...Dumbbell?"

"That head shrinker - Doctor McFarlin."

"Okay, what were you going to name them?"

She tightened her lips. "What possible difference could that make now? That was almost 25 years ago and they all got names given to 'em by someone else."

"Humor me, what were you going to name them?"

"Tom, Dick and Harry," she spat at him.

There was a knock on the door. They both looked at the door as the supervisor came through. He had a rather angry look on his face as he approached. "Look, I don't know what's going on here, but I don't have time for any ridiculous shenanigans. Just what…"

"Can you read?" shouted David.

"Well, of course I can…"

"Can you follow instructions?"

"Yes, but…"

"Then read what is on document and follow the instructions. I'm trying to take care of my client right now and I don't have time for ANY shenanigans - yours or mine. Is there anything else?"

"Well, no!"

"Good! Now can I get back to my business here?"

The supervisor shrugged his shoulders and looked around helplessly. "Sure! Whatever! The next bus will be the afternoon run at 2:30. Is that acceptable?"

"If there is nothing sooner, it'll have to do. Thank you."

Berg turned and left while re-reading the document.

Christine looked at him confused. "You're leavin' the prison on a prison bus?"

"No, you are. The bus transportation is for you."

"Huh?"

"It's all spelled out on the document I gave them."

Christine could not hold it anymore. "What's on that paper?"

"It's a transfer, for you, from here to a holding cell in town, until I can get a new arraignment, bail and a release for you."

Her shoulders sagged and she sat there, slack-jawed, in shock.

"I told you, I'm working on a new trial for you. I am going in with evidence that Mr. Reese never considered."

"But…bail…trial…WHAT?" She was beginning to panic. She had no idea what to ask or how or why. All she could think of was how mad Big Sugar was going to be when she found out.

"Now, we have a little while before the bus…"

"Forget the bus," she shouted, "I ain't goin' nowhere with you! I don't want no new trial. I just wanna be left alone."

His eyebrows went up. "In prison?"

She opened her mouth but all she could muster was a high-pitched squeak.

"The wheels are already in motion on this. I really don't think you belong here and I am going to do everything I can to get you out."

She laid her head on the table and groaned. She was still thinking of how mad Big Sugar was going to be and the beating she might get as a result.

"Now, again, we have a little time to go over a few more things…" He stopped when he saw a strange suspicious look on her face.

"I know what this is all about." She closed her eyes and shook her head. "You want to get me out." She started drumming her fingers on the table. "You want me out so YOU can profit. Well, I don't need nother pimp!"

He had a pained look on his face. He leaned back in his chair and spoke in a very solemn tone. "That word does NOT ever need to come up in any of our conversations again. It has no place in either of our vocabularies."

She raised her eyebrows mockingly. "What do you call it outside these walls now?"

"I am your lawyer. I am not trying to get you out to abuse you. I am trying to get you out in order to stop any abuse that you are suffering from."

"What difference it make to you? What're you gettin' out of it?" She shook her head and then stared down at the table.

"My job is to make sure that justice is served."

"And puttin' me out on the street with no means of support is servin' justice?"

He sighed. "You really don't know what is in those boxes."

She laid her head, face down, on the table. "Don't know and

don't care."

"You won't be stuck out on the streets. We could also start looking for your sons and then you could meet them and go through the boxes together - how does that sound?"

She looked up at him and narrowed her eyes. What boxes? What difference does it make what's in them? What does he really want? Why is he really doing this? Is he kidding - How could he possibly find my sons?

He asked more questions that were totally meaningless to her. She was getting more confused by the minute trying to figure him out.

The banter went on until the guard notified them that it was 2:15 and they needed to get her out to the bus. She was unhooked from the table re-shackled and led out to the waiting bus.

The entire time she kept on complaining that she did not want to leave. She just wanted to be left alone. As usual no one listened. Everyone else controlled her life.

During the bus ride, the same questions about his motives or intentions kept plaguing her. She finally decided that she could not answer them herself, so just wait and see what was going to happen. Ever since she had been first arrested, after the fire, not once had she been able to control or decide anything for herself. Everyone else made the decisions for her. The only time that anyone had listened to her and complied with her wishes was the doctor who refused the abortion.

The bus finally arrived downtown at the county courthouse. Christine and eight other passengers were taken to the basement holding area. Seven of the women were put in a large jail cell, while Christine and another woman were taken to interrogation rooms. David was already there talking to the air. She looked around the room - no one. He was not talking to her or either of her two escorts. Both of the escorts ignored him as they shackled her to the table, and then departed.

He continued his one sided conversation for a few more moments, then touched his ear. He looked at her and saw the puzzled look on her face. "Are you okay? Is there something wrong?"

"You settin' there, talkin' to yourself and you're askin' me if I'm okay?"

"I was talking on my phone."

She looked all around him as well as under the table. "I don't see no phone."

He looked at her slightly confused. "My phone tooth."

"What?"

"I was talking on my phone tooth."

She shook her head even more puzzled. "You're talkin' to your tooth?"

He pulled the tooth off of his right ear. "This! My phone tooth."

She looked even more perplexed. She chuckled nervously and cleared her throat. "That's a hearin' aid...ain't it?"

He pursed his lips. "Do you know what a cellular phone is?"

"My parents had a telephone. What's a cellar phone? Is it

different then a telephone?"

He pulled his cell phone off his belt. "This is a cellular, or cell phone. It is a completely wireless phone. It is connected, again wirelessly, to this phone tooth. I put the phone tooth in my ear and I can talk on the phone, totally hands free."

She looked even more doubtful. "Yeah! Right!" She smiled. She swallowed hard, wondering what kind of a nut she was being stuck with.

"Doesn't that prison have a television that you can watch occasionally and keep up with some of the new technology?"

Her shoulders sagged. "I ain't seen a television - let alone watched one - since I don't know when. Big Sugar usually keeps me busy…" She flushed and cleared her throat. "…doin' other things."

He put his hands to his forehead and rubbed up and down. "Wow," he said softly. "After we get you out of here, we are definitely going to have to work on your education."

"I don't want no education, I don't want no trial, I just want to be left alone." She closed her eyes and shook her head. "Why can't you just let me be?"

"Do you really want to go back to being abused by that person: Big Sugar?"

She stared down at the table. "At least there, I know the score."

The two of them sat in silence for a few moments. Christine heard the door open behind her. David stood up, smiled and walked around the table. A tall thin woman with brown hair pulled back into a pony tail walked up to David and they embraced. David looked at Christine, "This is my wife, Paula."

Christine gave Paula a smile and thought: 'Big deal.'

He looked at Paula. "This is Christine Lee."

"Oh," said Paula. "This is that case that has been keeping you busy all this time."

"Yes, she is the…"

At that moment a very loud gurgling sound came out of Christine. She grimaced and looked down at the floor.

David looked bewildered. "Didn't you have some lunch or something?"

"You had me in that room, hooked to the table right through lunch. I ain't had nuthin' to eat…" She looked away. "…or had a chance to go to the bathroom, since before I first seen you."

David went to the door, opened it and called a guard in. "My client needs a bathroom break."

A guard came in, unhooked Christine from the table and led her out to a toilet where she had no privacy at all. She was too tired to complain. She simply did her business and then was led back to the interrogation room.

David glanced at Christine then back to Paula. "Did you get hold of that guy Randall?"

"No. I got hold of that Randall WOMAN."

"Okay. Have the arrangements been set up?"

"Yes, she is waiting in the courtroom right now…on the clock."

"That figures."

After Christine was reconnected to the table, Paula pulled a brown paper bag out of her purse. From the bag came a plastic bag with a sandwich in it. Paula gave half the sandwich to Christine and the other half to David. He waved it away. "She needs that more than I do. I picked up a burger on the way back from the prison." Paula shrugged and set the rest of the sandwich in front of Christine.

Christine took a quick bite of the sandwich, started chewing rapidly and then stopped. She sat back in the chair, closed her eyes and concentrated on the different tastes in her mouth. She started chewing slowly savoring every new flavor, great or small, that hit her tongue.

"What's wrong, dear?" Paula was looking at Christine with a concerned look on her face. "You're crying."

Christine opened her eyes and flushed. She swallowed hard and realized she was crying. "It's nuthin'. I ain't…" She looked at the sandwich. "It's got *taste*. I ain't had nuthin' in my mouth that had *taste* in years. All the food at that prison is just so many different colored lumps that ain't got no taste." She sniffled a little. "This has taste." She took a smaller bite, closed her eyes and sat back chewing slowly, thinking only of the long forgotten tastes that were once again in her mouth.

"Enjoy." David said softly. "We have about 30 minutes before we have to be in front of the Judge." He looked at Paula, then back at Christine. "Enjoy all of it."

Christine noticed that his eyes seemed to mist a little. She shrugged it off and went back to the task of eating her best meal in years. After she finished she looked at Paula and meekly asked: "What was that?"

Paula looked slightly shocked, then confused. "That was a tuna fish salad sandwich."

"That's all?"

"Maybe it's the spices I added."

"What spices?"

Before Paula could answer, there was a knock on the door. Someone on the other side of the door called in: "The dockets are going fast. You need to get up to the courtroom now."

David and Paula scooped up all of the papers and shoved them into his briefcase. "We're ready," he called back.

A guard came in, unhooked Christine from the table and led her out to an elevator. When the doors closed and the elevator started moving, Christine felt her knees buckle a little. She looked at David and laughed nervously: "I ain't been in one of these critters in years," she said with a sheepish smile.

David leaned close to her ear and whispered: "Just remember, not guilty."

Her shoulders sagged. She shook her head. For over 25 years everybody had been telling her what to do and where to go. She was wondering if she would ever have any say on anything ever again.

14

Her case was called up and the bailiff brought her to the front of the courtroom next to David. They read off all of the information that she had hated hearing in 1983, and did not sound any better today. When the Judge asked for plea, Christine opened her mouth and belched. She bit her lower lip, looked at the judge terrified and then David. "Sorry!"

"Sorry about that, your honor," said David hastily. "My client just finished a hearty meal, before being brought in here. The plea is not guilty on all counts."

The Judge cleared his throat. "Mm-hmm. Normally, I have to hear it from the defendant. All things considered, I shudder to think of what else might come out of that mouth." He looked at the District Attorney. "Bail recommendations?"

"This woman has no family, no home, no money and nothing to keep her here. She is a definite flight risk. My recommendation is that she be held without bail."

'What a surprise,' thought Christine. 'Same garbage I heard 25 years ago.'

"My client does have a place to stay and I will agree to an ankle monitor on her," said David quickly.

"Oh really." The Judge glanced back and forth between the two lawyers. "And, just where is that?"

"My home."

The only one in the courtroom, who was not staring at David slack-jawed was Paula.

The Judge stammered a little. After getting back his composure he glared at David. "Mr. Murdoch. I do not have time for comedy acts…"

"Neither do I." David fired back quickly. "Now can we get a bail amount, Your Honor? Please."

The Judge's shoulders sagged. He cocked his head looking totally bewildered. "You're serious?"

"Yes! As you said, this is not the place for any comedy act."

The Judge looked at the Assistant District Attorney who was speechless. "Well. How refreshing. A defense attorney who puts his money where his mouth is." He waved his hand at the ADA. "Any objections now? His home. An ankle monitor. Well? We're burning daylight."

The ADA stammered a little. Then he shrugged his shoulders. "We are talking about two counts of second degree murder. I would recommend at least a million."

"Very well. Bail is one million dollars. Once bail is made, she will be under house arrest at the residence of Mr. Murdoch and she will wear an ankle monitor." He banged his gavel. He gave David another confused glance, and shook his head before calling the next case.

The ADA rushed over to David. "Have you lost your mind? That is the most unbelievable thing I've ever heard of."

David looked down his nose. "I made a promise. I intend to

keep it."

"Well, she is going to stay in jail because no one is going to put up that kind of bail - at least not for her."

At that moment, Paula walked up to David. "Here's the bail ticket for Christine."

David took it and smiled. "Well, Craig, it looks like she will be out of jail sooner than you think."

"No, no, no. You still have to make arrangements with a bonded security company for the ankle monitor. That will take a couple of…" He trailed off as he saw a dark haired woman standing next to Paula. "Evelyn Randall! Randall Security Services. What is going on? Did you already have this set up?"

David gave the ADA a huge closed mouth grin.

The ADA walked away muttering something about a snake.

David turned to Randall. "How much equipment is involved?"

"The main monitor and the ankle monitor. The main is hooked up to a telephone land line and it monitors the anklet."

"How far?"

"She has to stay within 50 feet of the main. Anything beyond that and it goes off. The police are called after the anklet has been beeping for 10 seconds and there should be a response within 5 to 10 minutes. Even if it is 10 minutes before the police get there, the anklet has a GPS monitor. They will be able to track her within 6 feet."

"I'll have to get my tape measure and find out just what the perimeter is so we don't have any incidents." He turned to Paula. "Did you get…?"

"Yes, dear," she said somewhat impatiently. "Over 500 feet of string and 3 dozen tent pegs."

Randall looked surprised as well. "You have been doing some very thorough pre-planning. What's this all about?"

David gave her a whimsical smile, "Justice. Can we be off now?"

"The string and the tent pegs are for justice?"

"No. We might have to establish the outside perimeter with string, so that she will know exactly where she can go outside. Can we please get going?"

"Sure," said Randall with a smile. "My van is in the east parking lot."

He kissed Paula. "See you at the house."

15

When they got to the big utility van, they found Christine already in the back, buckled in the side bench seats between two prison guards - one man and one woman. "What are you doing here?" David was a little bewildered. "She has been bailed out. We don't need you."

The woman gave him a stern look. "She has been bailed out under special circumstances. Until that anklet is on her and the main monitor is activated, we stay with her."

David looked at Randall who was nodding in agreement. He shrugged and climbed in the van. He looked at the male guard. "Do you mind if I sit next to her?"

Both guards answered simultaneously: "Yes."

David decided not to push the issue. He sat on the opposite bench and buckled up. Randall closed the back doors and went to the front. She got in the driver's seat and looked at her assistant who was working with a small device. "What are you doing with that?"

He looked up. "I measured her ankle. I'm adjusting it so it will fit her. I've never set up one this small before."

Randall looked back at Christine, then down at her ankles. She shrugged, buckled up and started the van.

"Don't you even THINK of taking the scenic route," said David sternly.

"Not a problem," laughed Randall.

"Hey, lawyer!" said Christine. "You said that you could help me find my boys."

"Yes."

"How long's it gonna take?"

He smiled and licked his lips. "As long as it takes and whatever it takes. I made you a promise and I keep my promises."

Christine felt a huge lump in her throat and her heart was racing. So many things had been taken from her, one way or another, and now here he was making noises about her finally getting something back. She did not care about freedom. She was now so used to being abused, that it no longer bothered her. The thought of just getting to see her sons…maybe talk to them, or even touch them. Hold them. Kiss them. Would they want to see her? Would they care? Would they turn their backs on her because of her being a convict? If just one of them would accept her that would be more than she had ever hoped for.

David saw the different expressions on her face as she muddled through her thoughts. "We have a wonderful thing called the Internet. It is absolutely amazing the wealth of information that is shared on it. We can find all kinds of other people who will help in a networking search for anything you want to find." He leaned forward and smiled. "I give you my solemn promise that you WILL be reunited with your boys."

She was having a difficult time breathing properly. She thought that it was blood pounding through her ears, until the male guard said: "What's that thumping sound?"

Everyone was looking around puzzled. The thump was getting louder and more frequent.

"Slow down!" Cried the assistant. "I think we're about to lose a tire!"

At that moment, they heard a loud bump, then a grinding noise and a much louder thumping from a piece of the tire that was slapping the interior of the fender well. Randall had a little trouble keeping the van under control, and let it lose momentum rather than slam on the brakes. When they finally came to a stop, Randall looked at her assistant. "Which one do you think it is, Dale?"

He groaned. "Which part of the van is leaning down?" He murmured sarcastically.

"Your corner, Dale," snickered David.

Dale unbuckled, opened his door got out and looked at the front right tire. He shook his head, leaned in the van: "It's a goner." He looked back behind the van. "There's pieces of it scattered all over the road."

Randall sucked on her teeth. "How long will it take you to change it?"

Dale gave her a helpless laugh. "That *was* the spare."

The female guard was looking out the windshield. "Isn't that a full service station just beyond that burger joint on the left?"

Randall looked where she was pointing. "It is. I guess if I go slowly we will be able to get there without much more damage."

"I thought he said the tire was totaled."

"I'm talking about saving the rim."

The half block trip took an eternity. Randall pulled in and Dale walked inside. A mechanic came out, looked at the tire on the driver's side. They did not have the same brand, but they did have the same size and the change would take about 45 minutes seeing as how they needed a new spare as well.

For safety purposes, no one could stay inside the van. Christine got unhooked from her seat and was now outside and being stared at by everyone who came by.

She looked at her female guard. "I gotta hit the bathroom."

David looked a little surprised. "You just went in the courthouse."

She gave him a mocking smile. "This time it's the occasion where even a man'd sit down."

She was led to the ladies room. They checked inside to make sure she could not escape. Then unhooked her hands and in she went. She just sat down and rubbed her wrists.

All of the questions that had been buzzing through her mind kept repeating themselves over and over. She could not figure what was David's motivation for getting her out and…inviting *her* into *his* house.

She heard David outside the door having another one-sided conversation. Obviously he was talking to his tooth again. She was very curious, and felt a little intimidated, by this technology. She did not have anything better to do, so she listened in on what he was saying: "Yes, just like the pictures…On the first page, dummy…

Right…Just give it to Paula…Not yours - Mine…Right…Have Gwen and Veronica gotten their stuff ready…Good."

Then Christine heard the security woman talking to David. "Are you nuts?"

"Hold on, someone else is talking to me, I'll have to get back to you." Then Christine heard an angry: "What?!"

"I heard you say that you would find her estranged children."

"Yes, so what's your problem?"

"Do you have any idea how impossible that is?"

"Do you have any idea how many adopted children there are out there that are ready to help network and surf and search and share any kind of information they have for that purpose? Everybody scratching everybody else's back to try to find out anything. There is also *Freedom of information* stuff.

"Okay, I understand that, but the chances are still very slim that you'll find anything."

"Would you care to make a wager on that?"

"You're kidding, right?"

"No."

"For me it's a no win situation. If you do find them, you win. If you don't find them I don't win because you keep coming back with: Still looking! Still looking! Still looking! Still looking! I never win."

"All right, put a deadline on it."

"Huh?"

"If you put a deadline on it, then if I haven't found them by that date, you are a winner."

Christine heard nothing but silence. She stood up and went closer to the door.

"Okay, I'll call your bluff. Today is April 17. If you have not found them by the fourth of July, I win."

With no hesitation Christine heard David give an emphatic answer: "Done!" Her heart nearly skipped a beat. He had promised earlier to find them, and now he had just made a bet on a hard deadline. She looked at herself in the mirror over the sink and saw a very frantic face. She was having a hard time breathing and could not even think of how far away July was.

While she was trying to digest all of the information, a sudden knock on the door nearly made her do what she had said she was going to do in here. "Hey," shouted the female guard. "Are you about finished in there?"

"What? Uh…yeah! I just need to wash my hands." She flushed the toilet, even though it had not been used. She turned on the faucet and splashed some cold water on her face. She looked at herself in the mirror again. "Who is this guy? What does he really want? Why me?" Baffling indeed. She cut off the water, dried her face and hands and opened the door. She had to go through the indignity of a ritualistic frisking (as if there were something worth stealing in a 6' x 6' bathroom, with nothing but a toilet, a sink, a mirror, a trashcan, a roll of toilet paper, and a stack of paper hand towels). Then back in the handcuffs.

While they waited for the tire replacement, Christine heard David and Randall haggling over the price of the security system that was to be installed. It seemed that the overall price, as well as something called extracurricular activities, was going to be the resulting reward for the wager. 'Right,' she thought. 'He's arguing over a few bucks on that security system after posting a 1 million dollar bond.' She was getting a headache.

Finally the van was ready, and off they went. She tried not to think. Whatever he was planning, she was going to find out anyway, sooner or later.

16

They finally arrived at the destination. The security van was directed around to the back of the house. Dale handed the ankle monitor to Randall. He then picked up a large box and stepped out of the van. He looked back at David. "I need to put big brother here, near a phone line, so…"

"Paula is coming out now. Tell her and she'll show you where it goes."

Dale looked out, then back at David. "Copy."

The guards finished unhooking Christine from the van, and led her out. When she saw the house she just stood there gaping. It was a huge two-story structure made of brown brick. There was a large patio in the back with a built-in brick barbeque, as well as a hot tub. She was standing in a massive back yard that had several tall shade trees randomly growing in the vast area. There was a high wooden fence which encompassed the entire yard which included a good sized swimming pool. The guards were noticeably impressed with the house as well.

"Uh-oh," said Randall.

"What's the problem?" asked David

"I didn't know that the house was this big. We may have to tweak the box to 60 or 70 feet."

"What kind of problem is that?"

"Oh, no big deal. Dale will be taking some measurements to make sure. That way there won't be any false alarms because she just happens to use the wrong bathroom or help put linen in a wrong closet that just happens to be too far away. She just won't have much space outside, and she for sure will not be able to go swimming. The pool is outside her electronic perimeter."

Christine was led through a large kitchen, through a hall and into a living room that was larger than her parents' house had been in total. She looked around in awe thinking that whatever punishment Big Sugar was going to deal out would be worth it if she had to live in this place for even just a few days of luxury. She sat down on a couch and sank down into what had to be the softest piece of furniture she had ever sat on in her life. She sat back and closed her eyes. Nothing seemed to matter anymore as long as she could just sit…here…forever.

Someone nudged Christine in the shoulder. She looked up and realized that she had been asleep. She wanted to smack the guard for waking her up. The nap had been glorious. She also noticed that while she had been asleep, the guards had removed all her shackles, without waking her.

She also noticed that David was no longer wearing his suit. He was wearing green hospital scrubs. She shrugged it off. It is his home, and he can wear anything he wants to at home.

Dale came in with the anklet. "Okay. I've set the box at 70 feet. From front to rear was no problem, but side to side…ho boy. As soon as we get it on her, it'll be activated and we're done."

Randall took the monitor and placed it around Christine's left ankle. Two little moves with a strange looking screwdriver and it beeped. It beeped several more times until a green light came on. "Now! As long as the light is green, you are within your perimeter. If you step outside of your boundaries, it will turn red and start making a lot of loud noises. If you don't get back inside your boundary within 10 seconds, the police will be called and you will be on your way back to jail. If you try cutting it off, the alarm goes off, and back to jail for you. I don't know how much of the yard you can walk around in but it is not much. Better for all concerned for you to stay inside. Any questions?"

Christine placed her left foot on her right knee to get a better look at the little parasitic machine on her ankle.

David looked at Randall with a smile. "I don't think we will have any problem with the boundaries."

Randall stood up and walked toward David. "Now! Why don't you tell her the truth about your futile search?"

David looked confused.

"You know what I'm talking about. There is very little chance of you finding her children and you know it. Tell her the truth. Come on, big lawyer man. Tell her."

David rolled his eyes and huffed. "I don't have to look very hard at all." He walked toward Christine with a smile. His eyes got misty. "I was hired to find you."

Christine decided to try a little casual finesse. "Yeah, by who? Who would possibly care that much about me?"

"Tom, Dick and Harry!"

At that moment Paula walked in the room carrying a baby.

She had changed into green hospital scrubs as well. She and everyone else in the room looked at David and gave a simultaneous: "What?!"

Finesse flew out the door. Christine was on her feet staring at him with shock, hope, anger and a little dizziness from standing so fast. She could not even think of what to ask or how. The only thing that she could think of was that if he was joking - somehow, someway - she was going to hurt him...badly.

"Sit down and listen," said David. "I'll explain it all to you."

"First, you're going to explain what 'the three nothings', have to do with all this," said Paula.

David looked at Paula with a bit of a strained smile. "I asked her what she would have named her sons and she said...uh... somewhat emphatically: Tom, Dick and Harry."

Paula snorted trying not to laugh. She bit her lip and looked at Christine. "Okay." She looked back and forth between David and Christine. She snorted again and turned away, rocking her baby.

David looked back at Christine. He held up a piece of paper. "Do you know what this is?"

Christine looked at it totally bewildered. There was very little writing on it. There were several smudges. They varied from almost visible to very dark. She stood there with her mouth open. She looked at David and just shook her head.

"It looks like DNA," said the male guard.

David looked at him. "Correct, Mister...?"

"Ellis. Sergeant Ellis."

"Ellis." David looked back at Christine. "Sergeant Ellis is quite correct. "This is DNA…*your* DNA. Now I know you are lacking in your knowledge of technology, but can you tell me if you studied biology in school?"

"I member somethin' bout DNA when I was in some biology class in juvie, but I don't member much bout it."

"Okay. What we can do with computers now is map out anyone's DNA. Once we have it in this form, the computer can compare your DNA to the DNA of someone else, and tell if they are related." He leaned forward a little. "Are you with me so far?"

"Uh…I think so."

"Good." He picked up another piece of paper. "Now, on this page I have the DNA of someone else. When compared to yours, the computer tells us that the two DNA's are those of people who are related, biologically. One is the parent - the other is a child. Since both of your parents are deceased, you have no other living relatives, then the second one has to be one of your children."

She felt her entire body trembling. "Who's the other DNA?"

He paused to take a long breath. "Dick."

She grabbed the second sheet. There was writing at the top and she wanted to see if it was the name of the person this DNA belonged to. Her vision was blurred by the tears in her eyes. She wiped her eyes and looked. "It's got *your* name written on here," she cried. "Who is this?"

His eyes started to tear up. "That is Dick." He fought a little to keep his voice from cracking. "And if you look…" He pointed to his left.

"...over there coming in from the foyer is Tom and Harry."

She looked at his arm. She nearly got whiplash from turning her head to see where he was pointing. Two men came walking into the room. Their faces and build were exact duplicates of David. One of them was wearing blue hospital scrubs. The other was wearing red hospital scrubs. The one in blue had a big grin on his face and moist eyes. The one in red had long tear streaks going down his face. They walked up and stood on either side of David. In a voice that sounded exactly like David, the one in blue spoke: "Hello... Mom." The one in red was too choked up to talk.

Several times she looked back and forth from the DNA papers to the three men standing in front of her. Her mind was totally blank. The papers fell from her hands. She reached up to touch the two newcomers just to make sure they were real. She could not muster anything more than a tiny whisper. "My babies?" She grabbed on to the red shirt trying to pull herself up. He immediately went down to one knee. The other two men followed suit, and they surrounded her completely in a group hug. Over and over again all she could say was: "My babies." She kept moving her gaze from one to another to another. She wanted to hug all three at the same time, but considering that there was an enormous size difference as well as the fact that she only had two arms, the logistics of that big hug were impossible. She held on to the arm of the one in blue with her right hand, David's arm with her left hand and pressed her face into the neck of the one in red. After a few moments like that she would then change grips and neck and start sobbing all over again.

The three men responded by touching her, if all they had was her arm, and hugging her if she had her face on his neck. This was the end of a long search to find their birth mother. Here she was and just to be able to touch her and be touched by her was a form of euphoria that none of them wanted to see end.

After several minutes of crying and spinning in the middle of her sons, she lost her balance. One of them caught her and she found herself sitting on a knee - clad in blue. The one in red was touching her right shoulder and David was touching her left.

She noticed that her nose had been running with all the crying. She tried to clean her face off with her hands. All three of them pulled out a small towel. One blue, one green and one red. She stared at all three for several moments. 'Which one do you take? No matter which one you take, you might hurt the feelings of the other two.' She finally gave up trying to decide and took all three and buried her face in them. Even though the towels were clean, she could smell them, her sons, on the cloth (along with a little cologne).

She wiped her nose and eyes. She looked from face to face to face. She had been crying so hard that she now had the hiccups. She started giggling as she looked at them and said: "You done growed."

"Oh, just a little bit," said the one in blue.

She put her arm around his neck and stared intensely into his eyes. "I really don't think that your name is Tom."

He chuckled. He took a deep breath and let it out. Then with a big grin he said: "Duane Bernard Murdoch, at your service."

She gave him a kiss. She looked quickly at David, then to

the one in red. "And your name?"

He tried to talk but was still too choked up.

"Daniel Edward Murdoch," said David softly.

Still clutching the towels in her right hand, she pulled him toward her and kissed him. She then stared into his eyes for several moments. She looked back at David. "Hey lawyer, you got a middle name?"

He smiled. "Louis."

She got off of Duane's knee and suddenly started hammering her fists on David's shoulders. "Why din't you tell me before?" She was almost in a rage. "Why'd you wait till now?"

David was momentarily surprised by her sudden attack. He grabbed hold of her wrists, pulled her to him and hugged her close. "What are you talking about?"

"Why didn't you tell me that you's one uh my sons before? That would'a saved me a bunch a worryin' on the way here."

David sighed and then smiled. "The reason I didn't tell you, is because 8 years ago when we started this quest to find you, we made a pact. We would not tell you, until all three of us were together at the same time. That way, like always, since there are three of us, and we share everything, we could share this moment. Not one of us would get the greater moment, not one of us would get a lesser moment. This moment is for *all* four of us. Any objections?"

She closed her eyes, bit her lip. She tried to say something in response but her emotions took over. She started crying uncontrollably and threw her arms around his neck with a new fountain of tears.

Off to the side, Randall turned to Paula: "If that tiny woman is the mother of those three leviathans, what did the father look like?"

"I don't know," said Paula. "It was a case of rape and I don't think it was ever solved as to who attacked her. I don't even know if there was ever a suspect."

Christine was once again looking from face to face to face. Then she was finally able to do something that she had been waiting almost 25 years to do. She took the three little towels that they had given her and she was finally able to wipe the tears off of the faces of her sons.

She was looking at David, when her expression turned to shock. She looked beyond David to Paula…who was holding a baby. "Paula."

"Yes, my wife Paula," said David bewildered.

"A baby!"

"Yes, my son Michael."

She stared at David wide-eyed. "I'M A GRANDMOTHER?" She was almost horrified. "I'm only 37 years old, I can't be no grandmother!"

Duane let loose with a hearty laugh, David smiled while Daniel looked down snickering.

She looked at Daniel to ask him if he was a father. Before she could ask she saw a woman standing behind him in a red dress. She was just a little taller than Christine, with light brown hair, large bright green eyes, a huge smile…and she was very pregnant. Standing down by (and trying to hide behind) her right knee was a little brown haired girl in a red dress, who had her index finger buried as far as she could get it into her left nostril.

Daniel cleared his throat several times before he could talk. "The big one is my wife, Veronica. The little one is my daughter, Cecilia." He placed his hand on Veronica's stomach. "This one we don't know what it is yet." He took Cecilia's hand and pulled her forward. The little girl tried to pull away.

Christine went down to her knees staring at the angelic little face. She was elated by the fact that this child was a blood relative - another relative. "Don't be afraid. I'm your…" She closed her eyes as she said: "Grandma."

Cecilia looked up at her father. "Another Grammy?"

"Yeah baby, now you have three."

Cecilia looked at her mother, then back to Daniel "What do I call her? I got Grammy Sandy and Grammy Lucy."

Daniel smiled. "This one is Grammy Chrissy."

Christine was losing her battle against a new round of tears. She looked into the big brown eyes of the child. Eyes that were filled with wonder. She suddenly realized that she had never talked to any child this young, since first being arrested. Especially not one that she was related to. She pulled Cecilia close and hugged her.

She felt the little girl struggle a little. "Why you crying?"

Christine looked deep into the young eyes. "Because I'm happy. So happy. Happier than I ever been in my life."

"But people cry when they hurt or sad."

Christine giggled. "Sometimes they cry when they're happy. Really, really happy."

"Why?"

She sighed. "Someday, you'll be old enough to understand. Right now, you just too young."

Cecilia stuck out her lower lip and frowned. "Mommy keep saying that to me."

Christine looked up at Daniel. "I don't know how to talk to someone this young."

Daniel chuckled. "You're doing pretty good so far."

She looked back at Cecilia. "She'll probably say that *a lot* for a few more years...uh...how old are you?"

Cecilia held up two fingers and tried to bend a third. "She'll be three in August," said Veronica.

Christine stood up and picked up Cecilia. Christine grunted and put the little girl on Daniel's knee. She placed her hands on her back with a pained look on her face. "That's something else I ain't used to." She rubbed her lower back. "Wow. Maybe I need to get in shape."

'Let's see,' she thought. 'David and Paula in front, Daniel and Veronica to the right.' She turned slowly to her left. Standing behind Duane was a woman wearing blue scrubs. Christine looked back and forth at Paula and the new woman.

Duane snickered. "Hey! She noticed!" He looked around

the room, then back at Christine. "Yes, Paula and Gwen are sisters." He gave David a condescending sneer. "But I got the better one."

David raised his fist and growled in a threatening manner. Duane responded in kind. They growled and shook their fists at each other for a few moments. Christine was terrified. She had seen too many fights like this in prison. She did not want to see something like this happen here. Not now - not in the middle of the best day of her life. She stepped in between them. "What're you two doin'? Stop! Please no fightin'…not now…not ever…not twixt you two."

The two men looked at Christine rather confused. Their glances went back and forth between her and each other. Then they both shrugged and snickered.

"Yes, Mommy," said David with a stupid grin.

"Okay, Mommy," said Duane with an equally stupid grin.

Christine saw a twinkle of some type in Duane's eyes. She felt his hand on the back of her neck, and all of a sudden both men leaned very close. Duane ran his tongue up the entire left side of her face, while David licked the right side. She stood there stunned for a moment, not sure what to do. There were numerous chuckles, snickers and laughs around the room. She looked back and forth at the two, who had huge grins on their faces. 'Maybe someone will explain this to me…when I get older,' she thought.

She looked back behind Duane. "Gwen?"

"Gwendolyn Marie Murdoch," said Duane. "My wife, and mother of my two boys. Joseph Charles Murdoch is the big one, Brett Matthew Murdoch is the little one."

Both boys' faces were duplicates of their father. Joseph, who was standing beside his mother, looked to be maybe a little older than Cecilia. Brett, who was in his mother's arms, was probably a little older than Michael. Christine was contemplating this, but figured that she would not have to guess at it. Her three big boys would be giving her all of that information freely. Both boys were staring blankly at Christine.

Christine started to move towards them. Brett turned away and hugged his mother, while Joseph kept his eyes on Christine.

"Joseph turns three in May. Brett is 11 months old," said Gwen.

Christine held out her hand to touch Brett. He pulled away and whined.

"Don't worry," said Duane. "There will be plenty of time for him to get used to you."

She knelt down in front of Joseph, and smiled - again fighting back tears.

He cocked his head to one side. "Are you my Grammy Chrissy too?"

She completely lost the battle against tears. She grabbed the boy and hugged him close. "Yes," she sobbed. "Grammy Chrissy."

Her mind was reeling. This morning she had been rudely awakened after another night of sexual abuse by other prisoners. After a rotten breakfast of sawdust flavored oatmeal, she had been dragged across the prison yard, practically naked. Then had been sexually abused in *The Back Room.* Then pulverized and nearly drowned by the fire hose in *the Pit*. Then dragged and redressed. Then she started on the most confusing journey of her life that was now the most wonderful day of her life. Now, she was finally reunited with her three sons, three daughters-in-law and four and two thirds grandchildren. Now there was family and mountains of love, with very little probability of any kind of abuse in the future.

While she was hugging her oldest grandchild, she felt three hands on her back, and was hoping and praying that this day would never end.

After crying herself out (hopefully for the last time), she looked into the eyes of Joseph. "Until today, I didn't even know you was here. I'm gonna make sure that I never forget you, your brother er any of your cousins."

She saw the three towels on the floor. She picked them up and stood up. Again she was wiping her face with the towels to get all the fluids off her face. She looked at David. "Is there any more surprises?"

David chuckled and looked around. "There will probably be some more, but not today. You look like you're pretty well emotionally exhausted. I don't know if you can take much more."

"As long as they's good ones like what I done already gone through - bring 'em on!"

Duane handed her a glass of water.

"What's that fer?"

"As much blubbering as you have been doing, you might be a little dehydrated."

She sat back down on the cloud of a couch, and drained the glass. Maybe he was right, her throat had felt a little dry. She looked back and forth from Gwen to Paula. "Can I hold a baby? That's somethin' I ain't done in a long time."

Paula walked to Christine with a smile. "Brett is just about a toddler, so Mikey, being the youngest, is definitely the baby." She frowned. "When did you ever hold a baby before?"

"I did some babysittin'…a long time ago. The biggest difference is that they was never related to me."

Paula handed Michael to Christine. Paula watched every move ready to make any corrections on how to hold an infant. "For something that you haven't done in quite a few years, you're doing it quite well."

Christine looked up and smiled. She looked deep into the eyes of Michael. All those years she had dreamed of how she would have cuddled and rocked her own baby boys. That was now impossible, but here she was with one of their babies. She slowly rocked from side to side while humming softly.

Off to the side, Randall walked up to David. "That ADA said you were something related to a reptile. I'm thinking of something more like an over-sized rodent. You played me! You had all of this already done and you knew it when you made that bet."

David was staring at her with an innocent *Who Me?* Look. "Ain't no bet like a sucker bet, is there? Yes, I had all of this set up. Yes, I knew about it when I took you. You never really gave me a chance to tell you, you just jumped down my throat about how it was almost impossible. I knew it was possible, because I had already accomplished it." He gave her a big toothy grin. "Looks like I win the bet."

"Well there are some special circumstances here…"

"That would allow you to back out on the bet?"

"You did play me!"

"You jumped to a conclusion - a *wrong* conclusion - and rode it hard." He leaned closer to her. "I…win…the…bet."

Michael started whining and kicking. "What's wrong?" Christine looked up at Paula.

"Don't worry, you haven't done anything wrong. It's feeding time and he knows it - and like his father - he *will* be fed…" Paula looked at David with a slight frown: "Now!"

Christine looked elated. "I can do that."

"No, he has a problem with his digestive system. He can't have anything but natural breast milk. He's incapable of keeping anything else down."

"No problem," said Christine as she unbuttoned her shirt. She pulled it open, bared her left nipple and held it to Michael's mouth. He took it and started suckling.

Paula had been reaching for Michael and now she just stood there, frozen in shock. She glanced around the room and saw that she was not the only one surprised by this sudden turn. She stammered a little, then stopped and engaged her brain to thinking. "Uhm… when was the last time you were…pregnant?"

Christine looked at Paula with some confusion on her face.

She scoffed. "I was only knocked up once, in my whole life. That was when I had my boys." She frowned. "Why?"

Paula shook her head. "But…that was 25 years ago. Uh… David will be 25 in November, and…you're still lactating…after all that time?"

"Uh…Yeah. So?"

"But that's impossible! After a very short time, if you are not suckling, you stop producing. How…? Uh…or dare I ask?"

Christine looked down and flushed. "When Big Sugar got wind of me having just give birth, she decided to become my owner - my agent - my pimp." She had a pained look on her face. "Anyone there in juvie who wanted a taste of real breast milk, had to pay her, and then I had to let them suck. When Big Sugar was removed from juvie, I thought it would be over, and Honey Kim took over as my owner. When she left there was Rolanda and then Carla. Always someone else to take over. Then, they sent me up to the Big House, and I thought it would be over. Ha! Guess who my cellmate was? Big Sugar! The whole rotten thing started over again and I had, no one knows how many people suckin' off my boobs." She stopped and giggled. "This, however, is the first time someone is suckin', what ain't got no teeth." She snickered. "It feels really different."

The female guard had been listening intently to all of this and could not hold back any longer. "What you're saying is not very probable. I know for a fact that you have been locked up in solitary at least three times. One of those times was for four months. You have also been in quarantine in the infirmary several times. You had to stop giving milk somewhere along the line."

Christine looked at the ceiling in disgust. "When I was 'isolated,' Big Sugar had told me to milk myself. If I come out of there with two dead pumps, she said she woulda found a way to get me pregnant again, so's I'd give milk again. She was makin' too much profit off my boobs to let it go."

David walked up: "And you are...?"

"I am Captain Margaret Melton, Head Hauncho of the guards at the prison, and second only to the warden."

"Okay, so what is your interest in this?"

"If she had stopped lactating, there would be only one way for Big Sugar to make sure she got pregnant again...one of the male guards. Yes, I do have an interest in this. Any intimate act between a guard and an inmate is a felony."

David spoke openly to the room: "Folks, would somebody get some very young ears out of the room - we may have a few serious discussions going on, possibly for some time."

Gwen and Veronica herded their children out. Paula reached for Michael with fear on her face, "Chrissy, she said that you were in quarantine a couple of times. If you had, or have some disease, it could easily be in your milk."

Christine jerked her gaze at Paula. She quickly pulled Michael from her breast. "Better to be safe," she said in a small voice.

"Yes, please," pleaded Paula.

After handing Michael to Paula, Christine took her newly acquired set of small towels and covered her chest with them, while looking around and biting her lip.

"Now," said Melton, "you claim that you were a wet nurse for some of the other cons. Did that go all the way back to juvie and was there anyone else involved?"

"Of course it was in juvie! I had them babies when I was 13 years old. They didn't send me up to the big house until I was 18."

"So you have been suckling other inmates since you were 13."

"Inmates, guards, strangers, anyone that they told me to let suck what appeared in *The Back Room*."

Melton was taken aback. She glanced around the room a little. "You said guards?" She looked at Ellis. "Please tell me that he is one of them."

Ellis muttered something under his breath. He clutched the butt of his gun, then let go of it. "I hope you get leprosy in your nose." He turned away. "Hag!"

Christine looked at Ellis and shook her head.

"Then, who? I need some names."

Christine thought about that morning's early encounter. She pulled her legs up to her chest. Slowly she named them: "Guernsey, Washburn, Turner…"

"…Richards, Upton and Lamberson," snapped Ellis.

Melton glared at Ellis, then looked at Christine with the unspoken question in her eyes. Christine looked at Ellis, then Melton and nodded. She walked over to Ellis. "And you know these names…how?'"

He grunted. "The Triple P's!"

Melton stared speechless for a moment. She shook her head and cleared her throat. "Did I come in on the middle of a conversation? Uh…Triple P's?"

Ellis growled in disgust. With a sour look on his face, he ran over the list again: "Guernsey, Lamberson, Richards, Turner, Upton and Washburn. We call them the Triple P's, because that's the bunch from Pennsylvania." He stared at her for a moment, waiting for some kind of response. "Do you remember when that idiot 'Bouffant Betty' was the governor?"

"I don't recall that being her name, but I know who you're talking about."

"Right, well, according to her, none of us dumb Texicans had a clue as to how to properly run any prison, or any of the judicial system. So, she brought all of those big-mouthed Yankees from Pennsylvania and New Jersey here to teach us dummies how to do everything, up to and including, how to properly urinate. Guernsey, Lamberson, Richards, Turner, Upton and Washburn: The *Phat-mouthed Philadelphia Phreaks,* or Triple P's. They have their own little clique, and no one else is allowed in - especially if you are originally from Texas. They do their own time schedules and cell block patrols. They don't care when or where *you* schedule them to be there, they go where they want to go and when."

"But how, I check all those schedules every week…?"

"They fabricate! You make a schedule, they don't stick to it. If any of us dumb Texicans try to say something, we get ostracized by *them* and none of our complaints ever seem to get to you, or you are ignoring them completely. If you want to get any accurate information, check their clock rings in the computer. If the clock rings are accurate according to what you scheduled, then they are controlling that too. If you don't believe me, check with Sanders, McGuffee, any of the Rodriguez brothers or the Hernandez brothers. Then check with the female guards."

Melton rubbed her temples. She turned to Christine. She made a few attempts at saying something, but could not seem to get a word out. Finally: "The six that were named - how often, or when was the last time that…they committed this felonious act with you?"

Christine hugged her knees to her chest. "This mornin'."

"THIS morning?" said David somewhat stunned.

"Yeah," said Christine, "that's why it took so long fer them to find me. Big Sugar was the only one what knew I was in *The Back Room.*"

With a little apprehension, Melton chimed in: "With who?"

Christine sighed. "This mornin', it was Turner, Upton, Guernsey and Washburn…takin' turns on me." She wrung her hands a little. "Before my last bout in quarantine, those two dykes, Campbell and Kowalski had a round of fun with me."

Ellis grunted. "Oh yes. The *Joisey Jills.*" He scratched his forehead. Those two dykes were a part of that package from the northeast as well."

Melton looked like she was ready to throw up from hearing all this information. "Are you telling me to check their clock rings as well?"

"Oh heavens no! I want you to do what you do best: Ignore the whole situation completely," Ellis said sarcastically.

Melton scowled at him. She flopped down on the couch next to Christine. "I came here to find out if this lawyer was for real, and I'm going to go away with a nightmare of an investigation."

A strange high pitched sound came out of Christine's mouth. She looked around in terror. "They're gonna kill me! I've been settin' here rattin' people out! When I go back to the prison...I'm dead!"

Melton sighed. "If we have to put you in the witness protection program, it will be done. Don't worry, we will see that you are protected."

David was disgusted. "Do you mean to protect her in the way you have been protecting her from being abused?"

Melton closed her eyes. "Look, somehow they have spun a very clever web of deceit. Their cover up is pretty good. They are using the prisoners code of silence, they are obviously threatening the other guards, they are using the greed of the prisoner bosses... they are very good at what they are doing." She put her hand on Christine's shoulder. "Someone has to come forward and break this chain of subterfuge. Once in the open, they have to back off."

Christine rolled into the fetal position on the couch. "I'm dead. There's gonna be pieces of me all over that prison. They're gonna take turns rippin' me apart."

David pulled Christine up and hugged her close. "I promise

you that we will protect you."

"You don't git it," she wailed. "When someone gets released, they usually come out with a message to others what still owe the bosses. They *will* come after me. If they can't get me, then they'll go after you or Paula or...Mikey, or one uh the other younguns." She looked into David's eyes pleading. "They won't stop. David, you done made this the happiest day of my life. When I fought against an abortion, it was because I wanted someone in this world, who was alive, and was related to me. I got three of you. Now, the three of you are married, with children, and I don't want to see any of you get hurt cause of me." She kissed his cheek tenderly. "Just let it go. For your sake...for Paula...and especially Mikey."

"Too late," said Melton. "The pillow has been ripped, in a windstorm, and its feathers are scattered everywhere. I have knowledge of an ongoing criminal conspiracy, and if I do not report it - I become part of it. THAT is NOT going to happen! Another thing - if you do not help me, you become a willing participant in obstructing an investigation."

Christine buried her face in David's chest. She started crying silently again.

David looked around contemplating ramifications, legalities and precedents. He rubbed Christine's back in the most comforting manner he could. "Paula," he called out. "We are going to need your Legal Secretary expertise in here."

Everyone sat in silence. The only sound was Christine's sniffling.

After several minutes, Paula walked in with a pen and legal

pad. "I had to turn Mikey over to Gwen. Okay, who is first?"

David glanced around. "Why don't you start with Sgt. Ellis? He seems to have a good working knowledge of this mess. We are definitely going to need as many witness accounts as we can get."

Randall broke in: "Are you going to need me or Dale for any of this? I mean we have heard a lot of things here…"

"It would be nothing but hearsay. If you don't have any first-hand knowledge, then your info is irrelevant and inadmissible. Thank you anyway, but no - have a nice day."

"I'll send you the bill; come on Dale."

After they left, David said, "Paula, in relation to the quarantine thing and all that, make a medical appointment for Christine to get a full physical so we can find out for sure about anything and get her taken care of properly."

"Yes, boss," said Paula as she made an annotation on her pad.

"Boss?" Christine looked at David confused.

"Yes, Paula is my legal secretary. I first met her at the law firm."

Melton listened in complete horror, while Ellis gave his statement to Paula. She was supposed to be in charge of keeping any abuse from occurring and it was going on every day right under her nose. She was finding out the hard way just exactly who it was that was in charge in the prison. The *Phat-mouthed Philly Phreaks* and the *Joisey Jills* were running everything. She wondered if she would still have a job after the investigation was finished.

Christine felt sick. She knew what kind of network the prisoners had. She knew just how vindictive and unmerciful they could be. Too many people had died in the prison for insignificant acts. She had committed the ultimate sin. Ratting on another con or crooked guard was the worst thing you could do because it would require absolute retribution. She would be marked for death, as would anyone else who got in the way.

"The horse is out of the barn." David spoke softly to Christine. "Captain Melton has to start an investigation, and Sergeant Ellis has given a statement. I understand that you are scared, but as an officer of the court, I have to see this through. We need you to make a statement."

"But, when I go back, they gonna kill me."

"You are not going back! I can guarantee that one way or another that will not happen. If you give evidence that blows the lid off this mess that will strengthen my case to keep you out." He smiled. "You haven't seen the ammunition that I have for keeping you out. I told you about the four boxes and the crime scene photos. You are NOT going back!"

She hugged him and sobbed again. This time she wasn't crying for joy, it was out of fear for her life, his life and the lives of all her grandchildren.

"If you ever want to take control of your life and stop letting others control you, you have to start somewhere," David said quietly. "Give us what you know and we'll go from there."

She wiped her nose and eyes. She looked into David's eyes with a pleading look. She sighed, looked at Paula and slowly started the sordid story. Other cons would abuse her, some of the guards would abuse her and then she started talking about other people that were brought into *The Back Room*.

Melton sat listening intently with a worried look on her face. When she heard the part about *other people*, she could not hold back. "Who are these *other people* that you are referring to?"

Christine looked at her and sighed. "I don't know. They never give me real names."

"Well, what names did they give you?"

Christine huffed. "There was Dark Lord, Spanky, Sex Master, Horny Devil, Temptress, Baby Jack…"

"Baby Jack?" asked Ellis. "What kind of name is that for a sex fiend?"

"Not everbody come there with an erection. Some of them wanted to be treated like a baby. I had to talk to them like they was a baby, and one of them I even had to change his…diapers. Do you know what it's like, changin' the diaper and cleanin' a 200 pound man?"

David broke in: "It doesn't matter what their perversion was or is, I doubt very seriously that we will find any of them in the phone book. Someone who is involved in that kind of illegal activity answers porn ads - covertly - they don't make them."

17

After Paula finished page 6 of Christine's statement, everybody started sniffing. There was an aroma wafting through the house that made everyone's mouth water.

David smiled at the two guards: "Since certain unexpected circumstances came up, we can set a couple of places for you two... we still don't know how much longer this is going to take."

They all got up and went in to the dining room. The table was huge, just like everything else on this property.

Duane took Christine by the hand and led her to a place at the middle of the long side of the table. The chairs all had padded seats and high backs. Duane pulled the chair back in a gentlemanly manner, and pushed her to the table after she was seated. Duane sat to her left, Daniel to her right and David directly across from her. Duane leaned close to Christine: "He got to spend some time alone with you this morning, so that's why he's on the other side."

Paula sat at the end of the table as Veronica and Gwen started bringing in the food.

Christine looked around confused: "Where's all the little uns? Why ain't they here?"

"It's late and they've gone to bed," said Gwen. "This meal right now is for the adults." She snickered. "Don't worry, you'll have plenty of time to play with your grandchildren later."

Christine looked out the window. Yes, it was dark. The day

that she finally met her sons and their wives and their children was coming to an end. "How long was I yappin' at Paula?"

"Long enough to fill six pages," said Paula. She turned to David: "How much of that do you think you can use?"

"Unless she can give us some exact dates on those incidents - not much." He placed both hands on the table. "That...is not the important thing right now. Right now, I'm ravenous. It's time to eat!"

Then Christine noticed what was on the table: A huge turkey, dressing, gravy, mashed potatoes, cranberry sauce, corn, green beans, peas, yams, and rolls. "This looks like a Thanksgivin' dinner," she said confused. "Ain't this April? Ain't Thanksgivin' usually in November?"

Daniel tenderly took her hand. "We just found our mother. You finally met your children. Can you think of a better time for giving thanks?"

More tears in her eyes. She still had the three towels in her lap. She picked them up and started wiping her eyes. "Stop makin' me cry," she sobbed. She looked at Daniel. "I'm hungry and I can't see food through wet eyes."

Before they ate, Christine witnessed something that had never happened to her before. Duane said a prayer over the food, then David, then Daniel. Each one mentioned her and the fact that the quest to find her was over.

After getting some food on her plate and a few minutes of stuffing her face, Daniel reached over and pulled her fork away as she was trying to stuff more in. "Hey Little Mom! This is not a race. You don't have any appointments tonight, or any tomorrow. No one is going to take the food away from you, so you don't have to overstuff your mouth."

She realized that she was eating her normal way. Get as much in your mouth as you can before Big Sugar grabs you and takes you off to some rendezvous. She tried to respond, but couldn't. She had crammed so much in her mouth, she could barely chew.

"Chew up what you got and swallow before you cram any more in," said Duane as he chuckled. "We are going to have to teach Little Mom some proper etiquette."

She sat there working over what was in her mouth (which was considerable). Usually at the prison, she never had been able to get that much on any given day, let alone one meal…or one mouthful.

Four times she forgot, and started moving more to her mouth. Each time, Daniel pulled the fork away, with a smile on his face. She finally left the fork on the plate and folded her arms as she worked over the large mass in her mouth. When she finally cleared her mouth, she heaved a large sigh. She looked at Daniel with pleading eyes. "Can I have s'more now?"

Daniel snickered. "One forkful at a time and swallow it before you get another."

As they continued eating, Christine, again, forgot several times and as she was moving another forkful to her full mouth, Daniel would gently take hold of her wrist and pull it away, with a smile. Each time he grabbed her wrist, everyone at the table would get the giggles along with Christine.

Even though some of the others at the table were interested in small talk, Christine was not. She was used to packing the food down, without any unnecessary conversation: Eat it now, because you might not get another chance for a while. By the time she had learned that she did not need to eat like a vacuum cleaner, she was so stuffed that she could not even think of putting anything else in her mouth.

David noticed her sagging eyelids. "It's getting rather late, would you like to see your bedroom?"

She looked at him somewhat startled. "My bedroom," she whispered with an amazed look in her eyes. She cleared her throat, smiled and said: "Sure!"

She walked (or rather waddled) out of the dining room into the living room. She stopped and looked around confused. "What'd you do to the furniture? How'd you change it while we was eatin'?"

David smirked. "That other room is the family room - this, is the living room."

She looked around bewildered. "One of these days I need a tour."

"Don't worry Little Mom, you'll have plenty of time to explore the house."

David turned Christine to her immediate left. There she saw a staircase. She thought about how she had just gorged herself and the staircase seemed to be an insurmountable obstacle. "You don't 'spect me to climb all the way up there do ya?" she said helplessly.

She felt something hit the back of her knees, and she yelped in surprise as she fell backwards - into David's arms. He picked her up in his arms. He said: "Don't worry about climbing any stairs today." He carried her up. The rest of the family followed. At the top he turned around to his right, another right and he stopped at the end of a long hall. "This door to my right is my bedroom. Of course I mean Paula and me." He walked a little way down the hall. "The door on the right is to Mikey's room - the door on the left is to the balcony."

"Balcony? You got a balcony?"

"Sure, would you like to see it?"

"Them security folks said I couldn't go outside."

"The boundaries are to either side of the house - not the front or back. The balcony is within your perimeter."

Someone opened the door and she was carried outside. She was ready to start crying again. She was awake, outside of a cell, it was nighttime and she could not smell anything that was remotely close to the stench of sweat and misery in the prison. David gently put her down. She walked to the railing and inhaled deeply several times in total euphoria with more tears streaming down her cheeks. All she could smell was vegetation and night air. There were no sounds of anyone screaming or crying, no guards stomping through the cell block - just the wind in the trees and crickets and cicadas giving a new symphony to free ears.

She felt two hands on her back. She opened her eyes to see Daniel and Duane. "The house directly across the street is where Gwen and I live," said Duane.

Daniel pointed to the right. "The house next to Duane's is

where Veronica and I live."

Christine started crying again. "What's wrong?" asked all three.

"Up till now, it never occurred to me that you lived in different houses. But now I know you do, and I can't go to either of tother ones."

"Not yet," said David softly. "Don't worry. Soon you'll be able to go anywhere you want."

She spun around and clenched her fists. "You sure uh that?"

David placed his hands on her shoulders. "I am absolutely sure of that."

"Then convince me!" she cried.

He went down to one knee and hugged her close. "Tomorrow. It's a lot of information, it's late and we are all tired. Let's go back inside and find your bedroom."

They went back inside. David continued the tour. "The next door to the right is the guest bathroom, the door at the very end of the hall is the guest bedroom and the last door on the right is your bedroom."

She walked into a dark room.

David clapped twice and two large floor lamps turned on. He clapped twice again and the lights went out. Two more claps - back on. "That is how you turn your lights on and off. You don't have to stumble through the dark or trip over anything. You can do it from anywhere in the room."

She tested the clap several times while staring in amazement. "I feel like I just come outta long, long sleep. I been sittin' in a cell while the world done passed me up and I feel like an idiot."

David picked her up and stood her on the bed. "Tomorrow we start your education. Tonight - sleep, rest and recuperate." He hugged and kissed her.

Duane and Daniel each took their turn giving her a goodnight hug and kiss.

"Oh, by the way, the door to the right goes to your private bathroom and the door on the back wall is to your closet." David smiled as he left the room. "See you in the morning."

18

The door closed and Christine was all by herself. She sat on the bed facing the door. To the left of the door was a huge set of drawers. Five drawers high and two wide. She was sitting on a queen-sized bed, with a nightstand on each side and the magic clap-on floor lamps next to each nightstand. There were two high backed, overstuffed chairs that were sitting angled but facing the bed. The wall opposite the bed had a vanity and an empty set of shelves. Beige wall to wall carpeting, beige quilt on the bed, dark brown dresser and nightstands.

Then she noticed that there were two nightgowns on the bed. One was white flannel with tiny pink flowers on it. The other was white silk. She decided that she was a little too dirty to put either one on until she had taken a bath.

She went to the closet and opened the door. It was dark. She tried clapping in here - all it did was shut the lights off in the room. She clapped again, got her bedroom lights on and looked for a light switch. It was directly to the left of the door. She turned it on. All she could do was stare back and forth dumbfounded. She was in the middle part of the closet that was bigger than a lot of the rooms she had seen. This walk-in closet was, at a minimum, twice the size of the cell she had been living in. It was just a little wider, but twice as long. It was carpeted, there was shelving for shoes, plenty of shelves for whatever ended up on them, lots of places to hang a mammoth wardrobe…and a couch. "I gotta couch in my closet. " She said out loud. She went and sat down on her closet couch, and took in the whole picture.

Time to go explore the bathroom, since she needed the use of a toilet anyway. The bathroom did not have a clap-on light either. Again she found a convenient light switch on the left. To her right was a set of shelves, directly ahead was the sink, to the left of that the toilet and taking up the entire back wall was a very inviting tub. This room was not carpeted, but there were several beige plush mats in the room. One by the sink, one in front of the toilet and a nice big one by the tub.

She started walking to the tub and noticed a clothes hamper on her left. Above the hamper was a towel rack with two big white bath towels on it. She reached up to touch the bath towels and noticed that she was still holding on to the three little towels the boys had given her. She walked over and put the little towels on the back of the toilet. She went back to see if the bath towels were as soft as they looked. She stopped - no, take a bath first and then touch them. She stripped off the prison garb and threw it all into the hamper.

Before taking a shower, she decided to check what the items were next to the sink. A bottle of liquid hand soap, a bottle of mouthwash, there was a tube of toothpaste with toothbrush, a comb and a brush.

She looked at herself in the mirror and was struck with horror when she saw the wild mop growing out of her head. The stark realization, again, that only this morning, she had been hit with a fire hose shower by Big Sugar, and she had not had any chance to do anything with her hair since. Normally it would not have made any difference - in the prison. Now it does make a difference.

She went to the bathtub, and was getting ready to start a shower when she noticed a bottle of bubble bath. All these years, she had only been able to take a shower, not a bath. Here was a bottle of bubble bath. She grinned. Why not? She had not been able to take a bath since... She turned the hot water on, plugged the drain and poured a little out of the bottle. Instantly the bubbles started building and an aroma hit her that she could not identify. She had no idea what it was but it smelled flowery - great! She turned on some cold to get a tolerable temperature in the water. The running water made her remember why she had come in the bathroom in the first place. After relieving herself she slowly slid into the tub. The warmth of the water engulfed her with more euphoria as the level of the water rose. The bubbles tickled parts of her body as they rose up as well. She reached over and turned the taps off. She felt that she did not need to go out to the swimming pool. This tub was so massive that she could probably go swimming right here.

She checked the other bottles on the edge of the tub. As soon as she found the shampoo, she started cleaning her mop. Then the conditioner.

The next bottle was liquid soap. She decided that there was enough soap in the water from the bubble bath, the shampoo and conditioner that the soap could wait for a shower. After giving herself a complete rubdown, she hit the plug and let the water drain out. Considering how large the tub was, it took quite a while for it to drain. She really did not want the bath to end but she was getting rather tired.

She slipped around in the empty tub a little trying to get out. It was then that she saw a rubber bath mat hanging on the wall above her head. She snorted - noted for future reference. She crawled out of the tub and pulled one of the bath towels down. It was even softer than she had imagined. She found that she was rubbing the towel on her, not to dry off, but just to touch the heavenly thing.

After she realized that she was dry, she tried to get some of the water out of her hair. She then threw the wet towel down, grabbed the other bath towel and wrapped herself up in it. Then she went to the sink, picked up the brush and steeled herself for the battle that was about to begin.

By the time she finished brushing and combing her catastrophic mop into a mild disaster, she was exhausted. She stumble into the bedroom, and did the clapping. She moaned in frustration when she realized that both the bathroom and closet lights were still on. She clapped, went and took care of the other lights and fell onto the bed.

The two nightgowns were still sitting there untouched. She was too tired to make a decision, and this was definitely not the first time she had gone to bed naked. She pulled the quilt, back flopped down in the bed and made a new discovery: A clean pillow. She sank her face into it and inhaled deeply. No smell. For the first time since her initial incarceration, she had her head on a pillow that did not reek of perspiration, vomit or excrement. She spent the next few moments smelling the two pillows in ecstasy. As she gave in to sleep, her last conscious thought was that this was the end of the most wonderful day of her life.

19

Christine woke up. There was plenty of light coming through the window over the bed. She was laying on her left side, which was unusual for her. She normally woke up laying on her right side. This morning, however, she woke up with her arms and legs wrapped around a big soft pillow. Another new experience: She had never been on a bed with two pillows before. She had no desire to get out of bed. She did not have the desire, but her over-stretched bladder and growling stomach were sending her another message. She stretched working all the kinks out of her body. She started scratching herself in random areas. She pulled the blanket off, lifted her right leg up high and rectally blasted about 400 PSI out into the room. She sighed with pleasure at having relieved herself of the pressure.

Then she heard a strange woman's voice: "Do you feel better?"

Christine sat up startled. She saw a woman sitting in one of the chairs. The woman was older with light brown hair that was graying at the temples. She was waving the smell away from her with both hands and had a rather disgusted look on her face. After dissipating the gas sufficiently, she now had a pleasant smile on her face as she stared back at Christine. She was wearing a loose fitting flowery green dress.

Christine looked around to see if anyone else was in the room. "Who're you?"

The smile on the woman's face got bigger: "I am Sandra."

Christine smiled weakly. "Okay." She contemplated for a moment. "Who are you?"

Sandra chuckled. "I am the woman who raised your sons for you."

Christine swallowed hard. She tried to say something but was not sure what to say.

"I have an idea what you want to say." Another smile: "No, dear, I am not going to try to take them away from you. I just hope that you are not going to take them away from me. You gave birth to them - I raised them. I am sure that there is plenty of room in those three big hearts of theirs for both of us."

Christine's eyes got misty. She felt a huge lump in her throat. She opened her mouth, but again could not say anything.

"You are welcome...I mean for raising your boys. That is what you were trying to do wasn't it, dear - Thank me?"

She laughed nervously, "Yeah, it was. I just...didn't know how to say it."

"Well, that's all right, dear. I understand that you have had a rather hard life and your education has been sadly neglected. You might need a little bit of educational upgrades as to the world of today. My experience is in raising three head-strong boys, but I think I could give you some decent advice. Of course, Gwen, Paula and Veronica will be able to give you some pretty good advice as well. Of course the first one you need to get some advice from is Veronica."

"What? Why her?"

"She is a beautician, and the way your hair looks - It might require a lot of attention."

Christine could not stop herself. "Are you married, er did you raise my boys alone?" She blushed and felt very embarrassed after asking the question.

"Oh, I am married, dear. You'll meet Ben later on. Ben is the one who was instrumental in finding your boys. When we found out that we were unable to have our own children, we started looking into adoption. When he found out about a set of triplets, he seemed to work some kind of magic and got us at the top of the list for adopting them. I always figured that one child would be hard to get. When I got three…well that was wonderful." She closed her eyes and smiled again. "I am rambling dear, uh, you are probably hungry and I'm just carrying on."

"That's okay. So many times the only thing that anyone wanted tuh say to me was something what was kinky or perverted. You can ramble on all you want…after I hit the bathroom."

Christine climbed out of the bed. She still had the towel partially wrapped around her. It fell off as she stood up.

"Oh my!" said Sandra. "I suggest that you put on the flannel nightgown before you come downstairs. Now that I see you, I think the silk one is too big and will hang on you like a sack."

Her shoulders sagged. "Too big for me! Gee, where've I heard that one before?"

"By the way, why didn't you put either one them on before

going to bed?"

"It was late and I was just too tired to make any decision."

When Christine came out of the bathroom, Sandra and the silk nightgown were gone. She picked up the flannel and put it on. This one was way too long as well. The sleeves were at least six inches beyond her fingers and it was made for someone at least eight inches taller. She sighed, rolled up the sleeves, and grabbed a huge handful of the bottom around her waist so she did not step on it. Time to get some breakfast.

When she finally got to the dining room, Sandra and Veronica were waiting. There was a plate with some steaming waffles sitting on the table.

Sandra looked thoughtfully at Christine's predicament. "Before you have some breakfast, let me do some adjustments to that nightgown. Here stand up on this chair."

Christine needed help climbing up because of all the extra material in the gown. "What are you going to do?"

"I'm just going to make a few quick adjustments now. I will fix it up completely later."   With that she pulled out a large pair of scissors, cut the extra off the bottom, and then cut the sleeves. "There, dear, now you won't trip over anything and you won't have to worry about your sleeves getting in the syrup."

"But…you ruined it. Now it looks like a hand-me-down rag."

"I am a professional seamstress," she said with a smile. "I will be able to make it look just like new after we find something else for you to wear."

After packing down the waffles and a large glass of orange juice, Veronica was giving some serious looks at Christine's hair. She sighed and shook her head. "I may just have to shave it all off and start from scratch. Before I do that, however, I would have to supply you with a decent wig."

Christine was not really worried about her hair right now. It had never really been a concern while in prison. She had lost a lot of her vanity over the years. "What I really wanna do now, is talk to David. He said he was goin' to tell me some things about the case. He's goin' to tell me why he's so confident that I don't have to go back to jail."

Sandra gave her another smile. "All right, dear, I will take you to him. Veronica, dear, if you are serious about a wig, I suggest you get started on it first."

Veronica cut a small piece of hair in order to match the color and measured the size of Christine's head.

"All right, dear," said Sandra, "let's go to David's office."

"What? I can't leave the house!" She pointed at her ankle monitor. "They said this thing'll go off if I leave the house."

"Don't worry. He works out of a law firm on the north side. He also has an office here at home. He is in his home office right now."

They walked out of the dining room and through the living room. On the far side of the living room was a door that Christine had not noticed last night. Sandra knocked on the door: "You're client wants to talk to you David." She opened the door and there was David talking to the air.

Christine walked in and shook her head. "He's talkin' to his tooth again."

Sandra looked at Christine totally bewildered. She shook her head and left the room.

David seemed a little upset with his side of the conversation. "I need that stuff there…I don't care what the obstacles are, I have to have the equipment in place…Did I ask you how much it was going to cost? …Get the stuff there so it will be there when we need to activate it…Just do it…If they have any problems, tell them to call me."

While that conversation was going on, Paula ushered Christine to a table and offered a cup of coffee. Christine could not remember if she had ever tasted coffee before. After trying it she was not sure that she ever wanted to taste it again.

David came to her with a big smile on his face. He picked her up and hugged and kissed her. "Good morning, Little Mom."

"Okay, good mornin'. Now, where's this special ev'dince that's supposed to get me a new trial and out of prison?"

He walked back to his desk, picked up a file and came back, while shuffling through papers in the file. He pulled out a photograph and put it on the table in front of her.

She sat there dumbstruck. She looked up at him. "A picture uh my daddy's lawnmower? You're tellin' me that a picture of daddy's lawnmower is gettin' me a new trial?"

He placed another picture in front of her.

She stared at it even more perplexed. "What is that thang?"

"That thing is called a jerry can."

She sat silently staring at him for a moment. "Whass a jerry can?"

"It is a gas can used primarily by the military."

"Well, then why didn't you just call it a gas can?"

"Because 'jerry can' specifies the style of can."

She closed her eyes and tried to put things together. "Izzat important?"

"The jerry can is the container that was used to bring in and pour gasoline all over your parents' house."

She glared at him.

"What? Why are you looking like that?"

"My parents? Why can't you say 'your grandparents'?"

He sighed. "Yes, they were my grandparents. I wish I could have been acquainted with them. I wish a lot of things had happened differently. They did not, so I am doing this and using my words as your lawyer, not your son and not their grandson. I have to give an argument from outside the family so that it will be accepted in court."

"Whatever. So howzis help me?"

"Before I answer that, I am going to do a little experiment." He walked over to a shelf. He picked up a small cardboard box, brought it to her and placed it in front of her. As she reached up to open the box, he placed his hand on top of it and said: "No, don't open it - pick it up."

She put her hands on either side and tried to pick it up. She could not budge it. She stood up and used all of her strength to pull the box closer to her body and tried to pick it up again. After two frustrating attempts, she looked at him in a questioning manner.

"Try again. I want you to pick it up and carry it around to the other end of the table."

She steeled herself and tried again. She held it against her chest and tried to walk. She made two staggering steps and dropped the box on the floor. She glared at him while panting.

"Is that the best that you can do with it?"

"Uh-huh!" She looked down at the box and back at him angrily. "Whatchoo tryin' to do, prove that I'm a wuss?"

He walked over to the fallen box, picked it up with very little effort and returned it to the spot on the table. "No. What I am trying to do is prove that you are incapable of picking up and carrying that kind of weight."

"Howzat help?"

"The jerry can. It holds 5 gallons of gas. Gasoline weighs six pounds per gallon. Five gallons of gas weighs 30 pounds. This particular can weighs twelve pounds. So we have 42 pounds of can and gas. At the time of your original arrest, you weighed a trifling 89 pounds. 42 pounds was almost half of your body weight. That full can weighed more than the box that I just had you try to pick up. According to your school records, you were not the strongest or most athletic in your Phys Ed class. Picking up and carrying a can that heavy was - and still is - very difficult for you."

She sat mulling it over for a few moments. "So what do the lawnmower have to do with that?"

"That lawnmower is a 'push' mower. When you do not have a gas powered lawnmower - why do you have a gas can for spare gas? The other equipment in the garage: A chainsaw - that is electric, a hedge trimmer - that is electric, an edger - that is electric. All the equipment in the garage was either manual or electric. Nothing in that garage was gas operated. Why would there be a gas can when there was nothing to put the gas in?"

She scoffed. "Even I could fight that guff. They could say it was fer the car."

"One of the things that survived the fire was the strong box where all the important papers were kept. The box was guaranteed to be fire proof and it lived up to that boast. Inside that box, we find a ton of gas receipts for the car. The car that he had was the type that had a 22 gallon gas tank. Not one of the receipts shows a fill-up of more than 10.6 gallons. Your fa…grandpa would fill up whenever the gas gauge got near half a tank."

"Yeah…daddy did always say that anyone who run out of gas was stupid. He said he'd never let that happen to us."

"Right! So why did he need a gas can? He didn't! Where did it come from? No one can come up with a good reason."

"Izzat all? I mean, that don't mean I couldn't or didn't do it."

"The can weighs 42 pounds when full. You could not pick up a box that I know for a fact weighs 40 pounds. The pattern of the gas being poured out, in the house shows a deliberate methodical act. You were bombed on barbiturates at the time…"

She stood up and screamed: "I didn't take any drugs! I've never took any dope…!"

He held up his hands to try to calm her. "Forget the source of the drugs! That is not what is important here! The blood test shows that you had a high concentration of drugs in your system when they took you to the hospital. The main fact here is - you were wiped out on barbiturates and because of that, you could not be deliberate or methodical in pouring gas all over the house, especially if you were slowed by the drugs. When someone has that much in their system, there is almost nothing that they can do in a deliberate or methodical manner."

"Okay," she said meekly. "I still wish that someone could tell me how the dope got in my system."

"That *is* another important question. I read the autopsy reports on your…my grandparents. There was a large amount of drugs in your system and in grandmothers system. There was a massive amount in grandfather's system." David leaned back and sighed. "There was a massive amount in his system and there was no soot in his nose, mouth or lungs. That means that he died from a drug overdose before the fire started."

She sat there stunned.

"Is that the first you heard of that?"

It was several moments before she could respond. "He was

dead before…? Both of them was doped…? Why din't no one tell me this afore?"

"Now you see why I am going to have Reese scalded for not doing his job correctly. Questions like that should have been asked - then! You should have been told a few more things and asked a few more things - then!"

"So you think that this is nuff to get me freed?"

He gave her one of his big grins. "I'm saving the really good stuff for the preliminary hearing. You needed a little convincing that I had something good. What I gave you here is minor. I am going to hit the prosecuting attorney with a barrage of heavy artillery in the preliminaries. Once I have done that, there will not be a trial, and you will be free."

"Well." She gave him a sarcastic smile. "Uh…why don't you tell me now?"

"First - I have to get some important things done here before I go downtown for a few other things, so unfortunately I don't have time right now. Second - Veronica wants to take care of your hair, and according to her, that is a major project. Third - Big Mom wants to measure Little Mom, so that Little Mom can have a decent wardrobe. Big Mom has not been able to use her seamstress skills in a while and she is just itching to get started."

"I wanna know more…now!"

He picked her up, hugged her and kissed her. He spoke directly into her ear: "I held back on the surprise that I was your son until my brothers were with me. That turned into something wonderful for all of us. Let me hold back on this so I can give you another wonderful moment."

She grabbed his ears and got her face close to his. "I wanna know more NOW!" She let a small growl out.

He started laughing. "I'm sorry! The difference in our sizes does not allow me to be intimidated by you."

She pulled on his ears a few times, growled a few more times (more in frustration rather that intimidation) and tried to come up with some kind of good argument. She finally let herself go limp in his arms. "Put me down, ya big ape."

He put her down after giving her another peck on the cheek. As she headed out of the room, Paula stopped her and said: "I made an appointment for a full physical on the 29th of this month - is that all right with you?"

Christine shrugged: "What else I'm gonna be doin'?"

Paula bit her lip. "Usually, I'm dealing with people who have a bit more to do." She smiled. "So the 29th is fine."

Christine smiled back. "Why not?"

"There is something here that puzzles me," said David: "Why did...Grandpa...have a lawnmower that was manual? Why didn't he have a power mower?"

"Daddy was cheap. Whenever er wherever he could get a bargain, he did. Besides, he said that usin' that mower was the only real exercise he got."

"But, who mows year round?"

"Oh c'mon! We *are* in south Texas. How often do you put

yer summer clothes away for the winter? I member a couple of winters where I never pulled out any winter clothes, other than a sweater. You can have a green lawn year round here, and so you got to mow year round."

David sat back contemplating the thought.

"We also had neighbors who were hippie propagandists for conservation and back to nature and all that organic junk."

David snickered. "Today they overuse the word: Green."

"Yeah, well they didn't gripe at Daddy that much because he had a push instead of a power mower. They growed all their own veggies and fruit in their back yard and they always griped to everyone else who did have gas powered stuff."

"So grandpa was trying to make peace with the neighbors?"

"No, he just didn't want to listen to their belly-achin'. They usually went to bed early, because they did some kind of sun worshippin' thing. When the sun went down, they hid in their house. Sometimes, around midnight, after they was in bed and Daddy had downed nine or ten cans of beer, he would go to the fence and say: 'I got somethin' here for you what's organic.' Then he'd pee through the fence into their cucumber patch."

David sat there with a strange look on his face. He looked off to the side in thought. He cleared his throat and looked back at Christine shaking his head. "Grandpa would have definitely been an interesting person to meet."

20

Christine came out of the office to see Sandra sitting on the couch. Sandra smiled, stood up and held up a tape measure. "Are you ready to be measured?"

"How many things you gonna make for me?"

"As many as you want, dear. I was retired from my job even though I didn't want to be. All those years and then suddenly I was obsolete. I did make a lot of clothing for the boys while they were growing up. Now, I don't get to do it very much at all. I never had a daughter, so this will be a pleasure for me."

"Whacha want me tuh do?"

"Stand up here on the ottoman so I can measure you."

Christine looked around the room puzzled. "What's an otto...what did you call it?"

Sandra was a little surprised. She looked back equally puzzled and then said: "This...the footstool."

"Oh. Why din't you just call it a footstool?"

"The style, dear. It's padded. That usually makes it an ottoman."

She climbed up and her shoulders sagged. "You must think that I'm a complete dummy. I hear words that I ain't never heared afore and don't know what you're talking bout."

Sandra started taking her measurements and annotating them on a pad. "No, dear, you just have not had enough exposure to a proper life." After making another note on her pad she looked up with her 'always present' smile. "I told you before that Ben and I could not have children, so we adopted three amazing little boys. I would have liked to have been able to raise a daughter as well, but I didn't get the opportunity. Now, if you would let me - I could be your guide."

"My guide in what?"

"Any questions that you have. I know that you lost your mother when you were only 12. You've had nothing but those nasty prisons ever since. I don't think the education you got there is up to any good standards, so if you have any problems...don't hesitate to ask."

Christine got a little misty eyed as she contemplated the thought of being mothered by this woman.

"All right, dear. I have all of the lower measurements. Now, I need you to step down so I can get the upper."

Christine stepped down. She was trying to wipe tears from her eyes. She had forgotten the three towels the boys had given her, so she had to use her sleeve.

"I was thinking of starting out with a nice pant suit for you. I'm just not sure what color you would want for it."

She wiped her nose on the flannel sleeve. "I want three. I want them all the same design. I want one in blue, one in green and one in red."

Sandra contemplated for a moment. "What shade? I mean with red you could get plain red, bright red, scarlet, crimson, candy apple…"

"Wait here!" Christine remembered where she had left the three towels. She ran to her bathroom to retrieve them from the back of the toilet. She ran back to Sandra and with the towels held out in front of her she breathlessly declared: "These is the shades I want!"

Sandra looked at them surprised. She cocked her head to the right while staring at them. "Where did you get those?"

Christine felt a sudden twinge of guilt. She could not understand Sandra's reaction. "Yesterday…my babies…I mean my boys give 'em to me. Why? What's wrong?"

Christine watched as at least fifteen different expressions crossed Sandra's face. Several times Sandra tried to say something, but stopped herself. Finally she closed her eyes and bowed her head. She took in a deep breath and sighed. Then she looked at Christine with her familiar smile. "It is fitting that you should have those. Those are the towels that the boys were wrapped in the first time Ben and I saw them."

Christine lost her legs. She collapsed to the floor. She was sitting staring at the towels. She slowly looked up at Sandra and then back at the towels. These were the first things that had touched her sons immediately after they were born. The same towels that she had seen for just a few fleeting moments so long ago. Now, they were also the very first things that her sons had given her after getting her out of jail. She buried her face in them and started sobbing.

David and Paula came out of the office. When they saw Christine on the floor rocking back and forth, with her face in the towels, David could only come up with: "What?"

Sandra looked at him in an accusing manner. "You didn't tell her what those towels were when you gave them to her, did you?"

David chuckled nervously. "No, we didn't. It just seemed right to give them to her."

Sandra had her hands on her hips. "Without telling her the significance?"

He shrugged. "It really didn't come up. She just needed something to dry her eyes. We each held our own out, and she took all three. What can I say? What can I do?"

"You can pick her up off the floor!"

"Yes, Mom." He stooped down and gently picked her up, went to the couch and sat her on his lap. "I'm sorry we didn't tell you the history of those towels. I didn't know that it would hit you that hard."

"I told you. Each one of you was wrapped in these things and taken out of the room. I got to hear each one of you use your first breath and cry and then you was gone. These towels is all I member of you three on that day."

"Well tonight we are going to pull out some scrapbooks and let you see our individual histories. Are we good now?"

She placed the blue and red ones on her lap. She held the green one up to his chest. She shook her head and looked back at

Sandra. "He was completely wrapped up in this thing. I couldn't see no arm or leg…nuthin' but the towel. Now it don't even cover his chest."

Sandra sat down next to David. "Yes, dear. All 4 pounds 3 ounces of him was wrapped in that towel."

"How much Duane weigh?"

"Duane was also 4 pounds 3, Daniel was 4 pounds 2."

Christine sagged against David's chest. "You're tellin' me that I had over 12 pounds uh babies inside me?"

Paula let out a pained moan. "Michael was 6 pounds 9 when he was born. I can't even imagine 12 pounds in there."

David looked at his watch. "I hate to break this up, but we have got to get downtown - NOW!"

Sandra shooed David and Paula out. "Well dear, I am going to need to get some fabric in order to make three outfits for you. Are you going to be alright?"

"Perfect." Christine curled up on the couch hugging her three precious treasured towels to her chest while smiling and sniffling.

21

While everyone else was gone from the house, Christine did her own exploring. She found the laundry room, just off the kitchen, and was surprised to see that the washer and dryer were very different than what was in the prison. There you counted the pieces of clothing that were put in the big washing machines, then the soap, then hit the only button it had - start. This one had several settings for the size of the load as well as type and water temperature. The prison dryers had one button - start. This one, like the washer, had several time and temperature settings as well as, 'air' and 'delicate.' She also noticed that the laundry was in different piles. At the prison it was undergarments and outer garments. She decided to leave the washing to Paula - or at least until someone could teach her how to use these machines.

She went back to the first room she had seen in the house. The family room seemed to her to be just another living room. She sat back down on the cloud of a couch. She curled up hugging the precious towels close to her chest. She let the couch swallow her up. She figured just a few minutes here and then she would go do some more exploring.

She was being shaken. She panicked and tried to bolt off the couch. She fell flat on her face on the carpet. She looked around startled and mumbling. Then she saw the surprised face of Sandra, and remembered where she was.

Sandra was not sure what to do. "Are you all right, dear?"

"Uh...yeah. Uh...wha happen?"

"You made the mistake of sitting on this couch. It seems to have an aura about it. If you are the least bit tired, it *will* knock you out. Did you have a nice nap?"

She got up off the floor and sat on the edge of the couch. "I guess I did whether I wanted to er not."

"Yes. You were mumbling something...what is Big Sugar?"

Christine looked down at the floor: "Muh owner."

"Owner?"

She sighed. "There's four differnt types in the prison: Bosses, soldiers, mules and toys. If you're a toy, you got an owner instead of a boss."

"Well what do they do?"

Christine looked at Sandra in disbelief. She shook her head. "The bosses, they controls everthing. They tell you what to do and you do it. The soldiers do all the fightin', the mules carry drugs and messages back n forth." She looked down and felt her face get hot. "You play wiff a toy."

"Well who determines who is in what category?"

"The bosses er the biggest, toughest, smartest n meanest. The soldiers is usually tough but not mean ner smart nough to be a boss. The mules are not tough enough to be soldiers and too ugly er mean to be toys. I'm a toy. Everyone else's tougher and bigger than me and so I got to do what they want...*anything* they want."

"But couldn't a toy be used as a mule?"

"No. Toys is too valuable as a toy. Mules get caught with some of the stuff they're carryin' and end up in solitary for a while. You can't get any profit ner fun from a toy in solitary, so the others do everthing they can to keep the toys out of trouble…so that they have something to play, or barter with."

"Barter?"

"Yeah," said Christine sadly. "Sex is somethin' that you can buy er sell in prison."

"But, I've heard of a lot of fights go on in prisons. How do you keep yourself or other…toys from ending up in the fight or getting hurt?"

"I went into the chow hall one time. I din't know they was a fight goin' on at the time. As soon as I got in there, someone grabbed me and pushed me up against a wall. There were three other girls there that I knew was toys, and at least six soldiers made sure that no one, who was involved in the fight, come near us. The six soldiers were from different gangs: Two whites, two blacks and two browns."

"Black, brown, white…what do you mean by that?"

"Blacks! You know, them Afro-Americans. Whites! Like you and me. Browns of course is the Mexicans."

"That sounds so prejudicial. How can they allow that?"

"You gonna go in to the prison and teach how everbody should be nice to everbody else? That ain't gonna happen in no prison."

Sandra hugged Christine. "I can see that this is causing you some pain. But I don't understand - if someone were to abuse me in such a manner, I think that I would become suicidal. How did you make it all these years without that thought?"

"I thought of it...all the time. It's just that you can't. The guards think they got a foolproof suicide pervention system...Hah! The cons have an even better system. They just wouldn't let me commit suicide. They was always watchin' me."

"Let's change the subject, dear."

"Good idea...thanks."

"I got the fabric and have cut some pieces. I need to check them on you for a proper fit."

While Sandra was placing and pinning and marking, Christine started thinking about some of the things that had happened in the last two days. She did not want to think of anything in the prison. She only wanted to have good thoughts. One thing kept bothering her though. "Yesterday, after I got to meet all three uh my babies, I met their families and...well, I can't git it out of my head." She stood there not sure what to say.

"Go on, dear, like I said, whatever is bothering you or whatever you need to learn, just ask. I would love to help you in any way that I can."

"Well, Duane and David looked like they was goin' to get in a fight. I've seen so many fights in the prison and people get bruised and busted up er crippled...er dead. I just couldn't let them do that to each other. How do I stop them from doin' it in the future? I just met em...and I don't wanna lose em...specially tuh each other."

Sandra snickered. "Don't let that bother you. They wouldn't hurt each other. They've never hit each other at all…well with the exception of the football field. All that silly posturing and growling. Don't let it bother you."

"Do you really mean it? They was just jokin'?"

Sandra did an imitation of the fighter stance and growling, and then giggled. "That's all it is, dear. Just a lot of noise and posturing."

Christine let out a long sigh of relief. "Good. For a while I was wonderin' if they might shank each other."

Sandra looked puzzled: "Shank, dear?"

"Yeah…a shank. It's a weapon."

Sandra looked even more puzzled. "How do you get hold of a weapon in a prison?"

"You make it. You take a comb, toothbrush er chicken bone and file one end to a point. Then you come up behind yer target and ram it into their kidney, heart or lung depending on whether you want to cause pain or death."

Sandra looked horrified: "Oh goodness! Did you ever…?"

"No, I'm a toy. Only the soldiers whack somebody."

"Yes. Well I think that that is a word we do not need to bring up again in future conversation."

'Where have I heard that before?' thought Christine. She shrugged and smiled.

"Was there anything else that happened yesterday that you

want to ask about, dear?"

"Oh yeah! After I told them to stop fightin', Duane and David *licked my face*. What's with this *lickin'*?"

Sandra closed her eyes and shook her head. "I don't know! All of a sudden they started doing that and it just infuriates me. More than once I've backhanded them for cleaning the makeup off my face, but they keep doing it. I wish I knew why they started it and I wish I could make them stop."

"So you're just as much in the dark about it as me?"

Sandra shook her head again and sighed: "Unfortunately yes."

After checking, fitting, pinning and marking, Sandra took all the pieces, put them in a suitcase and started heading for the door.

"Where you goin' now?"

"My sewing machine and all my other tools of the trade are in my house next door. My things are much too heavy to bring over here, and unfortunately you are not able to go over there, so I have to run back and forth with them. Don't worry, if you need anything all of the numbers are by all the phones in the house."

After Sandra left, Christine started exploring the house in order to find where the phone was. In her parents' house there had been only one phone. She was shocked to find that almost every room downstairs had a phone in it. Upstairs had one in the hallway just inside the balcony, and one in David and Paula's bedroom.

She looked at the listing beside each phone. There was 911, Duane cell, Gwen cell, Duane & Gwen home, David cell, Paula cell, Daniel cell, Veronica cell, Daniel & Veronica home, Ben cell, Sandra cell and Ben & Sandra home. 'Everybody has a cell. Is that anything like that tooth that David keeps talking too?' She felt afraid of touching the phone. She had not touched one since her incarceration. The technologies that were being used right in front of her scared her and this was one of them as well. How much had it changed since 1983?

She heard a knock on the door. She cautiously went to the door and peeked through one of the three small windows in the door. Veronica smiled back at her. She opened the door and saw that Veronica had a round box with a handle in each hand.

"Well, I found two wigs that should fit the bill to cover your head until I can do something with your hair."

Christine looked at the large boxes. She could not imagine how much hair was in each wig. The boxes seemed way too big for just a wig.

Veronica flopped down in a chair and sighed. She patted her stomach. "Three more months and this one is out. I can hardly wait."

Christine remembered her last few months of pregnancy and gave Veronica an understanding smile. Then she stared at the boxes.

"Don't be afraid, open them up and take a look."

She was expecting to see large gobs of hair in the boxes. She pulled the top off one and was surprised to find a neatly styled wig sitting on a plastic head. She pulled it out and was more fascinated with the head than the wig. Her mother had told her that a wig was a silly luxury and a total waste of money. Now, Veronica had bought two of them for her and each one was sitting on its own head.

Veronica looked at her. "Well, what do you think of the wigs?"

"Uh...nice." She had not really looked at the wigs, now she had to answer a question about them. One wig was styled, while the other was just long hair, hanging straight.

"Before we go trying them on, let's see what we can do with your hair."

The rest of the afternoon was spent in her private bathroom while Veronica shampooed, conditioned, combed, teased and did all kinds of other things that Christine could not understand. It had been so long since Christine had really done anything to or with her hair that she was just as ignorant about hair styling as she was about cell phones.

While the cleaning and styling was going on, Veronica was constantly talking about her life with Daniel and Cecilia. Christine paid close attention to every word. She wanted every single detail that she could get.

Finally after three hours of working with Christine's hair Veronica stood back up and huffed in frustration. "I may have to do what I originally said: Shave it all off and start from scratch. Sweetie, your hair is so damaged that there is almost nothing I can do to make it better. Let's go ahead and leave it as it is for a few days and see how you get along with it this way. If after a few days you can't stand it - then I'll get out the clippers and we'll go from there, okay?"

Christine just smiled and nodded. She looked at herself in

the mirror. Even though Veronica was ready to give up, Christine was still impressed and happy with the improvement.

22

Duane, Gwen and their two boys arrived at David's home first. Shortly after that Daniel came in with Cecilia. When David and Paula arrived, David made a phone call that Christine could understand - he used a phone instead of talking to his tooth. A few moments after the phone call was made, Sandra arrived with Ben. Finally Christine was able to meet the entire family.

Ben was a tall lean man whose face and hands had the leathery look of a man who had worked outside most of his life. His hands showed several old scars from what she found out was a result of him being a carpenter. His deep voice sounded as if it came from the bottom of a grave, but his bright blue eyes showed a very friendly attitude.

When Veronica asked what they all thought of her hair, the main consensus was that it definitely looked better than before. For the first time in years Christine felt a little twinge of vanity and blushed.

While the others sat around talking, Christine was able to sit down on the floor and play with the two grandchildren who could talk. It was a little difficult trying to please a boy and a girl, but she still enjoyed it immensely.

When dinner was ready, Christine again heard a long winded prayer before they were able to eat. It seemed that she was the only one who was impatient about eating. No one else said a thing or moved until the prayer was finished. 'Great,' she thought, 'the

Murdoch's have done turned my boys into Bible thumpers.'

Several times during the meal, Daniel, again, took hold of Christine's hand to keep her from cramming more into her overfull mouth. Each time he did it during this meal, she still got the giggles.

Duane looked at her a little puzzled. "Why are you still wearing a nightgown?"

"Uh, well, right now I don't got nuthin' else but that prison stuff. It's dirty and in the hamper in my bathroom. Other than that - I got nuthin'."

Sandra broke in: "Tomorrow is Saturday, and Veronica and I are going to go shopping for something else for her to wear. I'll need to see the underwear in that hamper so I can make sure I have the right size."

"Speaking of that clothing," said Paula, "we have to clean it and send it back. That stuff *is* the property of the state."

"They kin keep it," said Christine bitterly.

When they finished eating, Duane took Christine's hand. "Come on Little Momma. I won the toss, so I get to show you mine first."

Christine was at a total loss on how to take that statement. In the *Back Room,* "show you mine", usually meant that someone was about to drop their pants. "Show me yer what?"

"I have a scrapbook from when I was growing up and Gwen has been keeping one since we got married. We thought you might like to see some of the old photos and keepsakes of our lives."

Her heart started racing with excitement. "You mean startin' from when you was babies?"

"No," said David, "Big Momma has those pictures in her scrapbook."

Sandra lost the smile on her face. "You can call me Mom or Momma, I don't care. If any of you ever calls me *Big* Momma again, I will smack your face off."

There was some intense, fearful glances around the room by everybody – except Ben who was chuckling. The silence was broken by Christine. She looked up at Duane with a pleading look in her eyes. "Can I see the baby pichers first?"

He went down to one knee and hugged her. "Of course. You can do anything you want." He looked at Sandra. "*Mom*! Could you get your scrapbook for her?"

That ever present smile was back on Sandra's face: "Of course, dear."

While Sandra went to her house to get the baby books, Christine went to her bedroom and retrieved the three towels. Just thinking of seeing baby pictures started more tears and she figured that she might really need the towels now.

She came back down the stairs into the living room. Sandra was not back yet. She went to the couch and sat down and waited. Through the silence in the room, she could hear her heart pounding in her ears. She hugged the towels to her chest.

After five or six eternities, Sandra came back carrying four books. The books were placed on the coffee table in front of Christine. One was larger than the other three. The large one had pictures of all three, the smaller ones were devoted to each one of the boys. "Which one would you like to see first, dear?"

She reached for the big white book. It was almost too heavy for her. Ben and Sandra both helped bring the book to her lap. She made a silent promise to herself that she was going to try to keep the crying to a minimum. She wanted to see the pictures through clear eyes not tears. She saw that her hands were shaking.

Over the years of abuse that she had gone through, the only way that she had been able to tolerate it was by going to an imaginary world. When Big Sugar or Honey or whoever her owner was at that time had taken her to one of the "appointments", she would let her mind drift. In this world, she was in a house or a field, playing with three small boys. At first it had been the task of changing diapers, nursing them and helping them with their first steps. Later on it was playing tag or hide-n-seek or helping them with the alphabet, with boys about 6 or 7 years old. Every now and then mommy had to take care of a boo-boo or dry some tears or tickle them. Through all of those fantasies she had never been able to put a face on the three apparitions. Now she was about to open a book where she could actually see the faces that she had wondered about for so long.

She steeled herself with a long breath in and out. She opened the book and broke her promise about not crying. On the first page was pictures of each of the boys laying on "the" towels, still covered in amniotic fluids. She stared at the first page for almost an hour, memorizing each and every thing about the boys first moments out of the womb. She ran her fingers around their images of their bodies as she stared at the pictures. Under each picture was listed: Date, time of birth, weight and length.

Duane had his right arm raised and the left one by his side. He was facing slightly to the right as if looking at his hand. His left leg was covering his genitals while the right was stretched off to the side. The umbilical cord was hanging over his left side.

David had his left hand up by his mouth. There were some bubbles on the lips. His right hand was closer to his neck. His legs were bent up near his chest and the umbilical was slightly coiled around his naval before trailing off to his right.

Daniel was looking off to his left with his big brown eyes and his mouth wide open. His legs were sticking straight up with the ankles together. His hands seemed to be clasped across his chest.

All three were totally bald and had the big chubby cheeks from the baby fat. In Daniel's picture they had gotten someone's hand in it, as the 'someone' was trying to clean the fluids off of him. She was able to see just how small they had been at birth from the size of the hand. The towels did not seem to give a good comparison of size, but the hand did.

She felt big hands on her shoulders as she sniffled and sobbed while staring at the pictures.

She reached for her towels to wipe her eyes again. She looked in total confusion at a white towel. She nearly panicked looking for her treasures.

Paula was standing in front of her with the three precious towels. "Chrissy, these need to be cleaned. For almost three days, you have been wiping your eyes and your...nose on them. Let me run them through the washer and dryer for you." When she saw the look on Christine's face she added: "Don't worry, I'll take care of them and get them back to you as soon as possible."

She felt as if her children were being taken away from her again. She looked around and got comforting smiles from everyone in the room. She watched as Paula left the room with her precious treasures. She wiped her nose with the white one. It was clean and very soft...but it was just some useless ordinary towel.

She took a deep breath and started turning the pages. Ben and Sandra would give her a brief story behind each picture. She hung on every word they said as she started realizing, just with this book, how much she had missed. She did not care how long the story was behind each picture, because it was building new magnificent memories for her. She was learning about her babies' lives as they grew up. The tour through the scrapbook was not near as wonderful as the first meeting with her sons, however there was no place in the world that she would rather be right now. It was fantastic.

23

She woke up with a start. She looked around the dark room. She clapped her hands and the lamps obediently came on. She did not remember coming up to her room and going to bed. The last thing she could remember was going through the baby book. She sat there totally bewildered as to what had occurred during the tour through the scrapbook.

She saw that there was a different flannel nightgown at the foot of the bed. This one was red plaid, and looked smaller and therefore closer to her size. Since she had worn this flowery one all day yesterday and slept in it last night, it now had the overpowering aroma of an armpit. She got out of bed and stripped the old one off. She then realized that it was not just the nightgown that stinks.

She started heading for the bathroom for a cleaning when she noticed that the three baby towels were sitting on the vanity, clean and folded. She scooped them up and held them to her face. She could not smell her boys on them anymore, but they were clean. She walked into the bathroom smiling while hugging them to her chest.

When she finished her constitutionals, she got the old nightgown in order to put it in the hamper. When she opened the hamper, she saw that it was empty. She smiled as she thought of how there was nothing in here now that was from the prison.

She had herself another bubble bath, with her treasures sitting on top of the hamper.

After bathing, she took the brush and readied herself for another battle with her hair. She was amazed at how her hair was more compliant. Veronica had accomplished something miraculous. Not only did the brush go through a lot easier, some of the waves were still there.

She went downstairs to find something to eat. She got to the bottom of the stairs. She heard nothing and saw no one. She called out and listened. Nothing. She went to the kitchen, wondering where everyone was.

She could not figure out what to have for breakfast. Her assigned tasks in the prison had been in the laundry room. She had not cooked anything or been near a stove since a few feeble attempts in the home economics class in juvie. She found apples and milk in the refrigerator. There were some graham crackers in a container on the kitchen table. No cooking or preparation required there.

She was quietly sitting at the kitchen table with her makeshift breakfast when she was scared out of her wits by someone touching her shoulder. She looked up at the surprised face of David.

He put a box on the table and looked closely at her. "Are you okay?"

After a few moments her heart stopped pounding. She took a few deep breaths. "Where was you? I called out earlier and no one answered."

"I was in my office, sealing this box - Why?"

"Why din't you answer when I called?"

He chuckled. "The office is sound-proofed. I am a lawyer

and sometimes a client might drop by. There is that attorney/client thing and so I had the office set up so that no one can hear in or out. So, if you don't see me anywhere else in the house - come knock on the door."

She glared at him for a moment, then sat down to finish eating. "What's in the box?"

He sat down at the table. "Something that you don't want."

"Huh?"

"The stuff you were wearing when you first came here. Paula said that it had to be cleaned and then sent back. Remember?"

She scowled at the box. "Oh." She had a disgusted look on her face as she glared at the box. "Put that thing somewheres else. I don't want that junk near me."

He smiled and took the box out of the room. He came back, went to the refrigerator, poured himself a glass of orange juice and sat down next to her again.

"What happened last night? I member lookin' at them baby books and then all of a sudden I'm in bed and its mornin'. I don't member finishin' that book ner goin' to bed."

"You passed out. You seem okay now, so Mom was right. You were completely totaled from being emotionally exhausted. You had a whirlwind day on Thursday from being removed from the prison, and meeting an extended family that you did not know existed. Friday, you met Sandra and Ben and then the baby books - it was just an overload, and you zoned out. Sleep is a very good cure for exhaustion, so we put you in bed and let you sleep."

She looked at him with the most pleading expression she could muster. "I still need some convincin'. You tell me that you're savin' the good stuff fer the trial…but I need somethin' more. Give me somethin' more to hope with…and for."

"Look, take my word…"

She lost her temper and screamed at him about needing more information. When she finished her tirade, she had her fists on her hips and stood there fuming.

He had a slight smile on his face that broadened into a grin. He was still sitting and he leaned closer to her. She could not understand the sparkle of joy in his eyes.

"What did you say?"

She looked around confused. "I told ya…that I want more infermation," she said meekly.

His eyebrows went up. "What else did you say?"

"Huh?"

He cleared his throat. "What *else* did you *say*?"

"Uh…I…a few choice words, but…all I'm sayin' is that I need more infermation."

He pulled out his cell phone and punched a few buttons. He placed it up to his ear with that same triumphant grin on his face. "Hey, good morning, how you doing? Are you busy? Come on over…we've just had an interesting development." He punched a few more buttons on his cell phone. "Danny boy, your presence is requested over here. You're doing what? Drop it! Something interesting just happened over here. Yeah, see you in a few."

She started backing up. He reached for her hand, which she pulled back. He grabbed a handful of the gown, pulled her close, wrapped an arm around her waist and picked her up. As he carried her past the kitchen table she grabbed at her treasured towels. She got the blue and red, but the green one fell to the floor. She let out a slight cry of exasperation. He stopped, stooped down, picked up the fallen towel and handed it to her. Then he headed out to the living room. He sat down on the couch with his arm still around her and looked to the front door in anticipation.

A knock on the door. "Come on in," he hollered. Both Duane and Daniel came in with anticipation and curiosity in their eyes.

"Come in, sit down, and make yourselves comfortable."

They sat down still having questioning and confused looks on their faces.

David looked around with a big grin. "A few moments ago, she was telling me that she wanted more information on her defense in court. I told her - again - that I wanted to save the heavy artillery for the hearing itself. Well…she had a temper tantrum." He looked at her: "Now, what did you say in there?"

"What you said: I want some of that good stuff, so I kin feel a little better bout it muhself."

He pursed his lips and looked to the ceiling. "What else did you say?" He looked back at her.

She stared back confused. She looked back and forth at Duane and Daniel. She shouted helplessly: "Nuthin'!"

He now looked back and forth at his brothers. "She said a name."

She gave the best shrug she could while still trapped in his grasp. "So I said yer name - so what?"

He gave her one of his huge grins. "No! My name begins with a 'D'."

"Yeah! 'D' as in duh!" she said sarcastically.

"No! The name you called me begins with an 'A'."

She stared at him wide-eyed. She smiled and chuckled sheepishly. She looked around the room. "Did I call you… Alexander?" She asked in a small voice with a guilty look on her face.

Again the grin and a long: "Yes."

She laughed nervously and bit her lip.

"For a long time, we have been debating on how to ask you what you would have named us, if things had been different. I tried asking you before and you got very upset at the time. Alexander is a long way from Dick, so I don't think that Tom and Harry were what you meant either. The cat's out of the bag now, so…what would you have named us and why."

Duane and Daniel left their seats and were now coming closer to her. They both went down to one knee and inched closer, face first.

"Uh…well…you unnerstand that…I's only 13 at the time. I din't have much to go with…and I had…found out…by accidentally trickin' that Doctor Dumbbell into revealin' that you was boys…"

Duane was getting impatient. "Quit beating around the bush, what are the names?"

"He also asked why!" she snapped.

He nodded. "Yes, I guess he did - go ahead."

I had originally been thinkin' of names that could go either way...like Pat er Francis er Tracy. Then when he said boys...well, it got more pecific and I started thinkin' of home." She looked at Duane. "I named you after my Daddy..."

"My name ain't Daddy...unless you're talking about my two boys."

She put her hand on his cheek. "Gabriel! I named you Gabriel after my Daddy"

Duane leaned back and smiled. "I can live with that," he said quietly.

She glanced at Daniel, then up at David who still had a firm grip around her waist. "You two got my two granddaddy's names. Alexander was on my Daddy's side." She switched her gaze at Daniel and put a hand on his cheek. "Grandpa on Momma's side was Jeremiah."

Duane giggled. "Is his middle name Lamentations?"

"Huh?"

"You know - from the Bible."

She looked around at all three, remembering that Dr. Dumbbell had made a reference to the Bible as well. "Whatsa Bible got to do with this? I never read the Bible. I don't know what yer talkin' bout."

Daniel raised his eyebrows. "That is a good question, though: Do any of us have a middle name?"

"Um...I've never once thought uh that." She glanced at each one of them. "Is that really necessary? I ain't got one."

David finally let go of her. He slowly walked over to a book shelf. He pulled a large black book out and came back to her. "You say that you have never read the Bible? Now would be a good time to start."

She looked at it, then at each one of her sons. She stammered trying to think of something to say, but saw by the looks on their faces that she could not talk her way out of it. She took the Bible and placed it in her lap. She looked up at David.

David had a slight smile on his face. "You start at the beginning by opening it up."

"This is a big book. Can't I see yer baby books first?"

Daniel sighed. "You can see the baby books when Mom is here to give you a complete tour. There are a lot of those pictures that have a story behind them. Only she can give you those individual stories. We - on the other hand - can help you with a lot of questions that you might have about the Bible."

She looked at the coffee table where Sandra's books were laying. Her sons saw her gaze. Daniel sat down on her left side, Duane sat down on her right. Daniel opened the cover and Duane turned to the first page of Genesis.

She looked at each one of her sons. Their expressions told

her that this was an ultimatum that they would not give way on. She sighed and started reading. She read about the creation, Adam and Eve, a serpent figure, Cain and Abel, Seth, several people who lived a really long time, and Noah and the big boat. Then there were a group of nationalities that she had never heard of. She was just getting into a man named Abram. The door opened and in walked Sandra, Gwen and Paula with children and numerous bags in tow. Christine looked around expectantly. "Where's Veronica?"

Gwen flopped down in a chair. "She had a few appointments at the beauty shop that couldn't wait. She'll be here a little later."

Before Christine could close the book, Duane marked the page with a purple ribbon that was attached to the Bible.

Christine jumped off the couch and headed for the two older grandchildren. She went down to her knees and caught both Joseph and Cecilia in a big hug. They started talking about the escapades of being dragged to different stores all over the mall and how none of them were toy stores. They were both talking at once, and she was only catching bits of each conversation, but it was still a joy just to be holding them.

After listening to their stories for several moments, Sandra gently parted them from Christine. "The men can take care of the children for a while - we have some things to take care of."

Christine protested. "Why can't they come with us?"

Gwen picked Joseph up and handed him to Duane. "Because you are going to be trying on different clothing - including underwear - and *his* presence is not appropriate."

Christine looked at all the bags with apprehension. When

she was a child, she had hated getting clothing at Christmas time or for her birthday. Now, since her entire wardrobe consisted of two baggy flannel nightgowns, she could hardly wait to tear into these bags.

After resting for a few moments, the women gathered all the bags up and headed for Christine's bedroom. They walked in and started putting bags along the wall. As Sandra was getting ready to close the door, David held it open. She looked at him with her hands on her hips. "Are you planning on supervising or something? Don't worry counselor, she does not need an attorney protecting her in here."

Without saying anything, David simply smiled and walked to the closest nightstand. He placed the Bible on the stand. He turned and smiled at Sandra, walked to the door, turned around, smiled again and closed the door as he left.

Sandra took a quick glance at the book. "What part were you reading before we interrupted?"

"I just got to some guy named Abram."

Sandra nodded and smiled.

Paula dumped the contents of one bag onto the bed. Christine gaped in awe. She had never seen that much underwear anywhere outside of a clothing store or the prison laundry. Her bed was covered with bras. With the exception of six plain white ones, they were all different colors. She had heard of red, blue, green, brown, yellow and purple. These were apricot, ruby, burgundy, azure, sapphire, teal, sea mist, periwinkle, lime, jade, emerald as well as a few other words that she had never heard before.

After trying almost every single one of them on, she sat there frustrated.

Sandra noticed her consternation. "What is wrong, dear?"

She looked up helplessly. "Everthang looks so nice…but it itches like crazy."

Gwen giggled. "Don't worry, darlin', after all these things have been run through the washing machine with some fabric softener, you won't feel any scratchiness at all."

After seeing affirmative nods from Paula and Sandra, she was more than ready for the next bag of clothing.

About that time, Veronica walked in. "Did I miss anything?"

"No," said Paula. "We're just about finished with the brassiere and panties sets."

Christine looked forlornly at the one set that she had not tried on. She looked at the women surrounding her sadly. "I don't want that'n."

Paula looked confused. "What's wrong with it?"

"Well," Christine said sadly. "I don't mean tuh hurt no one's feelins', but…I don't never want tuh wear that color again…as long as I live…less'n I absolute gots to."

The other four women all looked at the orange bra and panty set. They all looked at each other with different types of consternation and sadness.

"That's quite all right, dear," said Sandra softly. "We understand. We won't make that mistake again."

Blue jeans, slacks, blouses, short pants, slips, bras and panties. After trying all of them on, she was ready for more.

The last bag had four different bikinis in it. Christine looked at the swimming suits sadly. She put them back in the bag. "I ain't wearin' nuthin' like at around here."

The other women again, all looked at each other rather confused. Gwen was the first to speak up: "Why not? Don't you want to go swimming in the pool when you get that silly ankle thingy off?"

Christine looked sadly at each of the other women. "Sure," she said with her head hung low. "But I don't wanna wear sumthin' like that, in front of my grandbabies."

Paula put her index fingers to her temples. "Why not? I mean…I - and Gwen and Veronica wear bikinis - why can't you?"

Christine turned her back to them and pointed to a large jagged scar on the left side of her ribcage. "I got that when I told Big Sugar that I was too tired tuh go pleasure some big Mexican dyke. She slammed me up against the bars and I got some 40 stitches in sewin' my back up." She turned around and pointed to another scar, just below her right breast. "I got thissun when I told Honey Kim that I din't wanna go on one of the appointments. Honey kicked me and busted two uh my ribs. I gotta scar cause some bone was stickin' outta the skin." She pointed to three other smaller scars. "I got a story buhind each one uh these as well. The main thing I'm tryin' tuh say is…I don't wanna havtuh explain these things to my grandbabies. You folks already know what all happened to me… and I can't hide much from you…but my grandbabies…they don't need tuh know."

"So, one piece bathing suits would be more appropriate," said Sandra.

"I spect so," said Christine solemnly. She sniffed as a tear went down her cheek.

While Gwen was separating items into piles for the washing machine, Paula was collecting some hangers from the closet. Sandra was fussing over a few of the items that did not fit quite right.

Christine could not hold it back any more. "Why izzer a couch in my closet?"

Paula looked at her, looked back at the closet and snickered. "It's not a couch - it's a loveseat."

Christine frowned. "What'sa differnce?"

"Size!" Gwen chimed in. "A couch will seat three or more comfortably, while a loveseat is only big enough for two."

"Okay, so it's a loveseat. Whyzzit in the closet?"

Sandra put her arm around Christine's. "This way you can sit in your closet while getting dressed and not have to go in and out while dressing."

Christine felt good. This was one of the few times that she had understood an answer and needed no further explanation about a word she had never heard before.

"Don't worry," said Veronica. "We are going to do everything we can to make sure that you become accustomed to life outside of that…place."

"Right," said Gwen. "We're going to teach you how to walk,

talk and properly put on makeup."

"Another thing," said Paula. "We need to work on your eating habits. I mean…why do you cram so much food, so fast, in your mouth? You couldn't possibly have time to taste, or enjoy it."

Christine sighed. She looked around a little and sniffed. She looked up at the four women and sighed again. "I never knew when I was goin' to get more to eat, or *if* I was goin' to be able to eat."

The four women all looked at each other somewhat confused.   Veronica was the first to speak up. "Wasn't there some kind of set schedule for breakfast, lunch and dinner?"

"Oh, sure, they was a schedule…but I never knew if I was gonna be able to get there, and if I was, if I was gonna be able to get something' tuh eat. They was a lotta times that Big Sugar would shove me into the *Back Room,* and I might be in there pleasurin' somebody, right through lunch er dinner. I din't know when I was gonna be able tuh eat again. So, I cram as much in as I can, when I can."

Gwen shook her head. "Did you miss that many meals?"

Christine huffed. "I don't know how Big Sugar done it, but somehow, she was able to keep me in the *Back Room,* during all kinds of counts that the guards done. She also kep me in there through meals and a couple uh times, through the night. I member that there was one time, I was in there fer two full days. I din't get no food at all. The only thing I was able to git down my gullet, was an occasional drink of water out of the fire hose, twixt customers. Just as soon as one customer would leave, another was comin' through the door. They let me go to *the Pit* and clean up a little, cause no one wanted me all sweaty er covered with…" She trailed off and cleared her throat.

All four women were now gawking at Christine in complete horror.

"The last customer that I pleasured that night, he come in with a carrot and a cucumber." She looked off to the side and blushed. Another tear went down her right cheek. "He bent me over a chair…" She closed her eyes and bit her lip. "He started doin' somethin'…" She turned even redder and looked around. She was wringing her hands a little. "…with my rear end." She sniffed. She cleared her throat. "While he had his attention…behind me…I looked at that carrot. I figured he wouldn't mind me takin' one little bite out of it…while he was busy…behind me. I picked up the carrot and took a bite. Then another, and another, and another…" She shrugged. "The next thing I knew, I was chawin' on that big brown nub on the end and I had done et the whole thing." She sighed again. "I din't even think about it…I picked up that cucumber and started chawin' on it…seein' as how he was still…busy…with muh butt. Anyway, I was lickin' the last of the juice from that cucumber, off muh fingers, when he finished…what he was…doin', behind me. Then he started lookin' fer them things. He got mad when he din't fine em. It was then, that I found out that he wanted to do somethin' kinky…to me…with them things."

Veronica covered her mouth with her hand and headed into the bathroom gagging.

Christine continued: "I found out later, that he did get another toy in the *Back Room*. He used them things on her…in whatever way he was plannin'. She ended up in the infirmary fer bout six days and walked real funny fer another five after she got out. The bosses decided that they din't want him comin' back, if he was gonna put a toy out of play fer almost two weeks, he weren't payin' enough fer that."

Sandra had tears in her eyes as she hugged Christine. "You poor baby. I can't even imagine the awful things that you have gone through."

Gwen and Paula joined in on a group hug, trying to be comforting to Christine.

"We're here for you Chrissy," said Paula. "I'm also sure that your sons will make sure that no one ever hurts you again."

After doing some gargling, Veronica came out of the bathroom and joined in on the group hug.

After several quiet moments of each one contemplating and sniffling, Sandra pulled away and wiped her eyes. "Ladies, there are some clothes to return and a large amount of laundry to be done."

Each woman gave Christine another big hug before they left the room.

24

29 April came and Christine was taken to a doctor's office with a security guard in tow. The wretched ankle monitor needed a special box close to it so that the alarm did not go off. There were several rooms that Christine had to go to in order to get all of the different examinations done. Everywhere she went - there was the chaperone.

Everywhere she went, they poked, prodded and gouged. They hooked her up to one kind of machine or another. They wanted urine and blood. She thought back to when she had awakened after the rape and could not remember anything like the equipment they were using here. She could not remember a lot of this stuff from the prison infirmary either.

After several hours of being examined (between long waits on a table in one room or another) the examinations were mercifully over. A nurse told Christine she could get dressed and leave.

She was then told that some of the results of tests would be back any time between now and two weeks. The blessing was that they were finished. She felt almost the same way she had after some of the sexual encounters in *The Back Room*.

Christine had not really been thinking much of the calendar. Since she had been thrown in prison as a lifer, for the most part, she had not really cared whether or not it was Monday, Wednesday, the

8th, the 15th, May or October. Time or date had not really mattered that much. Big Sugar always seemed to worry about that so why should Christine bother with it. There were a few "tells", however, they never really amounted to much, in the way of being important.

Duane, David and Daniel silently tiptoed into Christine's bedroom on the morning of May 11. They placed three large floral arrangements around her bed. The arrangements were full of roses and each had a big ribbon, with "Happy Mother's Day," on each one. They then tiptoed back out to the hallway where their three wives were waiting. The plan was to wait a few moments and then knock on the door.

"I hope she enjoys this," whispered Daniel.

Duane looked shocked. "Are you kidding? This is a day she'll never forget. Her first Mother's Day, out of prison, with her children."

"I wonder how long we should wait before waking her," said David.

They heard her sneeze. She sneezed again. She sneezed again. She sneezed again. All three of them looked at each other horrified.

"Oh no!" exclaimed David out loud. "You don't think…"

"Don't think," said Daniel. "Just do!" He quickly opened the door and ran in.

Christine was sitting up on her bed. Her eyes were swollen shut, her nose was red, she seemed to be clawing at her chest, while between sneezes her breathing was ragged and labored. Daniel pulled her out of her bed and carried her out into the hallway, and headed for a bathroom.

Gwen and Paula were close behind him. He placed Christine in the bathtub and turned to Gwen. "Get her undressed and bathed. Get any and all pollen off of her and wash the nightgown."

The two women asked no questions. Paula started pulling the nightgown off, while Gwen turned on the faucet.

Veronica was a little slower because of her pregnancy and with a very concerned look asked: "Is there anything that I can do?"

"Talk nice to Chrissy and give her some assurances as to what we're doing," said Gwen.

Back in Christine's bedroom, the three men were removing the flowers, the bedding and getting ready to vacuum the entire room.

"Boy, this is a kick in the head," said Duane.

"We didn't know," said David. "How could we have known?"

"So what do we do now?" asked Daniel.

David looked thoughtful for a moment. "Let her know that it was planned as a nice surprise. We found out the hard way that she's allergic to roses, so it didn't turn out so nice. Next, we see if there is something that she likes, that we *can* do for her for Mother's Day."

After thoroughly cleaning the room, the men went to David's bedroom. Christine was laying on her left side on David's bed with a towel wrapped around her. Her eyes were red and puffy. She could not breathe through her stuffed up nose and there were some rasping noises coming out of her throat.

The three men all knelt by the bed, feeling a little guilty about what had just happened.

"I'm sorry," said David. "We should have checked first, to find out whether or not you were allergic to anything."

Christine tried to say something and just croaked. She cleared her throat several times and then said: "What? Allergic? To what?" She coughed.

"Roses," said Daniel. "Didn't you know that you were allergic to roses?"

"Do, I did't. Dobody ever gave be roses before. I do't rebeber ever beig dear theb at all."

"Since we can't give you any flowers…" said Duane. "… uh, are you allergic to any other flowers?"

"I do't dow. Dothig like dis had ever happed before."

The three men looked back and forth at each other.

Finally Duane spoke up: "Well, is there anything that we can get you for Mother's Day that won't be a problem?"

She looked up at them through her red eyes. "Whed I was a little girl, by parets gave be a little stuffed toy. A buddy rabbit. It got burd up id du fire. Baybe you could replace by buddy rabbit." She gave the best smile that she could muster at this time.

One at a time her sons leaned over and tenderly kissed her on the cheek. She touched each of their faces as they kissed her. Then they all three got up and left, while the three wives continued checking on Christine.

Sandra and Ben had joined them all for a big Mother's Day meal. After eating lunch, Christine felt somewhat better.

"Well," said Sandra. "It seems that today, instead of my usual nine dozen roses, I got eighteen dozen. Don't worry though, Ben and I both changed our clothes before coming over."

Christine gave her a smile.

Sandra could see that Christine was still a little miserable from the allergenic experience. "The boys were trying to do something nice, so please don't..."

"Do't worry," said Christine with a smile. "I dow. I'b glad dey tried. I just wish dat I had dowd. I've dever had a probleb like dat before. I just did't dow. I still feel a li'l weak. Could you tell du boys dat I'b dot bad at deb?" She sniffed hard, trying to clear her nose.

Sandra hugged Christine. "I'm sure they know that, but I think it will be better if you tell them."

Christine sniffed hard. Her nose was finally unplugging from the morning event. "Okay."

That night, when Christine went to bed, she found two brand new pillows on her bed. All the bedding had been cleaned and the room smelled very fresh.

The next morning, Christine woke up, in her usual position laying on her right side. Directly in front of her face were three little stuffed toys. Three rabbits: One blue, one green and one red. They were about one foot tall and had silly grins on their faces. She pushed herself up to a sitting position, scooped all three bunnies into her arms and hugged them close. She closed her eyes and said to herself: 'I'm not gonna cry. I love this. I love my sons and this is one time I am not going to cry.' She sniffed a few times and felt the softness of the toys against her face. She giggled silently, opened her eyes and looked at the rabbits again. She sighed contentedly when she looked at the three grinning faces of her new treasures. The rabbits would not be anywhere near as cherished as the towels, but they were still wonderful treasures.

She put the rabbits back down on the bed beside her so that she could go to the bathroom for morning necessities. "Don't you little fellers go nowhere. I'm goin' to the bathroom and I'll be right back." She turned to the left side of the bed to get up and sat there frozen in shock. Sitting next to the left side of the bed was another stuffed toy. Another rabbit. This one, however was pink. It was in the same sitting up pose as the other three rabbits and had the same silly grin. But this one was over four feet tall. The ears were pointing straight up and with the addition of the ears, the rabbit was taller than Christine. She started giggling and crying uncontrollably.

The door to her bedroom came open and all of her sons, daughter-in-laws and grandchildren came in with big grins on their faces.

May 15 came around and she was given a clean bill of health. Now, she could nurse Mikey, without any fear of passing on some disease to him. Paula seemed somewhat reluctant about it, but gave in after seeing the results of the medical examinations.

Christine was constantly pressing David for more information, but he refused to budge. All he would tell her was that May 27 was the date of the hearing and she would get an earful at that time. He would then give her one of those exasperating grins and change the subject.

She spent most of her time looking through the scrapbooks. She would look at pictures she had seen a dozen times and still want to see them again. Sometimes she would sit there staring at a picture wishing that she had been there when it was taken. Other times she would sit in one of her sons laps, staring into his face, accepting what was now the present.

Many times she would sit, straddling their lap, with her face close to theirs. She would stare at each one of her sons closely. She was learning every little nuance of their face and their being. Sometimes she would put her arms around their neck and hug them close just to be holding them. Other times, her emotions would get to her and she would bury her face in their neck, while crying. Each time, no matter what she was doing, each one would patiently sit there and either answer her questions or just hug her back.

One of the real pleasures for her was that she was able to hug all three of them close and, unlike the times in *The Back Room,* she did not have to have sex with anyone. She was learning exactly what unconditional love really was.

The morning of May 19, David and Paula headed downtown for some legal stuff that they had to take care of. Christine was going to baby sit her youngest grandchild completely by herself. All four families were elsewhere doing something, so Christine was totally alone with Michael. She had volunteered to take care of all four of her grandchildren, but other plans had been made and she would have to wait until later for that big of a job.

She decided that since she was responsible for a baby, she had to stay away from the *sleeping* couch. Every time she sat down in the thing, she ended up taking a nap even if she had not been tired.

She was watching a sitcom while Mikey was nursing. He suddenly went limp. She looked at him closely. She listened. She could not hear any breathing. She laid him down on the floor, put her hand on his chest and tried to rouse him. She put her ear to his chest. No sound of a heartbeat.

A cold chill ran down her back as she scrambled to the phone. She picked it up and dialed 911. Nothing. She hung the phone up, picked it up and listened for the dial tone...nothing. Now she was close to panic. She ran to a different phone. This one was dead as well. She let out a small squeal of anger and frustration.

She did not remember picking him up, but she was hugging him to her chest and rubbing his back trying to see any form of activity. The phones were dead, and she did not have one of those cell phones or a talking tooth. She froze for a moment and looked down at her ankle monitor.

Without any hesitation, she ran to the front door, flung it open and was running across the front lawn. She got to the sidewalk before the monitor went off.

Since she had been virtually imprisoned inside, she had forgotten just how hot the sidewalk could get in a south Texas summer day. The grass line seemed to be the border for the monitor going off, so she could not step back into the grass. She did a painful dance running and hopping across the hot street to the front lawn of Duane's house.

She was frantically pacing back and forth while continuing to rub Michael's back. The ankle monitor continued the irritating beeping which only added to Christine's panic.

Finally she heard the wailing of a siren. The police car came speeding around the corner and skidded to a stop in front of Christine. Two policemen jumped out of the car, and immediately turned towards the noisy ankle monitor. They pulled their guns and aimed them at her.

"My grandson," she screamed, "he ain't breathin'."

"Put the baby down and back away!" shouted an officer.

She laid Michael down in the grass and backed away on her knees. "Please help my grandbaby, please!"

"Place your hands on top of your head, now!"

She obeyed the instructions, still pleading desperately for Michael.

While one of the officers put handcuffs on her, the other started examining Michael. "What did you do to him?" the officer asked angrily.

"I was just feedin' him and he stopped breathin' or movin'. I don't know what happen."

The officer that was doing the exam, started CPR.

The other officer got on his radio and called for an ambulance.

"So," said the officer, "why didn't you call 911?"

"I tried, the phones in the house is dead. This ankle thingy is the only way that I had to git anyone here."

While the one officer continued the CPR, the other put Christine in the back of the cruiser. He then went into David's house. He came out a few moments later and closed the door. He then walked around the house. As he finished his lap around the house, more sirens were heard approaching the scene.

Christine was surprised to see a fire truck come up before the ambulance, but she was glad to see any help arrive. The medical team took over on the CPR, while one of the firemen questioned Christine.

"What happened, did you shake him or strike him?"

"I din't hit him," she screamed. "He was nursin' on my boob and just suddenly stopped breathin'."

The fireman looked down at her chest. She looked down as well and saw that her shirt was still unbuttoned and there was a large milk stain on her left breast.

"Does he have any allergies?"

With that question she calmed down a little. "I dunno of any allergies. I just know that he can't have any food other'n natural breast milk."

The fireman looked surprised. "You say that you are his grandmother, but you were nursing him?"

She closed her eyes and clenched her teeth. "We don't got time fer a long story."

"Okay, okay, how old is he?"

"9 months."

Several of the team surrounded Michael, and Christine could do nothing but worry.

The officer that had gone into the house came up to her. "Which phone number should we call?"

"What choo talkin' bout? The phone inside is dead."

"I have a cell phone. I saw all those numbers listed by the phone and I need to know who the parents are so we can contact them."

"David and Paula are his parents, they'll know what to do."

The officer looked at his pad, looked to the keypad on his cellular and started punching buttons. He walked away from Christine with the phone to his ear and she could hear nothing of his conversation.

A few minutes later Michael was placed in the ambulance and it left with the siren blaring.

About the same time, another truck showed up with *Randall Security* markings on the side. After a short conversation with the police, the security agent opened up his laptop, hit a few keys and the annoying beeping on the ankle monitor finally, mercifully, stopped.

Christine could not feel any relief because she was still too upset about Michael. She had been taking care of him when he stopped breathing, and she felt guilty about his condition.

One of the police officers reached in the back seat, and

buckled her in. Both officers then got in the front and started the car.

As they drove away, she sagged down in the seat feeling totally depressed. "Where you takin' me?"

"You violated the terms of your bail. We're taking you back to the lockup."

"But I was tryin' to get help for Mikey! This ain't fair!"

"That's for a Judge to decide."

She felt horrible. The attempt to save Michael was planting her right back in jail. She felt too miserable to cry. Gone! That beautiful bedroom, the equally beautiful bathroom, all the wonderful clothing, a huge family that she was only beginning to get used to, but worst of all - she did not know what Michael's condition was or if David and Paula might blame her.

She was put in a special holding cell. One where she was separated from other detainees, for certain special reasons. She had no idea why she was special, but after seeing some of the women in the big cells, she was grateful for the treatment.

An eternity passed before David came to see her that evening. She was not concerned that she had to be trussed up in chains in order to see him, she just wanted to find out…anything.

David looked very concerned. She did not know what to read in his face as she was shackled to the table. Her primary hopes were that Michael was okay, and that David was not mad at her.

After the guard left the room, David looked up and cleared his throat. "It appears that Michael…has a genetic defect…in his heart. He stopped breathing because of it and…"

"Is he alive?" She was desperate to know.

"Uh…yes, he's alive. He's on life support right now…Paula is with him…so is Mom. They're checking his brain functions right now to see if he had any damage. If his brain wasn't deprived of oxygen for too long, then there shouldn't be any problems."

"What's gonna happen later on?"

"Well you're preliminary trial may be postponed…"

"Forget that! I wanna know bout Mikey!"

"Well…they are going to do the surgery to correct his heart problem in the morning. The procedure is one that they are very familiar with, so that shouldn't be a problem. What everyone is praying about now, is the brain scan. Fixing the heart will be simple." He clenched his lips and his eyes darted around the room. "If there is brain damage…then we aren't sure what will happen after that."

"I tried to get help fast as I could…but the phone…"

"Yeah. The phone. We're going to get you a cell phone of your own. At least that way, you'll have another option on getting help."

"What happened to the phone?"

"I don't know. I am planning on a few inquiries about it. I need a phone that I can depend on, and it seems that you do too."

"Are you gonna be able to get me outta here?"

"What? Oh yeah! Yeah! The only problem right now is a somewhat 'Gung Ho' Assistant District Attorney, who is trying to make a name for himself. He wants to do everything by the book, no matter what the consequences."

The two of them sat silently for a while.

He was more concerned about his son. He knew that no Judge could hold anything against her because her motive had been to save Michael. Getting her out would be nothing but a formality.

She was relieved that he was David was not mad at her. She did not share his optimism about getting her back out, however, she – once again – had no control of the situation and would have to rely totally on him to help her.

25

On 23 May, she was taken into court to determine what would happen next. The judge sat there listening with a rather blank look on his face through all the testimony. After hearing all of it he sighed, closed his eyes and shook his head. He sniffed and looked up at the ceiling. "Is there any more testimony?"

Both David and the ADA said no.

He leaned forward and looked at the ADA. "Why did this come to me?"

The ADA was quick to answer. "She *did* violate the boundaries, your honor."

"Were you listening? She violated the boundaries because that was the only way she could summon help. From what I have heard here, it seems that she got medical assistance there a lot faster than by calling 911, anyway."

"I understand that, your honor, but she still violated the terms of her release."

"Let me go back over this again: She was nursing the baby. He stopped breathing. She tried to call 911, but the phone was dead. The phone was dead because a *squirrel* ate the insulation off of the wire, disconnecting the wire and killing the squirrel and the phone line as a result. She used her ankle monitor to summon the police, who it seems responded faster than any ambulance could have. When the police arrived, she gave absolutely no resistance whatsoever, she explained what she had done and why. One of the officers started CPR on the child, saving the boy's life, because he started the CPR *in time*. Once the ambulance arrived, they were able to do an even better form of life saving procedures with their gadgets, widgets and doohickeys. The child has had a life-saving surgery performed on him as a result of what they found. She has not given anyone any guff of any type during all of this turmoil." He scratched his chin and looked at the ADA confused. "Why do you want me to revoke her bail? Everything she did was meant to save the life of the child. If she had done nothing, and let the child die, what would be happening then?"

"Your honor, I'm simply following procedure. She did violate the terms of her bail."

"She did it to save a child's life."

"I understand that, your honor, but we must follow procedure..."

"No, you are NOT following procedure, you're wasting this courts time. There are *some* things that can be handled at a lower level. My decision is that she suffer no consequences at all. Send her back home and reset the ankle monitor. Any costs of this procedure will come out of the funding for the DA's office. It should come out of your pocket, specifically." He banged his gavel. "We're done here."

They had to have a chaperone from the security agency with her on the way home to reset the monitor.

She was still confused about the phone. "A squirrel et the

wire?"

"The squirrel ate the insulation around the wire." David shook his head. "It seems that this insulation that they thought was so great, as far as saving money, is a feast for the squirrels. The little beasties love it. They start eating it and get so engrossed in their buffet, that they cannot tell the insulation from the wire. When their teeth hit the positive and negative, they cross the wires, get electrocuted and the wires short out. Result: Dead squirrel and dead phone. The phone company has been trying to put stuff in the insulation to make it more bitter or less tasty, but nothing has worked. They're going back and replacing all the new stuff with the old stuff that squirrels, or any other wild life, don't eat."

"How's Mikey doin'?"

"The surgery went well. They are going to keep him in the hospital for a few more days for observation. They say that the procedure is quick and easy, because of their familiarity with it, but it is still heart surgery."

"Wha bout his brain?"

"The scan showed nothing out of the ordinary. As young as he is, there is no way of really knowing about how his memory might have been affected. The only thing that we can do is observe him and see if he acts differently than he did before."

"How's Paula doing?"

He sighed. "She is a mother with her baby in the hospital following surgery. How would you feel?"

"I's never allowed to have that feelin'."

David flushed. He realized that it had been a stupid statement to make to Christine, however, he was not thinking as a lawyer right now - he was thinking like a worried father.

They arrived back at the house and her ankle monitor was reactivated. She stared at the thing somewhat disgusted and a little relieved. She did not like the idea of wearing it, however, it had been the main factor in saving Michael's life. She listened as they went through all of the procedures including the briefing on what her boundaries were.

After the security representative left, Christine went into the living room and found almost the entire family there. The only ones missing were Ben and the two oldest grandchildren. Paula was sniffling quietly. Gwen and Veronica were sitting off to the side looking rather embarrassed. Duane and Daniel were sitting next to each other looking rather smug. Sandra had an unusually stern look on her face. That ever present smile was strangely absent. David had noticed the uneasy feeling in the air and was waiting for the other shoe to drop when Christine came in.

Sandra switched her gaze towards Christine. Immediately the pleasant smile was back on her face. "Good Afternoon, dear. The other ladies have something to say to you. Just have a seat and listen."

David and Christine glanced at each other. David shrugged and sat down near his brothers. Christine sat down near Sandra.

Sandra patted Christine on her leg. She turned away from Christine: "Well ladies - who wants to start?"

The only sound was Paula's sniffling. Christine looked at each of the daughter-in-laws, then to David who was just as confused, Duane and Daniel who seemed to look even smugger.

Sandra leaned toward Paula. "Paula? I think you owe her the biggest apology and a big thanks for what she did."

Christine looked at Sandra totally confused. A thanks - yes, because of her quick actions in saving Michael's life. An apology? For what?

Paula looked at Christine and immediately looked down. She could not hold eye contact with Christine. She blew her nose and took a few deep breaths. A tear ran down her face. She opened her mouth to say something, but nothing came out. She shook her hands nervously and clenched her eyes closed. She took a big slow deep breath. "I didn't..." Again she seemed to lose her voice. "I didn't...trust you."

Christine was a little shocked and tried to say something. Sandra raised her hand in a signal for Christine to stay quiet.

Paula finally continued. "You had been out of touch for so long...I didn't know if I could trust you to take care of Michael." She gave David a worried look. "David made me leave Michael with you...I didn't want to. I had no idea how you might react to any situation. I thought you might fall back into some horrible action from the prison, if something strange happened." She leaned back, took another deep breath, and finally made eye contact with Christine. "You risked everything for my baby. When you ran outside, you were ready to give up every bit of freedom that you have had over the past few weeks to save my son." She buried her hands in her face and let out a few more sniffles. Her hands fell to her lap and she looked Christine in the eyes again. "I'm sorry that I didn't trust you…and yes, I owe you a huge amount of thanks for what you did for Michael." She put her fists up to her mouth and her body wracked with a few silent sobs. She took a few more slow controlled breaths. "I'm so sorry, I didn't trust you. Please, can you forgive me?"

Christine sat there stunned. She could not move or think. She looked at Sandra helplessly hoping for some kind of instructions.

Sandra was looking at the other two women. "Who's next?"

Veronica gave Daniel a guilty look while wringing her hands.

"I guess I am," said Gwen. She sighed and then sat up straight. "I didn't trust you either. I always made an excuse to take the boys to someone who was a little more professional at taking care of children." Her eyes started to tear up and she cleared her throat. She looked down at the floor. "What you did!" She shook her head and looked back up at Christine. "You showed me that you really care about…family. I hope that you can find it in your heart to forgive me too…for not trusting you." She looked around at Duane, Sandra and Christine. She clenched her fists in her lap and looked at Veronica as a few tears ran down her cheeks.

Veronica turned red. She saw that all eyes were on her. She looked Christine straight in the eyes. "Oh, I'm sorry too." She glanced around at everyone. "I had the same feelings. I wasn't sure that I could trust you with my little girl. But now I know that my little CC will be just as safe as if she was with me or her daddy." She looked at Daniel with a furrowed brow. "You showed us all that you really care about your grandchildren. I really don't know what words to use to say how sorry I really am for not trusting you, but

I hope that you can forgive me too. I really want to be friends with you."

Christine looked around at faces. She was dumbfounded. She slowly moved her gaze to Sandra. "What do I do?" She nearly choked on the words.

Sandra looked a little surprised. "What do you mean, dear?"

"Uh…they pologized…and…well…no one's ever done that. I mean, no one's ever apologized…tuh me. I don't know…what… to do."

Sandra looked even more astonished. "No one? Not ever?"

Christine just shook her head.

Duane snickered. "Well, Little Mom, you can either, slap them silly and tell them off, or you can hug them and tell them that you do forgive them."

Sandra huffed. "Oh, Duane! We're trying to be serious here!"

"I know…and I am serious. Hey, Little Mom, they know that they messed up and they're trying to fix it. So? What are you going to do?"

Christine looked at Duane, then Sandra. She then looked at David and Daniel trying to see if there was any advice from them. She slowly got up and walked over to Paula. Paula stood up with a face full of fear and anticipation. Christine looked back at Sandra anxiously.

Sandra silently mouthed the words and then cocked her ear towards Christine.

Christine looked up at the taller woman and swallowed hard. "I want to…I…uh…no one's ever said that they was sorry…to me. No one. You married my son, so I wanna be friends…with you." She looked back at Sandra who returned a stern stare. "I…suppose…no…I do…I do forgive you." She hugged Paula. Having a taller person cry on her shoulder felt a little awkward, but she held on tight till Paula got it out of her system.

Next she went to Gwen. She did not stammer as much with forgiveness here but she did have a little easier time with it.

When she went to Veronica it was even easier. First, because she was now practiced at it. Second because Veronica was much closer to Christine's height.

After all the hugging and sobbing was over she went back to Sandra. "I feel weird. I feel bad cause they din't trust me, but I also feel good because…uh…I feel good…and I don't know why."

Sandra's smile seemed to grow a little. "You have just grown a little closer to all three of them. You understand them a little better and they understand - and trust - you a little more. In the long run, you will be trusting them more as well."

Christine looked around the room at everybody. "Uh…I just got back from that there lockup. I think I need a bath…uh…I'll see yuh later."

She sat there soaking, in the warm water and thick bubbles, thinking. More new experiences. Not one, but three apologies. Apologies where someone was asking for forgiveness from a *toy*. It was usually the toy that had to apologize if you did not please your abuser. *They* had apologized to a toy.

Then they had looked to her for comfort. Comfort! There had been times that she had been in *The Back Room,* and all the customer wanted was to lay there and hold on to someone. Nothing had been said, nothing sexual, just hold on.

Each day seemed to be bringing more new things in her life that she was not ready for. She was feeling like a 12 year old again and was grateful for the mere existence of someone like Sandra with her tender words of comfort and wisdom.

Because of the "incident" with Michael, the ADA had postponed the preliminary hearing. David was very upset over this turn of events and tried very hard not to take it out on family. He was on the phone, sometimes, yelling, sometimes begging, but always pushing to "get the ball rolling" again.

Meanwhile, Christine was now doing her own day care with the other three grandchildren. They enjoyed her company and the fact that they did not have to go where there were some 40 other children. Joseph and Cecilia were getting a lot more attention than they would at the big day care center.

Even though little Brett was finally 1 year old, Christine kept in practice nursing him. She did it only when the two older ones were taking a nap. She wished that she could nurse the two older ones as well, but it would be difficult explaining that to their mothers.

On June 5th, Michael was finally brought home. Christine handled him very carefully, constantly listening for breathing and watching his eyes for any and all activity. He was the youngest of the four, but he had been the wonderful tool that had brought the entire family closer.

On the morning of June 11th, David came out of his office looking haggard and a little relieved.

"Finally!" He flopped down in a chair near Christine. "I got those bureaucrats to listen. The new hearing is going to be next Monday - the 16th." He looked at Christine and saw the look in her eyes. "No, I am still going to wait until the hearing to lower the boom."

If she had not been holding Michael at the time she would have thrown something at David. All she could do was sit there and boil in frustration.

26

The night of the 15th, Christine got no sleep whatsoever. She sat in the bed, hugging her knees all night. She got up several times to go to the bathroom, only to discover that once she was in there, she really did not need to relieve herself of very much.

Daylight started coming in slowly through the window. She got out of bed and went into the closet. Sandra had been turning out all kinds of wonderful pant suits and dresses for Christine. She had been, for the most part, sticking to the *blue-green-red* ideology. Today, she decided that since David was going all out to save her - green. Green pant suit, green underwear, pale green blouse and of course, green shoes and purse. The only thing she took with her that was not green was the treasured blue and red towels.

The chaperone from the security agency arrived early. She tweaked her laptop to Christine's monitor and sat patiently waiting for the family to go to the courthouse.

When they arrived at the courthouse, the usual occurred. Christine's ankle monitor set the metal detector off. After she had been given the once over with the hand scanner they were off to the courtroom.

On the way, they were stopped by a man who silently handed a note to David, and then simply walked off. David read the note and frowned. "That's weird. Usually you don't get a change like this at the last second."

"What's up?" asked Duane and Daniel.

"Different Judge. For some reason we have been switched from Whitley to Lassiter."

Daniel looked at David seriously. "Is that a problem?"

"No. It's just a little unusual. Probably nothing. Okay, according to this, Lassiter has his courtroom on the fourth floor."

The group headed to the fourth floor. Once David found the correct courtroom, they all filed in and sat waiting.

David was looking at a few things in his attaché case, when another man came in, walked up to David, handed him a note and left just like the other one. David frowned as he read the note. He sighed, checked his watch, got up and headed out.

Sandra saw the look on David's face. "Is there a problem, dear?"

He stopped, looked at her a little confused, shrugged his shoulders and then left the room. All of the family looked at Paula, who was sitting next to Christine. Paula could do nothing but shrug as well, because she had not even seen the note.

David looked at the enigmatic note. According to the instructions, he was supposed to go to the south smoking balcony, where he would be contacted. He walked out on the balcony where his nose was assaulted by several stale, partially full butt cans. He looked around and saw only one other man on the balcony.

The man was just under 6'. He was wearing an unremarkable tan suit with a black tie. A slight breeze was mussing his dark brown hair. He was looking at David in a condescending way. "Are you

Murdoch?'"

"Yes. Who are you?"

The man put a blank smile on his face and snickered. "John Smith."

David knew that he was being set up for something. "Look, I don't have time for all this covert nonsense - Mr. Smith. State your business, so I can get back to mine."

'Smith' looked over the edge of the balcony. "Succinct! Good! I don't have time for any more of your shenanigans either. This stupidity stops now - today. I don't know what you're trying to pull or why, but no more."

David stared at John confused. "What stupidity? What shenanigans? What are you talking about?"

"You, trying to be some kind of Clarence Darrow. You take it on your own shoulders to get some little trollop out of jail. Why? So you can look good? So you can take some 'nothing case' and make yourself look like a crusader for justice? No! You've upset a few apple carts. You've made waves. For what? Okay so you got the attention of certain people. Now that you have their attention, let the little bimbo go back to jail, tell them what you want, and everyone will be happy."

David put his hand to his forehead. He closed his eyes and then shook his head. "Did I come in on the middle of a conversation? I have no idea what you are talking about, around or hinting at. You need to start at the beginning, explain yourself and be a whale of a lot 'more clear'. If not, then I bid you good day and I'm going back inside to take care of business."

"Okay, stupid! You want to play stupid? I'll treat you stupid! That little hooker that you are trying to get out of jail - forget it. *I* made the changes in courts today. Whitley might have listened to you, but Lassiter won't. He's not even going to let you present your case. He was given a brief by *me* that had *my* instructions on it. You go in there, get embarrassed and the tramp is going back to a pimp in the prison. There were several deals that had been made where her "*talents*" were part of the agreements. They had to put them on hold, while *you* are playing your silly games. It ends - today! She goes back to prison and you go home and lick your wounded pride. Is that a little more clear…or do I have to dumb-it-down any further?"

David stared at him in utter disbelief. He looked up and took a long breath. "You obviously have not done your homework on this case. I am going to continue to fight for her until she is out of jail! She is innocent. I can prove it, so what you are asking is…"

"Hey moron!" John growled. "I am not *asking* anything! I am *telling* you! You drop it NOW! If you want to go in there and make a fool of yourself…well okay. I was trying to help you keep some shred of your dignity intact. If you want to be hard headed and go down in flames…I think I'll go in and watch the fun. Just remember - you were warned."

John walked off the balcony, and headed to the courtroom.

David stood there for a few moments in contemplation. Who *is* John Smith? Who are *they*? What applecart? Deals? He looked around the balcony. He raised his head, closed his eyes and said a silent prayer. He straightened his jacket, turned and went back inside.

He went back into the courtroom slowly. There were a few more people in the courtroom. John Smith was sitting on the back bench, arms folded with that condescending look on his face. There was a gray haired woman who was wearing a purple outfit that was very greatly overdressed for visiting or observing court proceedings. Sitting next to her was a much younger woman who was almost equally overdressed, in yellow. Another person that caught David's eye was a thin man with a mess of unruly snow white hair on his head.

Christine looked at David. She was a little concerned about what she saw. His swagger was gone. The content look was gone from his face. His brow was furrowed in deep thought. 'Oh well,' she thought. 'Maybe he's just putting on his game face.' She had seen some people act like that when they were gambling in the prison.

Her thoughts were interrupted by the bailiff making his announcements about Judge Henry Lassiter coming in. She did not like all this legal nonsense. All the rituals, traditions and fanfare had only gotten her locked up. She looked down at the floor as the Judge walked in and went to his seat. More ritualistic jabber, he banged his gavel and told everyone to sit down. It was then that she looked *at* the Judge. She did not notice that everyone else had taken their seats. She was ready to laugh out loud. Instead she just waved at the Judge and in a cheerful voice, said: "Hi, Mister Snake Man!"

All eyes turned to Christine - including the Judge. The first expression on his face was irritation. He opened his mouth to say something, and his expression changed to horror and then anguish. He tried to say something, but all that came out was a loud wheeze. He dropped his gavel, put his head down on his desk and covered his head with his hands.

David was just about ready to choke Christine into silence until he saw the reaction from the Judge. He looked at the ADA and saw a face that was just as confused as himself and the bailiff. He put his hand on Christine's shoulder, pulled her toward him and asked: "Mister Snake Man?"

Christine turned to David looking delighted. "Yeah! You member that you was asking me bout the customers that I had to service in *The Back Room*? Well, he's one of em. As a matter of fact, he's the one what helped me keep track of time. He's always there on Thursday evenin'."

Judge Lassiter was trying to get back some kind of control and composure. He picked up his gavel and pounded a few times. He was waving his hand at Christine, trying to get her to shut up. He was trying to say anything, but could get nothing to come out of his mouth but hoarse whimpering sounds. The Judge made some strange hand signals to the bailiff, who did not see them because he was more fascinated by what he was hearing from Christine.

"Okay," said David. "He was a customer. Why does he call himself, Mister Snake Man?"

Christine pointed to a spot on her stomach. "He got this crazy birthmark what starts right chere, near his belly button. It snakes its way down to his crotch, twixt his legs and then up to about the center of his right butt."

David looked at the ADA. "Well, Mr. August. My client has made an accusation and supplied a piece of evidence under the heading of 'distinguishing characteristics'. Shall we postpone our proceedings until we have proof of her information?"

The ADA was about to say something, when from the back of the room they heard a loud woman's voice: "The birth mark is there, exactly as she described it." It was the woman in purple. She was standing there, looking at the Judge with fury in her eyes.

The ADA ducked slightly with a surprised look on his face at the loud remark that came from behind him. "Who are you?"

Her gaze switched to the ADA, but her expression did not change. "I am Rita Lassiter. The soon to be EX-Missus Snake Man! I came here to see the revelations of how my husband does his job. Instead, I got a revelation of what he was actually doing all those Thursday evenings." She looked back at the Judge. "Pinochle! My foot! Penile adventures in pornography with this…person…is more accurate!"

"You his wife?" said Christine. "Ooh, he don't like you."

Rita looked at Christine. "What?"

"Well, it ain't you…I mean…he don't like the way you look. He told me about that group uh warts…"

"Silence!" shrieked Rita. She looked at the Judge. "You told her…? You beast! What else did you tell her?"

"You snore and you wear diapers." said Christine in a matter-of-fact tone.

Rita gawked at Christine and then shrieked again.

"That's enough," said David.

"Well he did say it," said Christine.

"Calm down Mom!" said the young woman in yellow. "Your blood pressure!"

The ADA looked at the court reporter. "Have you been taking this down?"

The court reporter, a young Hispanic woman, had a huge grin on her face. "Oh yeah! This is some of the juiciest stuff I've ever had a part of."

The ADA turned back to Rita. "I know this is REALLY messy, but I need you to give a statement in regards to what you've seen and heard and know. Uh…my assistant…Hannah Barnes, here will be glad to get your statement." He looked around nervously. "I know that you're upset…uh…okay, enraged. The sooner we get the statement, the sooner you will have all kinds of goodies to give to your…divorce attorney." He gave her a questioning glance and shrug.

"The statement will help rip that adulterous dog apart?"

"Along with what the defendant has said - oh yes. Your husband will be lucky if he is able to keep his freshly blemished skivvies."

Hannah was looking at Rita with fear in her eyes. "Shall we go to my office?" Her voice shook a little.

Rita took the arm of the girl in yellow. "Come Diane. We've seen enough of your father in action." She looked at Hannah. "Lead on, young woman! The sooner, the better!"

The ADA now turned to the bailiff. "Officer Woolsey, would you mind taking the Judge into custody and start processing him?"

The bailiff looked as if he was trying hard to keep from laughing. "What charges do I process against him?"

"Let's start with Misprision. That will be enough to knock him down, right now. As soon as we have all the other statements we'll figure out if there are any additional charges then."

Woolsey headed towards the Judge, still fighting hard to keep from laughing.

"Bailiff!" shouted August. In a deliberate low tone he said: "Please remove the Judge's robe from that *thing* before you process it."

Woolsey's expression immediately became serious. He gave a slight salute to August. "Yes sir. I understand."

"And bailiff…make sure that you read him his rights - twice - that way we will not have to worry about any technicalities."

"Yes sir."

"Thank you."

While all this was going on, David was eyeballing John Smith. Smith looked as if he had just been given a very unexpected and unwelcome prostate exam. His eyes darted around with a look of aggravation on his face. His gaze suddenly caught eye contact with David. Smith bared his teeth and he stood up. He whirled around to leave the room. As he was leaving, he pulled out his cell phone, and his thumbs were flying over the keypad. David was just about ready to do anything to figure out who was the recipient of Mr. Smith's text message.

As a whimpering Lassiter was taken out in handcuffs, August

sat down and looked at David. "Well! You said that I was in for a surprise. Was that it?"

David snickered. "Nope!" He looked back at Christine. "That one took me by surprise as well."

"Right! Sure!" August pulled out his cell phone and punched a few buttons.

"What's gonna happen now?" asked Christine.

"Very good question!" said Paula.

August started talking on his cell: "Are there any other Judges available? What? No, you'll probably get an earful on tonight's news programs...*all* channels! Come on, there has to be a mistrial or a plea bargain somewhere. Please get back to me... soon!"

David looked at August. "Do we wait here or...what?"

August sighed. "It's still early. Let's hope that the wait isn't too long."

Christine tugged on David's sleeve. "Did I do sumthin' wrong?"

August looked at her in shock. "You just defrocked a sitting Judge, in his courtroom, in front of witnesses, with corroborating testimony given at the time, and left him in a sniveling heap with no response to your accusations." August held his hands up as if trying to emphasize his statement. "I'm really not sure how to define that."

Duane perked up. "Exposed?"

David remembered the little prayer on the balcony. He

looked up and thought: 'A bit of a miracle that was desperately needed.' He sat down and hugged Christine. "As soon as I figure out all of what happened, I'll explain it to you. For now, let's just call it divine intervention."

Sandra had been taking all of this in. "Divine intervention? What do you mean by that, dear?"

"I'd like to know that too," said Duane.

"As soon as I figure out all of what happened, I'll explain it to you."

A man walked into the courtroom. "What happened in here? Hannah is in the office getting a statement from a *really* irate woman. She was supposed to be in here assisting you. Where's the Judge? What happened?"

August looked down at the floor and shook his head. "Mr. Hernandez, as I said, you'll probably be hearing about this on the news for some time. Right now, I need a Judge."

"But you have Judge Lassiter."

"HAD! Past tense! The news *is* the soon to be EX-Judge Lassiter. MISTER Lassiter is being processed right now for arraignment."

"Oh you can't leave me hanging. What happened?"

August groaned. "As soon as all the paperwork is done, I will let you get the whole thing in order for the trial on Ex-Judge Lassiter. But now…I need a Judge that has not been…what's the best word…?"

"Exposed!" said Duane emphatically…again.

August looked at the ceiling. "Good word. Appropriate. Accurate."

Hernandez looked around in anticipation of more dirt.

"Robert, go find me a Judge!" snapped August.

Hernandez huffed in frustration. He pulled out his cell phone and headed out of the courtroom.

Daniel looked around. "Hey are we allowed to still be in this courtroom? I mean, don't they have other cases to hear?"

David started laughing.

August groaned again. "Right now this is a courtroom with no Judge. It is, now, just another room until a new Judge can be found. We have no place else to be until we get a Judge...that still maintains his position...as a Judge."

A few moments later Hernandez came back in. "The Honorable Charles Poindexter just had a plea bargain end his case. He's available in number 37."

Everyone headed for the new courtroom. When they arrived, David was surprised to see the same white-haired man in this courtroom as well. He just shook it off as coincidence. The Judge had been busted, so this man had just gone to observe another case.

The bailiff started the routine of calling the court to order for the case. As the Honorable Charles Poindexter walked in, Christine started giggling.

David and August both heard her and simultaneously let out a: "What?"

Christine looked up at David: "That's the Horny Devil."

Poindexter looked at Christine with a frown, then shock. He dropped his gavel, put his hands on his head, turned his back to everybody and started heading back to his office.

"Freeze!" shouted August.

The Judge slouched down and leaned his head against the wall.

August looked at Christine dumbfounded. He looked at Poindexter, then back at Christine. "Was this another customer?"

She looked fearfully at August. "Yeah," she said in a small voice.

August growled slightly as he put his fists on the desk. "Does this guy have any distinguishing characteristics that you can remember?"

She looked up at David, who motioned her with his hands to say something. "Well he has this tattoo…" She placed her hand down by her pubic area.

"What?" said David? "On his penis?"

"No, it's above…the hair…"

David looked at her with anticipation. "Can you describe the tattoo?"

August flopped down in his chair. "Oh, I can hardly wait for that," he said sarcastically.

After she described the tattoo, the bailiff said: "The tattoo is there."

August looked incredulous.

"Don't look at me like that," said the bailiff angrily. "We work out at the same gym. I've seen him in the showers."

August stared at the ceiling while he gave this bailiff the same instructions that he had given the other bailiff.

Meanwhile, Sandra and Gwen both smacked Duane who had tears in his eyes from trying to stifle his giggling. They told him to settle down. This only started Daniel giggling as well. Veronica was having a difficult time stifling her laughs too.

"Oh, can you imagine what is going to be in the news reports tonight?" said David.

August looked at David and snarled. He hit a few buttons on his cell and put it to his ear. "You ain't gonna believe this...but...I need another Judge...for the same lousy reason." He put his hand over his mouth and whispered something into the phone.

Suddenly David noticed 'John Smith' beating a hasty retreat out of this courtroom as well, with his thumbs flying over the keypad on his cell - again.

"It is STILL only morning," said August. "What does your client have in mind for this afternoon...decimating the Federal Court Judges?"

Duane and Daniel finally got their composure back. They all waited talking quietly for a several minutes.

Finally, Mr. Hernandez came in. He walked up to August and whispered in his ear: "Why did you want me to find a Republican?"

August glared back and whispered: "That little bimbo

has just canned two Democrats. It's about time we beheaded a Republican as well."

"Well, I couldn't find a Republican, but I did get Judge Lang."

"Lang is a Democrat too."

"Yeah, but it is *Shiela* Lang. I mean a woman. What are the odds?"

August contemplated for a few moments. "Okay, which room?"

Hernandez stood up and announced to the room: "This case has been moved to courtroom 31. The Honorable Shiela Lang."

Again they all herded to the new courtroom.

…and…

The Honorable Shiela Lang (a.k.a. The Queen of Sin), was hauled off, in handcuffs, to be processed for "Misprision", by another giggling bailiff.

John Smith was looking very desperate as he left this courtroom.

August sat there glaring at Hernandez, with the veins in his neck standing out and pulsing. He leaned close to Hernandez. "Find me a Republican," he growled in a whisper.

"What's so important about a Republican?"

"Because we are running out of Democrats," snapped August.

Hernandez looked back with an equally angry glare. "Why don't you take that *person* to your office and show her that book? When she finds a Judge that she does not recognize, then we might have a better chance of getting this case moving."

August thought for a moment. He turned to David. "Mr. Murdoch. You and your client. My office…now!"

"Do you think that we are going to get this preliminary done today?"

"No," said August sarcastically. "I was thinking of asking for a change of venue, but we would have to go in front of a Judge to get that done and your client would probably bust that Judge as well. Right now, this courthouse is bleeding badly enough."

David looked at all his relatives. "You folks may as well go home. I'll let you know if anything comes up."

While the family left the building, David, Paula, Christine and her chaperone, headed for the office of the ADA.

David snickered a few times on the way there and was immediately slapped on his arm by Paula. "Don't you start that nonsense. It's bad enough what Duane was doing."

When they arrived at the office, August was sitting at his desk with his eyes closed, rubbing his temples. In front of him was a large brown binder. When he saw the others walk in he looked at David in disbelief. "I said just you and your client."

"Paula is my secretary and the security agent is here because of my client's ankle monitor."

August shrugged. He looked at Christine and smiled. "This

book is supposed to be a book of honor. In it, we place the pictures and a short biography of each of the Judges that are currently serving in this county." He closed his eyes. "Today, you have turned it into a book of mug shots." He opened his eyes. "I need you to look through it and see if you can find anyone else that was…uh…a little too close to you."

Christine looked at David apprehensively. David nodded, reached over for the binder and pulled it towards Christine.

She looked worried as she opened it up. "Okay, but I don't know what their real names is."

"That's quite alright," said August. "We do know them and so far your information has been…not just damaging…but…proven. I really don't care if some joker called himself 'Mister Tubesteak,' just look at the pictures and we will go from there."

"Cap'n Tubesteak," said Christine as she turned the pages without looking up.

"What?"

She looked up at August. "He calls himself Cap'n Tubesteak, not Mister." She looked back down at the current open page.

"Mister or Captain - doesn't matter. Just…check the photos."

Christine continued: "He's a real short black guy, with a funny accent." She looked up. "He is short…" She put her hand on her crotch. "…but, man is he packed."

August looked like a deer staring into oncoming headlights. He looked at David who had a bit of a strange look on his face. "Short? Funny accent?"

"Are they in alphabetical order?" David asked.

August simply nodded with a look of total helplessness on his face.

David took the book from Christine. He flipped to the back and started going forward. He found a certain page and turned the book so she could see. She got a big grin on her face and pointed at the picture. "Thass him! Thass Cap'n Tubesteak."

"Don't tell me," said August dejectedly. "It's the Honorable Jefferson Wickes. Right?"

"Yup!"

"Another Democrat," said August. He picked up the phone and dialed. After a moment, he asked for a Detective Ruiz. Moments later: "Hey Amigo, I need you to go arrest Judge Wickes...Yes, I said Judge Jefferson Wickes...No, I don't have a warrant yet... Yes, it is a reliable source...a VERY reliable source...Misprision...I don't have time for a long story right now...It's already hit the fan, Judge Wickes is just one part of the splatter...Thanks." He put the phone down and motioned for Christine to continue looking in the book.

She looked through it. When she got to the pages where the defrocked Judges were, the pages were removed. She found no more "clients".

August looked at the four photographs in front of him. "Well, they're probably going to be real proud of Snake Man Lassiter in Harrisburg, Pennsylvania, after the news media gets hold of this."

David looked at Paula. She looked just as stunned as he did.

"What did you say? Where is Lassiter from?"

August looked up. "Harrisburg, Pennsylvania, why?"

"Where is Poindexter from?"

He looked at the biography. "Uh…Reading, Pennsylvania."

"…and Lang?"

"What's with the hometown stuff?"

"Where is Lang from?"

August huffed as he looked at her biography. "Altoona, Pennsylvania." He checked the biography on Wickes. He looked up with a deep frown on his face. "Erie, Pennsylvania. What is going on? All four are from Pennsylvania."

"This may be part of another investigation."

August was looking agitated. "Which one? Who is in charge?"

"It's at the prison." David turned to Paula: "Who was that Guard Captain?"

"Milton…I think," said Paula.

Christine snickered. "Melton."

David looked at Christine a little surprised, then shrugged. He turned back to August. "Melton, head guard at the women's prison. She has started an investigation of the guards at the prison and the only ones under suspicion, as far as I know, are the ones from Pennsylvania or New Jersey. Are there any other Judges from either of those states?"

"I don't know, but I have the book right here…what do you mean about that investigation? How long has it been going on?"

David looked at Paula. She gave him a smug look back. "It was when our client was bailed out of prison - April 17."

"And this office is just finding out about it NOW? Have you got any other surprises that are going to pop up out of your shorts?"

David gave him one of those insincere grins. "No, I think we've done enough damage for one day. However, we will need a new date for the preliminary hearing for Christine. Soon, please. Time is getting critical."

August looked back and forth between David and Christine. "Check your current events file, buster! We're hemorrhaging Judges. As soon as I can find one, who is *not* terrified of *her*, I'll let you know. Let's not even mention the number of cases that those four Judges have been involved in that will probably have to be reopened or just…overturned."

David looked at Christine. "My dear lady, we have just knocked over an apple cart of monumental proportions." He looked back at August. "We need to keep her name out of the press. This was - to the media - a nothing case from the onset. Now, it's huge."

"Yeah, yeah, yeah. Don't worry. I'll just hit them with 'Ongoing Investigation,' and tell them to get lost." He sighed. "If they still want to push for answers, then we'll threaten them with 'Obstruction of Justice'. That one always seems to shut most of them off…and it should do it again…I hope."

27

The next few weeks, the media was having a feeding frenzy over the situation. Naughty Judges and the Whorehouse Prison, were common in the news. The tabloids were turning everything into a rumor mill that seemed to have no end to the possibilities as to who was behind the entire mess, including some avenging angel from one of the moons of Jupiter.

David on the other hand was getting more irritated over the delay in getting a new hearing. He would not tell anyone why, but something was bothering him about the extended time factors.

On July 7, 2008 Veronica gave birth to Benjamin Charles Murdoch. While all the adults were at the hospital with Veronica, Christine was babysitting some very impatient grandchildren who had no end to their questions.

Christine could not help but think of how she had never been able to breast feed any of her sons. Now she would have the privilege of breast feeding at least one child of each of her sons.

A few days after the birth, David and Paula were sitting at the dining room table eating breakfast. They were waiting for Christine to come down and join them. Michael had been fed and David was doing the crossword puzzle.

Paula looked up confused. "What's that noise?"

David listened intently for a few seconds. He turned to

Paula with an equally confused look. "It sounds like…Little Mom. It sounds like she's having a problem."

Paula picked Michael up as David headed towards the sounds. They found Christine at the bottom of the stairs, trying to move a coat tree that was kept near the front door. She was not having very much success.

David cleared his throat. "What are you doing?"

Christine looked up with anger on her face. "I'm tryin' to move this thing."

"Why?"

She stood up straight, panting. "Cause ever time I come down the stairs and I got my hand on the rail, one uh these knobs grabs my sleeve. I'm tired of bein' grabbed by this thing. I'm tryin' to move it so's I don't get grabbed by it."

"So you just need it moved a little bit…away from the banister?"

She sighed. "Yeah."

"Do you remember that box that I had you try to pick up?"

"Yeah."

"That box weighs 40 pounds. This coat tree weighs almost twice as much."

Christine looked up at him perplexed. "Why's it so heavy?"

"It's the base. It has to have a heavy base, so when you put several coats on it, it doesn't topple over. My brothers and I wear rather large coats and they are very heavy. We have to have a coat tree that is capable of that kind of weight."

Christine shrugged. "Okay."

David took hold of it with one hand, picked it up effortlessly and moved it about six inches away from the banister.

She had a bit of a sour look on her face. "Showoff."

"Is that enough?"

She looked at the new position. "I spect so." She suddenly put her left hand to her face and sputtered a little. She headed towards the dining room sniffling.

Paula had been watching and was standing there somewhat baffled. "Why is she crying? All you did was move the coat tree."

David got a little misty eyed. He sniffed and cleared his throat. "Don't forget, Darlin'. All those years in prison...no one *ever* did *anything* for her. They always did...whatever they wanted...*to* her. So now, even the most trivial of favors...to her... it's...monumental. She still doesn't know how to...accept a favor."

Paula stood there, sighed, shook her head and hugged Michael a little closer. "So, let's go in there and do her another favor with a good breakfast."

"Yes, let's."

Finally they were given a date. 30 July, 2008. Even though a date had been set, David still seemed upset over any delay. On July 15, David took Paula with her notepad out for some meeting that he would not say anything about to anyone.

When they got back that evening, Paula had a strange look on her face. She would not talk to anyone about what had happened. Her notepad was put in a sealed envelope that was then put in a safe.

Paula did not feel like eating dinner that night. The only thing she did was sit on the couch hugging Christine close with tears in her eyes. Christine was not sure who was being comforted or why, because the only thing that Paula said was: "You poor thing."

After Christine had saved Michael's life, Paula had been much nicer. Now, Christine was being spoiled by Paula. No matter what Christine said or did, Paula would not tell what had happened or give any indication as to why the treatment was so different.

The morning of July 30th arrived and as they were walking up to the courthouse, Duane could not control himself. "Hey, Little Mom, are you planning to cause another cataclysm in the county Judicial roll call today?"

Paula and Gwen both gave him an elbow in the ribs, which only made him and Daniel laugh harder.

The entire time David was looking high and low for the possible unwanted appearance of another "John Smith." They walked in the courthouse - no covert messages. They walked into the scheduled courtroom - still no covert messages. He started feeling less apprehensive, but refused to let his guard down.

Christine had noticed his uneasiness and just shrugged it off as a result of her dismantling the judicial roll call. When she sat down where her defense was to take place, for the first time in over two decades she started getting butterflies in her stomach. Before, there had been almost no future for her whatsoever because of the deaths of all known relatives. Now, she had an extended family. People who really seemed to care for her.

David sat there with his attaché case unopened. He looked at Christine, put his arm around her, moved his mouth near her ear and whispered: "Have you ever heard of a man named Dexter Hoffman?"

"No," she whispered back.

He cleared his throat. "Mister Hoffman is the man who raped you back in 1983." He let the information sink in. She stared back at him with shock and terror in her eyes. "I am very sure of this information."

"But how…?"

"The technology of today is better than what it was in 1983. They did take specimens from when you were raped in January of 1983. Those specimens were looked at closer with the forensic technology of today, and because of that, I have absolute confirmation of who raped you."

"Why're you tellin' me this now?"

"I wasn't sure how you would react to this information, and I did not want you fretting over it for any extended period of time. Do you feel that you have any problem of any type, in listening to him or seeing him?"

She could not say anything. She just sat there shaking from terror. She could not help thinking about all the times that she had been sexually abused in *The Back Room*, and had never felt this way.

Those acts she could remember, but for some reason, this seemed horribly different.

"You don't have to say anything, Little Mom. I can see it in your eyes. I do have to call him as a witness, but I can arrange for you to not have to listen to him. Does that make you feel any better?"

She still could not speak. All she could do was nod. She turned away from David trying to control her breathing. She had eye contact with Paula. The look in Paula's eyes was very telling. "You knew," she whispered. "You knew bout this Hoffman guy."

With a somber look on her face Paula nodded. "David did not want you worrying. I did all the worrying for you." Paula squeezed Christine's hand to give her reassurance.

Christine felt a tear go down her cheek. She reached inside her purse and pulled out the three treasured towels and buried her face in them. She looked back at David. He had been observing her. "Is it really necessary to have him testify here?"

Without giving anything away in his face he flatly stated: "His testimony is vital."

Mr. August walked into the room and went to the prosecution's desk. He looked at David and nodded. He then looked at Christine. He let a small grunt escape his throat. He folded his hands as if in prayer, looked skyward and shook his head, letting another small growl out of his throat before he sat down.

David got up and went over to August. He leaned down and they had a whispered conversation. August looked at Christine several times looking a little confused. August then motioned to the bailiff. Once the bailiff arrived at the table, he shrugged and nodded a few times. David came back and sat down with a warm smile on his face.

"Don't worry, Little Mom. There is a room where they can take you so that you don't have to listen to Hoffman's testimony unless you want to. The bailiff can take you in there and when Hoffman has finished then you can come back. Okay?"

She sat there chewing on the towels. She looked behind them at the rest of the family. "Can I have Duane and Daniel go in there with me?"

David looked toward the bailiff and motioned to him. The bailiff came over and David whispered to him. The bailiff motioned to August who joined this conversation as well. After several more moments of whispered conversation, August went back to his desk, and the bailiff went to his post.

David sat down and motioned to Duane and Daniel. He informed them of the plan to have Christine out of the room during Hoffman's testimony, and how she wanted their company while she was in the other room.

Duane shook his head in confusion: "Just who is this Hoffman?"

David cleared his throat and bit his lip: "The man who raped Little Mom and got her pregnant. The rat is our father."

That was the one thing that Christine did not want to hear. She pulled her legs up close to her chest and started crying. She felt two huge hands on her shoulders. Hands that she had become accustomed to over the last few months. Hands that were helping her adjust to life outside of the prison. Strong hands that she knew she could depend on for security and comfort. Hands that somehow, did not help calm her terror at this time. Still, she was glad that they were there. She sat there stewing and fretting until the bailiff made the ritualistic announcement that the Judge was entering the room.

Then comes the ritualistic reading of the charges.

As the prosecution was getting ready to start with his opening statements, David stood up and interrupted: "Your Honor, I must make an unusual request at this time."

August looked at David with his mouth still opened. He sat down and waited for the reason for the interruption.

The Judge raised his eyebrows and looked at David expectantly.

"Your Honor, I have a witness whose testimony is vital to the defense of my client, and who is also in the hospital in terminal condition. I ask at this time that the state relinquish just long enough for his testimony to be heard and then I will return the floor to the prosecution."

The Judge looked thoughtful for a moment. "Terminal condition?"

"Yes, your Honor, he is in the last stages of pancreatic cancer and could be dead at any moment."

"Any moment?"

"Yes, your Honor, his doctor has stated that he might last 6 weeks or he might not last 6 minutes."

"Do we have to go to the hospital?"

"No, your Honor, I have arranged a closed circuit conference through the television in this courtroom."

The Judge turned to August. "Any objections?"

"Your Honor, if the man is terminal, let's go ahead and hear his testimony now." He shrugged and sat down.

The Judge nodded.

David looked at Christine. "One other thing before we turn on the television."

The Judge looked slightly irritated. "Another favor?"

"Not for me, but for my client. This is the man who brutally, sexually assaulted my client several years ago, and she is very apprehensive about seeing or hearing him. I request that she be allowed to go to the other room so that she does not have to be put through any undue stress."

Before the Judge could respond, August stood up: "Your Honor, defense counsel and I discussed this before the proceedings. We have no objections to the defendant being taken back - in the company of two of her sons - to the seclusion room."

The Judge looked a little perplexed. "With two of her sons?"

Both lawyers nodded.

The Judge looked even more perplexed, but shrugged slightly. "Very well - bailiff, were you aware of this?"

"Yes, your Honor, they did inform me of this."

"Okay, whoever is going back there, get moving and let's get on with what we came here to accomplish."

The bailiff escorted them out. Christine, with tears going down her cheeks, held tightly onto two big arms as she left: Duane on her left and Daniel on her right. Of all the things that had happened to her in prison, all the things she had endured, she could not understand why this bothered her so much. She had painful memories of what people had done to her in prison. The attack that had occurred over 25 years ago was bothering her. Why? She could not remember the attack. She felt that her mind was just not functioning properly at all.

When they arrived in the room, Christine simply stood there holding on to those arms. She tried to say something several times, but could not make a sound. Duane and Daniel both knelt down trying to give her as much comfort as they could.

She cleared her throat and finally found her voice. "Duane… go back in there…please! Tell David…tell them all…uh…I don't wanna know. If you look like your father…I don't wanna know. I never saw that man. I don't have any recollection of what he looked like even if I did see him. I don't want to know what he looks like."

Duane looked down as if he were fighting back tears. He placed his hand on the back of her head and kissed her forehead. "Okay. Okay. I understand." He kissed her forehead lightly. He looked at Daniel: "Take care of her." He left the room.

Daniel sat down. He pulled her up onto his lap. This was a position that she was becoming very familiar with. All of her babies were so big that they held her instead of her holding them. He put his huge arms around her. She snuggled close to him still holding on to her towels. She had tears flowing down her cheeks and her lower lip was quivering. In the silence of the room, she could hear his breathing and his steady heartbeat. She just could not grasp why this was affecting her so much, but she was glad that she had at least one of her sons comforting her. She closed her eyes and tried to pull herself even closer to Daniel.

She yelped slightly when she was startled by a knock on the door. The bailiff opened it and they saw Duane standing there. "The guys' testimony is finished." He looked at Christine. "We can go back in now."

She looked at his face, into his eyes, she could not see any indication of what had transpired in the courtroom. She went back the way she had left - clutching hard on the arms of her sons.

They arrived back in the courtroom. It was deafeningly silent. She felt as if every eye in the room was piercing right through her. She looked at their faces to try to get some meaning. David seemed just way too calm. Paula seemed upset, but not very upset. Sandra had a fist up to her mouth and was being comforted by Ben and Gwen. Veronica sat there shaking her head. The prosecutor and his aide both looked like they had a very bad taste in their mouths.

After she had sat back down, David stood up. "Thank you, your Honor, for the indulgence. I now surrender the floor to the state."

August stood up and sniffed. He gave David a dirty look. He then turned to the Judge. "Your Honor...as a result of the testimony that we have just heard..." He gave Christine a side glance. "...the state is dismissing all charges against the defendant, Christine Lee."

Christine's jaw and shoulders dropped. She sat there dumbfounded. When the Judge started talking, she did not hear it, she just kept staring at the prosecutor.

"I agree," said the Judge. "What I don't understand is: Why did this come into a courtroom. You could have taken that testimony to the DA's office and not wasted this court's time."

David stood up. "Yes, I could have done it that way, but I didn't. I didn't because, on more than one occasion, my client has had to suffer the indignity of facing a Judge and being wrongfully persecuted for something she did not do. She was, and always had been, a victim in this case. I wanted her to hear it, in court, from a prosecutor and a Judge, that she was no longer being looked at as the perpetrator, who was guilty of things that she could not remember."

The Judge sat there contemplating. "All right." He took a long breath and was about to say something when he saw the look on Christine's face. She was still staring, flabbergasted, at Mr. August. "Hello, Miss Lee? Are you there?" He looked at David apprehensively.

David reached down and pulled her to her feet. As soon as he let go of her, she flopped back down in the seat like a sack of potatoes. He picked her up again and held her up. He took hold of her jaw and moved her head so she was staring at the Judge.

The Judge coughed a few times to hide the fact that he was laughing. "Christine Lee. The prosecution has dismissed all charges against you, and this court agrees. You are free to go with your record fully expunged of any criminal activity. We are adjourned." He banged his gavel and stood up.

The bailiff called the room to stand. After the Judge walked out, the family wanted to crowd around her, give her hugs and congratulations, and rejoice over David's courtroom victory. Christine, however was still staring stupidly at the wall behind the Judge.

David picked her up, sat her on the table, looked around the room, found the security representative, held up Christine's leg with the ankle monitor and motioned to the agent to get it off of her.

Without a word, the agent came forward, punched a few keys on the laptop and watched the ankle monitor go through a series of light blinking and beeping and then go dead. The agent then pulled out a key and removed the monitor.

"I want that machine of yours out of my house - now!" said David.

"Not a problem," said the agent. "I've already given it the order to shut down, and that has alerted our office to go get it…at your convenience."

David looked at the still astonished Christine. He snapped his fingers in front of her face several times until she reacted.

Christine looked up at David, still dazed. "Wha hapm?"

"You are free of any criminal charges and free to go do as you please," said David cheerfully.

She frowned. "What happened?" she asked desperately.

David's eyes danced and he stifled a laugh. "You didn't want to hear him, so I protected you from him and you are free."

She bared her teeth and gave an exasperated growl. "I din't wanna see his face, I din't wanna hear his voice. I *do* wanna know what he said."

Daniel came up to David. "If you're not going to tell her, tell me!"

David looked at Duane. "I think they're ganging up on me."

Duane just laughed.

"Hoffman confessed," said David nonchalantly.

Christine closed her eyes and held her arms out. "WHAT?!?!"

"Hoffman confessed," said David emphatically.

Christine growled in frustration. She grabbed hold of David's necktie, pulled herself up and wrapped her legs around his waist. She got her face as close to his as she could. "What happened?!"

"Hey, Little Mom, the position that you are in is so undignified," laughed David.

She growled again and started shaking the tie. He choked a little, sat down in a chair and cleared his throat as he pulled to loosen the tie.

"I can get that tie a lot tighter," said Daniel. "You better open your mouth and start talking, now!"

"Okay, okay, okay." David looked into the furious eyes of Christine. "I'll start at the beginning."

"You better start somewhere," fumed Christine.

"Dexter Hoffman is the man who raped you in January of 1983. He said that he had been stalking a certain woman, and thought that you were her. I guess it was kind of dark on that parking lot, and in the darkness, he got confused. Anyway, the day after the attack, he saw his initial target - intact. So, he checked the newspapers and that's when he found out that he had attacked you by mistake. The criminal mind works in strange ways, because, it did not bother him to brutalize an adult woman. When he found out that he had raped a 12-year-old girl that *did* bother him. He did not like the idea of being labeled as a child molester. So, now he, again with the idiocy of a criminal mind, decided to get rid of you, figuring that if you disappeared, then the police would have nothing to use against him."

Christine felt that she was getting even more confused. "But he raped me…what…how…he…wait…what's all this gotta do with my parents?"

"I am getting there. Patience, Little Mom. Like I said, the criminal mind works in muddled, strange, weird and idiotic ways. He started doing some stalking on you, in order to make you disappear. Well, guess who delivered the pizza to your house on March 1, 1983?"

Christine sagged against David's chest. "Oh no!"

"Oh yes. Mister Dexter Hoffman delivered the pizza. He was delivering for Carlucci's Pizza Parlor when your father called for dinner that night. He delivered it. He stopped on the way and liberally sprinkled the drugs all over the pizza that was to be delivered to your home. By the way, how many pieces of that pizza did you eat?"

Christine leaned back a little. "Do I look like I could eat that much? I had my one piece as usual."

"What about your mother?"

"Sometimes she'd eat two."

"And your father?"

She looked off to the side. "With Daddy, there weren't never any leftover pizza. He'd pack it all down."

"That is why he was dead before the fire started. He overdosed. He had just enough time to get to bed before he died. You and your mother were just knocked out. Anyway, he knew that you would all be out, so he waited until the end of his shift and went back to your house. Again, the criminal mind acts stupidly strange. He figured as long as he was there and that you were asleep, that he would rape you again and nobody would know, after the fire. He was the one who supplied that negligee. What he was doing, carrying around a…sexy woman's garment, I really don't want to know, but he did have it with him. After he had sex with you, he put it on you to see how it would look."

She clenched her fists hard against his chest. And closed her eyes.

"I can stop if you want."

She clenched her teeth. "No! I wanna know what happened."

"After he raped you, he started pouring the gasoline all over the house. He forgot about you and the negligee until after he had started the fire. He figured that it was too late to go back to retrieve it so he just left."

"His din't take me outside?"

"The only thing that I can figure, is that somehow during the sex act, you got stimulated. Enough stimulation to get out of bed and walk around. In the drug induced stupor, you had no idea what you were doing or where you were going and by sheer accident, or divine providence, you ended up outside. The firemen found you outside, saw that you were not functioning at your peak, had you put in an ambulance, and after you woke up - the rest you know."

"He meant to kill me."

"Yes, he was trying to cover up the fact that he had molested a child."

"Why din't he try to kill me afterwards?"

"You were in jail and harder to get to. Then, he found out that you were the one blamed for the fire, so he figured that he had gotten away with the whole thing. He just forgot about you and continued his criminal activities...until he got caught."

"Well, why din't anybody put my original attack against him?"

"With the computers of today, we have a better filing system. By the time the filing system had been set up in the computer, to compare crimes, the statute of limitations had run out on your rape charge. The only reason that I was able to get them hooked together was because of the fact that murdering your parents was attached to that crime, and homicide has *no* statute of limitations."

"But...how did you get them hooked together?"

"DNA. The negligee had your DNA all over it, and it had his DNA."

"But that was back in 1983. Din't the DNA get kinda rotten?"

"That is one of the miracles of science. It did not matter that the stuff in that negligee was over 25 years old. They were still able to match it up to him. Once that was done, I matched it up between your DNA and mine. You are our biological mother and he, unfortunately, is our biological father."

"Wait a minute. How didja get his DNA or mine?"

"Anyone that is in prison is in the system."

"But how didja know to check the prison system? I mean...I don't know what I mean. Why'd you check the prison system?"

David gave her a smile and hugged her. "Do you know how many sets of triplets were born in Texas in November of 1983? There were three born that month. One set in El Paso, one in Amarillo and then there was San Marcos. The one in El Paso was on the 18th of November. The one in Amarillo was on the 29th of November. Guess what day the triplets in San Marcos were born."

She leaned back and smiled. "Was it the 9th?"

"Good guess. I also found out that the birth was recorded as a medical emergency visit to the Juvenile Detention Facility. When I found that out, that is when I went to the prison files to find you."

She narrowed her eyes. "When did you find my DNA?"

"Last December."

"December?! But if you found out in December, why didja wait until April to get me out of jail?"

"Do you remember what that ADA said in April? He commented over the fact that I had everything all planned out in advance. He was right. I carefully planned it all in order to get things done as smoothly as possible. Whenever you always try to plan anything, you try to remove any X factor from your equation."

"What's an X factor?"

"Any unknown stumbling block that could foul up the whole plan. I found you, I found him, and I got into the evidence against you and him, and started asking questions." He pursed his lips and looked off to the side somewhat disgusted. "I asked questions that should have been asked 25 years ago. That idiot Reese never asked them. He never cared. Once I convinced a Judge that you had not received a fair trial, I was able to get things going full blast. Then there was the X factor about you being abused by the guards and the investigation that had to be started as a result. There was the X factor where you lambasted four Judges and the investigation that will be done from that."

"So the trial is over, I'm free and all them X factors is done."

He pulled her close and gave her a big hug. "I certainly hope so."

Duane tapped David on the shoulder. "If we are finished with the story telling and attaboys, let's get out of here and go take Little Mom to a restaurant. That'll be something she hasn't been able to do…for some time."

"I agree," said Daniel.

Christine finally let go of David's tie. She threw her arms around his neck and hugged him hard trying to fight off any more crying. She kissed him on the cheek and then slid off of his lap. She then turned to leave the courtroom.

Everyone was a little surprised to see her expression change to one of shock and horror. She pointed and said: "What's he doin' here?"

They all looked where she was pointing. The only other person still in the courtroom was the man with the unruly white hair. He was just sitting there staring off into space looking totally despondent.

David looked back and forth at the old man and Christine. "Do you know who that is?"

She looked up at David. "Doctor Dumbbell!" She spat angrily. "What's he doin' here?"

David closed his eyes and huffed. "What is his real name?"

"He's that head shrinker, Doctor McFarlin. He's the one what kept torturin' me in juvie. He's the one what kept on tryin' to get me to confess to killin' my parents. When they had that trial, as to whether er not I should remain in jail after I turned 18, that creep was the main one what burned me at that trial."

David thought for a moment. "There was a Dr. Bruce McFarlin on the DA's list of witnesses. He was supposed to be giving testimony as some form of a resident expert on your case."

"Expert! That skunk knows nuthin' bout me."

"The DA was going to put a lot of stock in what he was going to say. He has been working in the juvenile system for some time."

When David saw the fire in Christine's eyes, as she lunged at McFarlin with her claws ready for action. He caught hold of her belt from behind and yanked her off her feet.

"Leggo me," she screamed. "I'm gonna rip that maggot's face off."

David was having a hard time controlling Christine who had her arms and legs flailing around. She was trying to get hold of anything in order to get out of David's grip and get at McFarlin.

"No, you're not," said David. "We have worked too hard and too long to find you and get you out of jail for you to throw it all away now. You are especially not going to throw it away on someone who is *not worth it*."

"Wazzat thing in the room when you was listenin' to that other maggot, Hoffman?"

"Yes, he was. He has been here all along."

She turned her attention back to McFarlin. "Didja hear?" she screamed. "Didja? Didja hear, that I din't take any drug - voluntarily? Didja hear, that I din't start no fire? Didja? Answer me, you piece uh crap!"

McFarlin looked up at her sadly. He looked down at the floor. He spoke in a soft downcast voice. "I had to work with the information that they gave me."

"They give you trash. They give you what you's worth - nuthin'!"

"I had to work with the information that they gave me," he repeated pathetically.

"Crap! You owe me a mountain uh apologies. You owe me apology fer every time you called me a liar. You owe me apology for every time you opened your mouth, anywhere near me."

"I had to work with the information that they gave me, he repeated in total despondency."

"He won't apologize," said Duane flatly. "He can't afford to. If a head shrinker apologizes to anyone, then everyone will start questioning everything that ever came out of his mouth. Especially if he admits that he made a mistake with you or anyone else."

"If he don't give me any apology, I'll rip his tongue out," she said as she continued squirming in David's grip.

Ben grabbed hold of Christine's left hand. "He's not worth it! Look at him! He's pathetic! David is right. Forget that old fool. You can now start a new life, where he has absolutely no say at all."

Sandra took Christine's other hand. "You have won the war, dear. You are free. Everything that he said to you was wrong. He knows that now. What's more, he knows that you know, just how wrong he was. Find some way to forgive him in your heart or it will eat at you for the rest of your life, dear. Now, is the time to celebrate the rest of your life in freedom, not drag out horrors of the past and relive them."

"I had to work with the information that they gave me," said McFarlin even more downcast.

Christine looked into Sandra's pleading eyes. She calmed down and went limp in David's grasp. "Pumme down," she said quietly through clenched teeth.

David lowered her to the floor carefully. He kept an arm around her just to make sure because she was still fuming. Daniel moved ahead of the group, and used his body as a barrier between Christine and McFarlin. They all left the room silently. Christine never looked back at McFarlin. She simply stared forward as she departed the room.

McFarlin could do nothing else but sit there and feel sorry for himself. He had a few tears running down his cheeks as he sat there shaking his head. He sat there for several hours sobbing. When he finally stood up to leave, he was wondering if anyone was going to put him in a red suit. He also wondered if there had been any other children in that facility that he had talked into admitting to a crime they did not commit. He decided that it was time to retire. He did not want to ruin any more lives.

28

They walked out of the courthouse. Christine was clinging tightly to David's arm. They headed to where all their cars were parked. On the way to the cars, they passed by two policemen headed the opposite way. David felt Christine's grip tighten on his arm as they approached the police. She did not let up much after the two officers passed by.

When they got to the parking lot, everyone surrounded Christine. "So, what do you want to do now, with your new freedom?" asked David.

She looked around at everybody and weakly shook her head and shrugged. "I dunno. I…don't know what's out…here."

Duane pointed off to his right: "There's a park over there. Some pathways and trees and things. You could go over there and sit for a while and contemplate what you want to do."

"We have paid for parking in this lot for the whole day," said Gwen. "It's still early, we all called in to work so no one has anywhere they have to be today. We can all have time today to sit and smell the roses." She grimaced as she remembered the allergy episode. "…or some other flower."

Again as a group, they herded their way to the park. Christine could feel her heart pounding. She pulled her treasured towels out of her purse and clutched them close under her chin. Several people in the group were talking to each other, but she did not listen to them. They crossed the street and walked up to a pathway that led into the park.

"You are free to do what you want," said David. "You can take a walk by yourself or…whatever."

She took a few small steps onto the gravel pathway and turned back. She looked at all the smiling faces of the people behind her. She turned back toward the park and took a few longer steps. She turned back at them again with a larger smile on her face. She received more reassuring smiles from them all. She turned back to the park, took several deep breaths, opened her purse, shoved the towels in the purse, closed it and embarked on a new adventure in exploring this park – totally free.

As Christine disappeared around a clump of trees, Duane turned to David and looked him in right the eyes. "Are you going to tell her everything that that creep Hoffman said?"

David pursed his lips and shook his head. "I don't think so. Seeing her reaction to that McFarlin…I don't want put another burden put on her…at least not now."

Daniel joined in: "What are you talking about?"

"Hoffman's testimony," said David.

"Yeah, well I wasn't in the room. I was taking care of something *very* important. Would you care to enlighten me on what you're talking about?"

David glanced back and forth from Duane to Daniel. "He told the whole sordid story of what happened that night. He confessed to everything…and then, just before I shut the closed circuit connection off…" David cleared his throat to try to calm himself. "He asked me to bring her by the hospital, so that he could knock off another piece, just one more time before he dies."

Daniel looked at Duane. The look on Duane's face and a nod, confirmed David's story. "He actually had the gall to…?" Duane clenched his fists and shook his head. "Is there no…compassion or conscience in this guy?"

David just shook his head.

Daniel felt confused. "Why or how were you able to get him to confess anyway?"

"I made a deal with the devil," said David. "Somehow, he found out that she had become pregnant from his attack. He also knew that there had not been an abortion. How he knew is beyond me and he wouldn't tell me either. Anyway, I told him that I knew who the child was and would tell him who his child is, if he would tell the truth about that night."

Daniel raised his eyebrows and cocked his head. "Singular?"

"Yes, child. He does not know that there are three of us."

"Are you going to tell him?"

"Only if he gives it up, as to how he got all of his information."

"So…how did you fess up that you were his…biological offspring?"

"Well, after he confessed the events of the night, he asked when he was going to get to meet his *kid*. I said 'you already have.' For the first time since I met him, he looked surprised. When he got over the initial shock of that statement, he got a little mad and shouted: 'Who? When? Where?' He seemed rather upset. So all I said was: 'Me! Now! Here!' I think I finally got to him. That was the first show of emotion that I saw out of him."

"So, then he got promiscuous and you cut him off."

"No. Then he just laughed and said: 'So you're lawyering for your old lady, but not for your old man.' I told him: 'She didn't commit any crimes - you did.' He laughed again and said: 'You got me there.' That is when he got froggy and asked for her to be brought to him for...''

Duane put his hand on Daniel's shoulder. "Do you want to meet him?"

Daniel looked as if he had a bad taste in his mouth and simply shook his head.

Gwen came up to David. "Do any of us have to go and see that horrible man?"

David simply looked down and said: "Only if you want to. But, I don't see why anyone would want him to meet his other children...or his grandchildren."

Everyone was silent as all their glances went around the group, looking to see if anyone was going to consent to visiting Mr. Dexter Hoffman.

All of a sudden, they heard Christine screaming David's name. Duane, David, Daniel and Ben were all, immediately, headed in the direction of her screams at a dead run.

There were several clumps of trees in the park, so it was not easy to see exactly where she was. Duane was the first to see her. He pointed and everyone headed to her. She was running as fast as she could towards them. When they reached her, she was winded and half crazed with panic. She was panting and holding a piece of paper up to David. He took the paper, unfolded it and started reading it. Duane and Daniel went down to one knee and were trying to calm her. Ben was looking at the paper with David. The women caught up a few moments later.

"Slow down," said Duane. "Breathe slowly. Just calm down. We're here."

Daniel was rubbing her back and looking up at David somewhat concerned.

"What happened," Duane said calmly. "Just start at the beginning and let us know what happened."

"That man," she gasped. "He come up to me and asked if I was Christine Lee. I said yes, and then he handed me that piece uh paper and said: 'You been served - you better find yourself a good lawyer.'"

All eyes went to David.

"It's a subpoena," said David flatly. "Those guards that you accused of abusing you, the day I got you out of jail, have filed a lawsuit against you. Slander!"

Daniel hugged her. "They're calling *her* a liar."

"But they had me in *The Back Room* and were…takin' turns on me. I'm tellin' the truth. They're the liars. Can't you use the DNA stuff er somethin' to prove it?"

"I certainly am going to use something!" David looked

around the park. "I wonder who he was."

"Who are you talking about?" asked Ben.

"The subpoena is dated over two weeks ago. Whoever did this waited until she was alone to give it to her. He has had it for over two weeks and didn't have the guts to give it to her when she was in the company of any of us. Real brave individual."

Duane took the subpoena, read it for a moment and shook his head. "I don't get it. She just finished bushwhacking four Judges and these guys are going to try to call her a liar. Hasn't she…kind of put herself in a position of a reliable source as a victim?"

David sighed and looked up. "If the guards can shake her credibility, then the Judges will follow suit and try to destroy her completely. That could get all of them out of hot water."

"I hear that," said Daniel. "Wasn't there some corroboration from a wife, as well as all the distinguishing characteristics?"

David gave a slow growl. "If they bring one shred of doubt about any one thing, then their lawyers will jump down her throat on that one item, until they can blemish all the other points. It's a lousy manipulative witch hunt. Shake her up, in front of others on the witness stand, and then go for the kill. The date of the summons, for the preliminary, is Thursday, August 14. I have until then to get all of the DNA evidence from that *Back Room*." He looked down at Christine and smiled. "Don't worry about a thing. You have been totally honest in this entire sordid affair. I don't think that these liars will be able to destroy the truth, no matter what they do."

29

The next morning, Christine and Paula were both up early. Christine was feeding Michael while Paula was pulling a few things out of the cupboards in order get breakfast ready.

"He's a gettin' big," said Christine. "It's all I can do to have him sittin' on my lap. I don't think I can carry him around much more. Either that or I need to start workin' out with my boys…and get a stronger back."

Paula chuckled. "He won't get any smaller. Children never do." Paula looked at Christine sadly. "You know, this was supposed to be a celebration this morning, as far as your first day of real freedom." She shook her head. "I don't know, with that summons, if anyone can celebrate."

"Well…let's try somethin' new anyway."

"Like what?"

"How about you teach me to cook somethin'. I ain't cooked nuthin' since I was 12. I've heated a few things up in the microwave, but big deal. I want to cook somethin'."

"When do you want to start?"

"How bout now? What would be a good breakfast?"

Paula gave Christine a big smile: "Pancakes."

"Is that somethin' you gotta work at?"

"Bacon and eggs are simple. Just butter up the pan, crack open a few eggs, beat the eggs, a few spices, and heat the stuff up. You have to do some mixing and stirring, in order to make pancakes."

Christine got to do all of the work while Paula stood by watching and instructing. Pancake mix, butter, eggs, milk, stir the stuff into a huge mass of mush. Then pour some of it onto a hot plate and stand there for a while watching it until it is time to flip it. Then watch it some more until you finally pull the finished pancake off and start another one.

When David finally came in for breakfast, there was a big stack of pancakes ready for all. He pulled out a plate and set himself up with a large stack. Paula and Christine each took two and they all sat down at the table. They said the grace over the meal. David prepared his pancakes with butter and syrup. He cut a chunk out and almost had it to his mouth when he noticed that no one else was moving. Both women were staring at him with anticipation on their faces. He lowered his fork back to the plate and looked suspiciously at both of them. "What?"

"We just want to know if you like the pancakes," said Paula cheerfully.

He switched his gaze to Christine. He saw fear and anticipation in her face. "What is going on?" he said flatly.

Paula started buttering her pancakes. "Eat!" She poured some syrup on hers.

Christine still had not moved. She still had that terrified look on her face.

David slowly raised the fork to his mouth. From the look on their faces, he was expecting to find a mouthful of jalapeno and garlic flavored pancakes, or possibly some insect in the pancakes. He got the familiar taste of hot pancakes, butter and syrup. He chewed slowly and swallowed. He noticed that Christine still had not moved. "Something is going on and I want to know exactly what it is," he said sternly.

Paula was trying hard to keep from laughing out loud. "I didn't make breakfast, this morning. Little Mom did. Seeing as how this is the first time that she had ever made breakfast for one of her *babies*, she is a little concerned about what you think."

He cut a big chunk out of the stack crammed it in his mouth and again took his time chewing before he finally swallowed it. He reached over and patted her hand. "You done good. Tastes great."

Christine's shoulders sagged a little as she breathed a heavy sigh of relief. She closed her eyes and a tear trickled down her left cheek while a bead of sweat trickled down from her right temple. She looked at David, trying to hold back more tears as she started buttering her pancakes.

David looked sideways at Christine after swallowing another mouthful. "Are there more pancakes out there right now?"

Paula looked shocked. "Hey, just how hungry are you this morning?"

"It's not me," he said in a matter of fact tone, "I think that my brothers should share in the *first* breakfast that Little Mom prepared."

Christine looked up from her plate in shock. "Uh...there's

still a bunch more…batter. Uh…maybe I…" She looked down at her plate. "Oh! I don't know what to do! Uh…what…uh…should I do?"

"That's why I had you make so much," said Paula. "You can always make some for yourself later. Right now you have two more big boys to feed."

Christine got up from the table and scrambled into the kitchen.

David gave Paula a side glance as he pulled his cell phone out. "Got your cell on you?"

"Yes."

"I'll call Duane, you call Daniel."

With a satisfied smile on her face, she pulled her phone out.

Christine only had three large pancakes ready, as a big crowd formed in the kitchen. She gave them a helpless smile as she tried to figure out a way to get them ready faster.

Duane took a large stack out to the dining room, once they were ready. Daniel got the next stack. Ben and Sandra sat chatting with Veronica and Gwen, while the next set of pancakes went to Joseph and Cecilia. Gwen was next. She had Brett on her lap and every now and then she would give him a little mouthful.

After everyone else had been fed, Christine was finally able to get some for herself. She was almost too tired to eat, but she was too hungry to not eat.

Later on after everyone had departed, Christine and Sandra were alone in the kitchen cleaning up the aftermath of the meal.

Christine stood there sniffling as she washed a plate. "Why am I cryin'? All I did was just make a breakfast and I am blubbering like that first day I got here."

Sandra put an arm around Christine's shoulder with that ever present smile. "This morning you did an act of love for your babies, their brides, and your grandbabies. They all returned that act of love with the equal love of enjoying your act of love. You were never able to do anything for anyone in the prison who really loved you. You are now feeling what real love is like. You do something for someone you love and they appreciate it. That is what you are feeling, dear. The thanks that they expressed from *real* love."

"But...I had tuh make love a bunch of times in prison."

"That wasn't love, dear. That was a physical act of promiscuity. Love is not a physical act, it is a powerful emotion. Whoever was abusing you was acting out of lust. Do you get any enjoyment out of it at all?"

"No."

"Here, you did not have sex with anyone. But you saw eight adults and five children thoroughly enjoying and appreciating the effort of your labor."

Christine wiped tears off of her cheeks. "It feels real good."

"Yes, dear, it always does when someone appreciates you, and what you do for them."

"But...all that time...I was...I mean...I don't know what I mean!"

"Just get your thoughts arranged, dear."

"I made breakfast and now I gotta clean up afterwards. Why is this such a good feeling?"

"The big cauldron that you mixed the batter in was the first part of the preparation. Next, you cooked the batter to make it more palatable. Then you saw each one of them putting the pancakes on a plate, butter, honey, cinnamon and syrup to each of their individual tastes, and then enjoy eating it. Each dirty plate, now represents the task of nourishment for, those that you love, completed for this meal. The next meal that you prepare will be further extension of that love. One of the main things that I am trying to tell you, is that sex is not proof of love - doing something for someone that has all these steps is proof of love. Right now, you are washing the plates so that they will be clean enough for the next meal, then the next and so on. Love is doing for someone, over and over and over, and watching them appreciate what you do, even if it has become so redundant, that neither one pays that much attention to the act."

"It still feels better'n bein' used as a toy."

"Yes, dear. I don't doubt that at all."

They hugged. Christine could not help herself. She was happy but she could not stop sniffling. Sandra stood there, holding the embrace and patiently letting Christine get it out of her system. After crying herself out, Christine did not let go. The two of them simply stood there until Sandra finally said: "The rest of the dishes are not going to clean themselves."

Christine snickered, wiped her nose on her sleeve and went back to washing the dishes.

After getting everything done, Christine sat down at the

kitchen table and shook her head. "Do I gotta start gettin' a big lunch ready yet?"

Sandra chuckled. "No, dear. We'll let you get into the routine gradually. If you had been doing this as a wife and mom for several years, it would not seem such a chore. Gwen, Paula and Veronica might start getting a little jealous if you start doing it all."

Christine gave Sandra a sideways look to which Sandra simply chuckled: "Er they might just get lazy." She sat there contemplating for a few moments. "While we're talkin'...there is somethin' that I been wantin' to ask you for some time."

"Yes, dear, what is it?"

"Well, I read a few things about adoptions and...in most all cases they split up twins. Here, I give birth to triplets and all three ended up in the same house...same family. I mean...how?"

Sandra closed her eyes and tilted her head back. "I pestered Ben quite a few times on that subject. He would not tell me how he did it. Most of the time he just told me not to concern myself about it." She shook her head and turned her gaze back to Christine. "Just after we had finished celebrating the boys third birthday, I got a little angry with the frustration of not knowing. I angrily demanded that he tell me how he had done it. He got real serious and said: 'You don't want to know. The statute of limitations has not run out yet.' Ever since he said that, I have been terrified of asking him anything about it again."

Christine looked at Sandra with shock and fear on her face. She looked back over at the now empty sink. She felt a great need to wash something else. Or at least have something to do with her hands.

This was the first time that Christine had really heard of a chink in the armor of Sandra. The woman always seemed to be in control. She was nothing like any of the owners that Christine had been forced to endure in prison. They were vicious, condescending and merciless. Sandra was patient, tender and full of loving kindness. Christine hoped that someday, she could be just like that wonderful woman.

After Sandra went back to her house, Christine sat down in the living room with the boys scrapbooks. She had looked through each one dozens of times, but it was never tiring. She could remember everything that each one of them had told her about each photograph. Some of the stories had changed, but each telling was firmly planted in her memory. Her favorite, of course, was the one that Sandra had kept. She still could not get past the new-born pictures of the boys without sobbing.

That afternoon, when David and Paula got back home, David was looking very downcast. While Paula was taking care of a new diaper for Michael, David took Christine by the hand and led her into his office.

They both sat down. The suspense was killing her but she did not want to get pushy. She was thinking, but accidentally said it out loud. "What's wrong?"

He gave her a tired look. "What was in that back room that you keep talking about?"

She was taken aback a little. "There's nuthin' in there but a really stinky mattress and a few...whatcha mean - *was*?!"

He sighed. "There was a fire. According to the report from the investigator, there were several boxes of supplies as well as at least nine of the mattresses for prison cells in there. All of that stuff went up in flames."

"No! They was only one mattress and five chairs. Whoever was in there, would drape their clothes over a chair while they were doin'...whatever they was doin'...to me."

"Well, it seems that someone is covering and or destroying evidence. The day after you canned those Judges, *The Back Room* burned, and right now there is no evidence to back up what you are saying about the guards."

"What about the fact that I sacked four Judges? What about that?"

"You had corroboration in regards to distinguishing characteristics. Those Judges all pleaded guilty or no contest, because of that. These four guards are claiming that you are just trying to get vindictive with them, in the aftermath of scalding those Judges. They are saying that you made it up and are relying on your victory with the Judges to get them as well."

"Ain't there nuthin' that you can use?"

He threw his hands up and closed his eyes. "At this time... no."

She got up, went to him and hugged his neck. "What're they gonna sue me fer? I ain't got nuthin' sept what Sandra done made for me."

He pushed her back a little and looked directly in her eyes. "I still haven't gone over the full contents of the four boxes, have I?"

"Uh…no…you ain't."

"Well, that will have to wait. Right now, I have to see if I can find something in a few legal precedents, in order to build you up, and tear them down."

Paula came in. She could tell by the look on Christine's face that she had been hit with the hard news. "Would you like to take Michael for a walk?" she said with as much cheer as she could muster.

"What…outside?"

"Sure. While David and I are looking up precedents, you can do some exploring. You can do it now that you don't have that silly monitor anymore."

"But…he's too big. I can't carry him."

"I have a stroller. You can push him along and go exploring on Wilton Boulevard. If you get lost, you have your cell phone. You can just give us a call and let us know where you are."

Paula helped Christine get Michael ready. There was a large basket on the back of the stroller, where they put an extra diaper and a pair of pants, just in case. "I just changed him, so I think that he should be safe to handle, for a while."

"But…where do I go? What do I do?"

"You just go out to the sidewalk, turn left and Wilton Boulevard is only three blocks from here. Go buy yourself something, go get something to eat, get something frivolous that you don't need…or even something that you need."

Christine just gave her a scared look.

"Don't tell me, with all that you have been through, that you are now afraid of going outside."

"No…uh…I…ain't got no money. I ain't touched any money since…" She looked down embarrassed.

"Oh." Paula looked thoughtful for a moment, went to the office door, opened it and then hollered: "David, Little Mom needs some money!"

"For what?"

"She is going to explore on Wilton, while we're working."

He came to the door and looked at Christine. "How much do you need?"

Christine could do nothing but stare, wide-eyed and shrug.

David pulled out his wallet, opened it up and pulled out his cash. Paula immediately grabbed the entire bundle and headed towards Christine. "That should be enough," she said happily.

David grabbed the back of her belt and pulled her back. "Hold on there! That's all that I have right now."

Paula gave him a cheerful smile. "You can hit the ATM tomorrow."

"If I have to cough up - so do you."

Paula looked shocked. "But, I…I…"

"I, I, I, I, huh! Look, if I have to hand over the whole lot out of my wallet, you can donate too."

Paula wrinkled her nose at him and went to her purse. David followed closely behind. When she pulled her wallet out, David grabbed it and pulled all the cash out. He handed the clump of cash to Christine as Paula protested. "Hey, that's all that I have!"

With a smug grin on his face he said: "You can hit the ATM tomorrow."

She folded her arms and stuck her tongue out.

When Christine looked at the two huge wads of cash that had been handed to her, she just stood there staring at the money.

David looked at her quizzically: "Isn't that enough?"

She looked up at the two of them somewhat scared. "Uh… I…I never had more than $35 in my hand…ever…before."

David shrugged. "Happy freedom day. Now, you have something to play with and pay with." He then gave her one of his big smiles.

As David and Paula went back into the office, Christine sat down and looked at the money in awe. She had never seen a fifty dollar bill in her life. Now she had two of them in her hands. She started arranging the bills by denomination. Two fifties, nine twenties, seven tens, eleven fives and twenty-six ones. A new record - $431. She looked at the closed office door. She looked back at the money and swallowed hard. She shoved the money into a pouch in her purse and walked slowly to where Michael was sleeping in the stroller. She sank down to her knees in front of him. "Well baby boy, let's go explorin'." She got up, opened the door, pushed the stroller out and closed the door behind her.

The last time she had gone out this door with Michael, she had been half crazed with panic and barefoot. He was in critical condition and could have died. Now he was in better shape and sleeping. She was free to go anywhere without having to worry about any consequences.

She pushed the stroller to the sidewalk and sat there frustrated. She had to stop and think which was left and which was right. After pondering the concept of milk hand and sandwich hand, she turned left and headed to this wonderland called Wilton Boulevard.

When she arrived at Wilton, she realized that it was all stores. She had seen a lot of them before - from inside a car. It had been almost 26 years since she had been able to walk down a street and it now seemed exhilarating and frightening. Memories from so long ago, of hanging out with friends whose names she could not even remember any more.

She was not sure where to start. She looked to the right, across the street. A Liquor Store. She remembered an incident in prison, when someone had made her drink some kind of prison-manufactured "Jack". She had spent the next three days in the infirmary with the runs, stomach cramps and an overall rotten feeling, and had not been able to keep anything solid in her stomach. No interest there.

To the left was a large pharmacy store. She had seen several of these on different corners while traveling to and from the courthouse. So - why not? She headed inside.

Once again she felt totally lost. One wall from beginning to end was nothing but cosmetic paraphernalia. Her mother had told her that she was not allowed to mess with makeup until she was at least 15. Those days were long past and she just stared, baffled by what she saw. The only things that she could really recognize were tweezers, fingernail clippers and emery boards. Many of the rest of the things, she could only guess at what they were – or might be.

Another aisle was vitamins. All kinds of different types and brand names. Better leave that alone until she knew more about them. The next aisle was diet and weight loss items. She looked down at her skinny frame. She had reached her full height at age twelve. She was still only five feet tall and after giving birth her weight had gone back down to 89 pounds. There had been very little change in her physique since. There was nothing in this row that she needed.

When she got to the candy aisle - heaven! She did not know what to do or where to start. Candy bars and bags of lemon drops, gum drops, orange slices and other colorful and sugary messes. The basket on the back of the stroller received several entries from this aisle.

She found pastries, chips, sodas and a cooler full of different flavors of ice cream. She shook her head - too hot for walking home with ice cream.

There was one aisle where Michael woke up. Of course. Toys. He seemed to be an octopus. He would grab one stuffed toy, and she would pull it out of his hand and put it back. As soon as she turned back to him, she found that he had already purloined four more. She had to battle with him in order to get out of that aisle. She was grateful that all of the candy she had gotten for herself was in the basket behind him.

On the last aisle, she found all kinds of specialized bandages for knees, elbows, fingers and ankles. There were crutches and canes and some crazy little doo-dads for giving yourself a massage. She also found boxes of things that amazed, as well as interested her.

By the time she got to the cash register, the basket was overflowing. She pulled all of the items out of the basket and put them on the counter. The cashier patiently waited for each item to be brought out and up and slid it past a little box that beeped. Christine could not figure out what that annoying beeper was, but the cashier seemed to know what she was doing.

After emptying the basket of everything except the spare diaper and clothing she looked up at the cashier. The tall gray haired woman looked back at Christine expectantly.

Christine was confused. "What?"

"What about that?" The cashier was pointing down at Michael.

Christine's jaw dropped. Somehow he had been able to hide one of the toys, and was now chewing on it. She dropped to her knees and reached for it. He fought hard to hang on to it.

The cashier was looking at the battle with somewhat of an evil grin. "I don't think that anyone is going to want that after he's slobbered all over it."

Christine looked up at the cashier helplessly. She looked back at Michael. "Come on, Mikey. Grandma's gotta pay for it."

"Grandma?!" The cashier was staring at Christine in shock. "You're his Grandmother?"

"Uh…yeah…why?"

The woman looked skyward. "Why couldn't I have had some of those nice genes? Why did I have to get stuck with all the rotten ones?" She looked back at Christine and shook her head. She pulled out a pair of scissors and handed them to Christine. "Just cut the tag off, honey. I can ring it up from that."

Christine took the scissors and cut the label off. The toy was some kind of gray bird with a blue head and it squeaked. She took a quick glance at the label and winced. She was buying a "Doggy Chew-Toy" for her grandson. What would David and Paula say about that?

The cashier looked at Christine and shook her head. "You are a Grandmother!"

Christine cleared her throat. "Yes, Mikey here is one uh five grandbabies."

"How old is the oldest of these five?"

"Well, Joseph turned 3 in May, and Cecilia she'll be three next month."

"So, that's what all that candy is for."

Christine smiled and chuckled nervously.

The cashier shook her head. "The gene pool was sure nice to you."

Christine flushed a little. "Thank you. Uh…how much?"

"Oh, that's $71.48."

Christine felt guilty, giddy and elated. She had a fifty dollar bill in her purse and she was spending it. She pulled out a 20 and two ones and handed the money to the cashier. Back in 1983, she would never have thought of spending that much money. Her father would have had a stroke – or would have stroked her.

She again thanked the cashier, took all the bags and stuffed them back into the basket. She walked outside the store and looked around. There was no more room in the basket for anything else, so time to head back and put all of her goodies away.

When she got back home, she began to realize just what the differences were between inside and out. Since April, she had been confined to the inside of the house, where the temperature had always been comfortable. Now, she was perspiring heavily. She had been outside in the hot sun and pushing a stroller with a big heavy baby and several bags full of candy and other stuff. She walked into the house and felt a little renewed when she was hit by a cold blast of conditioned air.

She pushed the stroller into the living room and saw Paula heading from the kitchen to the office carrying two large glasses of iced tea. Paula stopped put one glass down and checked her watch. "You've been gone less than an hour."

"I know, but it's hot. I think I should do a little at a time until I get used to it."

Paula shrugged her shoulders. "Okay, sounds good." She picked the glass back up and continued to the office.

After Paula disappeared into the office, Christine rummaged

through the bags, looking for a certain one. When she found it, she ran upstairs with it and hid it in her room. Then, back downstairs to baby sit Michael and enjoy some candy.

She laid the bags on the coffee table and found the candy orange slices. She had to use her teeth in order to rip the bag open. She saw that Michael had been watching her bite the bag open. As she lowered the bag to her lap, he saw that the show was over and went back to contentedly gnawing on his bird.

She sat on the couch lotus style and popped one of the tart orange slices into her mouth. She chewed slowly and let a trainload of nostalgia flow through her mind, as she savored it. She ate another then another then another. She kept popping them in her mouth and letting each one bring back all kinds of memories prior to…!

She heard Michael whimper. She came out of her trance. That was his hungry whimper. She went around the coffee table, groaned as she picked him up and went back to the couch. He watched her as she unbuttoned her shirt and bared her right breast. As soon as the clothing was out of the way, he started suckling. She shook her head. "I wonder how much longer you gotta be on yer special strict diet."

Paula came out of the office looking at her watch. When she saw the two of them on the couch, she stopped. "Oh, you're already feeding him."

"He started his hungry whimper."

Paula sighed. "It's sure convenient having you around." She suddenly put her hand to her mouth and closed her eyes. She tried to say something but was too choked up. She quickly moved to the couch, sat down next to Christine and put her arms around both Christine and Michael. "No! It's not convenient to have you here, it's wonderful." She heaved a few sighs and bit her lip. "You saved my baby's life," she sobbed. She buried her face on Christine's shoulder and her body jerked as she tried to hold back her crying.

Christine wanted to return the hug, but she was using both hands to keep control of Michael. "Yuh welcome," she said. She breathed a long sigh. "Yer welcome," she said again as she leaned her head onto Paula's.

Paula's breathing became more controlled. She let go of Christine and leaned back on the couch. She pulled a bandana out of her pocket and was cleaning her face when she saw the debris on the coffee table. "What's all that?"

"I bought some candy and I et it."

Paula looked at Christine incredulously. "Eight bags of candy?!"

Christine looked at her mess, turned to Paula with a helpless looking smile. "It's a lot a memories."

"I'll bet!"

"It's been a long time since I had anythin' like that. I just couldn't stop eatin' em."

"You are going to be up all night."

"Why?"

"Eight bags of candy? You are going to have a sugar high tonight that won't end until tomorrow evening."

"Sugar high? Whassat?"

Paula shook her head. "You're going to find out tonight, sister."

David came out of the office stretching and yawning. "Are we eating in or out tonight?"

"I can get that meatloaf and some green beans ready real quick," said Paula.

"Sounds good. I thought you had to feed Michael."

"Chrissy already did it."

"Oh, good." He got a strange look on his face when he saw the coffee table. "What is all that?"

"Chrissy has already eaten as well. She got a bunch of candy and wolfed it all down."

He snickered. "My, my. Did you enjoy yourself?"

Christine just grinned and licked her lips.

Paula shook her head. "She'll probably be ricocheting from one end of the house to the other tonight."

"With her new found freedom, she has the right."

After taking care of Michael's need, Christine could smell the meatloaf. She went to the dining room and put Michael in a playpen next to the table. She looked bewildered when she saw only two places at the table. "Who's not eatin'?"

Paula came in with some steaming green beans. "Are you saying that you still want something to eat, after eight bags of candy?"

"Uh…yeah…why not?"

Paula and David looked at each other. They both shrugged and Paula headed back to the kitchen.

Christine had no problem eating a full meal - no problem until it was over. She felt stuffed. She tried to act normal, but she felt like she was waddling a little. She ambled up the stairs to her bedroom, and sat there suffering from the overeating. She decided that soaking in a bubble bath would help her relax.

30

David called a meeting of the family. Everyone came over. It was late and the children were all tired, so they napped while the meeting of the adults took place.

"I am about at the end of my rope," said David. "Someone has destroyed all of the physical evidence, in the prison, that I could have used to defend Little Mom against this slander suit. Right now, all I have is her word and her credibility in regards to burning those four Judges."

Duane looked up: "What about the investigation that that Captain of the prison guards is doing?"

"That is how I found out about the fire. She knows that Little Mom is a big part of that investigation and was going on that to build her case. She told me that after the fire, someone, somehow, *misplaced* all of the specimens and samples that had been taken from *The Back Room* and *the Pit*."

"Any other good news?" asked Ben.

"Before she massacred ex-Judge Lassiter in his courtroom, someone identifying himself as 'John Smith', gave me the impression that there is some skullduggery going on, under the table, in the whole system. He said that he had told Lassiter to throw my case out and that she was going back to prison, where everyone would be happy. They would be going back to their profiteering from abusing her and I should go off somewhere and mind my own business.

Just before I went into the courtroom that day, I said a little prayer out there on the balcony, asking for some kind of miracle. Right now, I can't think of anything else that will help this case, except prayer, because...I am completely...out of legal options. Whoever is covering for this unknown enemy has done a very thorough job. We have worked so hard, for so long and I can't believe that after all this time, we are going to get slammed by a bunch of manipulators, who...I don't even know who they are...but right now, they have the upper hand."

Gwen looked around confused. "Why isn't Chrissy involved in this meeting? Doesn't it affect her more than the rest of us?"

David just stared at the floor. "I don't want to scare her any more than I already have. She's aware of the dilemma, and has given me all the information she has. I don't know of anything more that she could add."

Everyone was looking expectantly around the room at all the other participants. There was hope that someone could come up with something. After several moments of deafening silence, Ben slid off his chair onto his knees and held out his hands. Everyone else followed suit. They formed a circle, joining hands, and started praying. A few were out loud, while several others were silent. At a certain point, they all finished and looked up. In silence, they stood up. Some wiped away a few tears. There were a few hugs. They all went their separate ways to their own beds.

Christine thought that a bubble bath would help - it did not. All she got was wet. She was too stuffed to do any of the ricocheting that Paula had talked about, and she was too wide awake to lay down and sleep.

Then she thought about her shopping trip and some of the purchases that she had hidden in her bedroom. It was late, so not much chance of being taken by surprise, while checking out her knew acquisitions. She got out of the bathtub, drained it, dried off and went to the bedroom.

She pulled out the hidden boxes and opened one, found the instructions and started reading. After reading it she felt really stupid. She felt that she might need a chaperone on her future shopping trips so she would not buy something that she had no use for - like a monitor that a diabetic would use to check their blood sugar.

She opened the other box and read the instructions. This one was more interesting. Right now, it might help answer a certain question that had been bothering her for a while.

Paula woke up. She sat up and stretched. She looked over at David who was growling slightly in his sleep. She went into the bathroom to take care of her necessaries. After a few minutes, she came out to see if any of her noises had awakened David. He was still sleeping soundly. She filled her mouth with mouthwash and went back into the bathroom while sloshing it around and gargling quietly.

She came back out into the bedroom, stretched again, inhaled deeply and was a little startled at what she smelled. She sniffed the air. She opened the door to the bedroom and sniffed again. The smell was stronger. She quickly went to check on Michael - not in his bed. She went to Christine's room and knocked - no answer. She opened the door and clapped. Christine was not there.

She ran to the kitchen. She arrived at the door, stopped and stared - somewhat confused and very curious.

Michael was sitting in his stroller chewing on a stuffed toy that Paula had no recollection of buying. He looked up momentarily when she came in and went back to gnawing on a toy bird wing.

Christine was taking a large completed pancake out of a pan and added this pancake to an enormous collection of pancakes that were in several piles on the table.

Paula rubbed her eyes. She walked over to where Christine was pouring more batter into the pan. "Did you have some trouble sleeping?"

Christine looked up and smiled nervously: "Uh…yeah. You was right. I ain't slept all night." She sniffed as she turned and looked at Michael. "You don't have to worry bout him, I already fed him."

"Huh…oh…thanks."

"I might have made somethin' else…fer breakfast…but I ain't learned how to make nuthin' else yet."

Paula heard the tone in Christine's voice. "Is there something else that is bothering you?"

Christine looked up from the pan worried. "I need to talk to David. I don't know if it's gonna help er not…but…well last night…" She waved her hands around trying to think. "Maybe David'll know what to do."

Paula took another look at the table full of pancakes. She figured that there was going to be another family breakfast, so go ahead and wake David up and go from there. She went back to her bedroom where David was still snoozing peacefully. She shook him several times. He gave very little response. She sighed, turned her back to him and fell back across his stomach. He grunted. She pulled herself up to where she was sitting on his stomach and started bouncing. He started growling, reached up and grabbed her and laid there looking at her in surprise.

"Oh, you're awake," she said cheerfully.

"I am now," he growled. "What's going on?"

She slid off his stomach. "Little Mom made breakfast - for *all* of us - again! She said she could not sleep because there is something bothering her and she wants to talk to you about it."

"You said that she was going to be up all night, ricocheting all over the house from a sugar high. Are you sure it's not just that?"

"No, she was up all night from the sugar, but that did not give her that worried look."

"Okay. I'm up. Why don't you call everyone?"

"Why should I make all the phone calls?"

"It's either that, or I'll put you on the bed and bounce on you."

"I'll make the calls," she said as she got up and rushed over to her cell phone.

After doing the morning ritual in the bathroom, David headed for the kitchen. The closer he got to the kitchen, the air got heavier with the smell of fresh pancakes. He expected to see maybe two or three dozen pancakes. When he walked in, and looked at the kitchen table he just stood there and gawked at nine piles of at least a dozen in each pile. He looked over at the stove where Christine had another pile of six more, with another two, half done pancakes cooking.

Michael saw his father and squealed while waving his bird. David went over to his son and picked him up. He then went to Christine. "Have you been a little busy - all night?"

She flipped one of the pancakes and looked up at David nervously. She flipped the other one and then faced him. "We gotta talk. I found out somethin' and I ain't sure if it's gonna help. You come up with a few surprises, and it worked out real good, maybe you can turn this into somethin' good as well…I hope."

Paula came in. "Hey, Chrissy! I think you have made enough for all of us. Please tell me that there's not any more prepared batter."

Christine looked into a big bowl near the stove. "There's maybe enough fer three er four more."

"Great," said Paula sarcastically. "Just what we need."

David looked over at Paula. "Can you finish these two on the stove while I take Little Mom into the office?"

Paula put her hands on her hip and gave him a disgusted look: "I have to set the table! Let her finish those and then you can have your meeting - no, I will not take care of Michael - you will have to take care of him during your meeting."

David gave her a wry smile.

After finishing the last two pancakes, Christine put them on the stack near her, turned off the stove and headed for the office.

David took one last glance at the collection of pancakes on the kitchen table, wondering, why there had been that much pancake mix in their larder.

Paula called Gwen, Veronica and Sandra. Each one seemed very surprised that they were having another family breakfast together so soon. Paula told each one that she would give further explanation after everyone was gathered. She did not feel like telling the story of Christine's sugar high more than once.

Duane and Gwen were the first to arrive and helped Paula with the table. Duane went back to his house to get more syrup and butter. After arriving, Daniel had to go back and get more condiments as well. Once everyone was there and settled, Paula had told the tale of Christine overdosing on sugar, and thus spending the entire night cooking pancakes. Since they did not know how long Christine's conversation with David was going to take, they all decided to dig in and start eradicating the mountains of pancakes.

David came walking into the dining room carrying Christine. He had his arms around her waist, and could not stop chuckling. Christine had one hand on his shoulder and was trying to push away from him, while the other arm was precariously holding Michael. She had a look on her face like she thought he was insane, and she would rather be anywhere else than in this big bear hug. David went to his seat, and sat down still holding Christine in his lap. Paula was not sure what was going on, so she retrieved Michael for his own safety (and her peace of mind). David turned Christine sideways on his lap after sitting down. He had his left arm around her waist.

He picked up his fork to start cutting into the stack, that Paula had already prepared, on his plate.

Christine turned to the other people at the table with a look of confusion and desperation on her face. She opened her mouth to try to say something and David crammed a forkful of pancake in her mouth. After pulling the fork out of her closed mouth, he noticed a little syrup dribbling down her chin. While still chuckling he wiped her chin and then went back to cutting with the fork again. He took a large mouthful and chewed it slowly. While doing that he hugged Christine close and just continued laughing.

No one else was eating except for Joseph and Cecilia. All the adults were staring in bewilderment at the giggling fool.

Finally he stopped the incessant giggling and looked around with a smug grin. "You remember what we did last night? All together we asked for a miracle. Nothing big of course, just something minor...like raising Lazarus from the dead, or parting the Red Sea...you know. Well, I think that our prayers have been answered...in a way that I wasn't expecting, but I'll take it."

Everyone leaned forward with anticipation on their faces.

David continued: "I can't tell you right now, I have to get a certain type of confirmation. Once I have it, I'll let you know. If it is true, then, by the grace of God, a major hurdle has just been *demolished*." He looked around happily at all their faces. "Enjoy what Little Mom has made for us, and maybe later on, she can learn how to cook something else."

Christine had finally conjured up the courage to chew up and swallow the mass that had been crammed in her mouth. "Can I set in my own chair now?"

He let her slide off his lap and then took another mouthful, while still grinning.

Christine looked at David confused. "Why can't I tell em?"

He leaned towards her. "Confirmation! I must have that, from a competent authority, in order to crush that wretched lawsuit against you and attack those dogs of mendacity that dared to upset your first day of freedom. Once I have that and we have talked to the DA, we can come back here and triumphantly give everyone *all* of the good news." Just before taking another mouthful he looked around the table. "And gloat!"

Christine huffed. She wrinkled her lips in a pout, picked up her knife and started buttering her short stack.

After swallowing another mouthful, David looked around the table. "Maybe you ladies can help her get a little dolled up before we leave. I want her to look her best when we ambush her opponents."

While they all downed as many of the pancakes at they could, there was very little conversation. They all kept looking at David with frustration, exasperation and suspicion on their faces.

While the women waddled up the stairs to Christine's room, to "doll" her up, the other men all started giving David some very stern looks. He got even haughtier and refused to tell them anything.

Christine could not figure out why he wanted to keep it a secret. She was about ready to blurt the whole story out, but her lawyer, who had so far not given her any bad advice, had given her specific instructions, so she remained frustratingly tight-lipped.

She came back down the stairs and all the men gave their approval at how she looked. Then everyone went their separate ways.

Paula gave up trying to pry any information from either David or Christine and headed to the child care facility with Michael, then to their law firm downtown.

Before getting into his car, David gave Christine a large travel mug full of iced tea and kept on insisting that she drink it. They got into his car and he started setting a destination on his GPS monitor. When the monitor was ready, David gave her a big smile, and they were on their way. Christine did not look at where they were going. She kept staring at the crazy little talking box that was giving David instructions on where to turn and when.

"Are you drinking the tea?" asked David.

"Why do I gotta drink this big mug? I ain't thirsty. This is a 52 ounce mug and I definitely *ain't* that thirsty."

"We are going to a doctor's office. The doctor will want some urine. Drink!"

She growled at him and started sucking on the straw. She still stared at the GPS box, wondering how it knew where they wanted to go.

They arrived at the doctor's office. "Have you been drinking the tea?"

She still had the straw in her mouth and she took a long gurgling suck on it. She popped the top off the mug, opened her door and held the mug upside down. Just a few drops came out. She then belched. "Satisfied?"

He put his hand behind her neck and kissed her forehead.

They walked in to meet a short, pudgy, Hispanic woman, in orange scrubs, with her hands on her hips. "Are you Murdoch?" She asked the question with an air of impatience.

"Yes, are you Dr. Lydia Fernandez?"

"Yes, now what's the emergency?"

"Let's get to the examination room, and I'll explain."

"NO! Before I go anywhere, I want an explanation."

David sighed and then took a deep breath. "My client, Christine Lee, was wrongfully incarcerated. While in prison, there were several guards who sexually abused her. On April 17th of this year, there were four of them, who she claims 'ran a train on her.' She now is pretty sure that she is pregnant." He pulled several plastic bags out of his pocket. "Each one of these bags has one of those sticks that women can use to check for pregnancy at home. All four show positive. What I need from you is some kind of confirmation that conception did, in fact, take place on or around April 17."

"Okay, I understand that, but four different men. It will take a few weeks before DNA comparison can be accomplished. What good will…?"

"Right now, I am not worried about any DNA. The main thing is to see if the child is at the right stage of development, from an April 17 conception date. If I confront them with an affidavit, from a qualified OB-GYN, that this *is* a 15 week old fetus, then it will tear their lawsuit apart."

Lydia looked up confused. "Lawsuit?"

"When she was acquitted, she made an accusation of the sexual abuse by the guards. They were able to destroy vital evidence, in the prison, that forensics could have used to destroy *their* case and enhance hers. Right now, the only evidence that I have *is* the unborn child."

Lydia nodded. "Let's get into the exam room."

They all headed through the reception area to a room with a collection of machines that scared Christine a little. All that time she was in prison, technology had been leaving her far behind. Catching up with all of this stuff, was a bit overwhelming.

Lydia turned to Christine with a smile. "Okay, Sweetie, behind that curtain, you will find a place to put your clothes and a gown. Go ahead, get undressed, and into the gown." She turned to David. "I can probably confirm the age of the fetus, but I don't understand the rush."

David looked up from a pad that he was writing on. "I want to get the stress off of my client. If I can hit those men with the probability that one of them *is* the father of the child, then 1: Their lawsuit goes bust, and the pressure is off of Christine, and 2: The DA can start prosecution on the four guards immediately for sexual abuse against her person."

"Pressure! Yes, when she is pregnant, there is a lot of concern and pressure on a woman. She doesn't need any more stress."

Christine came from behind the curtain holding the gown

closed. She was directed to get up on the table and Lydia got her into the stirrups, then put a sheet over her. Lydia then went to a box on the wall and pressed a button. "Raquel, are you here?"

A moment later they heard: "Yeah, what do you need?"

"I need you in exam 1." Lydia started turning on several different machines. She sat down between Christine's legs and looked directly in her eyes. "From what he is saying, this is a case of sexual assault. Now as a result, you have an option: Do you want to keep the baby?"

"Yes," shouted Christine frantically.

"Okay, okay, okay, calm down, it is a question that I have to ask. You have given me a firm answer, I will respect that desire. I do not want to get into a political or religious debate. You want to keep it, so, we do everything to make sure that this baby has the best chance possible."

At that moment a very thin Hispanic woman walked in, also wearing orange scrubs. "What do you need?"

"Open the book to 15th week, and check the printer."

Raquel placed a big gray binder on a stand next to Lydia, and flipped the pages. After getting it to the correct page, Lydia started putting on latex gloves while browsing the page. Raquel then went to another machine and turned it on. It made several strange noises as it warmed up. Christine was feeling even smaller and more ignorant because of all this technology.

"Okay, Christine, I am going to take a look inside."

Christine tried to close her legs, but was firmly locked in the stirrups. "How?"

Lydia held up a long white rod that had an electric cord attached to it. "I am going put lubricant on this and slowly insert it up into your uterus, so we can get a look at the baby. Your lawyer needs to know, as close as possible, how old the baby is, and this will help."

Christine looked at Lydia with a little concern. "I don't want to know."

"Huh?"

"If you're going to look at the baby, I don't want to know if it's a boy or girl. I want to be surprised."

Lydia smiled and chuckled. "Okay. I will not tell you anything."

"When do I get to pee?"

"Do you need to?"

David told me that you needed some of my pee. He made me drink a huge tub of tea on the way over here."

Lydia sighed and shook her head. "We are going to take pictures of the baby. The only thing that those home tests do, is prove you're pregnant. They do not tell the total development of the baby. Can you clinch for a few minutes?"

Christine clasped her hands on her forehead and bit her lip. "Yes." She looked at David and growled. He was too busy writing on his pad to notice.

Lydia inserted the rod and looked shocked.

"What's the matter?" Christine was asked frantically.

"How long were you suffering this sexual abuse?"

"It was over 25 years."

"Uh-huh. Okay. That explains that. Sweetie, when your time comes for delivery, we are going to have to go C-section. The prolonged abuse is obvious and…I think that vaginal birth is…out of the question."

Christine thought about how she had heard that before, and what had actually happened.

Lydia looked back and forth from the monitor to the book. She moved the wand every few moments and mumbled slightly to herself. "Raquel, is the camera ready?"

"Yes."

"Okay, capture!"

"Got it."

"Good, print."

"I'm going to need a minimum of four pictures," said David.

"All right," said Lydia. "Raquel?"

"Ready."

"Okay, capture."

"Got it."

"Let me get a different angle, there is something I need to see." She did her head bob several times between the monitor and the book. "Okay, capture."

"Got it."

"And we move it here…capture."

"Got it."

"Okay, print and we are finished." She removed the wand from Christine's interior and started to wipe the lubricant away.

"I'll do that!" said Christine. "Where's the bathroom? I gotta go."

Raquel and Lydia helped Christine out of the stirrups, and then Raquel took her to the bathroom.

Lydia looked up at David with her arms crossed. "Okay, big lawyer. That baby is right on time in the development for 15 weeks according to my illustrations. I will sign your affidavit. Conception on April 17 is a very strong probability. I would have a tough time trying to prove any other date…other than maybe the 16th or 18th."

David handed her the pad he had been writing on. "Do you think that this statement is about right?"

She took the pad and read. She stood there bobbing her head back and forth while making clicking noises with her tongue. "It's good, but don't you need this on some official type document?"

"I can use your letterhead. All I need is a word processor, and your signature and we're done."

"How are you going to hit them or try to get them to confess?"

"I will make four copies of your statement. There will be a picture of the fetus attached to each copy. Then they will be taken into separate rooms and confronted with the evidence. I will have to tell them that we don't have a clue as to exactly which one is the father, but that each one has a 25% chance of being 'daddy.' Then they will be told that because she conceived on April 17th - when they were 'taking turns,' the baby will be hard evidence that one of them *did* have sex with her. All four are claiming that, under no circumstances, did any of them ever touch her. Paternity will be established at a later date, and when it is, the law will come down on him, like the proverbial 'ton of bricks.' If, however, one or more decide to confess, now - then whoever starts talking first, gets the best deal from the DA."

Lydia angrily placed her hands on her hips. "Why that is just…devious, it is underhanded…it is disgusting." She placed both hands over her heart and grinned. "I love it! Do you think it'll work?"

"Divide and conquer has always been a powerful tactic in any fight – especially against some criminal element."

"Conquer well, Mr. Lawyer. Uh, do I add her to my list of patients now? Or was this just an act of convenience because I was available this early in the morning?"

David looked shocked. "I picked you because you took care of my wife, Paula, and you took care of my two sister-in-laws, Gwen and Veronica."

"Aiee! You are one of those Murdochs." She threw her arms out and hugged him gleefully. "I am so sorry I did not recognize you. Women I recognize, men I have a little problem with."

He patted her on the shoulder. "You are forgiven," he said

with a smile.

"Okay, I took care of your wife. How does that work with your client? Does she approve?"

"She is not just my client - she is my mother."

"No! I met your mother, Sandra."

"Sandra is my adoptive mother. Christine is my biological mother."

Lydia gave him the "not enough information" look.

"Later on I will tell you a long, long story. Right now, I need a statement printed up on your letterhead."

After getting all of the necessary paperwork, David called the DA's office with his paperwork and plan. Christine only heard one side of the conversation, so she was not sure what was going to happen when they got there.

They stopped at a Convenience Store. David took the big mug in and filled it. He paid, came back out and handed her the mug. "Drink."

She huffed. "Again?!"

"Mr. August has said that he wants a fresh Home Pregnancy Test, done with someone from his office witnessing it. There are two defense lawyers that are demanding the same thing. Drink!"

Her shoulders sagged and she had a big frown on her face as she took the mug, hugged it close to her chest and started sucking large mouthfuls through the straw. She let go of the straw long enough to say: "Next time, put some lemon in it."

31

When they arrived downtown, Christine was feeling waterlogged. She was also coming down from her sugar high and was having trouble staying awake. She was also feeling the effects of 52 more ounces of liquid in her bladder.

They walked into the DA's office. Christine saw the familiar Mr. August and felt a little concerned.

He read her body language and smiled: "Don't worry! Today, you and I are on the same side."

She gave him a quick smile and held on to David's hand a little tighter.

"Did you tell her that I need a fresh Home Pregnancy Test, just in case?"

"Yes, I told her, and prepared her," David said calmly.

August looked at Christine. "Are you ready?"

"Yes!" said Christine frantically.

August looked through a door to an adjoining office. "Breen?"

A woman's voice answered back. "Yes?"

"You remember that pregnancy test, I told you about?"

"Yes."

"She's here."

"Is she ready?"

"Yes!" shouted Christine even more frantically as she bit her lip and started dancing with a very concerned look of pain on her face.

A red haired woman in a black pin-striped business suit came in holding some latex gloves, one of the pregnancy test sticks and a plastic bag.

August smiled. "We'll hold the introductions for the moment. I don't think she cares what your name is right now."

Christine was led off to the bathroom while August perused the paperwork David had collected. "Interesting pictures. It sure is different than any ultrasound that I have ever seen before."

David told him about the wand and how it had been used.

While August contemplated it, Christine and Tina Breen came back in the office. "We have a positive," said Tina.

"Well, let's sit down and talk strategy," said August.

Christine saw a couch by the side wall, walked over to it and flopped down on it.

David looked at the two, August and Breen. "She had a very hard night because of anticipation, no sleep at all and I think it just caught up with her." He went over to check on her. "She's already asleep."

August got on his intercom. "John, Gary, Vera, I need you in here, now. We need to plan a mass decapitation."

Three more members of the DA's office came in. Tina and each of the others were each given a copy of Dr. Fernandez's statement. They all quietly read the statement and looked over the pictures. Once all four were looking up expectantly at August, he started. "Here's the plan. Each one of our suspects is in a different room. Tina, you get Washburn in room 5 - John, you get Turner in 6 - Gary, you get Upton in 7 - and Vera, you get Guernsey in 9. I'm going to be on the squawk box. I will give each one of you about 5 minutes to tell them the story and then I will hit them with the hard stuff. I will then turn off the sound and you can get their story - if anyone starts singing. Once we have that we'll take a look at their statements and go from there. Any questions?" He looked at all of them with raised eyebrows.

"How long are you going to give them to start squealing?" asked Gary?

"I haven't decided yet. You'll hear it on the box."

Everyone sat quietly, looking at all the other players in the room.

With an air of satisfaction, August proudly said: "Okay, my predators. Let's go for some jugulars!"

On the way to the interrogation area, David could not hold it back any more. "Why did you need confirmation on that pregnancy stick? Isn't the word of a highly qualified OB-GYN enough to convince you that she is most definitely, in the family way?"

"As I said, it wasn't me. It's two of the attorneys representing the four who are suing her. They wanted to see it for themselves. Tina can tell you that there were a couple of legal secretaries in that bathroom when she gave that stick a golden shower." August snickered a little. "Come on! You know how picky some of these defense lawyer types can get."

They arrived at the interrogation rooms and each one of his associates went to their appropriate room. August went to a booth, where they had the four rooms in question on monitors. A uniformed police officer sat there trying to reach an itch on his back.

August looked at the screens for a few moments. "Are we live?"

"Not yet, sir," said the officer. "Just say when."

"I'll give my opponents a few moments to go over the affidavit. Each one of my colleagues will give me a signal. When all four have signaled, we go live."

It did not take very long before all four had given a signal. The officer hit a switch and August started his part: "Okay, folks. You now know that this woman is pregnant. She came to be that way because of an illegal intimate escapade that took place on 17 April of this year. We don't know exactly which one of you is the father, but we are absolutely certain that it is one of you. If you want to be stupid and try to deny it, well, when the DNA tests are done…what can I say? Whoever it is that starts talking first - you get the best deal. The others can just suffer with what the law hits them with. If none of you are smart enough to confess, then all four of you will get the maximum that I can hit you with - no deals of any type. You have 30 seconds, as of now!" With that he turned off the intercom. He turned to David. "Well, that should separate the canaries from the fools. There's a stenographer waiting outside each room. If they get a signal from my colleagues, they will be in their pronto!"

They headed back to the DA's office.

"How long do you think it will take?" asked David?

August scoffed. "You have four of them in there, and each one will be wondering, in terror, how the other three will react. I would guess that at least two of them have cracked already."

David checked on Christine as soon as they got back to the office. She seemed to be sleeping peacefully, so he sat down at the conference table.

A few moments later, John walked in to the room. August looked in confusion at his watch. "Already? What's going on? Is someone trying to be foolishly brave?"

"No. This guy Turner has no courage whatsoever. As soon as you hit him with the ultimatum, he lost control of his bodily functions and then went completely catatonic. His lawyer is calling for a doctor to examine him now."

August looked at David with a dazed look on his face. David just shrugged in response.

August go over his temporary brain skid: "Let's hope that we have something a little more positive from the others."

"Oh, they are," said John. "I went to the booth. By the time I got in there, all three had a stenographer running the tape machines. I don't know which one started yapping first, but they are all three definitely cooperating."

A few moments later there was a knock on the door. "Come!" said August.

A man with a very sour look on his face walked in. He saw David and shook his head. "The slander suit against your client, just took a nose dive and augured into oblivion."

"Oh darn," said David sarcastically. "I was looking forward to embarrassing those men in court. Now, I won't get the chance."

The man gave David a look of greater irritation and growled in his throat. He sighed, turned around and left.

John left the room and was gone for almost an hour. He came back and had a very satisfied look on his face. "The other three are singing like a church choir. We're going to be busy with their information for quite a while. I heard at least fifteen other names of people who we are going to look into for prosecution, persecution and incarceration. Man, I love this job!"

August looked at David with a smirk. "I don't think that we will need her, for a while. If they give the right information, then it will be a confession where we won't need any more from her. Take her home and I'll contact you if we need anything."

David smiled and went over to wake her up. He made several futile attempts. He sat her up and she just sagged back down. He stepped back to reconsider what to do.

August had been watching and trying not to laugh out loud. "You weren't kidding when you said she had a hard night. She's pooped!"

David shook his head. "I didn't think that she was this far out of it." He picked her up off the couch, stood her up and started gently moving her back and forth.

She finally opened her eyes and looked around confused. "Wha? Lemme lone."

"We are going home now," David said, in order to try to bring her closer to consciousness.

She looked up at him through her daze. "Wha? Go home? Wha bout those guards?"

"They caved in when they found out you are pregnant. They're blabbing their heads off. Well at least three of them are."

She looked around dully at August, John and David. "Three? What about the slander?"

"Dead! You're in the clear."

She finally comprehended what was being said. She was still having a hard time waking up, but was more than ready to get out of any office of any prosecuting attorney. She had definitely seen enough of that. She picked up her purse and headed out, still weaving a little from being groggy. "Let's go."

David waved a bit of a salute back at August, who returned a smile and a nod.

Christine fell asleep, again, in the car. She slept the whole trip back home. When he pulled in the driveway, instead of waking her, he just carried her to her bed, and let her sleep.

32

Christine woke up. She looked around the room somewhat confused as to how she had ended up back in her bedroom. One of the last things that she could remember, was being in that bathroom, and urinating on one of those home pregnancy sticks, with an audience of four strange women watching her. After she had peed on the stick, all four stared at it until the results showed up. Three women had walked away irritated or downcast. That woman Tina had then escorted her back to the DA's office where David was waiting. She remembered being awakened by David after who knows how much time. Then they had gone to the car - now she was here. She had a fuzzy memory of some type where David was telling her that the lawsuit was dead. She hoped that statement was not a dream.

She checked her alarm clock. It was almost 4 o'clock. PM according to the light coming through the window. She got up and decided to change all of her clothing before trying to find out where David or Paula were. After changing, she checked Michael's room - not there. She went downstairs. She was in the house alone. She decided to watch a little television until someone came home.

David arrived home just after 5 PM and Paula came in shortly after that with Michael in tow.

Christine looked at David with a little helplessness in her voice. "Did I hear it er dream it?"

David frowned. "Hear what?"

"Is that nasty lawsuit…not gonna happen?"

He smiled. "When they found out that you are pregnant, three of them started confessing and naming a few names."

"Three? Whuh bout the fourth?"

"That guy, Turner, he went into shock and has not recovered. There is a doctor looking at him to determine what to do with him next."

"Whatcha mean?"

David scoffed. "When the going gets tough, the weakest link usually breaks. He shattered!"

"So…I'm in the clear? No more court dates?"

"The DA might need you to act as a witness for the prosecution. Other than that, you shouldn't have to worry about anything."

"*For* the prosecution!" She shook her head. "Wow!"

Paula walked in with Michael. She sat down opposite them. "Well, Michael has a fresh diaper. I've changed my clothes. It looks as if Chrissy is a little refreshed. The only one who has to get ready is you, David."

"Uh…ready for what?"

"Chrissy is not wearing that ankle monitor anymore. She isn't restricted to this house. Tonight, we are going to have dinner across the street at Duane and Gwen's." She looked directly at Christine. "When I say we, I mean everybody."

Christine felt like a fool. When she had gone on her

adventure down the street to the store, it had never occurred to her to visit Duane or Daniel. She tried to cover her act of stupidity with more conversation. "Tonight Duane? Uh…wha bout Daniel and Veronica?"

Paula smiled. "That will be tomorrow night. Then Sunday night we will all be Mama and Papa Murdoch's"

Christine started getting misty eyed. "Oh wow," she said meekly. "I can go…wherever I want to. Whenever I want to." She got up and walked to the door. Her hand shook as she reached for the handle. She opened it and walked outside. She smiled and tried desperately to fight back any tears.

David walked to the door. "Hey! Wait until I get changed. We'll all go together."

"Why?" asked Paula. "Why should she wait?"

Christine looked back at Paula. 'Why wait,' she thought. 'I can go where I want to go. Paula's right.' She turned back toward Duane's house and took a few small steps. She looked around worried. "You don't see no one round here, tryin' to subpoena me for nuthin' do ya?" She stopped, straightened her back, and started walking purposely across the street.

She, once again, remembered that first horrible trip across the street. Michael was in deep trouble and she was desperately all alone. Now, she was not alone, Michael was doing fine and she was going to see the home of her oldest son. She strode triumphantly up to the door and knocked.

A few moments later, Duane answered the door. He had a confused look on his face.

Christine felt a little confused too. "Whassa matter, wadn't you specting me?"

"I was expecting you - I just wasn't expecting you to knock. David, Daniel, Paula and Veronica don't knock. Neither does anyone else in the family. You don't need to knock either - just come on in."

She got misty eyed. She reached up, grabbed his shirt and pulled him down. "Come down here, you big gorilla."

He went down to one knee and she threw her arms around his neck. She sniffled a little while she was hugging him. He responded by gently rubbing her back. She leaned back a little and smiled at him.

"Come on in, Little Mom. I'll give you a grand tour of the place while dinner is cooking."

Paula came in. "David is a little late getting ready. He'll be here soon."

Duane nodded. "Veronica is in the kitchen with Gwen. They won't let me in there, but judging by the smell, I have a pretty good idea what the surprise dinner is going to be."

Paula gave him a side glance. "There is going to be more than one surprise tonight," she said mysteriously.

He looked at Christine confused. He looked up at Paula who was headed for the kitchen. He then looked up and shook his head. "Come on! Let's take the tour."

While on the tour, Christine finally found out something that she had been meaning to ask, but had not had the opportunity: What do you do? She never had to ask. During the tour, Duane showed her his work room. He was an architect. He had to explain what it was that he actually did, because "architect" was another word that somehow had escaped her education.

She saw a living room, a family room, a library, a den, a dining room, a big downstairs bathroom, Duane and Gwen's bedroom, the bedrooms for each of the boys, and balcony. It all seemed a blur and nonexistent when he showed her a bedroom that was for her. Her bedroom if she decided to spend the night here instead of at David's. This too, had a queen-sized bed, a chest of drawers, a huge walk in closet, a private bathroom and a giant pink bunny rabbit. There was a supply of clothing here as well. Sandra had been busier than Christine could have ever believed.

After showing her all of the things in the room, Duane spoke gently to her: "I understand that Daniel and Veronica have set up a bedroom for you in their house as well. You can spend the night, anywhere you want."

"Do you mind if I spend a little alone time in here? I wanna get my face cleaned up fore dinner," she said as she wiped her eyes.

He seemed to have a sparkle in his eyes. "You want to get your face straightened up?"

"Yes," she said softly.

He hugged her close and then ran his big tongue up the right side of her face. She groaned in disgust, and pushed him away wiping her face. She made several more sounds of disgust and punched him in the stomach. All she did was hurt her hand. To try to cover up that she had hurt herself, she looked up at him and growled with bared teeth.

He chuckled and leaned down a little. "I love you, Little Mom." He smiled and turned away. "I'll leave you alone to get cleaned up." He chuckled as he left.

She mumbled some more as she went into the bathroom to clean her face. After finishing there, she went back and explored the closet. More of Sandra's works all over this closet. She went to check on underwear and socks - fully stocked. She shook her head. All this had been going on and no one had given her a clue. The room in Daniel's house would not be as big a surprise, but would be welcomed with joy anyway.

She thought of the time before she had met David. One tiny shelved bed in a shared cell. All of her clothing had been supplied by the state and fit on less than two shelves in that same cell. Now she had three big bedrooms. She had three huge, fully supplied closets. A supply of outer and under clothing along with a collection of shoes, the likes of which she had never dreamed possible. She thought about how she had a third bedroom waiting for her that she had not seen yet. The differences between this and that cell were completely overwhelming.

Her stomach reminded her of why she had come over here to begin with. She took another look around the room, wiped more tears out of her eyes and then headed for dinner with the family.

She found them all in the living room and was surprised to find two more people in the room that she was unfamiliar with. A rather heavy set man with very thin white hair, and a woman who looked like an older version of Paula. She was introduced to Paula and Gwen's parents - James and Ruth Detweiler.

Christine sighed inwardly. More people to remember. She

wondered if she was going to meet Veronica's Parents tomorrow night.

David stood up and cleared his throat. "I know that I have been aggravating some of you with a little secrecy."

Before he could continue, Paula and Duane both chimed in: "Some of us?"

"Okay, most if not all of you. Yes, I have been keeping a secret, but now I'm going to reveal it." He pulled a plastic bag out of his pocket. Christine recognized it as one of the pregnancy sticks that she had given him when she told him about her suspicions being confirmed by the stick. He continued: "Little Mom surprised me with this little item here." He held it up. "It seems that we are going to have another addition to the family."

Paula jumped up angrily. "What are you talking about? How did you know?" She looked at Christine. "What are you doing, going through the trash?"

Christine was totally surprised by Paula's outrage and was trying to push herself behind the cushions in the couch. "I...what? What trash? Whatcha talkin' bout?"

Paula's tirade continued. "I wanted to surprise everybody and now you have spoiled my surprise."

David looked at her flabbergasted. "How did you know?"

"I think that I would be the first to know!"

He closed his eyes and put his hand to his forehead. "But...I didn't tell you. I didn't tell anyone."

"What are you talking about?" raged Paula

David took a step back. "What are *you* talking about?"

"The fact that you're telling everyone that I'm pregnant. I wanted to be the one to tell."

David looked at her wide eyed in surprise. "You're pregnant?"

She was taken aback by his response. "Yes," she said confused. "Isn't…that what you were…going to say?" she said meekly.

He bit his lip and snickered. "No. I didn't know that you're…" He held up the stick. "This isn't yours."

Paula's jaw dropped. "Well then…whose is it?"

He looked at Christine and pointed. "Hers."

Paula looked from David to Christine to the stick. She bit her lip and looked around the room. She smiled nervously and was not sure what to do with her hands. She opened her mouth to say something but couldn't. She swallowed hard and smiled again. "Chrissy…is pregnant?" She again inventoried the faces around the room. "Chrissy is pregnant!" She wrung her hands a little. "So am I." She held her hands out, gave a helpless smile with an equally helpless laugh. "Surprise!"

David laughed as he embraced Paula. Others around the room stood up and went to Paula to congratulate her.

Christine was still sitting on the couch hugging her knees. "Is everything alright now?"

Duane laughed hard. "Yes, Little Mom. I think that some of the confusion has been sorted out."

Veronica looked at him. "What do you mean by some of it?"

"Well, I have a pretty good idea of how Paula ended up in the family way - what I am confused about is Little Mom." Duane looked directly at Christine. "Who…when and…how?"

Christine looked around the room worried.

David sat down next to her and put his arm around her. "I'll answer that one. The morning that I got to the prison, that person 'Big Sugar' had taken Little Mom to a back room. In there, a few prison guards had made a deal with Big Sugar for sexual pleasures with Little Mom. I surprised them by showing up. In the haste of trying to hide - from me - what had happened to Little Mom, Big Sugar never tried to clean her out. Little Mom was cleaned off and looked like a drowned rat, when I first saw her. In all the confusion of getting her out of the prison and the new trial and all that, Little Mom never thought about any internal cleansing. Well, it seems that it worked out for the best. When I confronted those four guards with that fact that Little Mom had conceived on April 17, and had confirmation from a qualified doctor, they started confessing to what they did to her, as well as other inappropriate activities in the prison and they dropped the slander suit. Are we all up to par now?"

Sandra came and sat down on the other side of Christine. "Are you going to keep the baby, dear?"

Christine looked up at Sandra and then each one of her boys. "I refused to get aborted 25 years ago. I ain't bout to get one now."

"Did the doctor say when you are due to deliver?"

"She said that it would probly be some day in January. She din't give me no exact date."

Sandra looked at Paula: "When are you due, dear?"

Paula was finally able to smile now that the confusion had been cleared up. "The closest estimate right now is February 10."

Duane shook his head and snickered. "We are going to have a little brother or sister. Plus, Paula is going to add another baby to the clan as well. This family is definitely getting bigger."

Daniel came over to Christine. He went down to one knee, pulled her up off the couch and hugged her quietly. Christine put her arms around his neck. She heard him clear his throat several times as they just held the embrace. To be held in the arms of any one of her sons was always a pleasure.

That evening as they dined, the conversation completely revolved around maternity clothing, what to plan and how, for all concerned. Two of the grandchildren had numerous questions.

Sandra looked at Christine puzzled. "I understand that you became pregnant because of that nasty time in that room, but…how did you manage to keep from becoming pregnant before? I mean… if you were being abused by a lot of others, how in the world did you manage to not get pregnant before this particular time?"

Christine pursed her lips and hung her head low. She cleared her throat and looked up. "Big Sugar'd take me in to *the pit* and stick the nozzle of the fire hose up inside me and turn it on."

All of the women in the room winced.

Sandra was horrified. "A…fire hose? But…that would be devastating. I mean…the pressure from that hose…it just…don't know what I mean."

"That nozzle got different speeds. I don't know who rigged it or how, but it's got about 8 different speeds - anythin' from dribble to blast. Anyway, Big Sugar'd let the water run through me fer a few minutes and I never got knocked up until that day I first met David."

Veronica shook her head. "How do I get that picture out of my head?"

"I wish I knew of a way," said Gwen.

33

The next night, the entire clan had dinner at Daniel and Veronica's home. Christine got to meet Veronica's parents: Charles and Lucy Hunt. She found out from all the conversations that Veronica had a few brothers and sisters. Christine was having a hard enough time keeping the ones she had met straight. A few more would have to wait until she could memorize the ones she knew now.

Once again, she got the answer to the question of occupations. Daniel was some kind of Construction Engineer. He would go to a construction site and check all of the work against the requirements annotated on the blueprints. He left Christine a little dumbfounded in his explanation, but eventually, by dumbing down his explanations, she got the general idea of what he did.

During this party, Christine decided to ask something that she had been wondering about. She had all three of her sons here and now that she knew their occupations, she was still a little confused. "How come you boys ain't playin' in perfesional sports? I mean yall three are big enough and strong enough...so...how come you ain't in sports?"

Daniel sighed and started his story. "We did do football and wrestling when we were in college. As a matter of fact, that is how we all three got scholarships into college. During our junior year, however, at the end of the season, when we got into that bowl game..." His voice cracked a little. He looked up at the ceiling and swallowed hard. "During the third quarter…I got blindsided…and had to be carried off of the field. It turned out to be…a career ending injury to my left shoulder. I can still workout and stay in shape, but…after that injury, I could never make it in the pros."

David cleared his throat. "During our senior year…in the fourth game of the season…" He looked off to the side and cleared his throat. "I ended up having someone land on me…after I went down. They told me that I had received a career ending injury to my right hip." He sighed. "Just like Daniel, I can still do workouts and stay in shape…but no contact sports of any type…if I still want to be able to walk…in my golden years."

Duane was looking down at the floor. "Three games later, the seventh game of the season, was my Waterloo. One of five times in my lineman's career that I ended up carrying the ball. An opponent grabbed hold of my ankles and…I have never felt pain like that in my life. Now, I know, that of the three of us, I will never win a foot race. My career ending injury. Papa Ben had always told us that we needed to have some kind of other major that we were working on in college. When each of us got hurt, we were still able to concentrate on "other than physical education". That is why none of us is in any professional line of sporting affair."

Christine sighed. "Well, at least you was smart nuff to listen to Ben and have somthin' that yer good at. Lookin' at you, I know that if you had been perfessional sportsmen…youda been real good."

The Monday after all of the family reunions took place, she was taken to the DMV, where they filled out the paperwork, took her picture and she was given a temporary form. She was, for the first time in years, getting a State ID card that had nothing to do with a prison.

After the day at the DMV, Christine walked up to David with a sad look on her face. She sniffed and wiped her nose. "In all of this here excitement and meetin' new folks and new revelations and all that...I forgot."

David was confused. "Forgot what?"

She bit her lower lip and looked up at him. "You know where my parents are buried?"

He looked a little surprised. He contemplated what she had said. "No. I will definitely look into it though. I'd like to know myself."

Several days later, Duane took Christine to a store with all kinds of strange electronic devices. He got her a phone tooth of her own. She was fascinated with this crazy gizmo. She spent the next few days using up a considerable amount of her minutes trying to get used to the unusual gadget. There was a thing in the instruction booklet that told her how to do a conference call. She decided to try it. She was sitting in the living room at David's house. She had all three of her sons on the line at the same time. Even though they knew that she was devouring huge quantities of their minutes, and they had nothing fresh to talk about, they patiently let her get used to her new toy, and all the things that went with it.

David was in his garage, Duane and Daniel were each in their home, when all four of them heard a loud crash. Christine was startled by the noise and was not quite sure what to do about it.

"Sounds like someone was in an accident," said David calmly. "Do you think we should go out and investigate?"

"Might be a good idea," said Duane.

Christine was not willing to go out and look at some vehicle accident. She had seen enough suffering in prison.

There was another crash and squealing of tires.

They all heard Daniel through the phone: "What's going on...a demolition derby?"

There was some more squealing of tires and another crash.

"Something is not right," said David with a little concern in his voice.

Christine looked out the front window of David's house and at that moment, a badly damaged car pulled up onto David's front lawn and stopped. She was, at first, just startled. Then she saw someone get out of the car and start looking around. Her blood ran cold as the woman who got out turned and met eye to eye with Christine...it was Big Sugar. At first Christine was frozen in shock. She could do nothing but stare. The big woman started lumbering towards the front door. Christine ran to the door and locked the deadbolt. "It's Big Sugar," she screamed into the phone. "She got out and she's here!"

"Get back away from her," came an order through the phone. "Head to the back yard!"

Christine was still in shock. The last person that she thought she would see...here...was Big Sugar. 'How could someone with her record get paroled? ...get a car? ...find out where I am living?'

Her thoughts were racing.

Big Sugar slammed into the front door. It held...with the first hit. When Sugar hit it again, the door and the frame started fracturing. Christine ran into the living room and hid behind a couch. The third hit slammed the door open as splinters flew everywhere. Big Sugar came in and saw Christine peering over the back of the couch. A big evil grin crossed her lips.

"I just got out and I ain't goin' back. Gonna need a good stable of whores, like you, my little milkmaid, in order to go somewhere and live high on the hog." The huge woman started lumbering towards Christine.

"You can't touch me here," cried Christine. "I'm free now! I don't have to do anything you say...anymore!"

Big Sugar scoffed. "Course you are! And I'm the Queen of England. Don't give me any garbage or I'll have to do things I don't want to in order to get you to obey. You're valuable, but only if you're intact. A few bruises won't hurt that much, as long as I can profit off you." She stopped with a strange look on her face. "You still a wet nurse?"

"What difference would that make to you? I've been acquitted. I am totally free. I go where I want and when I want. I don't have to answer to anyone - especially you," she cried desperately.

"Well, the way you talk certainly done got better. Whoever your new pimp is, he's definitely a good teacher in highbrow talkin'."

"So I sound better, so what! My family has been teaching me how to talk better. Maybe I still can't say some of the big words because I don't know what they mean, but I am not a hooker anymore. That says that you don't have the right to do anything you want to me. I am free - totally free."

"You expect me to believe that after all this time, all of a sudden someone just says 'all charges dropped?' I may be crazy and vicious, but I ain't stupid."

Christine kept dodging around furniture trying to buy time until one or all of her sons showed up. She knew that they had to be hearing this conversation and would do something. Her main problem was that Big Sugar could still move fast and was still highly proficient in brutal confrontations. She tried to keep talking in order to give her boys more time. "What do you think Honey Kim, or that big black woman are going to say about you? They always tried to lay claim to me."

Big Sugar stopped, got a strange look on her face and laughed. "Honey Kim? That slant-eye is out of the picture - permanently! Fore I left, I busted her neck. Did the same to that big fat black sow. From now on, I don't have to worry about either one of them...or that big wetback. From now on, you mine. I do with you what I want and you do what you're told to do." She stopped for a moment and smiled. "I killed that stupid guard, with the big butt as well. That's her car I'm drivin'."

Christine was shocked by this news but she knew she did not have time to stop running. She did everything she could to keep a piece of furniture between her and Big Sugar. "No one has any claim on me. I told you, I was acquitted. The state has no hold on me and neither do you. I am free." Christine was wondering what was going on. Surely all three of her sons had heard what was going on. What was taking them so long to respond?

"You think I can't cover that? All I have to do is find one murder in prison that wasn't solved and make you a suspect. You'll be back in the system in no time and that freedom is gone. You either belong to me, or in prison. *That* is the bottom line."

With that, Big Sugar shoved the chair that was between them away. Christine, again, had forgotten just how strong Big Sugar was. The woman had lost nothing over the years. Big Sugar grabbed Christine, got her in a hammer lock and pulled her up. "Okay now, let's go to your new home. If you're free, I don't have to worry about any Parole Officer. You're mine free and clear."

At that moment, David finally walked in. "I don't think that she is going to go anywhere with you."

Big Sugar just scoffed. "Hey big blubber, back off. I've knocked down bigger trees than you. You think I'm gonna to let her go to some other pimp after all this time? No chance! She's mine!"

"He's not a pimp, he's my son," screamed Christine.

"Yeah, right. Some of these fast talkers seem so smart, because you are so dumb." Big Sugar let go and faced off against David. "Okay, *son*, let's see how badly you want to keep your mommy."

Christine remembered all the fights she had seen Big Sugar take part in. "Be careful, she's dangerous!"

David heard the warning, but was still not ready for what the lumbering hulk was capable of. Big Sugar attacked before he could even think about defense. She bent over, charged and slammed into his stomach knocking him back completely off balance. He went down hard. She then punched him in the back of the head. She backed off and shook her hand in pain. Apparently his head was harder than she suspected and all the punch did was hurt her. She grabbed Christine by the hair and started pulling her towards the door.

Christine was able to glance out the front window and saw Daniel coming across the lawn with Duane not far behind. She pulled back as hard as she could to possibly give her other two sons a little more time and to distract Big Sugar as much as possible.

Big Sugar switched from pulling Christine by her hair, back to the painful hammer lock on the left arm. She ended up getting to the door just in time to see Daniel. Big Sugar looked up and was startled by seeing the man, she had just knocked down in the living room, now coming through the front door. She backed off a little with surprise on her face. Then she saw Duane come through the door as well. "Well," said Big Sugar with a bit of a laugh, "You punks don't b'lieve n fightin' fair, do ya?" Big Sugar grabbed Christine by her waist and tossed her up onto the stairs like a rag doll.

Christine was momentarily stunned as she hit a stair, face first. She could hear some talking between the combatants however her upper lip was throbbing in too much pain to understand what was being said.

David had recovered a little and was standing again. He saw that his brothers were here and they were ready for some hard, rough business. "Be careful," he said. "This crazy thug is even tougher than that offensive tackle from A & M."

Duane scoffed. "If it's as tough as it is ugly, then we might be in for a rough time…but I don't think so."

Big Sugar sized up each one and got ready. "I'm tougher 'n' what any uh you ever been up against. I'm gonna knock all three uh you down and maybe even kill ya. This is gonna be fun." She backed off a little to her right in order to be able to see all three of them.

Duane was to her right, David to her left and Daniel directly in front. Duane gave a small move of his eyebrows and all three charged. *They* were not ready for *her*. She had been in life-or-death struggles. The triplets had not. She grabbed both Duane and David in headlocks, raised a knee against Daniel and spun around. The spin, along with the knee, sent Daniel awkwardly around her and to the floor. At the end of the spin, she let go of both men and they went sprawling to the floor as well.

Christine had recovered slightly from the pain and now turned around and saw a horrible sight in front of her. Big Sugar was still standing and all three of her sons were on the floor. Primordial instinct and rage took over. She felt a fire in her that she did not know she could ever have. Fury and adrenalin took over as one single thought seared through her brain: *"You're hurting my babies."* She grabbed the first thing in reach - the coat tree. With no effort at all she picked it up and screamed as she charged toward Big Sugar. The big woman turned around still cackling at the triplets. Her laugh turned to shock, about half of a second before the base of the coat tree slammed into the right side of her face. She was spun around as the wall to her left was splattered with blood, saliva and teeth.

Daniel had been able to get up by now, seeing as how his injury had been his shoulder. Duane and David were having a little tougher time due to hip and ankle injuries.

As Big Sugar was spun around, Daniel slammed his fist right into her mouth, which ended up in extracting a few more teeth. His punch spun her back around facing the enraged Christine. She now swung the coat tree back the other way, catching Big Sugar in the left side of her face, shattering both the upper and lower jaws, and now the front window was decorated with blood, saliva and some more teeth.

Duane and David had been able to get up by now but were both a little hesitant to get in the way of a swinging coat tree.

Again, Big Sugar was spun around by the blow and again Daniel nailed her in the face with another hard punch that had 345 pounds of raging righteous indignation behind it. This time Big Sugar was floored as she spun back around.

The wrath in Christine subsided as quickly as it had begun when she saw all three of her sons now standing and Big Sugar on the floor. She now felt an agonizing pain in her left shoulder that knocked her to her knees.

Big Sugar was trying to push herself up. Daniel came around her, raised his fists as high as he could and came down with a double sledge hammer punch to the back of her head that flattened her again. He backed off a little shaking his left hand and grimacing in pain. She again tried to push herself up. Daniel did a pile driving punch, again to the back of her head, with his right fist, which again flattened her. She started pushing herself back up. He growled in frustration and stomped, as hard as he could, on her left hand. She went down again. Somehow, again, she tried to push herself up with just her right hand. He looked around and saw the abandoned coat tree. He picked up the coat tree, raised it high and slammed the base of it down on her right hand. Everyone in the room heard the bones in her hand crunching. She was making all kinds of strange grunts and groans, trying to get up on her elbows while trying to look around at her opponents.

Someone shouted: "Everybody, freeze!"

All the people in the room looked to the front door. Three policemen were coming into the living room with their guns drawn and ready for business.

"I'm the home owner, here," said David quickly. "That big, fat lump on the floor is an intruder. My two brothers and I were trying to subdue her and stop her from abducting our mother."

Four more police officers came through the front door. One with stripes on his sleeve looked around and said: "Does anyone know who this…intruder is?"

Christine was gasping a little because of the pain in her shoulder. She looked up at the policeman. "Cassiopeia Tinkle!" She shouted it with great pleasure. "Her name is Cassiopeia Tinkle." She turned to look in Big Sugar's eyes. With a huge grin on her face she taunted. "Cassiopeia Tinkle is your name. Do you hear me, you pig? I said your real name: Cassiopeia Tinkle! I'm calling you Cassiopeia Tinkle right to your ugly face!" Christine looked back at the police. "She scaped from prison and came here to do nasty things to me."

One of the police looked at the injured woman. "I thought

it was a joke!" He looked at his colleagues. "When they radioed the BOLO that we were looking for someone named...Cassiopeia Tinkle...I thought they were joking. Are you serious? Is that really her name? Considering the condition of her face, how can you make a positive identification?"

Duane groaned a little from the pain. "What's a...BOLO?"

"Be on the lookout," said David.

"Oh, okay."

"Yes, that's her name," gasped Christine. "I've known her for almost 25 years. Up until April, we were...roommates...ever since 1988. I know that pig...too well."

"Okay," said the officer in charge. "Well, it looks like we're going to need at least one ambulance. Is there anyone else who needs medical attention?"

At that moment, Christine passed out from the pain in her shoulder.

Christine woke up feeling very groggy. She was, once again, in an all too familiar hospital room. The pain in her arm was gone. Then she realized that she could not feel anything. She looked down at her left arm. Her shoulder was heavily bandaged. She tried to talk to one of the people in the room, but her mouth did not work. She just laid back and closed her eyes.

When she woke up again, she had her feeling back and she could hear people talking in the hallway.

"Are you back?"

Christine was startled momentarily. The voice was from Sandra, but Christine had not noticed her until she talked. Sandra had been sitting by the window. When Christine had stirred, Sandra got up and approached the bed. "What happened? Are my boys okay? Where's Big Sugar? Was anyone else hurt?"

Sandra held up her hands and giggled. "One at a time, dear. Apparently that horrible woman had some very nasty plans for you. Your three boys stopped her."

"How did she get out?"

"According to what we've been told, she murdered a guard, stole her car and…for some reason she made a bee line to you…and we still don't know how she knew where you were. The police are still trying to figure out how she knew what the navigation system was or how she knew how to use it. She had a pair of bus tickets for you and her to New Orleans. She thought that she was going to take you there and do…heaven knows what."

"Where is she now?"

"She's in intensive care. When Daniel hit her, he did some major damage. They're not telling us very much about her condition. The police keep asking us if we know how she got there…how she found you. Either she's not talking or she's still unconscious."

"What about the boys…are they okay?"

"Daniel broke two bones in his left hand when he hit her. Duane and David just aggravated their old injuries. They're doing fine. They're not really hurt badly."

"How did I get here?"

"The ambulance brought you here, they gave you something for the pain and you had some kind of nasty reaction to it."

"What do you mean - reaction?"

"Well, dear, it's Monday. That horrible woman came in on Saturday morning and you were completely out of it all day yesterday. It's now after 2 PM on Monday."

"Is my baby okay? With all the pushing around that Big Sugar did and the drugs that I was stoned on…"

"Don't worry, dear. One of the first things they did was check the baby. The baby is fine, the boys just need to take it easy for a while, and you need to heal. We can all be thankful that everyone we care for is in good health or healing well…and that nasty woman is out of our lives. By the way, what did you do when you were younger? They said that your left shoulder looked like it had some kind of old injury - the type of injury that football players or wrestlers have from over exertion or twisting the wrong way.

Christine thought back to the last time her arm had been in a sling. She had been wrestling with several custodians over refusal to wear a red outfit. "I did something stupid when I was young."

"Did you get it taken care of?"

"Only with a sling."

"Too bad. They might have saved you from a little suffering now. I still think that you're in better condition than that horrid woman."

"Daniel didn't kill her?"

"No, dear. She is badly hurt, but not dead. According to

David, because of the fact that she murdered a prison guard, the State of Texas is going to go for the death penalty. She killed that guard, stole her car and came after you to kidnap you. She escaped from prison, after killing two other inmates and crippling another. She assaulted you, she broke in to David's house, plus a few other things that only David seems to understand."

Christine rubbed her left shoulder. "So, I am healing. How long is that going to take?"

"The doctor will have to give you all that information, dear. When it comes to making clothing that fits properly - I am the genius. When it comes to other things, I leave that up to those experts to explain. Right now, I'm going to go tell some of the others that you are awake and not babbling, like you were yesterday."

After Sandra left, Christine sat there contemplating. Big Sugar would be hard pressed to try anything again. Soon enough she would be on death row and would soon be permanently out of the picture. Four of the inmate bosses who had fought for power in the prison and ownership of her and other toys, were permanently out of the picture. They were all dead or crippled, so she was now safe from them. The guards who had abused her were buckling, and she had the destruction of four judges on her tab. Maybe things will finally be getting better…she hoped.

The boys came into her hospital room with Ben behind them.

"So that was Big Sugar." Duane shook his head. "I still don't understand what made her so tough."

"It was the life that she lived," said Ben.

David shrugged. "What do you mean?"

Ben sighed and then snickered. "When you boys were playing football or wrestling...it was never life-or-death. There was always a referee standing there with a whistle. When the ref blew his whistle, you always knew that it was time to stop. Stop all combat by both you and your opponent. She never had a referee anywhere. If she ever stopped, she could have ended up dead... or crippled. She was always fighting for her life. You boys never did...until you faced off against her."

34

Labor Day of 2008, the entire family was having a big barbeque in Ben and Sandra's back yard. A lot of Veronica's family and others from Paula's were there as well. Christine was having a difficult time trying to keep all these people associated with who and where.

Christine and Paula were sitting with two other women, Cathy and Betty, who were related to somebody in this crowd, who were pregnant as well. Yes, the family was big and getting bigger.

Paula looked at Christine. "Have you been reading the Bible that David gave to you?"

"Yes, I get a few chapters in every now and then."

"What book are you in right now?"

Christine looked a little desperate. "I…uh…I can't pronounce it."

"Spell it," said Betty cheerfully.

"Well…uh…H, A, B, A, K, K, A, K, U, K, U, A, K…uh…" She threw her hands up in exasperation. "It's a bunch of K's and vowels."

All three women snickered.

"I've heard at least three different ways to pronounce it," said Cathy.

"Keep reading," said Paula. "You'll learn more each time you do."

Later on, when it came time for everyone to dig in and eat, Christine was not sure which table she would be sitting at. She ended up at the same table with all of the grandparents. She had met Veronica's parents as well as the parents of Paula and Gwen. Now she was meeting in-laws of other in-laws and it started getting really difficult to keep track of who belonged where.

She thought back to her childhood. Her parents had both been 'only' children. She was an 'only' child. No siblings, no aunts or uncles. Her grandparents had all died before she was 9 years old. Here was this huge family. They all seemed to know who was related to who and how. They had grown up in this crowd. She had not. She was still very glad to be a part of it all.

In milling around through the crowd, she found a group where she recognized everybody and headed for that. She did not care what they were discussing, she was, in some part, tired of talking to someone and wondering, to herself, 'who are you?'

Duane had just finished a bowl of ice cream and was cleaning his hands. He looked at David seriously. "When are they going to have the trial for that Tinkle broad?"

David shook his head. "Not soon enough! One thing I did find out was that the Korean woman is going to be released from prison."

Several people in the group chorused a big "What?"

David shooed a fly away. "She is being released, because according to the DA, it's almost impossible to care for a quadriplegic in jail."

Daniel shook his head. "Quadriplegic! I'm amazed, her neck was broken, but she survived. How did she survive?"

"She's probably just too obstinate to die," said Ben. "I still don't understand why they're going to release her."

"Okay! Is everyone paying attention?" David looked around the group to make sure that they were. "Prisons do not have the facility to take care of a quadriplegic. Also, one of the reasons for a prison is to incarcerate someone so that they cannot cause any more harm to others. Remember? She is now totally helpless. She can't hurt anybody anymore, except with the possibility of verbal abuse. Why keep her in jail and cost the taxpayers a fortune in medical care of her. The burden of her medical care is now in the hands of her family."

Duane looked shocked. "She has a family that cares?"

"Yes, she does. She has a husband and a child."

Christine let loose with a somewhat involuntary "What?! Are you kidding? She was pregnant as a teenager in juvie. Are you saying that she was married at that time?"

"Apparently she was a child bride, in an arranged marriage. Some old Korean custom that she didn't care for. She apparently got herself thrown in jail in order to *not* have to put up with being a wife. It's now the only thing she has as far as being taken care of, and being a quadriplegic, she has no choice."

"For her, that's a fate worse than death," said Christine. "If she can't control, manipulate and abuse - she's not alive."

On Friday, September 12th, 2008, the entire family had another big party. Christine was celebrating her 38th birthday and the first birthday since first being incarcerated that she was free. She fully understood the symbolism of the cake only having thirteen candles on it. She spent most of the day with tears of joy constantly flowing down her cheeks. Once again Cecilia was a little confused by all the tears, when Grammy Chrissy was supposed to be happy.

They were all sitting around the table looking at the remains of the birthday cake and all the dirty dishes. Several people talking at once while discussing the birthday celebration and a few other things.

Christine was looking around rather confused at what she was seeing. At first no one noticed it, then someone, then someone else then a few others. Eventually all the adults were looking at Christine's frown wondering why she seemed confused. Finally Christine broke the ice: "Duane, why are you sitting next to Veronica?"

Veronica looked rather shocked. She looked at the man with his arm around her. "This is Duane?"

"Yes," said Christine rather befuddled.

Gwen gave a little squawk. "If he's Duane, who am I with?"

"That's David," said Christine.

Paula looked at the man next to her: "You're Daniel?"

All three men looked somewhat guilty and surprised. They glanced back and forth at each other nervously. "She can tell us apart," said David rather shocked.

Sandra snickered slightly. "Are you telling me that you really *can* tell them apart, dear?"

Christine held out her hands looking a little surprised herself. "Of course, can't you?"

"No, dear," said Sandra. "Well sometimes...I've never really been able to tell them apart all of the time. How is it so easy for you?"

"Well, it wasn't at first. Then I really started looking at them. Once I got to study them, then it became real obvious."

"What is obvious?" asked Veronica.

"Their differences," said Christine in a matter-of-fact manner.

Paula was looking at each one perplexed. "They don't have any physical differences that I can see."

Christine shook her head. "It's not just the physical difference, they have different attitudes as well."

"Like what?" asked Gwen?

Christine pointed at Duane. "He's the prankster. He always looks at the funny side of everything and concentrates on that." She looked at all the faces around her. "David is the serious one. He is also very frustratingly secretive. He is more serious than secretive though." She put a big smile on her face. "Daniel, he's the passionate one."

Daniel looked affronted. "Passionate?" He looked around as if he had just been the victim of the most horrible insult of his life. "Passionate!" He huffed. "I'll show you passionate." He walked up to Christine, hooked his hand into the back of her pants, picked her up and headed out of the house, carrying her with just one hand.

Christine was helplessly dangling from his grip, trying to figure out where he was going. She looked forward and noticed that he was heading for the big swimming pool in David's back yard. She grabbed his leg with one arm and started panicking a little. "No, no, no, no, no, don't do it!"

He did not slow down. Everyone was following him giggling.

Christine was able to get her legs wrapped around his left leg. She could not break his grip, but she was trying desperately, not to let him get away with what she feared. He trudged on effortlessly towards the pool. When he reached the side of the pool, he looked down at her with a huge evil grin on his face.

She looked up at him almost terrified. "Don't you do it."

He reached into his right hip pocket, pulled out his wallet and tossed it on the ground. Then held up his left leg, the leg that Christine was wrapped around, as high as he could and leaned forward, falling into the pool. Christine let out a long scream as she disappeared, into the pool still wrapped around his leg. After a very few moments everyone realized what she was screaming about - Christine did not know how to swim and Daniel had plunged into the deep end of the pool. She flopped around desperately trying to get some air. He got her head above the water line and pushed her up to the side of the pool. She grabbed on to the side of the pool sputtering and hacking up water.

She looked at Daniel with fire in her eyes. "Don't you ever

do that again!"

"You really don't know how to swim?" he asked incredulously.

"No!" she spat back through her wheezes. "I never had the chance to learn."

"Well, happy birthday, Little Mom. We are going to teach you." He pulled her away from the side and closer to himself. She grabbed around his neck in a panic. He started moving towards the shallow end slowly while trying to ease her fears. "Don't worry, I'm not going to let anything happen to you. We are headed for the shallow end."

"It doesn't look any shallower to me," she cried.

What she did not realize was that he was bending at the knees and waist so that still only his head was above the water line. She had her arms around his neck and her legs wrapped around his chest, as high as she could get. She was making all kinds of squeaking noises in her throat, still terrified of the situation.

"Now, we're at the shallow end," he said calmly.

"It doesn't look shallow to me," she spat.

He stood up. The water was now just below his waist and she was completely out of the water. She looked around and started to calm down a little. He hugged her close and whispered in her ear: "As I said, I am going to teach you how to swim." He then howled as she sank her teeth into his ear.

Meanwhile, back on the edge of the pool, Gwen and Paula were looking at their husbands. "Just how far does this switching of places go, with you clowns?" asked Gwen. "Have I ever been in bed with David or Daniel?"

"No, no, no," said Duane as he shook his head adamantly. "I would never do that. Fooling you or Paula or Veronica on some little thing is fun - going to bed with either of *them* - that will *not* happen."

"Can we believe that?" asked Paula.

"Absolutely!" said David. "That sort of thing is not funny. If we ever did do something like that…well it's just unthinkable."

"I wonder just how far you clowns really will go," said Veronica.

With that Duane and David looked at each other. Duane was standing between Veronica and Gwen. David was standing between Veronica and Paula. The two men smiled real big at each other and then shoved all three women into the pool. After a good hard laugh, they threw their wallets to the ground and both did a cannonball dive into the pool.

"Oh mercy!" said Sandra as she looked at what was unfolding in front of her. "What possesses you people?" She looked off to the side as she heard something hit the ground. It was Ben's wallet. Her eyes got real big as she felt Ben's arms around her waist. Before she could muster a protest, she was going into the pool with Ben.

Then Joseph and Cecilia were in the water as well. Certain mothers were glad that they had hired a babysitter to watch the younger ones during the party. All they had to do here was take care of two young ones who were capable of walking.

The next day started out normal. Christine had finally dried her eyes and was able to get a good look at some of the presents she had received.

Shortly before noon, she went out to the garage with David and Paula. They were planning to get a certain area cleaned out. Probably so that they could store some more junk in there. They had conned Duane and Daniel to come help with the project (seeing as how there were two pregnant women in this house and they might just need a little more baby equipment, overall).

David found an old baseball bat that he decided he could part with, but Christine could not. She had never been able to watch him play. She had seen pictures of the three boys in their football, baseball and wrestling outfits. This was something that she could hold on to as memorabilia.

She carried the bat into the house, and was going to put it somewhere in her bedroom. When she got to the bottom of the stairs, there was a knock on the door. She leaned the bat against the wall and answered the door.

A tall woman with brown hair (and gray roots), stood there with a pleasant smile on her face. She had on a yellow pant suit that looked very expensive. She had a briefcase that matched her suit. She held out her hand for a handshake. "Hi there, I'm Melissa Kilgore. I'm looking for a Ms. Christine Lee."

"I'm Christine," she said as she shook the woman's hand. "What's up?"

"Oh, good, I don't have to go searching for you. I need to talk to you about a few things that concern you. I hope that you have some free time right now. Can I come in?"

Christine shrugged. "Sure. Come on in. Have a seat."

They walked into the living room and sat down. "Now, Christine - can I call you Christine?"

"Yeah, that's my name," she said, still suspicious of what was going on.

"Good. Things always seem to work better on a first name basis. Now, Christine, I understand that you are pregnant and that you are around your 21st week. Is that correct?"

Christine was a little surprised at this woman's knowledge, and she became even more suspicious. "Yes, so what?"

"Well, I'm from Parent Planners Association, and I am here to discuss the realities and options that should concern you."

"Did I ask? Do I need to listen to you?"

"Oh you must know all that is going on. Now, let's see. You are single and you are now, what, 37 years old?"

"38."

"Alright 38. Now, a pregnancy at your time of life and due to the fact that you are single, there are other options that you seriously need to look at. One of those options is abortion…"

"WHAT?!" Christine was no longer sitting. "No way!"

"But, my dear, you don't understand…"

"No! You don't understand. Back in 1983, I was pregnant and a bunch of high-and-mighty bureaucrats, tried to have my babies carved out of me then. Well I didn't get an abortion then, because I didn't want to."

"But things have changed. You were young and healthy then. Your baby was put up for adoption and probably had a better life as a result. Now, you're much older…"

"I gave birth to triplets, you pig! Yes, the state took my babies away from me, yes they had a better life, because I had no way of taking care of them, but that is no reason to kill this baby now."

"It's not a baby, it's just a blob of protoplasm," snapped Melissa. "Where have you been getting this? Don't tell me you've been listening to a pack of those radical religious cultists."

"No, I've been reading a few things in that Bible…"

"Oh, good grief! A Bible. That's all old stuff and doesn't really apply to anything today. What I've got here…"

"Is a bunch of garbage that I'm not going to listen to? They told me in 1983, that I should have an abortion. I didn't! Guess what? As a result of that fact, almost 25 years after they were born, my babies came looking for me. They found me in prison. They found me and they rescued me. Now, I'm not rotting in prison anymore, for something that I didn't do. If it hadn't been for them, I would still be stuck there, with no hope for the future. My babies rescued me! No one else cared. Who would have rescued me, if I had had them carved out back in 1983? Huh? Where? I think I'll go with my history and keep the baby. NOT FETUS! BABY! A living human being. Since my other babies pulled me out of that hellish prison, I wonder if I'll have to depend on this baby to come rescue me again!" By now Christine was shrieking at the woman. "Get out! You have nothing to say that I need to hear! No way are you going to carve this baby out of me!"

"I am not leaving until you listen. You don't understand what could happen to you or the fetus as a..."

"I don't have to be told by anyone, anymore, how to run my life. I am totally free now and you are a nothing! Anything you have to say is nothing! Your statistics and propaganda is nothing! Get out and stay out!"

By now, all of Christine's screaming had attracted the attention of everyone in the garage. They were quickly assembling in the living room, assessing what was going on.

Christine pushed Melissa as hard as she could. Seeing as how she had very little practice at fighting, she was not able to move Melissa in any way at all. Melissa simply gave Christine a disgusted look, and pushed back. Christine was unceremoniously flopped onto the floor.

David advanced with his fists ready. "You had better watch what you're doing. This is my house, and that's my mother and you don't treat me or anyone that I am related to that way in this house."

"Well then, tell her to try to act like a civilized person," said Melissa. I came here to give her some information and make her understand the entire situation and I'm not leaving until I have done what I came to do."

"I distinctly heard Little Mom tell that hag to get out," said Duane. "Don't that make her an intruder, now?"

David stopped and looked back at Duane. "Yes it does." He looked back at Melissa. "Unless you get out NOW, you are legally guilty of criminal trespass."

"That does not apply to me," scoffed Melissa. "I am here to do my work and it WILL be done, no matter what you people do. Try calling the police - they will be on my side."

With the conversation going on between David and Melissa, only Daniel noticed Christine heading to the stairway and picking up the baseball bat. As Christine raised the bat and headed for Melissa, Daniel grabbed Christine, picked her up and pulled the bat out of her hands.

Christine yelped as the bat was pulled away from her. She flailed her hands at the bat, trying to get it back. "DAV...DUA... DAN...whoever you are, PUT ME DOWN. Gimme that bat, I'm gonna bust her skull in."

Melissa considered Daniel's actions as a rescue attempt for her. She looked at Christine in total disgust. "Stop acting like a child. You are going to sit down and listen to what I have to say and that is all there is to it."

Daniel looked at the bat in his hand. "Wrong! I took it away from her, because you might be able to defend yourself from Little Mom. You won't be able to defend yourself from me. *I* am going to crack your skull with this thing."

Melissa started backing up, looking around the room for some help.

"Oh no! No, no, no, no, no," said Duane. He walked up to Daniel and took hold of the bat. "It's my turn." He looked at David. "You got her out of jail *and* out of that lawsuit." He looked back at Daniel. "You rescued her when you mangled that big fat sow." He jerked the bat out of Daniel's grip and turned back to Melissa with a diabolical grin on his face. "Now…it's my turn to rescue Little Mom from some…unnatural."

Duane started walking slowly towards Melissa, with an evil laugh coming from deep in his throat. He took a practice swing with the bat. The bat made a loud swish as it cut through the air, and Melissa's eyes got even wider. She threw her custom made briefcase at him. He swung hard and it was immediately turned into shattered debris as it came apart and the contents were scattered all over the room.

Melissa turned to run and in her panic slammed into the wall. She went down leaving a patch of blood on the wall. There was blood coming from her nose and mouth.

Duane got hold of her and held her down on the floor, with the business end of the bat near the bridge of her nose. "The first thing you are going to do, is clean up your mess. All that garbage that came out of your case, is messing up my brother's house. Then you are going to take yourself and your trash and never come back."

David came up: "And don't think, for one second that any police would be on your side. I am the home owner here. My mother ordered you out and I will respect her wish. Do not try telling *me* the law, because I *am* a lawyer. When Little Mom ordered you out and you refused to leave, then, at that moment, officially and legally, *you are* criminally trespassing. Clean up your crap and get out and don't ever come back…and don't you dare bleed on my carpet."

Melissa pulled a small kerchief out of her left sleeve. She held it to her face as she crawled around gathering up pamphlets, pens, documents and the remains of her day planner. The whole time she was collecting her things, she was under extreme scrutiny from the triplets. Duane stood there twirling the bat in his fingers. David was smacking his right fist into the palm of his left hand. Daniel, who was wearing a tank top, stood there flexing his muscles. When she finally got everything she could find in the bottom part of the briefcase, she covered it with the badly mangled lid. She finally stood up and retreated out of the house, with Duane on her heels. She got to her car, unlocked it and threw what was in her arms into the back seat, climbed in, started it and burned rubber as she left.

Christine walked up to Duane. She took the bat from him. She looked at the bat for a moment and then looked up at Duane pouting. "I wanted to hit her."

All three men cracked up. Duane knelt down, hugged Christine and said: "Maybe next time."

They all went back into the house. The three men still laughing, and Christine still pouting while holding the bat close. They walked in to see Paula standing there with her hands on her hips, looking perplexed.

David looked back at her. "What?"

She held up a box of condoms. "Where did this come from?"

"I think that atrocity didn't pick up all of her trash," said Daniel.

"You may be right," said Duane.

David looked around the room. "Be ready for more surprises. We had all better start looking around under everything. I don't want any of the children finding something that they don't need to be handling."

While everyone else got down on their hands and knees and started searching the room, Christine took the bat upstairs to her room. She had a triumphant grin on her face as she headed for her room. She had finally been able to see one of her boys actually swing a bat. It was not a sporting event, but it was still very satisfying.

Christine came back downstairs to see that the search was still on. David and Duane were holding a couch up in the air, while Paula was retrieving something that was under it. After they set it back down and finished their search, Christine sat down on the couch looking rather dejected.

Daniel sat down next to her. "What's wrong, Little Mom? We were victorious over that hag."

Christine sighed. "She's right. I don't have any way of taking care of myself. I had nothing in prison and now that I am here, I have nothing that I could have possibly gotten by myself. I have to depend on you guys for everything."

David walked up to Christine. "I don't know why I have been putting this off...other than just not wanting to let you go. I think that this might be a good time to get those four boxes and let you look through them. You are not as destitute as you think you are. Unfortunately, the boxes are at the office and I can't get them until Monday."

"I'd like to be there, when she opens those boxes," said Daniel.

"Same here," said Duane.

Christine looked at them confused. "Why?"

Daniel hugged her close. "Whatever is in those boxes, is part of your history. That makes it part of *our* history…or legacy, if you want to use that word. I think that this might be just like when we first got to meet you back in April. Another glorious shared moment for all of us."

Christine took hold of his hand and held it up to her chin. She looked up at David with pleading eyes.

David chuckled. "Okay. Monday afternoon, after work…all of us gather here so she can explore the boxes with us…together."

Monday could not come soon enough. Then when Monday arrived, she had to wait all day for David and Paula to come home with the boxes. She had Michael with her and tried to feed him at least nine times in the morning alone. She changed his diaper several times, even though he did not need changing. She could not sit down at all. She paced constantly until Daniel showed up at the house. He came in and stretched, then sat down, turned on the television and started watching the news. Duane and Gwen showed up a little later on, with their children in tow. Veronica showed up with her children and now Christine had her two oldest grandchildren to play with. Anything to keep her busy, doing…something. Someone came through the door while she was occupied playing a board game with Joseph and Cecilia. Christine nearly jumped out of her shoes until she saw that it was Ben and Sandra.

Christine looked around the room. "Who else is coming here, today?"

"My parents said that they would be here, but it might be late," said Gwen. She looked at Veronica. "Any word from your folks?"

Veronica shrugged. "They had some prior commitment and might be able to make it later."

Christine wondered why her life was becoming a spectator sport for all her new relatives. She headed into the bathroom. She had gone in there at least 15 times since people started arriving. If for no other reason, than to try to get her head on straight. This was one of the few times she actually had to relieve herself. While she was washing her hands, she heard one of her boys call out that David had arrived. She bolted out of the bathroom with her hands still wet.

She ran into the living room and stopped short. She was somewhat disappointed when she first saw them. She was expecting four boxes, the size of footlockers. All four were small square cubes, about 14 inches on each side. They appeared to have been taped shut, several times. They were all sitting on the coffee table. She sat down and stared at them, now almost afraid to look in them.

David used a box cutter to open the first one. He pulled the flaps back and set it directly in front of her. Paperwork. Piles of paperwork. Receipts dating back to 1968, when her parents had been married. Tax forms, credit card receipts, a payment book for the mortgage and one for the car.

She looked closely at the mortgage book. "Looks like the payment is a little overdue. It was supposed to be paid on March 21, 1983. What do you think happened to the property?"

David shrugged. "Foreclosure. Your parents were dead, you had no income, no living relatives and you were the primary suspect according to the police. I remember checking on it and the property was foreclosed in April 1983. The car was repossessed in March, so all that was left from the fire is this stuff."

She picked up two handfuls of paper at random. "How did all this paper survive a fire?"

"Your father…"

Christine snapped at him: "Your Grandfather! Remember? I am your mother. He was my father. So?"

David flushed. He looked down at the floor and cleared his throat. "Grandpa…had purchased a fire proof safe. It lived up to its reputation. They had to destroy it in order to get into it and find out what was in it, but it did its job and kept the contents intact."

Christine went to the second box. More paperwork. This, however, was a little more useful. She found her birth certificate, her Parents birth certificates as well as their marriage license and wedding certificate. She also found some other papers that she wasn't sure what they were. She held them up and looked questioningly at everyone in the room.

"Those look like stock certificates," said Daniel. "We'll have to get with a broker and find out if they are worth anything."

"I didn't own any stock," said Christine. "Each one of these things has my name on it. How come?"

Ben leaned forward and picked one of them up off the table. "I think that your parents were looking out for your future. The fact that they put them in your name means that there is no probate. You own them outright. If these are stocks that haven't tanked like some stocks have lately, then they could be worth 20 to 50 times what is marked on them as their original face value."

Christine pulled out a checkbook. "Is this what I think it is?"

David took it and opened it. "It's a checkbook that shows a balance of $650.85. I'll have to check and see if the account is still open. There hasn't been any activity on it since your...my grandparents died, so the state may have absorbed the assets. The other one in there is a book for a savings account."

She looked down at the book he was talking about and picked it up. She found two more under it. "There's three. Why three?"

David shook his head. "I can understand having accounts at different banks - just in case - but three accounts at the same bank?" He took all three and looked closely at them. "Okay, this one is a general account for the family, this one is a Christmas account. You can only get the money out in December, so that everyone will have plenty of presents at Christmas. The third one, they set up as a college fund for you, Little Mom. From what I see here, at the time they died, they already had almost $15,000 set up for you to go to college."

Duane shook his head. "Stocks and a college fund. They were good planners. I wish that I could've met them."

The rest of the second box was filled with more receipts

for items purchased. They also found warranty information for a television, the refrigerator, the stove, the washer and the dryer. The instruction manuals were all in this one as well.

The third box brought more tears to Christine's eyes. For the first time in several days, she pulled out her treasured towels. In this box, they found seven old scrapbooks, and her parents wedding album. She held the towels up to her mouth as she slowly turned the pages. The only relatives that she had known up until last April. Her parents and her grandparents were all in the pictures.

Other people were looking at the other seven, when suddenly Gwen yelped. She was holding the book open with one hand and had her other hand over her mouth as she stared wide-eyed at one of the pictures. "Chrissy, who is this pictured here?"

Christine did not get up. She wiped her eyes and said: "Momma showed me how she labeled the pictures. If you want to know who is in a picture, you just pull it out of those corner thingies. The names of whoever is pictured there is written on the page under each picture. Why?"

Gwen carefully pulled the picture out. "Let's see…according to this, the couple here…uh…Walter Tyler and his wife Lydia."

Daniel was losing patience. "What's so special about them?"

Gwen held the picture up for all to see. "Well, take a look!"

Sandra and Paula were the first to get a good look and both gasped.

Now Christine was losing patience. "What?!"

Sandra took the picture from Gwen and passed it to Christine.

"What is his relationship to you, do you know?"

Christine took the picture, without really looking at it. She set it down and went to the back of the wedding album. "My Mom was kind of a stickler about ancestry. She put a bunch of information in the back of the wedding album." She started perusing a page in the back of the album. "You said his name was Walter Tyler?"

"Yes," said Gwen.

"Tyler, Tyler...here it is. Okay he was on my Father's side. He was my Father's, Mother's, Father. My Great Grandfather. Walter Horatio Tyler and Lydia Louise (Carpenter) Tyler. Why?"

While the conversation had been going on, Duane had picked up the picture and was shaking his head. "Well, Little Mom. You said that you didn't want to know...but I'm going to tell you anyway."

Everyone looked at Duane with a chorus of: "Huh?"

"Little Mom told me that if we looked like our biological father, she did *not* want to know." He looked at Christine seriously. "We don't! Look at the picture."

Christine finally took a good, long look at the picture. She bit her lower lip and the tears started flowing freely. After a few moments of sniffling, she wiped her eyes and nose, took a deep breath and one by one, took a good long look at each one of her sons. "If there was ever any doubt in my mind about you not being my sons - it's gone now. You look exactly like one of your Great, Great Grandfathers - on my side of the family." She handed the picture back to Gwen. "Be very careful with that one."

The entire family spent several hours with this box, learning quite a lot about the family tree. They nearly wore out the back pages of the wedding album, trying to categorize each relative that was pictured in the other seven books. Christine's mother had been able to obtain information on some of her ancestors, some of them going back as far as nineteen generations.

Daniel frowned at Christine. "How come you didn't tell us some of this information before?"

"I thought that all of this had been lost in the fire. I didn't know about that special safe. I had no idea that any of this stuff survived. Momma was the one who was obsessed with the family tree. At that time, I really didn't care. Now...well it seems to have made itself important."

After looking through the scrapbooks for a while longer, they turned their attention to the fourth box. David pulled some smaller boxes out of it, as well as more credit card receipts.

Sandra picked up one of the boxes. "Is this possibly your Mother's jewelry?"

Christine was frowning in confusion. "Momma and Daddy weren't too big into jewelry. The only jewelry that I remember either of them wearing was their wedding bands." She opened one of the boxes. There were some pendants, necklaces, petite gold and silver chains as well as a few rings. "I've never seen this stuff before. I didn't even know they had this, or where it came from. Like I said: They didn't wear jewelry in front of me, and they told me that I didn't need it either."

Another box had several pocket watches in it. Another had

wristwatches with rather worn out wristbands.

Daniel took a long look at the pocket watches. "Is it possible that these belonged to some of the people in those albums?"

All that Christine could do was shrug. There were no indications on any of them as to how old they were or who they might have belonged to.

Veronica was looking at a box that had been set aside. "Happy Birthday, Chrissy."

Christine frowned again. "Huh?"

"This one…" said Veronica. "It's marked for you, for your sixteenth birthday."

A pink jewelry box, with a somewhat crushed pink ribbon wrapped around it was presented to Christine. She snickered and shook her head. "Mom always gave me pink stuff. My favorite color is white. She was determined to make me like pink."

"Well, dear, it's a little late for your sixteenth birthday," said Sandra. "I think, however, that you can safely open it now."

Christine got a quizzical look on her face and shook the box near her ear. Nothing. She shrugged. "David, you got that box cutter?"

David cut the ribbon on the box.

She opened it and looked puzzled. "Two keys? Two keys taped to an envelope." She set the box down and pulled the envelope out. She pulled a note out of the envelope and read it. "These are keys to two safety deposit boxes." She looked up perplexed. "What's a safety deposit box?"

David shook his head. "Because of the fact that the message is almost 26 years old, probably nothing now. Someone would have to pay rent for the things, otherwise...the bank probably opened them, long ago, and they've been rented to someone else."

Daniel shook his head as well. "There was a reason for it back then, but things have changed dramatically since. No point in even speculating on what might have been in those things."

Christine looked a little downcast. "So whatever they had set up for my sixteenth birthday...I'll never know what it was."

"Yes, you will," said Ben.

All eyes turned to Ben in confusion and suspicion. He was staring up at the ceiling. His arms were folded over his chest. He pursed his lips and looked down. He placed his hands on his knees and looked around the room at all the faces. "Are you all ready for a long story?"

The room was totally silent.

Ben just stared into space and started: "I've known about Christine...all along. I guess the best place to start, though, is with the problem that I have. As you know, I can't produce children. My dear wife wanted to be a mother and I could not help. The next best thing was adoption. You talk about all of your internet and search engines and all that, well, back in the 1980's, I didn't have any of that. I had to use other methods to find out what I wanted and needed to know. Using those methods, I found a young girl, in juvenile detention, who was totally alone and pregnant. I also found out - don't ask how, you don't want to know - that she was carrying triplets. I figured that this was the jackpot. If I could get to be number one on that adoption list, I would get maximum return for minimum input - three for the price of one. So, I pulled every string that I knew how to pull and got just what I needed, and here you three are.

I researched everything I could about this girl. I found out about her parents bank dealings. The accounts as well as the safety deposit boxes. I followed her, as she was moved from juvenile to adult detention. In 1988, when she was put in the adult facility... for, in all probability, the rest of her life...I figured that the banking that her parents had set up, would or should go to her children. We have that law that says: You cannot profit from any crime that you commit. So, the fact that I could prove that you three boys are her children...that would mean that any money or property, would bypass her, and go to you.

I thought...wait until the boys turn 21. Then I will tell them about those accounts...and her...and we'll see if we can probate the accounts. The money and property would go to you boys, as legal heirs, to any Lee property, that was still tangible.

The only problem there, was that in order to keep the accounts active, there had to be *some* activity, on the accounts. I found that there is another law that says: If an account goes dormant for several years, then the state can absorb the money. All I had to do, to keep them active, was occasionally make a small deposit into each account. The safety deposit boxes - just pay the annual rental fee. Anybody, anywhere, anytime can make a deposit into any account. The only person, or persons, who can get the money out, or find out the balance, is the legal account holder. I didn't care how much was in there, I just knew that, after 21 years, there should be a sizeable amount, in all of them.

Then, you boys turned 16, and that's when you started your quest: Find Mom!" He cleared his throat. "I…never helped you. I…tried not to…hinder. I really did not know what to expect…either way. I was not sure what to say. Did you really want to visit your biological mother in jail? I didn't know…how that would affect you. Did you want to have your children, talking to their grandmother, through prison bars? I had no answer for that. A big part of me was hoping that you would not find out. I knew, however, that one day, I would have to tell you something. I had done everything I could to teach the three of you to finish any job you start. Now, that was coming back to haunt me.

I…really, sincerely believed that justice had been done. I… had no idea of how badly…this little woman had been wronged." He finally changed his gaze. He looked Christine directly in the eyes. "Words cannot express, how elated I am, that you are not guilty of those crimes. Words, also, cannot express, how sorry I am, for not coming forward with this information sooner, seeing as how I now know the full picture. If I had had the slightest notion that you were innocent, I would have moved whatever mountains were in the way, to get you out of jail, and reunite you with your boys.

Anyway, I watched the three of you do your searches. I initially did not think that it could happen, because of how impossible it had been in the past, for any adoptee to find their birth parents. Freedom of information, the internet, people networking and all the other new laws and technology, sure knocked those road blocks down."

Ben looked around the room at all the faces. "When you finally found her, I was at a total loss as to how I was going to tell any of you, my big secret. The closer you boys got to finding her, the deeper it got for me. As the saying goes: '*When you're in over your head - stop digging!*' I had to stop digging sometime... No time like the present. Once you started looking to find out who has been paying for those safety deposit boxes, you would have found out anyway."

Christine sat there with her three towels pressed tightly against her chest. Tears were streaming down her face. "You've known...all along," she said in a shaky whisper. "You knew...from the start...where I was...who I was. How could you have let me just sit there and rot?"

"Again...I thought, the lawyer that the state appointed to you had done his job...proper." Ben looked at David. "If you hadn't kept the information on that Hoffman character, such a big secret, I would have told this story, a long time ago."

David sat up straighter with an angry, indignant look on his face.

Before David could say anything, Ben raised up a hand to stop him. "I am not blaming you for anything. I know that attorney-client privilege and all that. Unfortunately, it seems to have worked against you in this case. It did help get her out, but...if I had known sooner...well...no point in dwelling on what might have been. She's out of jail, and the truth about what I knew and know is out as well."

David had not changed his posture or demeanor. His eyes narrowed slightly as he said: "What about the taxes?"

"You don't need to worry about that either," said Ben. "I went in each year and talked to an accountant in the banks. I told them that I did not need to know the balance, I just needed to know how much to pay in taxes on the interest." He tightened his lips a little. "I always added another dollar or two, and paid the taxes in her name."

Christine could not hold back anymore. She screamed and charged at Ben, dropping her treasured towels on the floor on the way. "You knew! You knew and you never told me or them!" She leapt into a straddling position on his lap and started pounding on him with her fists.

Duane and Daniel started towards her to halt her attack, and both stopped and stared in confusion, when they saw that Ben was making absolutely no defensive move against her flailing fists. Even after she bloodied his nose and split his lip open, he just sat there taking the beating with his eyes clenched shut and his arms relaxed at his sides.

After several moments of beating him, she slumped to the side sobbing. Daniel pulled her off of him, and carried her back to the couch. He held her close in his arms as she continued her long anguished sobs.

Ben finally opened his eyes and looked around the room.

Sandra pulled out a handkerchief and started cleaning the blood off Ben's face. "Why didn't you stop her? She could have hurt you badly."

"She needed to vent," Ben said flatly. "She needed to get all of it out of her system. I'll worry about asking forgiveness later."

Duane retrieved the towels from the floor and put them in Christine's hands. He then turned to Ben: "She could have been out of jail, a long time ago! Eight years ago! Why couldn't you have trusted us then?"

"No, she wouldn't," said David.

Now everyone turned to David. "I had planned to go into another line of work. The main reason I became a lawyer, was to see if I could use the legal system to find her. If he had blabbed the story to us eight years ago, then…I probably would have never become a lawyer, I never would have used the search on the DNA, I never would have found Hoffman, and we would be visiting her - in jail - with *us* thinking that she was guilty." He shook his head with a disgusted look on his face.

Christine had stopped her wailing. She sat there with the towels covering her face. After a few minutes, she lowered the towels and noticed the blood on her hands. She got up and headed for the kitchen. "The towels need cleaning," she said to no one in particular.

Veronica put her hand on Daniel's shoulder. "Don't leave her alone," she pleaded.

Daniel jumped up and followed Christine.

"I need to get you into the bathroom," said Sandra to Ben. "Come on, you need to get cleaned up."

Christine went through the kitchen to the washroom. She stared off into space as she put the three towels in the washing machine, put a small bit of soap in and then started the washer. She then sank to her knees and just sat there, staring. She did not move as the washing machine went through each of the cycles. When the machine finally stopped, she got up, opened it, pulled the towels out and placed them into the dryer. Then again, she sank to the floor.

Daniel sat there the whole time, not sure what to do. He was afraid to talk to her even though he desperately wanted to say something comforting.

Shortly after the towels were put in the dryer, Sandra walked in. "How is she doing?"

Daniel shook his head. "She seems to have gone zombie on us. The only thing she cares about right now is the baby towels."

Sandra sighed. She saw the dried blood, still on Christine's hands. She looked up at Daniel and said: "I'll be right back." She left the room and came back shortly with a wet rag. She sat down next to Christine and started cleaning the blood off her hands. Christine showed no reaction at all. "Daniel will you leave us alone, dear? We have some girl talk to do."

"Are you sure?"

Sandra gave him the "Mother's glare." An expression that says no words, but speaks volumes. A look that only a mother could give and only the child understands fully. He made a slight grunting sound, pursed his lips and walked out. She continued cleaning Christine's hands. "Well, dear, we've had quite a big surprise today."

Christine still showed no reaction.

"It does make one wonder. What would have happened if Ben had told his story, years ago? What would have happened? Would the boys have visited you in jail? Would they have let their children and wives visit you? David did say that he became a lawyer to try to use the legal system to find you. He did it. If he had known, when he was 16, that you were in jail, would he have become a lawyer? Would he have ever been able to find that horrible Mister Hoffman? I don't know."

Christine still showed no reaction.

Sandra continued: "I think that the boys would have visited you, and they would have let you meet your grandchildren. You would have been able to see all of your grandchildren…through prison bars…all except Michael, of course."

Finally Christine reacted. She frowned as she looked at Sandra. "Why wouldn't Michael visit me?"

"He would have been dead," said Sandra in a matter of fact manner.

Now Christine looked shocked. "Why?"

"If you had not been here to babysit Michael, he would have been in a day care center. There would have been an adult there, but that person would have had her attention split between nine or ten other children. If she had checked on Michael, all she would have seen was a baby, quietly sleeping in a crib. She might not have noticed the lack of breathing for quite some time, and by then, it would have been too late. Would some attendant at a day care center have reacted as fast, or cared as much as you did, dear? I think not. You, dear, are the *only* reason, that Michael is still alive." She finally finished cleaning Christine's hands.

Christine sat there trying to think of something to say. She could not do anything except sit there with a shocked look on her face.

"Just think, dear, you might have spent an additional eight years in jail, just so that David could get you out at just the right time, in order to save Michael's life."

Christine wiped new tears out of her eyes. She sniffed a few times, and tried to come up with something to say.

"Do you think that eight years of your life was worth saving the life of one of your grandchildren?"

Christine sniffed hard and wrung her hands in her lap. "It's hard to argue, when you put it that way. Do you actually think that no one would have been there to save Michael if I...?"

"I can't think of anyone, other than Paula, who would have cared enough, to do what you did, dear."

Christine felt like she was getting a headache from all this thinking.

"Another thing, dear: Consider the fact that you became pregnant at just the right time, in order to have a growing piece of undeniable evidence against those prison guards who abused you. Once they found out that there had been no form of birth control done on you, they gave in to the inevitable. Plus, what happened with those judges?"

Christine sat there trying to somehow come up with any argument against Sandra.

"Well, the Lord was looking at the big picture."

"Do you actually think, that there is some big plan, somewhere that could have put all of that into play?"

"Who knows what is in the mind of God? All I can say

is that there was some pretty good timing involved here. Divine intervention? Coincidence?"

"But if that's the case, why did my parents have to die? Why did I have to get attacked, back then and end up in jail?"

"I don't have all the answers, dear. I can only go with what I have seen happen. The speculations, of what might have been, could go on forever and drive everyone insane. But as I said, who else would have done what you did for Michael?"

Christine slumped down. She put her head on Sandra's lap and hugged her legs and started sniffling again. Sandra rubbed Christine's back.

Sandra continued: "All that time you were being abused by all those people in the prison. You had no power, of any type back then. Now, you have all the power."

"What?"

"Well, dear, everyone is rather upset with Ben. Right now, you have all the power. If you refuse to forgive him, then your boys might not either. If you do forgive him, then it will be a lot easier for them to forgive as well."

Christine sat up. She looked at Sandra with shock and disgust on her face. "Why should I...?" She stopped and huffed. "For Michael? For me? For what?"

"For everyone's sake, dear. Remember, he was thinking of the boys. He was trying to do what was best for them. They were his main concern. You could say that he made a big mistake in not telling them, but he was at least *trying* to be a good father..."

She giggled. "...unlike someone who would pee on someone else's cucumbers."

Christine would have collapsed if she had not been sitting on the floor already. In a loud whisper, she said: "David told you about that?"

Sandra laughed a little. "Yes, he did, dear. All three of them tell me a great number of things. Your father must have really been something."

"I'd give anything if I could talk to either one of my parents right now," she said sadly.

"As I said, dear, you hold all the power. Are you going to forgive Ben for his mistake or not?"

Christine straightened up and looked as serious as she could. "No! I will not..."

Sandra looked a little shocked and was about to say something.

"...not until the dryer is finished," said Christine flatly. She then gave Sandra a sideways glance and smirked.

Both of them snickered. They hugged and giggled a little.

"How soon will it be finished, dear?"

"I don't know, it doesn't have a clock on it. It just buzzes when it's finished."

They sat there hugging each other, waiting for the buzz.

Christine walked back into the living room with Sandra close behind. She held her treasured towels tightly up to her chest. Ben, who had an ice pack held up to his mouth, stood up with a worried look on his face.

"Oh, sit down," said Christine impatiently. "Everybody here is taller than I am. I'm tired of looking up at people. I'm getting a crick in my neck."

He sat down on the edge of the couch.

"I've been thinking…and…okay, maybe what you did was not exactly right…when you look back on it. I guess I might have done the same thing…if…" She let her words trail off. She cleared her throat. She looked around the room at her sons and their families. She bit her lower lip. "In the future, will you please not hold any secrets back…where my babies are concerned?" She cleared her throat again. "You did a good job raising them…and…I thank you for that. But…please, anything that concerns them…I need to know…and I'm starting to ramble." She sat down next to Ben.

"Hindsight is always a kick in the pants," said Ben. "Maybe if I had done this, then, or maybe if your lawyer had done something different. The speculation can drive you nuts. Don't worry though, from now on, anything that I can think of, I will let you know…" He dabbed at the split in his lip. "…no matter how much it hurts."

Sandra came over and pulled his hand away from his mouth. "Stop playing with that - you're going to start it bleeding again."

The air in the room seemed a little less thick. Everyone seemed to be breathing a little easier.

"One other thing about my boys…" Christine looked at Ben with a very worried expression on her face. "…what did you do?"

Ben looked as if he was waiting for more. When he did not get any he closed his eyes and raised his eyebrows. He opened his eyes and looked at Christine with trepidation. "What, *what* did I do? I mean what are *you* talking about?"

Christine took a deep breath and sighed. "Sandra told me that you did something illegal…to get the boys."

"I…what? No, I didn't."

"She said that she asked you how you had been able to get all three of them. You said you didn't want to tell her because…well… the statute of limitations had not…run out."

The expression on Ben's face slowly turned to a smile. He put his fingers to his forehead, brushed his hair back and started chuckling.

Christine got a little irritated over his reaction. "What's so funny?!"

Ben stopped laughing. With a big smile on his face he looked Christine directly in the eyes. "I did say that I would tell you the truth, didn't I?"

"Yes you did!"

He cleared his throat. "Illegal? No! Unethical? Maybe. I did pull all the strings I knew how to pull. I called in every favor that I could find. I had done a lot of favors - as a carpenter - for a lot of people. I used that friendship to get this done. I didn't do anything illegal at all."

Both Christine and Sandra looked confused. "Then why… why did you tell her…?"

Ben sat there smiling. "In the thirty-two years that we have been married, that was the *one and only* conversation that we had... where I got the last word in."

Sandra stood there with her mouth wide open. She looked around the room looking a little dazed. She drew in a deep breath. "You rat! All this time...I thought...you rat!" She looked around the room making several huffing noises, trying to think of something else to say. She finally just sat down with her arms folded across her chest and shaking her head and making all kinds of disgusted huffing noises.

Everyone stood there in silence. Duane was the first to shatter the hush: "So! Are we going to find out what's been hidden in those safety deposit boxes, for over a quarter of a century?"

"I don't think that they will let us go in there en masse," said David. Why don't we limit it to the three brothers, with Little Mom? Once we find out what is in them, then we'll decide what to do."

"Take an empty briefcase with you," said Paula.

She got several strange looks from everybody.

"Well! You don't know how big they are, what's in them, or what you might want to bring home now. Take it, just in case."

"One medium and one large," said Ben.

"And you know that...how?" asked Daniel.

"Prices. When I paid the rent on them, I looked at their price list. The prices matched up with one medium and one large."

"How many sizes do they have?" asked Duane.

"Four: Small, medium, large and drawer."

"But…how do I get in?" Christine looked around somewhat confused. "I mean, my parents got the boxes, but I never knew about them until now. What do I have to do to be able to get into them?"

"We go to the bank and check on it," said David. If we need to get the things probated, we will. Who knows what they planned for you? The fact that they had these keys for you, for your sixteenth birthday, maybe they had something already planned."

36

They arrived at the bank. Christine was ready to climb the walls in anticipation. So many things that she had not known about her parents were coming in to the light. Bank accounts, stock certificates and mysterious gifts - what next?

They walked up to the vault. A small gray haired woman in a uniform sat at the desk reading a book. She looked up as they approached. "May I help you?"

"Yes," said David. "My Mother wants to check her boxes."

"Box numbers?"

Christine looked fearful. "I forgot. It's been a while."

"Do you have your keys?"

Christine pulled the keys out of her purse and handed them to the guard.

The guard looked at them as if she had never seen a key in her life. "Just how long is a while? I haven't seen keys like this since we put in the new system 10 years ago."

"It's been over 25 years."

"Could I see some identification, please?"

With a big stupid grin on her face, Christine handed her Texas Identification Card to the guard. This was the first time that anyone had asked to see it since she had received it in the mail.

The guard pecked the keyboard to her computer. "Yes, we have two boxes." She looked up at Christine. "What are the other names on the list?"

She looked up at David: "Who else would be on it?"

"Try your parents," said David.

She looked at the guard. "Uh…Gabriel and Annette."

The guard looked back at the computer screen. "And your mother's maiden name?"

Christine was a little surprised with that question but answered: "Bryce."

The guard nodded in satisfaction then did a double take looking at the screen. "My, it has been some time since you've been here." She hit a button on an intercom. "Pete, will you come out here, please?"

A very chubby man came out of the vault, picking his teeth with a toothpick. "What's up?"

"We have a customer here who wants to check her boxes."

"Okay, what's the problem?"

"Well, neither box has been opened since September of 1981."

Pete stood there with his mouth open. He glanced back and forth from his colleague to Christine. He licked his lips. "I'll get the oil can."

"While he is doing that, Ms. Lee, I need you to sign the roster. While you are looking at your boxes, we are going to need to set up new keys. Since your boxes haven't been opened, since we started the new system, the old keys will work, but we still need to put in new locks...now that we have the chance."

Christine shrugged. "Okay. Uh...can I put my sons on the list for the boxes?"

"Yes, you can, but it will require the permission of all three of those who already have their names on the boxes."

She let out a small squeak. "They're...dead. How do we...?"

"Who is dead?"

"My parents...they..."

"I'll need to see the death certificates."

David placed the briefcase on the desk, opened it, pulled out a file and handed the file to the guard.

"What are you - a lawyer?"

"Yes, I am," said David with his big smug toothy grin.

She read the documents slowly. She then clicked her tongue. "Okay. It's all here. Now I need your sons to come in and fill out a signature card."

"These are my sons," Christine said cheerfully.

The guard looked up at David. "Your son is your lawyer. That is definitely convenient." She pulled out three cards. She wrote the numbers of the boxes on the cards and then passed them out. "Please fill these out."

While they were writing, Pete showed up pushing a cart. "I've got the new lock bolts and the oil for the old ones. Which boxes are we going to?"

He was given a slip of paper that he quickly looked at. "Okay, which one first, ma-am?"

Christine looked back at her sons.

Duane quickly responded: "Go ahead, we'll be in there in a few moments."

She looked back at Pete and shrugged. "I guess we'll go with the medium sized one first."

He looked back at the numbers again and headed into the vault. "Follow me."

Christine disappeared around a corner while the sons continued with the paperwork. A moment later she came back. "Is anyone finished with their form?"

"I am," said Daniel.

"Well come on in, I need your help. That thing is heavy."

Daniel looked slightly confused. "How heavy?"

"Very!" shouted Pete.

The three men glanced back and forth at each other. Daniel shrugged and headed into the vault. He found Pete standing in front of an open box. He and Daniel pulled the inner box out and they nearly dropped it. Daniel took a firm hold on it and weighed it in his grip. He raised his eyebrows as he looked at the box. "Grandpa was *not* a wimp."

"Sir, you can put the box on the cart and I'll wheel it over to the private room for you."

"What about those lock bolts?"

"Oh, don't worry about that. While you're checking your stuff, I'll replace the bolts. It only takes about three minutes."

As he pushed the cart to one of several doors inside the vault, Duane and David came in. Pete opened a door and looked at the three big men. "It might be a little tight in there, but as long as you're all friends, I think you'll be okay." He pushed the cart into the booth, Daniel lifted the box onto the counter, Pete took the cart out of the booth and then Duane, David and Christine squeezed in.

"I don't know if this is going to work," said Christine as she was being crushed between two of them.

Duane lifted her up and sat her on the counter with the box. "Is that better, Little Mom?"

She snickered and jabbed him in the stomach with her elbow. She then opened the box: Coins. Small, large, silver, copper, gold, dull, shiny and all wrapped in individual clear plastic envelopes. The box was stuffed with coins. Each one pulled a few coins out and started looking at them closely.

"I've got a Mercury dime and an Indian head penny," said Duane.

"I've got several silver dollars," said Daniel. "All from the 1800's."

"I've got a Buffalo nickel and...some big coin that's... foreign," said David. "I don't have a clue where it's from. Far east…I think."

"So what do we do with them?" asked Christine.

"We need to take them to someone who knows coins and get them appraised," said David. "I don't know how we're going to get them all out of here though."

"What's the matter?" scoffed Duane. "Is a few coins too heavy for him?"

"It's not me! It's the briefcase. I don't think that *it* can handle the weight."

Daniel chuckled. "Why don't we pick…oh I don't know… two dozen of them at random. Take those to some coin collector or gold shop and then go from there."

"Sounds good," said David.

Duane nodded.

Christine just stared at the coins.

Each one grabbed a handful of coins and put them in the briefcase.

"Let's go see about the other box," said David.

After putting the first box away, and getting the new key - off to the next box.

Pete was spraying the keyholes with WD-40. He inserted both keys. He had a few problems turning them. After finally getting the door open, he looked up at the triplets: "I wonder if this one is going to be as heavy as the other one."

Daniel reached in and pulled it out. He hooked two fingers into the handle and held it up easily. "Not even close."

They left Pete to take care of the new lock bolts and headed back to the booth.

Again, since there was very little room in the booth, Christine was lifted up onto the counter. She got on her knees and put her hands on the box. She opened it and found a gift-wrapped box on top. She pulled it out and looked at a card that was attached to the ribbon. Her shoulders sagged a little as she read out loud: "Happy sixteenth birthday to our darling daughter - love from Mom and Dad." She looked up at her sons in a forlorn manner, and slowly started tearing away the wrapping. Inside was a dark blue box, the type that jewelry came in. She looked up at her sons again, only this time there was a little fear and suspicion in her eyes. "How much money were my parents hiding? Whatever is in this box...it ain't no small bauble." She opened the box and all four of them stared wide-eyed at a diamond studded tiara. She held it up and shook her head. "This thing must have cost a fortune. Where did they have the money for this?"

"It's an heirloom," said Duane. "I remember seeing something like this in a couple of the photographs from those scrapbooks."

David looked in the top of the box and found a small envelope. He pulled it out, opened it and found another note inside. "He's right - according to this it is an heirloom that has been in the family for several generations. Your parents were hoping that it would really be something for you to show off...when you wore it...to your...senior prom."

She looked up at David and her eyes started tearing. Duane was the closest to her and he hugged her close, as she started sobbing quietly. The prom…something else that Hoffman had cheated her out of.

While Duane comforted her, David and Daniel started an inventory on the rest of the contents of the deposit box. More heirloom jewelry. Several necklaces, rings, bracelets, cameos and other pendants.

"She's going to owe a fortune in inheritance tax," groaned Daniel.

"No, she won't," said David. "Her name was already on the boxes, so it was joint ownership. When the other two on the list died, she just absorbed the assets. And, even if they do try to hit her with inheritance tax, the tiara looks to be worth more than any of the other stuff, so they can't charge any tax on that. It was already marked as a gift for her."

It took several weeks, however they took the time. Between cash-on-hand, bank accounts, coins, jewelry and stock certificates, they found out that Christine Lee was a very wealthy individual. David had to check on all the taxes involved and was pleasantly surprised to find out that he had been correct. Since her name was on most of the accounts, stocks and safety deposit boxes - and because Ben had paid some taxes throughout the years, what she owed in taxes was very little. Her parents had left her very well off, but she had not been able to enjoy any of it until now.

She sat there in David's home office looking at the list and the bottom line. Her sons and daughters-in-law surrounding her. She looked around at them with a very large, smug grin. "Get ready, all of you. I am going to spoil my grandbabies...rotten. Of course there will be some for each of you and whoever is growing inside me right now."

Duane snickered. "Right now, if you want to, you can afford to buy your own house and live alone."

"NO!" screamed Christine.

Everybody in the room was taken aback at her reaction. Daniel went to her to try to calm her. He went to one knee as he held his arms out to her. She grabbed two fistfuls of his shirt and pulled herself closer to him, while glancing back and forth at all three of her sons. "No!" she pleaded.

All three men gathered closely around her, on one knee, all three confused as to what had struck such fear in her.

"Don't let it happen," she cried. "Don't you ever leave me alone again!"

No one in the room could think of what to ask her.

"I don't ever want to be alone again. I was alone when I was attacked on that mall parking lot. I was left totally alone when that cockroach killed my parents. That lawyer, made me feel alone when he told me to plead 'no contest' to those charges. I was alone in that constant battle against Dr. Dumbbell. I was alone in juvie, until I met Rebecca. Then she died and I was alone again, to be used and abused by Big Sugar, Honey, Rolanda, and a bunch of others." Tears started streaming down her face. "Then the same thing again, when they sent me to the big house. I was alone when Mikey nearly died. I was alone again, when that creep handed me that subpoena. All the worst things that have ever happened to me have been when I was alone. Don't any of you ever leave me alone again."

Daniel hugged her close. David and Duane put their big arms around all, for a group hug.

"You have a bedroom in all three houses, for as long as you want," said Duane.

"I don't think that any of our wives will object to a permanent live in babysitter," said Daniel.

"Hey, Little Mom," said David. "We will do everything we can to make sure that you are never alone."

37

Christine walked up to David. "Will you take me to the hospital to see that Hoffman creep?"

David looked at her puzzled. "Why?"

"I just want to get some things off my chest and let him know how badly he hurt me and…maybe a few other things."

David narrowed his eyes at her and stared at her trying to read her face. "Is that all? I mean, is that really all you want to do?"

She gave him one of those shocked innocent looks. "Of course," she said with her voice shaking a little. "What else would I want to do?"

"I don't know," he said as his suspicions grew. "What are you hiding behind your back?"

She looked a little surprised. "Nothing," she said with a guilty look.

He tried to look around to her right side. She had her arm behind her back and moved slightly to keep him from seeing what was in her right hand. He looked up at her face with a stern look. "What are you hiding?"

"Nothing!" she snapped.

He quickly wrapped his arms around her and grabbed her right arm. She tried desperately to fight back, but of course she was no match for his speed and strength. He felt the baseball bat in her hand, and held onto it firmly. "What makes you think that you need this?"

"You know what he had done to me…twice. I need something to defend myself."

"You are not going to go anywhere with that bat."

She scowled at him. "Like I said, I need some kind of defense against him."

Holding on to the barrel of the bat, David lifted it high. She grunted a little as she held on to the handle. He lifted it higher and she grasped as hard as she could when her feet left the ground. They glared at each other for a few moments. She had to adjust her grip a little in order to hang on.

"I am your mother, and I am telling you to let go of the bat," she huffed.

"I am your lawyer. As your lawyer, I am telling you that you are not going anywhere near any hospital with this bat."

She clenched her teeth and growled at him. He changed his grip on the bat to his left hand and raised the bat a little higher. She wrapped her legs around his waist and tried to pull the bat out of his grip making a few grunts and growling sounds as she yanked. She glared at him while he gave her nothing but a deadpan stare.

"You don't need to go there anyway. He died sometime last week."

She looked shocked. "Huh? Why didn't you tell me?"

"It didn't seem important at the time. You didn't want to see him anyway. I doubted that you wanted to grieve for him, so I just let it pass."

She let go of the bat and placed her hands on his shoulders. She had a hurt look on her face. She scoffed in disgust unwrapped her legs from his chest and let herself down. She looked around and sniffed. "Can I have the bat, so I can put it away?"

"Yes," he said as he lowered his arm and gave her the bat.

She walked away dejectedly.

Paula came into the room. She watched Christine walk away then turned to David. "I didn't hear anything about him passing. Are you sure he's dead?"

"Nope," said David. "I don't know if he is still alive or not. I just don't see any point in her getting into any more trouble because of him."

"Oh," said Paula as she got closer to David. "You don't play fair," she whispered.

"Sometimes I can't afford to fight fair."

One day while Christine was looking through one of the scrapbooks - again, David walked in. He sat down beside her and hugged her close. She looked up at him and saw the expression on his face. She felt a little troubled. "What?"

He sighed. "I found your parents."

"What? Where?"

"After the state finished their autopsies, the two of them were put in a cemetery for paupers. A few months ago, it might have seemed a little overwhelming, financially, to do anything. Now, if you want them moved out of that cemetery and put in a proper burial site, with a proper funeral, I'm pretty sure that you can afford it."

"When?"

"Whenever you want. I'll make the arrangements."

She swallowed hard. "Will it include everything for a real funeral for both of them?"

"Absolutely."

She once again lost control of her emotions and buried her face in his chest as she silently cried.

David stroked her hair. As tender a voice as he could muster he asked: "Do you have any idea where you would like them to have their final resting place?"

"Yes," she answered softly. "There's that big cemetery on the northwest side of town. Every Spring, it's just one huge, endless field of bluebonnets. All of my grandparents are buried there. My parents need to be with their parents."

"I know which one you're talking about. I'll check on cemetery plots and such…tomorrow. I'm sure that we'll be able to find something very nice for them."

A few days later David came down to breakfast. Paula and Christine were already there eating. He sat down silently and shook his head. "I contacted that idiot Reese," he said flatly. "I told him what had happened to you and how I exposed the truth…truth that he totally ignored."

Christine looked thoughtful for a moment. "So what happens now?"

"I am going to file a lawsuit against him and I am also going to start the proceedings to have him disbarred."

Paula looked rather puzzled. "Are you going to let him try an offer before you file the lawsuit?"

"I did. He offered $25,000 and Christine has to sign a gag order. She would never be able to talk about, or testify against him for any reason, if she takes the offer."

Christine choked on a sip of milk that she was drinking. "$25,000? That's ridiculous. He let me rot in prison for all that time and now he wants to sweep me under the rug for a lousy thousand dollars a year for all the time I was in prison?"

David scoffed. "I told him that he was going to have to add at least three zeroes to the figure before we would consider the offer. He wants to do it the hard way. So be it. I will enjoy taking him down and knocking him out of the profession."

"So will I," said Christine.

"One thing," said David. "We are going to have to stand in line in order to get him."

Both women looked at him confused.

"What line?" asked Paula?

"It seems that Little Mom is not the only person that Reese diddled. I was fortunate, in the fact that I filed a lawsuit first. The other people who got scammed are going to have to wait until our lawsuit is done. We, however, are going to have to wait until the

IRS is finished with Reese."

Christine looked confused. "What's the IRS?"

Paula nearly choked on a mouthful of food.

David was momentarily stunned by the question. "The IRS, my dear Little Mom, is the Internal Revenue Service. They are the ones who screw everyone in the country as far as taxes are concerned."

"So what puts them at the head of the line?"

"Because they are pressing criminal charges against him. Ours is a civil suit. The fortunate thing about the IRS hitting him first is: While they are chewing on his derriere, all of his financial assets are frozen."

Christine looked even more confused. "So?"

"He can't get to any of his money," said David with an air of condescension. "Right now, if he were able to use his assets, he might flee the country, and then we couldn't get to him. Or, he might try to hide his assets. He's staying right where he is and the money is staying where it is until we will be able to really stick it to him, after the IRS is finished."

Christine sat there with a big evil grin. "Good!"

38

Meanwhile in a hotel room, somewhere in Waco, Texas, a meeting. John Smith was sitting there with a scowl on his face. Another man came out of the bathroom, zipping his pants.

The partner sat down at the table across from John. "Are you still thinking of trying to go at her again?"

John looked up angrily. "What does it look like? A crummy little hooker has gotten the best of me. She has single-handedly destroyed a network that took years to set up. We can't just sit by and..."

"And WHAT!? The ones that we lost, were lost because they put their fingers, as well as other body parts, in the till. If those judges hadn't been playing hoochy-coochy, with her, they would still be in their positions. If the prison guards hadn't been running trains on her, *they* would still be in their positions. They were like a dope peddler, who samples his own merchandise. Eventually, you go too far and you get caught."

"I know, but, I still can't accept the fact, that I was beaten by *one* little hooker. We were controlling..."

"Again, you're not looking at the big picture! It turns out, that she wasn't alone. You thought that lawyer, was trying to get some big name for himself, with some Clarence Darrow ploy. Now, we find out that, the little hooker, is *his* mother. His and two brothers. That guy is not going to let go. I mean, think about it:

You got that Big Ugly...or Big Sloppy...or whatever that whale's name is...you arranged to let her escape, gave her the information on how to find the hooker and even supplied her with a car and a navigation system. You got her some bus tickets, in order to make them vamoose somewhere else...quickly...and what happened? Her sons happened, and we still aren't one step closer to repairing the damage."

"Well, they are there, and I think we should do something about them."

"AGAIN, you are not looking at the big picture! The judges screwed themselves. The guards screwed themselves. You, screwed the Big Stupid, by not giving her the whole story. Big Stupid screwed herself by killing a prison guard on her way out. Then she screwed us by killing or crippling three inmate bosses on her way out of the prison. Think about it. We're having enough trouble, with the judges and the guards. If they talk, we have even more problems. Making them keep their silence is expensive enough. The loss of four prison inmate bosses, has hurt even more."

"Her name is Big Sugar. I didn't tell her to kill anyone. I told her to get out, get the hooker and then get lost. She's the dummy who went on the killing spree. So, are we going to put out a contract on her?"

"No need. The State of Texas has had a bellyful of dead bodies that are scattered in her wake. That prison guard is *absolutely* a crime that warrants the death penalty. They have to execute her to show the other inmates that you don't get a plea bargain for killing a prison guard. Funny thing about it is that when they give her that 'last meal', they are going to have to give it to her as soup. Seems that when she faced off against the three sons of that hooker, she lost all but two teeth…and those two don't meet."

"What if she tries to tell them about us…for leniency?"

"Then we do make a contract."

"So, what do we do about the hooker? Do we take her out?"

"If you take her out, you have to take out the sons and daughter-in-laws and their siblings and parents and children…no. That would be a *very* expensive blood bath that would get too much attention on us. That will start an investigation, that we might not be able, to get out of."

"Are you saying that, we should just walk away?"

"No! I am saying, RUN! Look, every business, suffers a loss, every now and then. *Learn* from the setback, and learn to cover all the bases, in the future. Tell the judges to keep their hands off, tell the guards the same thing. Find a way, to keep a tighter leash on the inmate bosses."

John Smith sat there stewing for a few moments. "That lawyer…he has seen me. What about him?"

"As long as you don't stir up any more mud, he won't have anything to go on. Leave town, leave Texas, and head back to where you were before. Learn and rebuild. Everyone in the business, knows that there's an occasional…unforeseen circumstance that knocks a few holes in your agenda. Holes that are anywhere from insignificant to…catastrophic. It happens! You can either learn from the mistakes made…or become a casualty, yourself."

John Smith looked at the airline ticket laying on the table.

"So, I go back and start all over again."

"Right. All of us review this and learn…and move on."

"What if she…?"

He was stopped by an angry glare, from his partner.

John sighed. "Okay. You're right." He picked up the ticket. "I'm headed to the San Antonio airport…"

"No, you're not. We don't want you heading south…at least not now. That ticket flies you out of Dallas."

He looked the ticket over. "Okay. I get the message."

"I hope you do," said the partner. "Other associates, of ours, in the organization, might not be as patient as I am. If you don't get the message - well, remember that idiot, Taylor?"

John rolled his eyes. "Oh yeah! Who could forget that?"

"He did *not* get the message! Now, I have a few other loose ends to tie up here and then I'm headed back home as well. Let's rendezvous in Aruba in two weeks, so we can start planning another set up here in Texas, without a bunch of oversexed judges and prison guards…or any other of those idiots from Pennsylvania or New Jersey. It's tough starting the business over again from scratch, but we have some "learned lessons" to consider."

John Smith sighed and left the room.

39

In keeping with their promise of never leaving her alone, they included Christine in their choir practice at church. Rarely had she darkened the door of a church. She did continue reading the Bible that David had given to her. She was sitting in a pew, reading it. She had finished reading another book called *John.* Earlier she had read a book titled *John.* Now she had just finished a fourth book called *John.* Did they have a problem with books named *John*? Why didn't they combine them? She had been told that once she finished reading the Bible, she would then have to start *studying* the Bible. All three of her sons, her daughters-in-law, as well as Ben and Sandra told her that they would help her with it.

She was a little aggravated at the family over what they had done. She had come home from the Obstetrician, with a weird picture that they took of the baby, even though it was still in the womb. She was not sure how, but the grainy picture did show the baby inside her. All the rest of the family was familiar with those pictures and every one of them had figured out, from the picture, that the baby was a little girl. Now there was a pink basinet, a pink crib, a pink diaper changing station and Sandra was pounding out all kinds of dresses for the baby on her sewing machine. She had not wanted to know, until the baby was born, however, now she did and so, in keeping with what she would have named the boys, the new little one would be named after Christine's mother: Annette.

She rubbed her eyes and looked up at what they were doing in their choir practice. They seemed to be having a little trouble finding a good key (whatever that was) for the soloist on *"Be Thou My Vision."* She sat there a little despondent, because she was so ignorant about music and religion…among other things.

She contemplated what had been happening since she got out of prison. In the courtroom Dr. Dumbbell had been exposed to the truth by that Hoffman creep. He had realized that he was totally wrong and that Christine was the one telling the truth the entire time. For the rest of his useless life he would be questioning the possibility of whether or not he was ruining another life by making all kinds of accusations based on something from a third party. He would never be sure of himself again because he just might be erroneously accusing another innocent child of wrong doings.

Dexter Hoffman was another one where his life, what had been left of it, had been turned upside-down. He was a hardened criminal and among even the worst offenders, the lowest scum of all was the child molester. David had made sure that since he had confessed to committing sexual assault on Christine – twice when she was only twelve years old – that he was to be labeled as a child molester and not just a sex offender. He died knowing that his legacy was that he *was* the lowest of the low.

The four Judges that had been defrocked would never be able to find a decent enough way to hide their shame or guilt. They had been on a pedestal that stated they were supposed to be the pinnacle of virtue and trust. They had violated that trust repeatedly every time they visited the prison and had their way with any of the inmates. If they ever got out of prison, they would be shunned wherever they went.

The prison guards were in the same boat as the Judges. They

had been so haughty and arrogant and now they were just another number in the prison roll call. Police, guards and Judges did not have any form of a nice life in prison. They were marked from the time they got there…until the time they died. In the investigation, following Christine's revelations, they had given up the names of nineteen male guards and eleven female guards who had been profiting on the "open season" sale of sexual favors by inmates to anyone who comes along. A new form of screening was set up to determine the suitability of a person to be a prison guard.

That incompetent lawyer, Reese, was another domino to fall in the line. He now had more woes than Christine had ever encountered. She had been on the bottom and did not know, until now, what it was like to be on the top. Reese had been so high up there and now everyone he had known or misrepresented was after his hide. His money was gone, his family was gone, his freedom was gone, his integrity was gone and his occupation as a lawyer was finished. Just like the Judges, he had fallen from a very high pedestal.

She remembered the roll call of all of the ones in juvie and the Big House who had been her owner. Big Sugar, Honey Kim, Rolanda and Carla in juvie. Big Sugar, Honey Kim, Consuela and that big black woman who had made Christine call her "Massuh". Big Sugar had killed or crippled all of Christine's ex-owners and was now on death row for murdering a guard when she escaped. Big Sugar and Honey Kim had both been released from juvie and then continued their criminal ways and ended up in the big house as a result. Big Sugar was one of those habitual offenders who thought that she was above the law and did whatever she pleased. Honey Kim committed a crime on purpose, to return to prison, in order to have a way to keep a barrier between her and the husband that she had been involuntarily matched up with from an arranged marriage.

Christine wondered if she should go visit Honey Kim just to gloat. No, David would never allow that. Sandra would not be too happy about something like that either. They kept on preaching to her about forgiving all of those people who wronged her in so many ways. She felt now that she did not need to worry about that because the state and federal governments were after them for all kinds of transgressions that Christine did not even know about.

The most satisfying of all of those things was when she had been able to sit there and call Big Sugar by her real name, over and over, and Cassiopeia Tinkle could not do anything about it but grunt and get mad…and take it. That was something that Christine could always look back on and smile.

All of the monsters that had abused her were now the ones on their knees – or dead. She had a lot of hope for the future with her loving family (and a fortune that her parents had set up for her future). Here she was - a 38 year old, pregnant ex-con, who knew so little about the world, outside of prison. According to all her relatives, her best bet, in learning everything about life, was in this Bible. She put the book down, stretched and sighed. She had just finished reading another short, confusing book called *Jude*. She picked up the Bible, trying to position it to read it around her ever enlarging stomach, and started reading *Revelation*. 'Here's to hope,' she thought. 'This one *should* be easier to understand, because of the title.'

www.ingramcontent.com/pod-product-compliance
Lightning Source LLC
Chambersburg PA
CBHW071644260626
47170CB00001B/228